IN THE HEAT OF PASSION

Zach's breath was warm against Adria's face, his hands strong and forceful, his eyes as dark as the night. Adria's throat caught and she couldn't look away. Spellbound, she held his gaze and knew in an instant that he was going to kiss her. Her heart squeezed. Unwanted desire—wicked and wanton—crept stealthily through her blood.

"Damn you," he whispered hoarsely, his face so close to hers she could see smoky desire in his eyes.

"Zachary—"

"Why are you doing this?" he asked before he lowered his head and his lips crashed over hers in a kiss that was almost brutal and his fingers wound in the thick strands of her hair. Anger and passion sizzled through her blood. She tried not to respond, to push him away, but her hands were useless against his broad chest and he ground his mouth over hers in a way that was wickedly possessive and seared her to her very soul . . .

Books by Lisa Jackson

TREASURES
INTIMACIES
WISHES
WHISPERS
TWICE KISSED

Published by Zebra Books

TREASURES

Lisa Jackson

Zebra Books
Kensington Publishing Corp.
http://www.zebrabooks.com

ZEBRA BOOKS are published by

Kensington Publishing Corp.
850 Third Avenue
New York, NY 10022

First Printing: February, 1994
10 9 8 7 6 5 4 3 2

Printed in the United States of America

For the record I'd like to acknowledge and thank the following people for their help and encouragement: Nancy Bush, Anita Diamant, Sally Peters, John Scognamiglio and Larry Sparks.

Prologue

Portland, Oregon

October 1993

ADRIA

If only she could remember.

If only she knew the truth.

If only she were certain she wasn't on a fool's mission. She glanced up at the dark October sky and felt the gentle wash of Oregon mist against her face. Had she ever tilted her head back and let the moistness linger on her lips and cheeks? Had she stood on this very corner, across the street from the old Hotel Danvers, holding onto her mother's hand, waiting for the light to change?

Traffic rushed by, cars and buses spraying water as tires splashed through puddles. Deep in the folds of her cape, she shivered, but not from the cool autumn air, or the breath of a breeze rolling off the dank Willamette River only a few blocks to the east. No, she shivered at the thought of what she was planning to do, her destiny, or so she'd been told. She knew she was in for the battle of her life.

But she was committed. She couldn't give up now. She'd traveled hundreds of miles, been through emotional hell and back, and spent days searching her soul during painstaking, laborious hours in libraries and newspaper offices throughout the Northwest, reading every chronicle, article, or editorial she could find on the Danvers family.

Now her plans were about to come to fruition. Or ruin. She stared up at the hotel, seven stories of Victorian architecture, which had once been one of the tallest buildings in the city and now was dwarfed by its concrete and steel counterparts, great skyscrapers that knifed upward, looming over the narrow city streets. "God help me," she whispered.

Without waiting for the light to change, she dashed across the street, the hood of her cape blowing off with a strong gust of wind. Daylight began to fade as the cloud-shrouded sun settled behind the westerly hills, hills that were still rich with green forests and dotted by expensive mansions.

Though the Hotel Danvers was closed to the public, as it had been for the past few months while it was being renovated and brought back to its turn-of-the-century grandeur, she walked through the lobby door that had been propped open for the workmen. The renovation was nearly complete. For the past two days she'd watched as delivery vans had brought tables, chairs, and other furniture to the service entrance of the grand old building. Today, linens, glassware, even some food had been delivered in anticipation of the grand opening, which was slated for the weekend.

The entire Danvers clan, Witt Danvers's first wife and his four surviving children, were rumored to be in town. Good.

A cold fist of apprehension tightened in her stomach. Ever since learning of the hotel's closure and reopening, she'd planned her introduction to the family, but first, to test the waters, she needed to speak with the man in charge of the hotel's face-lift: Zachary Danvers was the rebel of the family and second son to Witt. According to every article she'd read about the family, Zachary had never quite fit in. The Danvers family resemblance, so evident in his brothers and sisters, had skipped over him and during his youth he'd had more than one brush with the law. Only the old man's money had kept Zachary out of serious trouble and gossip had it that not only was he the least favorite of Witt's children but was also nearly cut out of the old man's will.

Yes, Zachary was the man she needed to see first. She'd studied his photographs so often, she knew she would recognize him. A little over six feet, with coal-black hair, olive skin, and deep-set gray eyes guarded by heavy brows, he was the one son of Witt Danvers who didn't resemble his father. Leaner than his brothers or the bear of a man who had sired him, his features were as chiseled as the cliffs overlooking the Pacific Ocean. He was a rugged man, rawhide-tough with a cruel mouth that was rarely photographed in a smile. He bore a scar over his right ear that interrupted his hairline and his broken nose was testament to his violent temper.

Telling herself it was now or never, she walked into the lobby. Two men were staggering under the weight of a long couch wrapped in plastic. She heard other workers talking in the background, saw hotel employees and workmen scurrying to and from the dining room and kitchen located opposite the front doors. The smells of cleaning solvent, turpentine, and varnish greeted her and the whine of a skill saw screaming through the vestibule was muted by the rumble of industrial vacuums.

As the workmen shoved the couch near a huge fireplace, she paused in the lobby and eyed the hotel that had once been the most opulent in Portland, a place for dignitaries and town fathers to gather, where decisions were made and the shape of the future had been planned. Biting her lip she gazed upward to the intricate stained-glass windows that rose over the outer doors where they caught the last rays of daylight and cast a pool of amber, rose and blue on the tile floor in front of the desk.

She swallowed against a lump that closed her throat, this hotel was her legacy. Her birthright. Her future.

Or was it?

There was only one way to find out. She headed for the wide, curved staircase that swept upward to the balcony.

"Hey, you! Lady, we're closed!" The voice, deep and male, was coming from a big, burly man poised on the top of a high scaffold positioned under the second-floor landing. He was fiddling with the chandelier situated over the lobby desk.

Ignoring him, she started up the carpeted steps.

"Hey, I'm talkin' to you!"

She hesitated, her gloved hand trailing on the banister. This wasn't going to be easy, but the electrician was only a small stumbling block. The first of many. With a determined smile meant to disarm him, she turned and squared her shoulders. "Are you Zachary Danvers?" she asked, knowing full well he wasn't.

"No, but—"

"Are you related to the Danvers family?"

"What the hell?" Beneath the brim of his hard hat he scowled at her. "No, of course not, but you can't go up there!"

"I have a meeting with Zachary Danvers," she insisted, her voice filled with chilly authority.

"A meeting?" the electrician repeated, obviously not believing her bluff.

Tossing her hair away from her face, she stared at him without giving an inch. "A meeting."

"That's news to me. I'm his foreman and he didn't mention no meeting." His scowl grew dark. Suspicious.

"Maybe he forgot," she said, her stomach grinding as she forced a cold smile. "But I need to talk to him or a member of the Danvers family."

"He'll be back in a half hour or so," the man said reluctantly.

"I'll wait for him. In the ballroom."

"Hey, I don't think—"

Without another glance in his direction, she hurried up the remaining stairs. Her boots were muffled on the thick carpet and her breath was shallow, a sign of her case of nerves.

"Shit," the man muttered under his breath, but stayed atop his perch and turned back to his work. "Goddamned women . . ."

Her heart was beating so fast she could hardly breathe, but at the top of the landing, she turned unerringly to the left and gulping in a huge, calming, breath of air, she shouldered open the double doors. The room was dark. Her throat closed in on itself and with her gloved fingers she fumbled for the light switch.

In a glorious blaze, the ballroom was suddenly lit by hundreds of miniature candles suspended in teardrop-shaped chandeliers.

Her heart nearly stopped at the sight of the polished oak floor, the bank of tall, arched windows, the dizzying light from a million little bulbs that reflected in the cut crystal.

Her throat clogged and she blinked back tears. *This* was where it had all happened? Where the course of her young life had been thrown away from its predestined path and into uncharted territory?

Why? She chewed on her lower lip. Oh, God, why couldn't she remember?

October rain slid down his hair and under the collar of his suede jacket. Dead leaves, already sodden, clung to the sidewalk and were beaten with the thick Oregon mist that seemed to rise from the wet streets and gather at the corners of the buildings. Cars, delivery vans, and trucks roared by, their headlights feeble against the watery illumination from the street lamps.

Zachary Danvers was pissed. This job had lasted too long, and wasted too much of his time. Working here made him feel like a damned hypocrite and he was thankful the job was just about over. Muttering oaths at himself, his brothers, and especially at his dead father, he pushed open the glass doors of the old hotel. The smells of lacquer and cleaning solvent wafted through the lobby as his boots rang against the Italian tile of the foyer. He'd wasted a year of his life here. A year. All because of a promise he'd made at his father's deathbed a couple of years ago. Because he'd been greedy. And because he'd loved to see Witt Danvers beg.

His stomach soured at the thought. Maybe he was more like the old man than he wanted to admit.

The hotel manager, a newly-hired nervous type with thinning hair and an Adam's apple that worked double time, was laying down the law with a new clerk behind a long mahogany desk, the pride of the lobby. Zachary had discovered the battered piece of dark wood in a century-old tavern located off Burnside in a decrepit building. The tavern had been scheduled to be razed, but Zach had decided to take the time to have the bar restored. Now the once-scarred mahogany gleamed under the lights.

All the fixtures in the hotel had been replaced with antiques or damned-close replicas and now the hotel could boast an authentic 1890s charm with 1990s conveniences.

The advertising people had loved that turn of phrase.

Why he'd agreed to renovate the old hotel still eluded him, though he was beginning to suspect he had developed a latent sense of family pride. "Son of a bitch," he grumbled under his breath. He was tired of the city, the noise, the bad air, the goddamned lights and most of all, his family, or what was left of it. Zachary Danvers itched to leave.

"Hey, Danvers!" his foreman Frank Gillette yelled from his position on the scaffold twenty feet above the lobby floor. He was tinkering with the wiring of a particularly bad-tempered chandelier. "Been lookin' for you. There's a woman here, in the ballroom. She's been waitin' here over an hour."

Zach's eyes narrowed a fraction. "What woman?"

"Didn't give her name. Claimed she had a meetin' with you."

"With me?"

"That's what she said." Frank started down the ladder. "All she'd tell me was that she had a meetin' with you and she couldn't talk to me as I wasn't a—and I'm quotin' here—'member of the Danvers family.' "

Frank hopped to the floor and dusted his hands. He drew a wrinkled handkerchief from his back pocket and rubbed it under the brim of his plastic hard hat.

From somewhere near the kitchen there was a crash and rattle of silverware that echoed through the hotel.

"Christ!" Frank's head snapped up and he narrowed his eyes at the kitchen. "Damn that Casey."

"Is she a reporter?"

"The woman?" Frank fumbled in his pocket for his cigarettes. "Hell if I know. As I said, I'm not a Danvers, so she wouldn't talk to me. Not that I wouldn't mind spending a little time with her."

"Good-looking?"

Frank said, "Beyond a ten."

"Sure."

"Look, all I know is that short of bodily hauling her pretty ass out of here, we got a problem. No one's supposed to be on the premises. If she slip and falls and breaks her neck and OSHA finds out—"

"You worry too much."

"You pay me to worry." Frank found his crumpled pack of Camels and shook out a cigarette.

"Just finish the job. I'll deal with the insurance people and the woman."

"Good." Smiling as he clicked his lighter to his cigarette, Frank inhaled deeply. "Now, let's see if this bitch works. Hey, Roy, turn on the damned juice." Reaching around the desk, he flipped a switch and stared at the chandelier. Lights shaped like candles blazed for a second before flickering and dying. "Fuckin' wiring," Frank growled, his face turning red, his cigarette bobbing between his lips. "Goddamned fuckin' wiring. I told that half-wit Jerry to use . . . oh, hell!" Exasperated, he shot out a stream of smoke. "Roy, turn it off again!" he roared.

"I'll go talk to the mystery lady."

"Do that," Frank growled as he started back up the scaffolding. Zach didn't doubt that by the grand opening, everything would work perfectly. Frank would see to it, if he had to hold two wires together himself.

From the stairs, Zach glanced around the lobby and thought of his father. Witt Danvers. A royal pain in the ass. The only surviving son of Julius, one of the great timber barons of all time, a poor man who had amassed a fortune with the saws, augers, axes and the sweat of other men. Witt had kept up the tradition, using chain saws and trucks and winches and the sweat of other men to line his pockets.

Right now, Witt would have been proud of the son he'd disowned half a dozen times. Not that it mattered. Witt Danvers was dead and cremated, his ashes spread across the rolling forests of the Oregon hills two years ago. A just end to a timber baron who had spent all his years raping the land. Witt had been a man who had seen what he wanted and taken it. Anyone who'd gotten in his way had regretted opposing the wealthiest man in Portland. Including his second son.

Through the rough suede of his jacket, Zach rubbed the scar in his shoulder, the result of being the son of Witt Danvers. His jaw tightened. It had taken him years to come to terms with the old man and now it was too late to make amends.

"Rest in peace you miserable bastard," Zachary said, his lips flattening as he opened the ballroom doors. His father had always treated Zach differently from the rest of his children. Not that he gave a damn now. Zach had his own business, his own identity. The noose of being the son of one of Portland's wealthiest men didn't seem quite so tight.

He took two long strides into the ballroom, then stopped dead in his tracks. The woman was there, dressed in a flowing black cape and matching knee-length boots. She turned at the sound of his entrance and before she could say a word he knew why she was waiting for him.

Glossy black curls swirled away from a flawless face. Round blue eyes fringed by lacy black lashes stared straight at him. Thin black brows arched inquisitively. He felt as if his heart had stopped for a second as she smiled, showing off finely carved cheekbones and a strong, slightly stubborn chin.

His breath seemed to stop somewhere in his lungs.

"You're Zachary," she said, as if she had every right to stand in the middle of the ballroom—*as if she belonged.*

Zach's throat was suddenly dry and hot and forbidden memories struggled to the surface of his mind. "Right."

"Danvers," she supplied, her voice low, her lips tightening just a fraction. Tossing her hair away from that gorgeous face, she smiled slightly and with her hand extended walked slowly toward him. "I've been wanting to meet you for a long time," she said, forcing a smile. "My name is—"

"London," he supplied as every muscle in his body grew taut with the pain of the past.

"You recognize me?" Hope lighted those blue eyes.

"There's a resemblance. I guessed."

"Oh." She hesitated, the wind suddenly out of her sails.

"But that's why you're here, isn't it?"

"Yes."

"You think you're my long-lost sister." He couldn't hide the cynicism in his words.

Those clear blue orbs clouded and her hand, the one she'd offered and he'd ignored, dropped to her side. "I think so. To tell you the truth, I'm not a hundred percent sure. That's why I'm here." She seemed to find her confidence again. "For a long time my name's been Adria."

"You're not sure?" he threw back at her. For a minute he could only stare into those wide blue eyes—eyes like another treacherous pair that had seemed to see right through him, but quickly his senses came back to him in a rush. Why did he think for even a second that this woman could be London? Hadn't he been close to enough elaborate frauds to smell one a mile a way? So she looked like his stepmother. Big deal. "My sister's been dead for almost twenty years," he said in the flat tone he reserved for liars and cheats.

"Half-sister."

"Doesn't matter."

She sighed and wrapped her arms around her middle. "I just wanted to see if I remembered this place—"

"London was only three."

"Four. Almost five. And even four-year-olds have memories . . . maybe just impressions, but memories nonetheless. . . ." She glanced toward one corner. "The band was over there in that alcove, and there were plants . . . trees, I think, near the windows . . ." Her eyebrows bunched together as if she were trying to catch hold of a fleeting memory. "And there was a huge fountain and an ice sculpture—a . . . horse, no, not just a horse, a *running* horse, I think and—"

"You've done your research."

Her lips tightened. "You don't believe me."

"I think you'd better leave." Zachary cocked his head toward the door. "London's dead. She has been for over twenty years, so take whatever it is you're peddling and go back home, before I haul you out of here and drop you on the front steps with the rest of the drifters and panhandlers and garbage."

"How do you know London's dead?"

His throat closed and he remembered with gut-wrenching clarity, the accusations, the fingers thrust in his direction, the suspicious looks cast his way. "I'm serious. You'd better leave."

"I'm serious, too, Zach." Ramming her hands in the voluminous folds of her cape, she took one last look around the huge room, then faced him again. "You may as well know, I don't give up easily."

"You don't have a prayer."

"Who's in charge?"

"Doesn't matter." His voice was hard, his features drawn with brutal resolution. "You can talk to my brothers and sister, my mother or the attorneys who are acting as the gods of finance in my father's estate, but no one's going to give you the time of day. You may as well save your breath and my time. Take my advice and go home."

"This could be my home."

"Bull."

"It's too bad Katherine isn't alive."

Zachary blood ran cold at the mention of his beautiful and much too young stepmother. There was an unmistakable resemblance between the young woman standing so arrogantly before him and his father's second wife, Katherine—the Kat—the woman who'd made his life a living hell for years. "Is it really too bad, or is it damned convenient?" he asked, keeping his expression bland.

She blanched a bit.

"Get out."

"You're afraid of me."

"As I said, 'Get out.' "

She held his gaze for a heart-stopping second, then strode through the ballroom doors and down the stairs. Zachary moved to the windows and watched as she walked onto the street, her strides long and full of purpose, her head ducked against the thickening rain.

She'd be back. They always came back. Until the power and money of the Danvers family drove them away and they gave up their farfetched dreams of stealing a little bit of the old man's treasure.

Good riddance, he thought, but, as she disappeared around the corner, he felt a premonition, like footsteps of the devil crawling up his spine, and he knew with absolute and bone-chilling certainly, that this one—this imposter posing as London Danvers—was somehow different from all the others.

PART ONE

1974

Zachary

1

"Happy birthday, darling," Katherine Danvers whispered into her husband's ear as they danced across the polished floor of the ballroom. From the alcove near the corner, a small dance band played "As Time Goes By" and the melody whispered through the crowd. "Surprised?" she asked, nuzzling him, her satin heels moving in perfect time to the music.

"Nothing you do surprises me." He chuckled low in his throat. Of course he'd known that she'd reserved the ballroom of his hotel under the fictitious name of some sorority. He hadn't spent fifty years learning to be the shrewdest businessman in Portland without picking up a few tricks along the way. He gave his wife a playful squeeze and felt her breasts, beneath her black satin dress, press closer to him. A few years before he would have become aroused just by the scent of her perfume and the knowledge that beneath the gown she wore absolutely nothing—just the dress and a pair of stiletto heels.

She pouted prettily as the pianist played a solo. Her black hair gleamed under the muted lights from chandeliers suspended from the cove-shaped ceiling and her eyes, a deep blue, glanced coyly at him through the sweep of thick dark lashes.

There had been a time when he would have given away his fortune just for one night in her bed. She was sensual and smart and knew exactly how to please a man. He'd never asked her how she knew so much about the pleasures of love when he'd met her. He'd just been grateful that she'd taken him as her lover, bringing back the lust that he'd thought he'd lost somewhere near middle-age.

A kitten who liked to be cuddled, Kat metamorphosed into a wildcat in bed and for a few years her raw sexual energy had been enough to satisfy him. He'd married her and remained faithful and managed to bed her every other day in the early years. But his desire had been short-lived, as it always was and now he couldn't remember when he'd last made love to her. A hot fire crept up the back of his neck at the thought of his impotence. Even now, when her thighs were pressed intimately to his and her tongue touched a sensitive spot near the back of his ear, he felt nothing, no hint of wildfire in his blood, no welcome stiffness between his legs. Even a little harsh foreplay didn't bring him to an erection anymore. It was a miracle that they'd managed to conceive a child.

Suddenly angry, he swirled her roughly away from him, then jerked her back into his arms. She laughed, that throaty little laugh that bordered on nasty. He liked her laugh. He liked everything about her. He only wished that he could throw her on the dance floor and take her the way she wanted to be taken— like an animal, with four hundred horrified eyes watching as he proved that he was still a man and could satisfy his wife.

She'd tried all her tricks. Flimsy negligees. Peek-a-boo bras that outlined her nipples and long black garters that flicked at her shapely thighs. She'd coaxed him with her tongue and dirty words, slapped playfully at his butt and balls, but nothing she did aroused him anymore and the thought that he couldn't manage an erection, might never have sex for the rest of his life, cut a hole in him that burned like dry ice and scared the living hell out of him.

The song ended and he pressed forward, bending her spine in a low dip, so that she had to cling to him, her eyes staring up into his, her black hair sweeping the floor that had been littered with pink rose petals. Her breasts, heaving with exertion, threatened to spill out of the deep cleavage of her dress.

In full view of the audience, he pressed a kiss to that glorious hollow between her breasts, as if he were so randy he couldn't stand it, then yanked her to her feet. Laughter and applause erupted around them.

"You old dog, you!" one man shouted and Kat blushed as if she were an innocent virgin.

"Take her upstairs. What're you waiting for?" another middle-aged boy yelled. "Isn't it about time you two had a son?"

"Later." Witt winked at the crowd, content that they didn't know his secret and secure that Kat would never breathe a word of his shame. A son. If this crowd of friends, relatives, and business acquaintances only knew.

There would be no more children, damn it. He'd sired three sons and a headstrong daughter from his first marriage to Eunice, that wop-loving bitch. With Katherine there would only be London, his four-year-old daughter and favorite child. He made no apologies for caring more about his little girl than he did all of his other children put together. The other kids—some of them adults now—had caused him so much heartache and their mother . . . Christ, what had he ever seen in Eunice Prescott—a skinny woman with a sharp tongue who'd thought sex with him had been her duty—nothing more than a chore? He'd decided she was frigid, until . . . Hell, he didn't want to think about Eunice and that damned dago cheating on him behind his back—laughing at him.

Angered at the turn of his thoughts, Witt escorted his wife to the center of the room where, beneath the glimmering lights of the chandelier, an ice-sculpture in the shape of a running horse was beginning to melt. Nearby a tiered fountain of champagne gurgled and splashed.

The band started playing "In The Mood" and a few brave couples strayed onto the dance floor. Witt snagged a fluted glass from a silver tray and drained the champagne in one long swallow.

"Daddy!" He glanced up and found London, her black curls dancing around her face, her chubby arms outstretched. Dressed in a navy-blue dress with white lace collar and cuffs, she ran up to him and threw herself into his waiting arms.

He hugged her tightly, the velvet of her dress crushed against him, her legs, encased in white tights, clamped around his waist. "How do you like the party, princess?"

Her crystal-blue eyes were round and wide, her cheeks flushed with the excitement of the festivities. "It's loud."

He laughed. "That it is."

"And there's too much smoke!"

"Don't tell your mother. She planned this as a special surprise and we wouldn't want her to feel bad," Witt said, grinning as he winked at his daughter.

She winked back, then snuggled her pert little nose into his neck and he got a whiff of baby shampoo. She tugged at his bow tie and he laughed again. Nothing could make him as happy as this dynamic whirl of precociousness.

"Hey, that's my job," Kat said as she smiled and gently nudged London's fingers from Witt's neck. Kissing her daughter's crown, she said, "Leave Daddy's tie alone."

"How about a dance?" Witt asked his young daughter and those little lines between Kat's eyebrows, the ones that suggested silently that she disapproved, appeared. Witt didn't care. He drained another glass of champagne and twirled a laughing London onto the dance floor. The child, his princess, squealed in delight.

"Sickening, isn't it?" Trisha observed from her position near the band. She leaned against the glossy top of the concert grand and petulantly sipped from a fluted glass. She was allowed, having just turned twenty-one.

Zachary lifted a shoulder. He was used to his old man's theatrics and he really didn't give a damn what Witt did anymore. He and his father had never gotten along and things had only become worse when Witt had divorced his first wife and eventually married a woman only seven years older than his oldest son, Jason, Zachary's brother. Truth be known, Zach didn't really want to be here, had only come because he was forced. He couldn't wait to escape the smoky, loud ballroom filled with boring old people—suck-ups every last one of them.

"Dad can't keep his hands off Kat," Trisha said, her voice slurring a little. "It's obscene." She took another swallow. "The lecherous old fart."

"Careful, Trisha," Jason said as he joined his brother and sister. "Dad probably had this place bugged, compliments of the Republican party. The Danvers Hotel might have something in common with the Watergate."

"Very funny," Trisha said, tossing her long auburn hair over one shoulder. But she didn't laugh. Her blue eyes were flat and bored and she continually scanned the crowd as if she were looking for something or someone.

Jason fingered his mustache and his eyes narrowed. "You know half the people here would like to see the old man fall."

"They're his friends," Trisha argued.

"And enemies." Jason rested a hip against the piano as the band took a break. He watched his father, still holding London, playing the crowd, moving from one knot of bejeweled guests to the other, never once setting London on her feet.

"Who gives a shit?" Zachary asked.

"Always the rebel." Jason smiled beneath his mustache, that know-it-all smile that bugged the hell out of Zach. Jason acted as if he knew everything. At twenty-three Jason was already in law school and was seven years older than Zach, a point he never let his rebellious younger brother forget.

Zach tugged at the tight collar of his tuxedo shirt. He couldn't stomach Jason any more than he could his sister, Trisha. They both cared too much about the old man and especially about the Danvers's family fortune.

Leaving Jason and Trisha to worry and fret over Witt's affection for London, Zach passed several groups of people passionately arguing about the impeachment proceedings against President Nixon and the rationing of gasoline.

He didn't care about either.

After grabbing a champagne glass from an unattended table, he sauntered over to the bank of tall, arched windows that overlooked the city. Drinking from the forbidden cup, he felt a bit of satisfaction as he stared through the glass to the hot July night. Traffic flowed in a steady stream along the street. Taillights winked and blurred as cars and trucks, still moving despite the gas crunch, labored through the city and over the yawning Willamette River, a sluggish black waterway that separated the west side of the city from the east. Steam rose from the city streets and the humidity level was high.

In the distance, beyond the expanse of city lights, a ridge of mountains, the Cascades, guarded the horizon. Thunderheads that had been gathering all day blocked out any view of the stars and the quick sizzling forks of lightning added unwanted tension to the brackish night. Zach finished his champagne and, hoping no one would notice, half buried his empty glass in the soil surrounding a potted tree.

He felt out of place, as he always had with his family. This black-tie affair thrown by Kat made him all the more aware that he was different from his brothers and sister. He didn't even look like the rest of the Danvers clan, all of whom were fair-skinned, blue-eyed and were favored with varying hues of light to dark brown hair.

He resembled his half-sister, London, more than anyone else in the family. Which didn't win him any points with Jason, Trisha, and Nelson, his younger brother, all of whom on one occasion or another professed to hate the princess.

With a snort, he considered London. He didn't care much about the kid one way or the other. Sure, she bothered him. Any four-year-old was a pain in the ass, but she wasn't as bad as the others made out. In fact, Zach found it amusing that she was already showing some of the traits Kat had perfected over the years. It wasn't London's fault the old man treated her like some kind of priceless jewel.

As if she'd read his mind, London pushed through the crowd and grabbed hold of his leg. He turned to tell her to get lost, but by that time she'd discovered his glass, pushed deep into the potting soil.

"Leave that alone!" he whispered in a harsh voice. She glanced up sharply, a naughty twinkle in her eye. God, if he could just step out on the balcony and grab a smoke—another vice of which his father and stepmother disapproved though Kat was never without her gold cigarette case and Witt enjoyed his share of cigars smuggled in from Havana.

She dropped the glass back into the dirt. "Hide me from Mommy!" With a wicked little giggle, she ducked behind his legs.

"Hey, don't get me involved in your stupid games."

"Shh. She's coming!" London hissed.

Great. Just what he needed.

"London?" Katherine's husky voice drifted over the slow strains of a ballad.

Behind him, London tried to smother a giggle.

"London, where are you? Come on now . . . it's time for bed. Oh, there you are!" Katherine sidestepped a group of men, her practiced smile well in place. Waving her fingers as she passed, she tracked down her wayward daughter with the precision of a bloodhound.

"No!" London cried as her mother approached.

"Come on, sweetheart, it's nearly ten."

"Don't care!"

"You'd better do what she says," Zachary offered, his gaze flicking slightly to his stepmother's. He knew what the old man saw in his young wife. Katherine Danvers was probably the sexiest woman Zachary had ever met. At sixteen he understood about unbridled sexual desire. Hot and thundering, it could eat a man up and cause his brain to shrivel.

"Come on." Katherine leaned down to pick up her daughter. The silk stretched across her shapely rump and her breasts seemed to bulge a bit, as if they might fall out of her plunging neckline.

"I'll get her into bed," another woman, London's governess,

Ginny Something-Or-Other, offered. She was a small, plain woman in sensible shoes and a drab olive-green suit. Next to Katherine she looked frumpy and old, a dowdy matron, though she probably was probably just over thirty, not much older than Kat.

"I don't want to go to bed," London insisted.

"She's being a pill." Katherine looked up and noticed one of the waiters motioning toward her. With a sigh, she turned back to her daughter. "Listen, honey, it's almost time to bring out the birthday cake; you can stay up and watch Daddy blow out his candles, then you have to go upstairs."

"Can I have some cake, too?"

The corners around Katherine's mouth tightened, though she said, "Of course, darling. But then you go with Ginny upstairs. We've got a special room for you, right by Daddy and Mommy's and we'll be up later to tuck you in."

Mollified somewhat, London headed back to the party and Katherine straightened, smoothing her dress over her hips as Ginny followed her wayward charge.

Zach hoped that Katherine would hurry to the band leader and order the musicians to strike up "Happy Birthday To You," but she inched her chin up a fraction and eyed her stepson. Zach was three inches taller than Kat. Nonetheless, she had a way of making him feel small. "Stay away from the booze." She plucked his empty champagne glass from the dirt and twirled the stem between her long, slim fingers. Even while reprimanding him, she was sexy as hell. As if she knew her power over him and any man who wasn't blind, she puckered her lips sweetly, then waggled the glass under his nose. "We wouldn't want anything to spoil this party for your daddy now, would we? If you were to get caught with one of these, there could be trouble."

"I won't get caught."

"Don't think you're so smart, Zach. I saw you swilling champagne, and I don't think I'm the only one who was looking in your direction. Anyone else could have seen you, including Jack

Logan. You remember—he's with the police department. I think you two have met before."

Zach's teeth clamped together. Hot embarrassment climbed up the back of his neck. "As I said, I won't get caught."

"You'd better not, because, if you land your cute little butt in jail or end up in the juvenile hall again, Witt won't bail you out. So"—she smiled sweetly—"use your head."

As she sauntered away, mingling with one group of guests after another, Zachary seethed. His blood boiled through his veins and he fantasized about wrapping his fingers around her neck and shaking some sense into her, but he couldn't take his eyes off her ass and the way it shifted beneath the shimmering black silk of her dress. She moved slowly, as if each step were a deliberately sensual movement designed to make him squirm. The rose petals were crushed beneath her heels. Her smooth back, visible to the curve of her lower spine, was unblemished and supple, and he imagined it would arch perfectly beneath the right man.

He felt an erection beginning, and turned away from her image. Half the time he thought she put on a sexual show for him intentionally. Other times he told himself that it was his imagination, that he was finding sexual overtures in the most innocent of gestures.

To cool his blood he placed his head against the window. Steam was fogging the inside of the glass. The room was so damned hot he felt that he was suffocating and his blood still pounded at his temples. At sixteen he was still a virgin, which wasn't a big deal, unless he had to spend any time alone with Kat, something he tried to avoid.

Stuffing one hand into his pocket to hide the swell in his pants, he walked to the nearest tray of filled glasses, grabbed one and downed it quickly, all the while staring at his stepmother. She didn't seem to see him. Buoyed by his newfound source of rebellion, he sauntered over to another unattended tray, snatched another glass and downed the champagne in one gulp. A few drops drizzled along his chin but he didn't care.

The room began to get warmer still and he loosened his tie. A flush stole up his face and he felt a little light-headed. He was definitely getting a buzz. Well, good. He didn't want to be here anyway. Might as well enjoy himself.

Halfway through his next drink, he felt a smooth hand close over his arm. He jumped and champagne splashed down the front of his jacket and shirt. Kat's long fingers dug into the muscles beneath his sleeve. Her eyes were dark with rage, her full lips clenched in fury. "You just don't know when to give up, do you?"

He shook off her arm. "You can't tell me what do."

"No?" She arched an eyebrow in a sexy gesture that scared him spitless. "Mmm. We'll see."

He finished his drink to spite her, but she didn't seem to mind. In fact, her face changed into a soft smile and her eyes caught the reflection of the chandelier, sparkling up at him. With an innocent grin, she linked her fingers through his. "Dance with me, Zach."

Zach, despite the friendly cobwebs in his mind, smelled trouble. "I . . . I don't dance."

"Sure you do. It's easy."

"But I can't—"

She leaned closer to him, put her lips against his ear. "People are staring. Come on."

His throat was suddenly desert-dry. "Katherine, I really don't want to—" But she was right. He felt the burning weight of the gazes of curious onlookers. He wanted to die. From the corner of his eye, he saw Jason staring at him, his expression unreadable. Trisha was downing champagne and God-only-knew what else. She smiled drunkenly at Zach's discomfiture. Witt, his father, was still dancing with little London and too busy to notice that Zach was trapped.

"Really, Katherine. I don't want to—"

"Oh, you want, Zach," she said, leaning closer to him, pressing her hip against his groin. "I can tell. And I'll let your father know if you don't give me just one little dance."

Guiltily, Zach glanced at Witt but the old man seemed oblivious to the fact that his son, the one who always gave him so much trouble, was being led to the dance floor like a horse to slaughter. He couldn't imagine dancing with Katherine, feeling her body pressed close to his. His blood was already roaring through his system. As they reached the dance floor, she turned, molding her body to his, beginning to sway in rhythm to the music.

Her hips were pressed intimately to his and her breasts seemed crushed against his chest. "Now, isn't this better?" she murmured in a husky drawl and he closed his eyes, fighting the lust that burned through his body, feeling his stiffening erection even as he tried to deny it.

"Let me go," he begged.

"You don't want to go." She shifted slightly so that her lower abdomen was hugging his. God, she had to know that he was hard. "I can tell."

"Don't—"

Holy Christ, his right hand was on her bare back, feeling the silky texture of her skin, the sleek movement of her muscles. Was it his imagination or did she make some low sort of wanting sound deep in her throat?

"You lied," she whispered, her breath ruffling the hair covering the tops of his ears.

He was dying inside. So hard he ached, he couldn't think straight. A part of him warned him to back off, but the other part, puffed up by male ego and sexual desire, couldn't stop fantasizing. He wondered what she would do if he rubbed up against her; let his hand slip beneath the black fabric of her dress. What would happen if he slowly let his mouth and tongue wander down the delicate column of her throat?

As if she understood his need, she lolled her head to one side, exposing more of her white skin, showing off just a little more of her gorgeous bosom.

"Mind if I cut in?" Witt's voice seemed to reverberate through the ballroom and Zachary started, dropping his hands guiltily.

He tried to put some distance between his body and Kat's but she
held him close.

Turning slumberous eyes toward her husband, her lips
twisted into a wicked grin, she whispered, "Thought you'd never
ask."

Witt's face was flushed. His eyes thinned on his rebellious son
as Zachary took a step back and London, who was still clinging
to her father, was plopped into Zach's empty arms. "Stay away
from the champagne," Witt said. "It would be a hell of an
embarrassment if Jack had to arrest you here. Now, give London
a spin on the floor and ask one of the Kramer girls to dance—
they've been watching you all night."

Gulping, Zachary wished he could knock the old man's lights
out. When he glanced at Kat she was laughing, her eyes twinkling with naughty amusement. At his expense. His fingers
clenched into fists and if it wasn't for the fact that he was holding
London, he might have made an already ugly situation worse. It
was as if his father and stepmother had conspired together to
make him look a fool.

His shoulders tensed and heat surged up the back of his neck
to spread through his face. Though several girls in expensive
dresses were trying to capture his attention, Zach didn't even
give them the time of day. He handed London to her nanny, and
wished he could hit something . . . anything.

Ripping his tie from his neck, he wanted nothing more than
to leave the goddamned hotel and cool off. Spoiling for a fight,
he left the dance floor. How could he have been such a fool?
How? Because of Kat. Damn the woman! His fists curled in angry
impotence. He had to get out of here.

Jason, drink in hand, found Zach insolently leaning a shoulder
against one of the pillars near the door as he plotted his escape.
"Don't let her get to you," Jason advised.

"Who?"

"The Kat." Sipping his drink—bourbon straight up—Jason
smiled.

"What do you mean?" Zach asked, trying to sound nonchalant.

Jason snorted and cocked his head toward the dance floor. "I saw that little exhibition."

Mortified, Zach gritted his teeth.

"Christ, she can be a bitch." Jason raked an impatient hand through his thick, chestnut-colored hair. "I know what she's up to, saw her coming on to you. She damned near laid down and spread her legs right in the middle of the dance floor." He took a swallow of his drink and stared at Kat and Witt. "It's some sort of game with her."

A muscle worked in Zach's jaw. He felt the angry tic and couldn't control it.

"She did it on purpose, you know. Decided you needed putting in your place, which, I might add, she did."

"I hate her."

"Don't we all?" Jason replied, his eyes following his stepmother as she danced. "But she might just be the most incredibly sexy woman on this planet. People talk about Raquel Welch or Ursula Andress being so damned irresistible. Obviously those people haven't met our stepmother. I wonder what she's like in bed."

"I don't want to know." Zachary scowled and refused to look at the object of their discussion.

"Sure you do. Every man here would like a little piece of the Kat." He flung a brotherly arm over Zach's shoulders. "But she doesn't play her games with them. No way. For some reason she's picked you to toy with. If I didn't know better, I'd think she might have her sights set on you."

"Oh, Jesus! No way!" Zach said, though his heart skipped a beat.

"I'm not so sure. She sure hasn't come on to me like she just did with you and I've seen her, when she thinks no one's watching. The way she looks at you. Christ, it's hot."

"Stop it."

"But you can't mess with her. If Dad ever found out—"

"Cut it out, Jason," Zach said, suddenly anxious. First Kat and now his brother. "I'm not going to mess with her."

Jason lifted a shoulder. "Everyone's always said you were different, I guess Kat just wants to find out if it's true."

"God, Jason, listen to what you're saying! No, don't! It's sick."

"You know what you need to do?"

Zach didn't answer.

"Go out and get laid." Leaning closer to Zach, he pointed a finger at a swarm of teenaged girls, curls piled high on their heads, their makeup right out of *Seventeen* magazine. Compared to Katherine they seemed young and gawky and . . . desperate. "But not with Kat. Like I said, the old man would tan your hide if he found out. But Alicia Kramer is so hot for you she can barely stand it. I'll bet she's creaming all over herself just looking at you."

"Stop it!" Zach hissed, but Jason laughed, obviously pleased that he'd gotten such a violent reaction.

"I'm telling you, sliding into her would be like sticking it into hot pudding."

"For Christ's sake, cut it out!" Zach slid a glance in Alice's direction and caught her hopeful gaze. She was a petite girl with big boobs and a bad complexion she disguised with thick pan-cake makeup. Her teeth were straight, compliments of the braces she'd worn for two years. She wasn't bad looking. She giggled and blushed when she caught Zach's eye. But Zach wasn't inter-ested in the daughter of some big-shot banker. No way. Com-pared to Kat, Alicia seemed like a child.

"She's so horny she can barely keep her dress on. Look, I can tell you from my own experience that the Kramer girls are definitely hot-blooded. My guess is Alicia will give you a ride you'll remember for the rest of your life."

"No thanks," Zach replied.

"I'm telling you, little brother, it's time. I can hook you up with—"

"Forget it, Jason."

Jason grabbed his arm. "Really, Zach. I know how you feel, like a powder keg ready to explode and believe me you can only take it so long." His voice lowered a little. "There's a girl I know . . . well, a woman really. She . . . well, she knows just what to do to make a man feel good. She's expecting me tonight."

"A whore? Are you talking about a whore?" Zach demanded, shocked, yet a little intrigued. Did Jason really know a prostitute? Holy shit!

Jason took his arm and steered him to a quiet corner of the room, far away from the guests and the linen-clad tables of food and drink. "Now, just listen. This girl, Sophia, she's . . . well, believe me, you'll like her. She's a good person."

Zach snorted. "Good people aren't whores."

"I mean it. She's not a streetwalker. In fact, she does this because she likes it. She's always ready."

"Oh, God—"

"She's pretty and clean and will only do what you want to do. You can fuck her brains out if you want to, or, if you'd rather just talk . . . she'll listen. Really. It's up to you." Jason's voice was filled with brotherly concern.

Zach knew he should walk away, but he couldn't. An honest-to-goodness hooker. Waiting for Jason? A hooker who would just listen?

"I know you and I don't always see eye-to-eye, but this time, for the love of Christ, listen to me. You need a woman. Bad. And it can't be Kat." Frowning slightly, he reached into his pocket, pulled out a room key and pressed the cool metal into Zachary's sweating palm. "Three blocks down. The Orion Hotel. Sophia. Don't worry about money. It's all been arranged."

"I don't want—"

"Do yourself a favor. Forget about Kat. Get laid." With a friendly smile, Jason headed toward the bar, leaving Zach to clutch the damned hotel key in his clammy fingers. Swallowing hard, he opened his hand and stared down at the key to room

307, the key to his manhood, the key to his freedom from Kat.

Suddenly aware that any number of his father's guests could have overheard his conversation with Jason, Zach jammed his hands deep into his pockets and wondered how many of the other people at the party had witnessed his humiliation on the dance floor. How many eyes other than his brother's and his father's had seen Kat's lips brush against his ear, or watched as his sweaty fingers had itched to delve beneath the zipper of her dress to grasp one of those firm buttocks? Jesus, he had to quit thinking about her like this! The key felt heavy in his pocket.

The band broke into "For He's A Jolly Good Fellow." Though his mind was still on the mysterious Sophia, the hooker with a heart, Zach watched as a huge cake in the shape of a fir tree was wheeled into the room on an elaborate cart. Fifty candles arranged in a string, like holiday lights decorating a Christmas tree, had been placed upon the needles of green frosting. Tiny flames flickered and danced as Witt, with Katherine and London's help, blew out every last spark.

Laughter and applause erupted and Witt, like a bridegroom, cut a fat piece of cake and fed the gooey concoction to his wife. Everyone cheered and Zach thought he might get sick as Katherine returned the favor, then smiling up at her husband, licked her fingers daintily.

By the time London was hustled upstairs to one of the suites reserved for the Danvers family, the old man was starting to look a little tipsy. He hazarded a hard glance Zach's way and even in the crowded room, Zach read the warning in his father's eyes. His heart sank. From years of experience Zach knew that Witt had not forgotten that his young wife had been flirting with his son. Nothing escaped the old man and sooner or later, there would be hell to pay. Zach already bore several scars on his backside from the slap of his father's belt. By this time tomorrow, he'd probably wear a few more—at least psychological scars. Witt Danvers was nothing, if not brutal. He wouldn't spare Zach's feelings and would let his rebellious son know that he was no good, didn't live up to his expectations, would never amount to anything in life.

So who gave a shit what the old man thought?

The key pressed hard against his thigh.

Witt and Katherine began dancing again and his father's attention was diverted from his second son to his wife. Zach seized the opportunity for escape. Without a glance over his shoulder, he wended his way past loud groups of guests, slipped through ballroom doors to the landing where he stopped to catch his breath and fight the dizziness in his brain from too much champagne.

What was he doing? He couldn't just leave the party. The old man would come unhinged.

More unhinged.

Good.

Maybe Witt Danvers might even worry a little.

Before he changed his mind, Zach steadied himself against the rail and hurried down the wide staircase.

"Hey, Zach. Where're ya goin'?" Nelson, his younger brother demanded. At fourteen, Nelson, now hanging halfway over the rail, his shaggy blond hair flopping over his eyes, idolized his hellion of an older brother.

"Not now," Zach growled. He didn't need the kid's adoration any more than he needed Witt's disapproval.

"But—"

"Just keep quiet, Nelson. Okay?" Refusing to acknowledge Nelson as the kid ran down the stairs, Zach strode through the front lobby where club chairs, brass lamps, and glossy dark tables were positioned around a massive fireplace. Past the lobby desk and a forest of potted palms, he walked quickly, trying not to think about the ramifications of his actions when Witt discovered him missing.

Outside, the night was humid. The smell of the river, musty and dank, drifted on air so still it seemed to cling to Zach's skin. He yanked off his jacket and began walking fast, heading north, trying to cool his blood and clear his head.

What he was contemplating was crazy, and yet, he'd consumed enough alcohol to feel bolder than usual. So what if the old man found out? What could he do? Kick Zach out of the Danvers's family mansion, force him to live with his mother? That thought was a bitter pill to swallow.

Deep down, a part of him still cared for the woman who had borne him, but she didn't deserve that love, not after she'd abandoned them all and left them in the lonely house on the hill with Witt. Zach didn't know the full story, but the gist of it was that Witt had caught his wife in bed with his most hated rival, Anthony Polidori. She'd been carrying on with him for years and rather than expose herself, or her lover to the media, she'd had no choice but to accept Witt's terms for the divorce: he'd get the kids and most of the wealth, she'd receive a stipend and be spared the ugly scandal of testifying in divorce court that she was an adulteress. Her social position had been spared; her children's lives had not.

As much as Zach professed to despise the old man, he did have a grudging respect for Witt Danvers and the power he seemed to possess over the people of this city. As for his mother, Zach felt little but loathing for Eunice, the woman who had shamed his father with an affair that had ripped out the old man's soul. It had been Eunice who had wounded his pride so badly that eventually, though it was years later, Witt had fallen into the open arms of Katherine LaRouche, a woman whom he'd met at the Empress Hotel in Victoria, British Columbia, a woman he'd married within the week, a woman, who, Witt had explained to his children, was from a wealthy Ontario family, a woman whom he adored, a woman who would be faithful to him, a woman who was twenty years his junior. Their new mother.

The family had been in shock, the Danvers's lawyers nearly apoplectic, but the damage had already been done. Katherine LaRouche, whoever she was, had managed to become the bride of one of the wealthiest men in Portland. She'd seemed proper enough then, Zachary thought, remembering back, and the change in her attitude toward him had come subtly over the years. As he'd reached adolescence he'd felt her watching him more closely, caught her eyeing him whenever his shirt was off—either when he was swimming in the pool in his cut-off jeans or riding one of the horses bareback. As his muscles had developed, so had Katherine's interest in her stepson.

He'd told himself that he was imagining things, that it was only his newfound awareness of his own masculinity that had changed his perception, but now he wasn't so sure. And Jason had voiced the same suspicions.

Sighing through his nose, he shook his head, to clear it. With one hand, he felt the key in his pocket and his stomach tightened into a hard ball of apprehension. What if he actually went into the Orion Hotel, took the elevator to the third floor, rapped hard on the door and it was opened by a withered old woman without teeth who smelled bad? What if the damned door was opened by a man? A queer dressed up as a hooker? Oh, Jesus! What if this whole arrangement was a setup, the result of Jason's twisted sense of humor?

He gritted his teeth and glanced behind him as he reached the Orion. No one seemed to have followed him and no one other than Jason would guess that he was here. Somehow he found strength in his anonymity as he lingered on the steps of the high-rise that jutted upward, washed by floodlights, white concrete slicing into a sky as black as obsidian.

Hesitating a fraction of a second, Zachary locked his jaw, squared his shoulders, threw open the hotel's front door and decided it was time he became a man.

2

The hotel corridor was empty, a long hallway of gold shag carpeting and metal doors painted to look like wood. The Orion had none of the charm of the Hotel Danvers, but Zach didn't care. Swallowing back the urge to turn tail and run, Zachary let the stairwell door bang shut behind him and walked, heart knocking, toward room 307. To Sophia. His destiny.

Before he lost his already-faltering courage he rapped sharply on the door and waited.

"It's open," a cool, feminine voice called through the metal.

Oh, Christ! Zach's heart nearly stopped. He reached for the knob with clammy fingers and threw open the door.

The woman was lying with her back to him. Sprawled sensually across the bed, wearing only a black bra and a lacy black belt with long garters that dangled over a scanty pair of panties, she stretched. Zach could see the hollows in her smooth rump and long thighs and his mouth turned to sand. "You're late," she reprimanded gently.

Zach's diaphragm slammed up against his lungs and he could barely breathe. Heat radiated from his groin.

Turning slowly, allowing him a glimpse of full breasts crushed into a bra several sizes too small, she smiled up at him with a come-hither look that evaporated when her gaze met his face.

"Who're you?" she demanded. Her dark eyes shadowed with fear. "Get out!" She cast an anxious look around, as if searching for a weapon, or clothes to cover her body. "Get the fuck out!" She reached for a pink silk wrapper and started ramming her hands frantically down its sleeves.

"Jason sent me."

She froze. "Like hell," she muttered, her black eyes disbelieving. The robe still gaped enough so that he had a view of the hollow between her ample breasts.

Zach's throat closed in on itself and he prayed to God that his voice didn't squeak. "He's still at Dad's party and—"

"Dad's?"

"I'm his brother, Zachary." He started to stick out his hand, knew it to be a mistake and wished he could just drop dead of a heart attack. She was a hooker, for God's sake, a professional and he was a bumbling, tongue-tied, green, virgin! She could probably smell it.

Suspicion lingered on her features. "You don't look like him."

The bane of Zach's existence. "I know." Still he didn't move.

"Close the damned door."

Zach kicked it closed but didn't bother with the bolt.

Scooting closer to the headboard, trying to hold the robe closed over her dark skin, looking as if she might bolt for the door at any minute, she asked, "Why'd he send you?" She tossed a thick rope of coal-black hair off her face. "Jesus, you scared the living shit out of me."

"I didn't mean to."

"Well, come in," she ordered, obviously agitated.

Carefully, afraid she might jump up and run down the hall screaming rape, he walked across the orange carpet and eased himself onto the foot of the bed.

"Jason sent you?" she asked, reaching onto the nightstand for a crumpled pack of cigarettes propped against a half-finished drink. She shook out an unfiltered Pall Mall and her hands only trembled a little as she struck a match and cupped the tip of her cigarette. She waved the match out, sucked in deeply, then, with the cigarette still dangling from wet, pink lips, let the smoke drift out of her nostrils and plucked a piece of tobacco from her tongue. "Why?"

"He, um, he had to stick around. Dad wanted him there."

She arched a fine black brow as she drew on her cigarette again and finally lifted it from her lips. "But he didn't want you?" she asked skeptically.

"Jason's the oldest," Zach said, as if it explained everything, which, it did. Jason had been groomed from the day he was born to be heir to the Danvers fortune. Nothing had changed just because Witt had sired a second son.

The whore smiled. "So he's the favorite."

"London's the old man's favorite."

"Ahh. Jason's talked about her. The little kid. What is she, about three?"

"Almost five." Zach didn't see that London's age mattered at all, especially considering the situation. He was in a hotel room with a prostitute and they were discussing his baby sister! Well, hadn't Jason said she liked to talk? Somehow he'd expected the conversation to be a little more sensual.

Sophia set her cigarette in the ashtray on the bed stand, then picked up her drink. Swirling the melting ice cubes with one long, violet-pink nail, she stared at Zach, letting her eyes rove up his half-buttoned shirt to his windblown hair.

"Jason wants you to take his place?"

"That seemed to be the plan."

She took a swallow from her glass and the tip of her tongue rimmed her wet lips. "Are you a virgin, Zachary?"

The question hit him like a slap in the face. "Of course not."

"Mmm. Then you've had . . . many women?" She sipped her drink, trying to smother a smile.

"My share," he said, realizing that they both knew he was lying. Hell, what did you say to a prostitute when she asked you things like that?

"You ever had a blow job?"

His head snapped up. Was she for real, or was she teasing him? He stared straight into her dark eyes and wondered if she was laughing at him. His gut tightened as she set the glass on the night table, allowing the robe to gape open and reveal her big breasts. He couldn't help but stare.

He was already beginning to get hard, but he didn't try to hide his erection. The robe fell off one of her shoulders and her skin looked soft and smooth, moving easily beneath the silky ebony strap of her bra.

"So what're we going to do about this?" she asked, as she settled back on the bed, the pink wrapper no longer clutched in her fingers, her navel and the top of lacy black underpants visible. When he didn't reply, she inched closer to him, first with her toe, then with the rest of her, sliding slowly down the bed, rumpling the coverlet with her rounded buttocks. Her eyes were hot, dark mirrors seeming to reflect the torment of his soul. She seemed to stare past all the lies he'd told her as she pulled herself up to her knees and moved her head close to his. She smelled of perfume and smoke and bourbon.

"So you won't tell me, eh? Well, just let me know when I do something you don't like, okay?"

She pressed her hot, wet tongue against the shell of his ear and he groaned. The swelling between his legs began to ache and as her tongue dipped into his ear, he wondered if he might embarrass them both by coming in his pants. "Come on, baby, what're you waiting for?" she whispered in a whiskey-smooth voice.

The invitation was impossible to resist.

He grabbed her and pressed his lips hard to her slick, pink mouth, smearing lipstick in his anxiety, tossing her back on the bed so he could feel her under him.

"That's my boy," she growled as he shoved the robe off her and stared at her beautiful breasts. Round, dark nipples pointed upward through the sheer lace, inviting his hands and mouth and Zachary, finding her so willing, couldn't stop himself.

His thumb grazed a nipple and she arched, her butt coming off the bed, her naked abdomen slapping against the inseams of his pants. Her fingers found the buttons of his shirt and the wall of skin beneath. She lifted herself up and playfully nipped at his few chest hairs, causing him to lose himself in the wonder of her touch. Already dizzy from the champagne, Zachary felt the room spin as she touched him, her magic fingers caressing his bare skin, her tongue slick and hot as she slid down further.

He groaned as she breathed across his groin and he closed his eyes in ecstasy as she began to minister him. But as eagerly as she'd started, she stopped just as suddenly, jerking up her head.

Zach sensed trouble. He opened his eyes and found her staring at the door. He reached for his fly.

Bam! The door burst open. The knob banged against the wall. Sophia screamed, bucked beneath him, and tried to writhe off the bed. "No!" she squealed, trying to push him away.

Zach, still foggy, glanced toward the door. For a second he couldn't move, but Sophia, scrambling, managed to slide away from him.

Two men, one tall and dark, with bad teeth and oily hair, the other shorter and skittish, with a pockmarked face and a crooked nose, were standing in the doorway, dark menacing figures silhouetted by the lights from the corridor.

"Get out of here," Zach commanded.

They didn't move.

"I said—"

"Shut up!" the oily one cut in, stepping inside.

The short one slid a glance at Sophia, then kicked the door shut.

Zachary rolled off the bed and onto the balls of his feet. The smell of a fight hung heavy in the air and he stood between the men and the bed, torn between some silly chivalrous desire to protect the woman and the urge to run like hell out of the room. He stood his ground, staring down the men. "Call security," he ordered Sophia.

"Danvers?" The shorter one with shoulder-length brown hair asked.

"Yeah?" Zachary's guts shredded. These thugs knew his name? How? The whore! This had to be some kind of setup.

He reached for the phone. The tall man kicked it away from him.

"What the hell—"

Zach spun away, but he was too late. With the agility of a jungle cat, the tall intruder grabbed Zachary's arm and wrenched it behind his back. Zach twisted and writhed.

"Cool it, you dumb fuck!"

Zach kicked, the heel of his boot connecting with the man's shin.

Wind whistled between the attacker's teeth. "You son of a bitch! You lousy little bastard!" The man yanked hard on Zach's arm.

Pain screamed through his shoulder. He heard a sickening rip and his muscles turned to fire.

"Help me out, Rudy!"

From the corner of his eye, Zach noticed Sophia scoot backward on the bed. Her face was white with fear as she tried to grab the receiver that dangled from the phone.

"No way, sister," the shorter man—the one called Rudy said, as he yanked the cord from the wall.

"Please—" she cried.

"Shut up!" the thug snarled.

Zach kicked his attacker again. "Let go of me!"

"No way, Danvers. You fucked up one time too many." His lips twisting in malevolent glee, he wrenched Zach's arm.

Agony jarred through his body. Zach screamed.

"You tryin' to kill him, Joey?" Rudy barked.

"Maybe." Joey slammed Zach's face with his meaty fist. The blow landed with a sickening crunch. Pain exploded behind Zach's eyes as blood spurted down his shirt, spraying Rudy.

"Hey, watch it—" Rudy stared at Zach's pulpy face for a minute, then glanced up at his partner. "Oh, shit! Hey, man, I don't think this is the right guy. This one, he don't look like—"

"You're making a mistake!" Sophia cried, clutching the blankets around her, her lips trembling.

"I don't think so." The big one wasn't convinced. He growled next to Zach's ear. "Let's do it, Rudy! Quit screwing around!"

Zachary struggled, throwing himself toward the door. From the corner of his eye, he saw Rudy reach into his pocket. A flash of silver glinted in the lamplight. Zach's guts twisted with a numbing fear. He heard a resounding click and he nearly wet his pants. A switchblade!

"Okay. Cut him," Joey said, his foul breath warm against Zach's head.

"No!" Zach struggled even harder, hurling his weight sideways, throwing his attacker off balance.

"I said, cut him!" Joey yelled.

Rudy's switchblade sliced through the air.

Sophia screamed.

Zach flinched but felt his scalp slitting open above his ear. White hot, the pain nearly blinded him. "Stop!" Blood poured from the wound, over his eyes and face.

"This isn't the right guy," Rudy said wiping the blood from his weapon on his pants. "I've seen Danvers—"

"Don't matter! 'Sides he's claimin' to be him."

"Shit!"

Blindly, Zach kicked.

"Who cares who the fuck he is," Rudy finally agreed. The knife plunged into Zach's shoulder. Pain shrieked through his arm. He retched. His body sagged heavily. *They're going to kill me. I'm gonna die just like a lamb being slaughtered.* Zach struggled, but he could barely move.

"He said he's Jason Danvers, now let's just get it over with," Joey said.

Jason? They thought he was Jason? "Zachary." Zach spat words and blood from behind loose teeth. He tried to break free and his knees buckled. "I'm . . . I'm . . . Zachary Danvers."

"He's telling you the truth!" Tears rolled down Sophia's white face. "He's not Jason! For the love of God, just leave him alone!"

"Not Jason?" Rudy repeated. "I knew it!"

"Shit!" Joey let go of Zach and jerked the knife out of Zach's shoulder. The wound burned like acid. Zach dropped to the floor, banged his head and couldn't move out of the sticky blood pooling beneath him.

"I told you he was the wrong guy. Shit, man, why don't you ever listen?" Rudy hissed. He pointed at the bed where Sophia was still huddled in fear. "You—get some clothes on and get out of here."

"But the boy—" Sophia whispered.

"He'll live," Rudy snarled, casting a dark look toward Zach before eyeing the whore again. "Unless you want to explain what you're doing up here with the half-dead son of Witt Danvers, you'll move your sweet little ass out of here."

Don't leave, Zach tried to say, but the words wouldn't form over his thick tongue. He watched three sets of feet, her small bare ones, the others in black work boots—moving in slow motion away from him. Footsteps scuffled on the shag carpet. Blood seeped from his body to the floor. He tried to lift his head.

"Bastard!" He saw the shoe, felt a hard kick in the groin and curled into a ball. Bile sprayed up the back of his throat. "Stay put, Danvers! You'll live longer."

A tide of black swirled around his eyes, though he willed himself to stay conscious. He saw the door to room 307 open, then close and he gave in to the warm, dark void that swallowed him.

Katherine's feet ached, her head throbbed and her eyes burned from cigarette smoke. The celebration had been a success and Witt, if he hadn't been surprised, had put on a good show of acting astounded at his wife's carefully planned party.

Seated on one of the chairs near the empty stage, she ignored the litter on the floor and took off one of her spiked heels to rub the bottom of her foot.

Soon dawn would be streaking the eastern sky and still a few guests lingered, talking, laughing, refusing to call it a night.

"Come on upstairs," Kat suggested to her husband as she slipped her toes into her shoe again. "London will be up before we know it." She stood and stretched, aware that after hours on her feet, her hair tangled, her makeup all but gone, she was still beautiful and sexy. She caught more than one male gaze lingering on the swell of her bosom.

Witt, having consumed champagne for hours, yawned and wrapped a meaty arm around her shoulders. He was heavy, this big bear of a man, and she staggered under the combination of his sagging weight and too many glasses of champagne.

Hours before, while she was getting ready for the party, she'd dressed with care and planned to seduce her husband, no matter how much work it was, but now she was tired, her feet ached, her head pounded and she wasn't interested in anything but falling into the huge bed in their suite and sleeping for at least a million hours.

She helped Witt into the elevator. For a few hours the guests, dressed in their finest clothes and jewelry had forgotten about OPEC, the impeachment proceedings, and the horrible state of the economy. Even Witt had given up talking about the problems in the timber industry, thank God, as speeches about old growth, clear-cutting, runaway fuel prices and the like bored her to tears.

With a groan, the elevator moved upward, only to shudder to a stop on the seventh floor. "Come on, birthday boy," she said, still supporting him as they reached their suite with its panoramic view of the river. She didn't much care about the view as she unlocked the door, snapped on the lights and helped him to the king-size bed that had already been turned down by the maid. Witt fell across the silk sheets like a heavy sack of potatoes.

"Come here," he said thickly, reaching for his wife as she pulled the draperies shut.

Katherine giggled. "Want me?"

"Always," he assured her. "I love you, Katherine. Thanks."

Tears stung the back of her eyes as the drapes snapped shut. She did care about him. "I love you, too, honey."

"I wish I could . . . I mean . . ."

"Shh. It doesn't matter," she said, and meant it at that moment.

Sex was important, but it wasn't as valuable as love. Kat could find sex anywhere, but she'd learned long ago how stingy people were with love. Leaning over, she rumpled his hair playfully and placed a kiss on his cheek. "I'll be back in a minute. I just want to check on London."

"Me, too," he said, his foggy eyes clearing a bit as he thought of his little girl.

Kat sighed. As much as she adored London, a tiny part of her was jealous of the attention Witt lavished upon his youngest daughter—their only child. As Witt pushed himself upright in the bed, Kat cracked open the connecting door, allowing a thin shaft of light from their suite to pierce into the room occupied by London and her nanny.

At first she thought her tired eyes were playing tricks on her, that she'd drunk too much champagne and her cloudy mind wasn't focusing, but as she stepped into the smaller room, her heart began to hammer, thunder in her ears. She fumbled for the switch. Suddenly the room was flooded with light.

Both beds were empty; neither had been mussed. The sheets were turned down and two mints sat untouched on the pillows.

Katherine's throat constricted in a mind-numbing fear. "London?" she said weakly.

Sagging against the door frame, Kat glanced at the closet, standing open, and noticed that there was nothing inside—no clothes, no bags, no shoes, as there had been earlier. There wasn't a trace of London or Ginny.

Dear God, please let this be a horrible mistake. She stepped into the room and felt a chill as cold as November. *Don't panic!* London was here. She had to be. But something was wrong and a black fear started crawling up her spine, clutching at her heart.

"Witt?" she called, surprised at the calm in her voice. After all, this was probably just a mistake. The nanny moved London to another room—to make sure that Witt and Katherine had the privacy they needed. "Witt!"

"Whaaaa?" Witt weaved to the doorway and propped a shoulder against the frame. "What's going on?" he asked thickly and Kat knew a moment of absolute desolation—as if her soul had been stripped from her.

"Call security! There's something wrong here—London and Ginny are gone. Probably in another room, but call the security guards and the manager just in case." Her mind, always so cool and dependable, was running away with her to horrible nightmares concerning her child, but she tried her best to stay calm and reasonable. There was just a mixup. That was all. No reason to become hysterical, not yet. Then why were her knees knocking? *Oh, God, please don't let anything happen to my baby!*

Witt strode into the room, knocked over the lamp, and swore. Suddenly comprehending that his daughter was truly missing, he began tearing the dresser and bed apart, as if he could find his precious child or some evidence of her in the room.

"Leave it alone! For the police!" Kat threw herself at him. "Just call the damned security!"

"She's not gone," Witt said, suddenly stone cold sober. "She can't be. She's in this hotel. In the wrong room." He opened the door and bellowed into the hallway, "Jason! Zach! For Christ's sake get in here!" Turning to Katherine, he said, "We'll find her. And that damned nanny. And when I do I swear I'll strangle Ginny Slade for this little prank!"

Witt's words were bold, but his face grew ashen and Katherine knew the cold, jabbing fear that she might never see her daughter alive again. Guilt and fear took hold of her. She loved London, she did. With all her heart. All the times she'd been jealous of her little girl because of the attention she received from her father flitted through her mind and she wondered, vaguely, if she were being punished. She didn't believe in God, but . . . Oh, please, please, let her be safe! She ran back to her room and with shaking fingers dialed the main desk. Before the clerk could answer, she said, "This is Katherine Danvers. Send up security. Room 714. And call the police. London's missing!"

* * *

Witt loosened the top two buttons of his collar and stared out the window to the city he'd loved, the town he'd trusted. The street lights, skyscrapers, and traffic looked the same as they had on any predawn Sunday morning, but now the town seemed sinister and menacing. Portland, his home, had turned on him.

He saw his reflection in the plate glass, ghostly and faint over the eastern skyline. His face was ravaged and drawn, his eyes haunted, his shoulders slumped. He looked eighty rather than fifty.

Whoever had taken his baby would pay, but a gnawing fear tore at his mind. What if they were never found?

He wouldn't think such dark thoughts. Of course she'd be found. Of course she'd be fine. She was London Danvers, for Christ's sake. That part bothered him as much as the loss—that someone would dare defy him, someone who knew how to wound him until he was bled dry.

He reached for his wife's pack of Virginia Slims and lit up, hoping that sucking in smoke and inhaling nicotine would help. It didn't.

Turning back to the suite he saw the faces of his family, tired and drawn, with dark circles and eyes dark with fear. Everyone was accounted for except London. And Zach.

A loud knock jarred through Witt's head. "Police, Danvers! What the hell's going on?"

Jason opened the door and admitted Jack Logan, who only a few hours before had been downstairs at the party. Jack, an honest cop before he'd met Witt, was now firmly trapped in Witt's gold-lined pockets. Four officers were with Detective Sergeant Logan.

"We got a call that London was kidnapped," Jack said, eyeing the group, taking mental tally and coming up not one, but two Danvers short.

"Looks that way." He stubbed out the damned cigarette in a cut-glass tray, then showed the police London's room.

"Jesus, Mary, Joseph," Logan muttered under his breath. The

room was dusted by experts, then Logan returned to Witt's suite, where he, along with another officer, Sergeant Trent, began his interrogations.

Questions were fired at each of the family members, sometimes together, sometimes individually. Logan trusted no one.

While the officers were still scribbling on their pads, Logan demanded a list of the people who had attended the party. He wanted names and phone numbers of the guests, the staff, as well as the band members, florists, and caterers. Who were the delivery men? With what agency did Katherine book the entertainment? What about the baker and the ice sculptor? Were there any reporters or photographers present?

Who was Ginny Slade? Where did she come from? Did she have any family? What were her references?

What was her relationship with Zach?

"She has none!" Katherine said emphatically, her cool confidence shattered. Eyes rimmed with streaking mascara, she glared at the detective sergeant. "Zach isn't involved in—"

"He's missing, isn't he?" Logan countered, his lips thinning thoughtfully. "You call that a coincidence?"

"For Christ's sake, he's only sixteen. How could he be behind something like this? He was probably kidnapped as well," Witt interjected and Logan sent him a harsh look that silently called him a fool.

"That boy's been in and out of trouble since he was twelve, Witt. Face it. I've had to cover his ass more times than I can count."

"Nothing like this," Witt said quietly, though deep inside he felt a gut-wrenching fear that Logan was right. Zach had a chip on his shoulder the size of Mount Hood and he'd never gotten along with anyone in the family—even London, though the precocious child had hung on his every word. "You know who you've got to arrest, Logan. The wop is behind this one."

"You don't know that."

"Like hell!" Witt bellowed, suddenly snapping. The tension in the room was getting to him and he felt as if his nerves were strung as tight as winch cables.

Logan, still staring at Witt as if he were a buffoon, ran a gnarled hand through his snow-white hair. Logan's face was lined and ruddy, weather-beaten by the winds that had blown incessantly down the Columbia River Gorge while he pounded a beat on the east side for ten years. Tiny lines webbed beneath the skin of his nose, adding a reddish tone created by a lifelong love affair with Irish whiskey. A no-nonsense man, Logan seldom threw any punches. It had taken years for Witt to get the goods on the man, make him bend the rules a bit, and take a simple bribe. Logan had fought him, but when push came to shove and Logan had needed help with his drug-dependent daughter, Risa, Witt had gotten the girl quietly into a private clinic and made sure that the story hadn't found its way to the news stations or been printed in any of the local papers.

Logan had been a trusted friend and ally ever since. But he still spoke his mind. "If you ask me, Zach knows what happened to your little girl, Witt." The detective glanced at Kat who had turned a paler shade of white and looked as if she might faint. "Any reason why he'd want to harm her——?"

Katherine let out a whimper. "He's just a boy . . ."

"——or at least scare the bejesus out of the both of you?"

"Shit, no!" An uneasy feeling tightened in Witt's guts. He and Zach had never gotten along. They'd been oil and water for years and the fact that Zach didn't seem to have one Danvers characteristic made Witt suspicious of the boy. There had always been rumors . . . ugly rumors suggesting that Zach wasn't his son. Then there was the problem with Kat . . . Witt had seen her dancing with her stepson, leading him on, whispering in his ear only to shut him down. Maybe out of vengeance . . . Hell, no! Zach was the only one of his older children who seemed to like London. And he was sixteen, for crying out loud. Sixteen!

"It's been known to happen," Logan was insisting. "One kid gets jealous of another——"

"No way. Zach's probably up to his butt in trouble, but he didn't take London."

"Think about it," Logan suggested, then started ordering some of his men to talk to everyone remotely associated with the Danvers family. Other officers were ordered to interrogate everyone staying at the hotel, then told to check the records and contact guests who had stayed in the hotel for the last three months.

While each family member was interrogated a second and third time, the detective sergeant kept track of the investigation via walkie-talkie. His men were situated throughout the building and checking every available space in the hotel as well as working the grounds and spreading through the city, reporting anything remotely suspicious on the streets.

Informants were contacted, and anyone with an arrest record for kidnapping was in for a shock, though Logan suspected that this case was different. This wasn't the work of penny-ante crooks, this was different and deadly.

Logan was a practical man, a cop who had fought his way through the ranks to make detective sergeant. He hadn't earned his position because of his education or his sophistication; he'd built his reputation by the simple fact that he always got the job done. Over the course of his twenty-odd years with the force, he'd been called a mule, a terrier, a dirty Mick, and a self-centered bastard, but the bottom line was that he got results. Crusty and cantankerous, with four-letter words being the essence of his vocabulary, he'd devoted his life to cleaning up the filthy streets of Portland.

He called 'em as he saw 'em and in his book, Zachary Danvers was a bad seed. Maybe not even Witt's son. Rumor had it that Zach was sired by Anthony Polidori and though Logan didn't give much credit to most of the gossip he heard, he did believe that where there was smoke there was fire. He'd caught more than one slippery criminal on the anonymous tip from an informant, the "gossip" of the streets. So maybe the grudge between

Zach and Witt was stronger than the old man wanted to admit. Maybe Zach hated the man who had raised him. Considering the feud between the Polidori and Danvers families, anything was possible.

The sooner Zach was located, Logan was convinced, the sooner he'd locate London and when he did his score with Witt Danvers would be even. Members of the family, swathed in hotel robes, hair mussed, smoking cigarettes, sat in the chairs and whispered quietly, hoping not to set off Katherine, who, arms wrapped around her middle, stared sightlessly out the window, a neglected Virginia Slim dangling from her fingers.

Trisha chewed at the corner of one fingernail. Jason paced from the window to a small table and back again. Nelson was wide-eyed and nervous, as if he was on speed, Witt thought with distaste. Everyone was there except London, her nanny Ginny, and Zach.

Witt stared at the bleary-eyed faces of his children and wished to God that little London was safe, just misplaced. He hoped that the child, upon being hauled away from the party, had protested by "running away" to some hidden corner of the hotel and that Ginny, the idiot of a nanny, rather than lose face and admit that she'd lost his most precious possession, was tearing the hotel apart, searching for her missing charge. But he knew in his heart that he was wasting his time on empty hope. The child was gone. Abducted and kidnapped and probably worse. His back teeth ground together in frustration as he wondered where she was— if she was still alive. He couldn't let his mind wander too far along that dark path, or he'd lose ever bit of his sanity.

The police, except for Jack Logan, left the room.

Kat ran the fingers of one hand through her rumpled hair and glanced sightlessly to her husband. With effort she stubbed out her cigarette. "I think we should do something."

"Logan's got his men searching the building. He's going over the guest list with a fine-tooth comb. He'll question anyone who was in the hotel."

"That's not good enough!" she said with a deadly calm that belied her ravaged emotions. "My baby's gone, Witt. *Our* baby. Gone! Disappeared!" Blinking back tears, she walked to her purse, pulled out her gold cigarette case and fumbled with the catch. She lit up again and wrapped one arm around her, as if warding off a chill.

"What do you want me to do?" He felt so damned helpless and he hated the feeling. He was always in command, the man in charge . . .

"Use your influence, for God's sake. You're the richest man in this city, so you shouldn't sit around here waiting for the police to fumble all over themselves. Do *something*, Witt. I don't care who you have to bribe or threaten. Call in the goddamned FBI! Just find my daughter!" Her hands shook as she took another drag on her cigarette.

"They've already called the feds—in case she's been taken over state lines. And I'll do anything I can to find London, you know that. Believe me, I'm trying."

"Well, try harder!" She squashed out her half-smoked Virginia Slim in a glass tray. "She might be with Zach," she said, not for the first time, though at one point she'd defended the boy. She'd been the first to suggest that Zachary was involved, then changed her mind as if the thought were too distasteful. "Maybe Zach's got her somewhere and this is just a prank . . ." She must've noticed the skeptical expression on his face. "Well, he's involved, then. You know him, Witt, always in trouble . . . walking on the wrong side of the law . . . like his father."

Stung, Witt held his tongue. The crack about Zach's paternity struck home, but he didn't call her on it. He'd never believed, never let himself think for one minute that Zach had been sired by Polidori. A bitter taste filled his mouth at the very thought. It was possible, but, no, he wouldn't believe that the boy he'd considered his second son for all these years had filthy Italian blood running through his veins. But he wasn't going to argue the point with Kat. There was no reasoning with her now and he had to keep a calm head, no matter what else.

Nelson, his youngest son, looked scared. Witt had never much cared for the boy; at fourteen he was still a scrawny kid, who seemed to take after him, but always reminded Witt of his first wife, Eunice. There was something about Nelson that was . . . odd. Unsettling. "Why didn't you tell me Zach didn't come upstairs?" he asked the boy and Nelson swallowed hard, avoiding his father's eyes. "You were supposed to be sharing a room."

"Dunno."

"Where is he?"

"Dunno."

Witt let out a sigh and stared at Nelson with an intensity that had made loggers with inch-thick hides squirm. "You know where he is."

"No!"

"But you know something," Witt prodded, sensing that the boy was holding back. Hell what a bunch of headstrong kids he was raising.

"I, uh, saw him leave the party," Nelson admitted sullenly, looking as if he thought he was Benedict Arnold, for Christ's sake!

Witt didn't move. "Leave? When?"

Katherine walked over to Nelson. "Just after Witt cut the cake, isn't that right?"

Nelson nodded mutely.

So Kat had kept her eye on Zach. "Was London with him?" Witt demanded, already knowing the answer.

Nelson shook his head furiously, his long blond hair brushing the back of his shoulders. "He left alone, didn't want to be bothered."

"Why didn't you tell us this earlier?" Katherine seemed tense enough to slap the boy.

"I didn't want to get him in trouble."

"London's missing!" she screamed. She was at the breaking point, nearly hysterical, not making a lot of sense. "I don't give a damn about your brother getting his ass in trouble again!"

Witt stepped between his son and young wife. "We don't know anything. Not yet. Let's not go jumping to conclusions."

"That kid's always had a mean streak," Katherine said. "I didn't want to believe it, but I wouldn't put it past him to—"

"Enough!" Witt turned his attention on his oldest son who had watched the exchange with a hint of amusement on his lips. "You think this is funny?" he roared.

"No."

A muscle ticked in Witt's jaw. "You act as if you know where your brother is."

"Probably meeting a girl," Jason replied, then shrugged indifferently. "He's always horny. My guess is he's spending the night with someone he picked up."

Katherine looked stricken.

"Come on, Dad. Don't pretend you don't remember how it was when you were sixteen and horny as hell. Zach just wanted to get laid."

Witt could barely remember, but he didn't give a damn. Not now. Not when London was missing.

3

Sirens.

Somewhere in the distance sirens screamed through the night. Horns honked, people shouted and the pounding in his head wouldn't fade. Slowly Zach opened an eye. The floor tilted and for a second he didn't know where he was. He tried to move and pain ricocheted down his arm. He was woozy and his head felt as if it weighed a ton.

Gritting his teeth, he got to his knees and saw the dark stain of blood—his blood—on the cheap carpet. The room swayed. He was dizzy, his mind a blur until he saw his bloody reflection in the mirror over the bureau. The Orion Hotel. Room 307. Sophia. All at once he remembered everything, the pretty girl, the hoodlums barging in and nearly killing him.

Why?

Because the thugs had thought he was Jason.

That bastard. He'd been set up. By his own brother. Zach pulled himself upright and staggered into the bathroom. His head throbbed, his gut ached from being kicked and his shoulder felt as if it were aflame, but somehow he managed to twist on the faucets and splash some water onto what had once been his face. He looked like hell. His eyes were already beginning to blacken and swell shut, blood crusted in his nostrils and clotted over his lips. One cheekbone was crushed and a clean slice ran from the top of his head and down to his cheek.

His monkey suit, the tuxedo Kat had bought for him, was torn and stained with blood and mud.

Shame and rage grappled with each other as he glared at his

reflection. Jason had lured him with a whore—a lousy whore—
and then let Zach take the fall. Jesus, he could have been killed.

But he hadn't been. He was alive and though he'd probably
have to be stitched up at a hospital, he'd survive long enough to
beat the living shit out of his brother. With a white terry cloth rag
emblazoned with a black O, he cleaned his face, wincing when
the warm water touched the knife wound. He didn't dare mess
with his shoulder, couldn't afford to have it start bleeding again.
Besides, he had to leave quickly. No way did he want to try and
explain what had gone on here or give the thugs another chance
at him. He'd have to sneak back into the Hotel Danvers and up
to his own room without being spotted by anyone.

That shouldn't be too hard. According to his watch, it was
almost four-thirty, nearly dawn. Witt's party should have wound
down to nothing. Anyone who was still awake would be too
drunk to notice Zach slinking in.

And then he'd hunt down his older brother and beat the piss
out of him. Jason had a lot to answer for.

He slipped out of the room unnoticed, took the stairs to the
first floor and while the desk clerk had his back turned, Zach
crossed the lobby, hurried past the magazine stand where some
old coot was hoping to sell the early edition of the newspaper,
and was out the door.

A summer storm had hit. Warm rain lashed from the sky,
puddling on the sidewalk and drizzling down the back of Zach's
neck. Ducking his head against the wind, he started back toward
the Hotel Danvers. He hunched his shoulders and his legs felt as
if they were made of rubber.

As he rounded a corner, he noticed the police cars, six or
seven of them, parked in front of the hotel like vultures hovering
over a dying sheep. Blue and red lights flashed against the side
of the building and a dozen uniformed officers milled around the
grounds.

Zach stopped dead in his tracks.

His anger turned to fear as he realized what had happened.

Joey and his pal had probably left Zach and attacked his older brother right in his father's hotel! Jason was dead! Oh, God! without realizing what he was doing, Zach started running, forcing his heavy legs forward, unaware of the sight he made, unafraid of the police with their riot sticks and guns. His footsteps pounded on the wet cement and he dashed across the cross streets, ignoring the early-morning traffic, mindless of the brakes squealing and the horns honking as he flew toward the hotel.

Jason. Oh, God—

"Hey, you!" a loud male voice yelled.

Zach didn't pay any attention. He sidestepped between two parked cars.

"Kid, I'm talkin' to you. Stop!"

Zach was barely aware of anything except the fear that gripped him and a burning sensation in his shoulder.

"Police! Freeze!"

He skidded to a stop as the words sunk in and whirled on the two officers who approached him. They emerged from one of the cars, their weapons drawn, no-nonsense written all over their features.

"Hands in the air! Do it!" Zach slowly raised his one arm. The other hung limply at his side. "Shiiit, look at him, will ya, Bill?" the one with the loud voice said. "Looks like our boy here got himself into a fight. What happened to you? Haven't seen a little girl, have you?"

"What?" Zach figured they must be talking about Sophia, but he kept his mouth shut. Something wasn't right and he didn't trust the cops.

The stocky officer—Bill—smiled without a trace of humor in his suspicious eyes. "Don't you know who this is, Steve? This here's the Danvers kid. The one who's supposed to be missing."

"Zachary?"

"Yeah, so what?" Zach snarled.

The policemen exchanged glances and Zach's blood ran cold as ice. The tall one, Steve, said, "So where's the girl?"

"What girl?"

"Your sister."

Trisha? London? "What about my sister?" he asked. "Where's Jason?"

The stocky one took hold of his arm and Zach nearly fell into the street. "Jesus, get your hands off me!" He sucked in his breath through loose teeth.

"Look at this, Bill." The officer opened the front of Zach's jacket, shoving aside the expensive lapel with his riot stick, showing off the sticky purple stains of blood. "You okay, kid?"

"Let's get him up to his old man. There was a paramedic in the hotel—with the mother. And the old man's called his personal physician. Come on, son, through the back door. We don't want the press to get a picture of you looking like this, do we?"

"What happened to Trisha?" Zach asked, dazed. The two thugs, Joey and Rudy, they'd found his sister. She'd been drunk and . . . Oh, God. Rage burned through his blood.

"Maybe you can tell us," Bill said as he hauled Zach in the direction of the service entrance. "My guess is you've got one helluva story."

"I don't give a good goddamned what time it is," Witt yelled, his patience worn thin. London was missing. His precious little girl—gone without a trace! His heart had nearly stopped at the news and he'd been foggy, but after six cups of coffee he was clearheaded and he knew who the bastard was behind the kidnapping. "I want you to send a car over to Polidori's house. You wake up that goddamned wop and find out what he knows about this!" Witt yelled at Logan.

"Back off, Witt. We'll question Mr. Polidori, after the search of the hotel is complete."

"You bet your ass you will," Witt said, reaching for the humidor of cigars he kept on the desk of his office on the main floor of the hotel. Katherine was sleeping, thanks to Dr. McHenry and several sleeping pills. Witt lit up and stalked around his massive desk. "You've checked all the rooms?"

"Twice," Logan snapped. He had no patience for Witt's inference that he and his men weren't capable of doing their jobs.

"And the service elevator—"

"And the boiler room, the linen closets, the conference rooms, the rest rooms, even the air shafts, elevator shafts, maintenance rooms and freezers. We also checked out the parking lot, restaurant, bellboy's closet, wine cellar and every goddamned nook and cranny this old hotel has. It's been renovated half a dozen times and my men have gone over every set of blueprints hoping to find some secret room that everyone here's forgotten about. Take my word for it, Witt, she's not on the premises."

"Then what're you waiting for?"

"I still haven't heard from the men outside. We're covering a ten square-block area, talking to people on the street, checking other buildings nearby and literally beating the bushes."

"You're wasting your time," Witt growled impatiently. "Polidori's—" He glanced up and saw two officers and Zach, bloodied and beaten, stumble into the office. Witt's guts twisted. The boy's face was the color of chalk and a nasty cut had ripped his skin open near his ear. He was still bleeding and his nose was a pulpy mass. On his feet in an instant, Witt rounded the desk. "Get the doctor," he ordered a policeman, then faced his son. "What happened?"

Zach glanced suspiciously to the police. He ran his tongue over dry, swollen lips. "What's going on?" he asked, squinting against the light. "Did something happen to Trisha?"

"Hell, no! What're you talking about?"

"They said, the police, that she was missing—"

Witt's guts twisted. "They were talking about London."

"London? But she's only a kid—" Zach swallowed hard.

"You weren't with her?"

Zach, stricken, shook his head.

"Christ." His entire world was collapsing and he knew where to put the blame.

"What happened to her?" Zach asked.

"She's missing," Witt said.

"Missing?"

"Ginny, too. They're gone. That's all we know." Through his silent fear, Witt forced himself to turn his attention to the boy who was nearly beaten beyond recognition. "Are you all right?"

Zach gritted his teeth. "I'll live."

"So how'd this happen?" Witt demanded, then picked up the phone and dialed three digits. "Is McHenry still there? I sent a man for him. Well, just tell him to come down here, on the double. Yeah, my office. What? Oh, it's Zach. He's back and he's been roughed up. Looks serious." He slammed down the receiver and motioned two police officers off a green leather couch. "Come on, you'd better lie down. Looks like you've lost a lot of blood."

"I'm okay."

Witt felt his temper snap. "Just do it, okay? For once in your life, Zach, don't fight me. Lie on the couch and let McHenry examine you, for crying out loud!"

Zach looked like he was about to snarl back a hot retort, but instead he sat on the couch as Dr. McHenry walked through the door. A spry man nearing seventy, he'd been Witt's physician for years and the best doctor money could buy. McHenry knew his stuff, but he could be trusted to keep his mouth shut, which made him invaluable.

"I'd hate to see the other guy," the doctor quipped, as he helped peel off Zach's shirt. Witt's stomach turned over at the sight of the ugly wound, red and angry, that sliced down Zach's skin.

"Okay, Zach, start talking," Witt said, sitting on the corner of his desk. He reached for a fresh cigar while the old one smoldered in his overflowing ashtray. Zach, sullen and wincing as the doctor attended his wounds, didn't say a word. As usual, Zach seemed to be rebelling. Witt let out an angry cloud of smoke. "Look, Zach, I don't care what you think of me. Hell, nothing matters but London's safety, so you'd better tell me what happened to you tonight. Your sister's life could depend on it."

Zach sent him a look of pure hatred, but Witt didn't care. He turned his gaze to the detective sergeant and stared Jack Logan straight in the Irishman's eyes. "And nothing that we hear in this room goes any further, right?"

Logan nodded curtly, and satisfied, Witt settled back in his chair. "We're listening, Zach."

Zach closed his eyes, hoping the room would stop swimming. He wanted to lie, but didn't and told his story, with only two slight changes. He didn't admit that his stepmother had turned him on during their dance at the party and he kept Jason's name out of the mess. He didn't rat on his brother and claimed to have made the arrangement with Sophia himself. Why, he wasn't sure. Maybe he wanted to kill Jason himself. Or maybe he held some latent brotherly affection for the older brother who had been a thorn in his side for as long as he could remember or maybe he was just scared shitless.

Doc McHenry didn't say a word as he worked over Zach. He grunted to himself as he applied ointment and something that burned like hell, then began stitching his shoulder back together and tended to the gash above his ear. Once satisfied with his stitches, he worked on Zach's face. "You're nose is broken again, kid, but it'll give you character in your old age," the doctor said, cleaning off the dried blood. Each time he touched Zach's nose, Zach nearly passed out all over again. "This is something for the pain." He found a hypodermic needle in his black bag, rolled down the waistband of Zach's pants and punched the needle into Zach's butt. "And another tetanus booster."

Zach refused to be mortified that McHenry had shown his ass to his father and several of Logan's men. He didn't give a damn what the old man or the doctor did to him. It wasn't any worse than dealing with the cops.

Finally Detective Sergeant Jack Logan—one of Portland's finest, and, in Zach's opinion, a paid off prick—had his turn. Zach felt the skepticism in Logan's eyes as he asked questions, noticed the way two officers shared a dubious look when he told them about the whore. No matter what he said, he knew they thought he was lying.

Oh, Logan went through all the motions, recording the conversation while the officers took a few notes, but Zach read the bored disbelief in the old policeman's eyes.

"These men who attacked you," Logan finally said as McHenry packed up his doctor's bag. "Rudy and Joey?"

"That's what they called each other."

"You ever seen them before?"

"Never."

"He's got to go to the hospital," the doctor interrupted.

Logan didn't miss a beat. "Look, Doc, we're trying to find Witt's little girl. I shouldn't have to tell you that time is critical. We just need Zach to come down to the station and look at a few pictures, that's all."

"I'd advise against it."

Witt's frown deepened. "Zach?"

His mouth tasted foul, his head thundered and his shoulder throbbed like holy hell, but he nodded to his father. "I'll go."

There was nothing further McHenry could do. He pulled Witt aside, warned him about something, but Zach couldn't make out what. They rode in a squad car to the police station and seated in a small room with flickering fluorescent lighting and the thin smell of stale cigarettes and old coffee, Zach flipped through pages of mug shots and stared at black-and-white pictures through a haze of pain.

"What about this one?" an officer would ask and Zach would focus only to shake his head. There were more people in the room than had been in the hotel. As the hours passed, officers would come and go, glancing at him as they strapped on weapons, took statements, or told dirty jokes.

"Him. What about him?"

The questions didn't stop and Zach stared at photograph after photograph—grainy black and whites of men he'd never seen. He thumbed the pages, shook his head and thumbed some more. His father was in the room, creating a haze of smoke from his cigar, pacing, looking as if he wished he could tear someone, anyone, limb from limb.

The pictures started to look alike and swim before his eyes. His back ached and he felt as if he hadn't slept for a hundred years. Smoke collected near the ceiling as the men talked among themselves, changing shifts. One officer sat on the corner of the table, watching his reactions, while another went out for coffee that tasted like it had been brewed in the sewer.

Zach slumped in his chair and craved a cigarette.

"That's it. Nothing," a burly officer said over a yawn as another, a slim woman who had just come on duty, started gathering the books.

"I guess Rudy and Joey aren't in the book," Officer Ralph O'Donnelly said as he squashed out the butt of his cigarette in his empty coffee cup.

"Rudy?" The woman glanced from Logan to Witt.

"Yeah, the kid, here, heard their names." Officer O'Donnelly stood and stretched. His back popped loudly.

"Why didn't you say so?" she asked, searching through the books again and flipping one open. She shoved the open pages under Zach's nose. "Look again."

Every eye in the room was on Zach, as aching, he ran his finger under the pictures and forced his eyes to each face. They blurred for a second, but he kept looking and he felt the air in the room charge. "I don't think—"

"Look again! Imagine your man clean shaven or with different-colored hair or whatever," Logan muttered angrily.

Zach gritted his teeth, eyeing the mug shots, knowing that there wasn't a clue on the page when he stopped at a shot on the bottom row. The hair was different, longer now, and a beard and mustache in the photo covered what appeared to be a pock-marked jaw, but the eyes, the cruel malicious eyes, were the same.

His throat barely worked as he laid a finger on the incriminating shot. "I think—"

"Rudolpho Gianotti," the woman officer said with a satisfied grin. Zach got the impression she liked beating the men at their own game. "A speed-head who hangs out with Joseph Siri."

"Wops," Witt ground out. He strode across the room and glared at the mug shots. Red in the face, he trembled. "I bet they're connected with Polidori."

"Bingo," the woman said. "The vice squad is checking them out: drugs and prostitution, maybe even some penny-ante gambling."

"I told you!" Witt growled, kicking at the leg of the table. "When I get my hands on old Anthony, there's gonna be hell to pay. Let's go!"

"Whoa!" the woman officer said. "We're not talking about the old man. These guys"—she tapped a short-clipped nail on Rudy Gianotti's mug shot—"are involved with the kid. Mario."

Witt's eyes darkened to the color of midnight. He hated the son as much as the old man. "Bring him in, Jack. Let's talk to him."

"We will," Logan assured him, "but first, let's find Gianotti and Siri. See what they have to say, what they know. Then we'll round up Mario Polidori."

"And his old man."

"Maybe."

Witt's face twisted into ugly rage. "He's behind it, Jack. I told you that from the beginning. He took my little girl and God only knows what's happened to her."

"Don't worry, Witt, we'll find her." Logan's voice lowered and Zach didn't really care what was said. The room was spinning, his head reeled and his bones seemed to melt. He blinked to stay awake, but blackness enveloped him. With a moan, he slid from the chair and lost consciousness before he hit his head on the cracked linoleum floor.

Two days later, Zach woke up in a hospital room, his shoulder on fire, his mouth tasting like puke. He couldn't breathe right because something—cotton wadding he guessed—was rammed up his nostrils. Bandages swathed his head and held his shoulder together and everything reeked of antiseptic.

"You look awful."

He turned quickly at the sound of Jason's voice and pain seared down his arm. Memories—Sophia, the thugs, the switch-blade and London—seared through his mind. "You bastard," he said, his tongue thick. "You set me up." He tried to raise up again, yanking hard on the IV that was taped to the back of his hand.

"You've got it all wrong. Zach, I'm sorry. I had no idea that—"

"Liar!"

Jason squeezed his eyes shut for a second. "It's true, I knew I was in a little trouble with Sophia's pimp."

"A little trouble—those guys wanted to cut off my balls!" So angry he could barely talk, Zach silently swore at himself for being such a fool, falling into Jason's lust-filled trap. "You make me sick!"

"I didn't know they were going to be there."

"Like hell!" Zach turned away and stared out the window. He could see the sky and the wake of a jet as it streamed across the blue vastness. Jaw clenched so tight it ached, he refused to look at his brother. The starched pillowcase felt rough against the wounds on his face. God, he hated hospitals. Almost as much as he hated Jason right now.

"Dad thinks Polidori's behind London's kidnapping."

Zach didn't respond. The feud between the Polidoris and the Danvers had existed for generations. Anything that went wrong in Witt's life was quickly laid at the feet of Anthony Polidori, whether deserved or not.

"We haven't heard anything new. Not even the FBI has an answer. No one's asked for ransom and Jack Logan's afraid that London may have been taken by some terrorist group—you know—like the Patty Hearst abduction."

"Logan's a prick."

"But he has a point." Jason walked around the end of the bed, forcing himself squarely in the middle of Zach's line of vision. "Look, I know this all looks bad, Zach, and I feel . . ." His face screwed up as he searched for the right word. Shaking his head, he said, ". . . well, I feel responsible, I guess."

"You should."

"But I really didn't think they'd come after you."

"You knew they'd be there."

"No way, man! I swear. I only knew that Sophia was waiting for me. I had no idea that her pimp would be pissed off enough to send some goons with switchblades." He tugged anxiously at the corner of his mustache. "You gotta believe me, Zach, if I'd had a clue, I wouldn't have sent you to the Orion."

Zach let out a sound of disgust.

Jason sighed loudly. "I don't blame you for not believing me, 'cause the truth of the matter is, I'd already decided not to meet with Sophia. I would have avoided the place like the goddamned plague, but I didn't think you'd get cut. I thought you'd get laid, that's all. I swear it. You gotta believe me."

Zach didn't. He'd been a fool to trust Jason the first time and he wouldn't make that mistake again. He shifted his gaze to the metal bureau near the bed.

"If I could change things, man, I would." Jason thrust one hand into his pocket and rested the other on the bureau. "You may as well know, things are bad at home. Dad's on the warpath against Polidori. Kat's usually either drunk or on sleeping pills and Valium. And Trisha. Well, she's a basket case, but what else is new?"

Jason moved into Zach's limited field of vision but Zach wouldn't give him the satisfaction of looking up at his eyes.

"As for Nelson; you're a hero in his eyes."

Zach gritted his teeth.

"Yep," Jason said, grabbing the jacket he'd draped over the back of the one chair in the room, "Nelson thinks that anyone who makes it with a whore, then gets cut by a switchblade is some kind of goddamned hero."

* * *

"Zach?" Her voice was familiar and brought back warm memories from a long, long time ago. In his mind he heard childish laughter and smelled the scents of cinnamon and hot chocolate and the jasmine of her perfume. Somewhere, maybe on the back porch, a dog barked. But it had been so long ago. . . .

"I came as soon as I heard."

Groggily, Zach opened an eye. The lamps had been dimmed. Only the night-light illuminated the hospital room, though from the window, the reflection from the security lights guarding the parking lot splashed against the wall. He squinted and saw a movement before he made out the features of a tall, big-boned woman in an expensive blouse and skirt. His mother. Eunice Patricia Prescott Danvers Smythe. She stood on the far side of the rails of his hospital bed. A dozen emotions riffled through him, none of which he wanted to examine too closely and his head throbbed. "Wha—what're you doing here?"

Her eyes were sad, filled with a lifetime of grief for the mistakes of her youth.

"Nelson called . . . explained what happened and I took the first flight out of San Francisco." She reached across the rails and folded her long, cool fingers over his hand. Her grip was strong, the lines around her face desperate. "I'm so sorry this happened, Zach. Are you all right?"

He'd never been all right. They both knew it. "What do you care?" he said, drawing his hand away and forcing his thick tongue to form words.

She winced, but didn't move. "I do care, Zach. I care lots. More than anyone you'll ever meet."

He snorted.

"You don't believe that I love you," she said, her voice losing all inflection. "You never did."

He closed his eyes again and wished he had the strength to cover his ears so he wouldn't have to hear her lies. If she'd loved him, really loved him, she wouldn't have left him with Witt.

He didn't reply, just pretended, as he had for years, that she didn't exist. It was easier that way. Her rejection didn't hurt anymore. He'd had a long time to recover and heal. She could say what she wanted, Witt had bought her off, paid her enough money so that she gave up her children.

"I thought you and I shared something special," she said on a tremulous sigh. He felt, rather than saw, her move to the window and wondered if she played nervously with the strand of pearls at her throat, the way she used to when she was discussing Witt. How long had it been since he'd trusted her? Eight years? Nine? Maybe never. "I hate to admit it, Lord knows a mother shouldn't, but you've always been my favorite. Of all my children, you were the one closest to my heart."

"Don't lie to me, Mom. We both know you've never had a heart."

Her intake of breath was swift. "Zachary, don't you ever—" As quickly as her anger had come, it disappeared. "I suppose I deserved that."

What a bunch of crap! Why didn't she just shut up? Yet he couldn't stop listening.

"I would never have left you, but . . . well, your father made sure I couldn't get near you kids. You probably don't believe this, but it was a horrible price to pay. I've regretted it . . ."

He closed his eyes. He wouldn't trust her. She'd carried on her affair with Polidori for years, knowing the inevitable consequences. In Zach's mind, she'd turned her back on her children, on her husband, on her life, for a fling with a man who used her just to get even with Witt. Zach didn't believe for a minute that there had ever been any love between Anthony Polidori and his mother. No, what they'd shared was sex, pure and simple and that thought turned his stomach. Polidori had chosen Eunice to best his opponent and Eunice had slept with her husband's sworn enemy for a quick thrill in a life devoid of any kind of excitement. She'd had the affair to prove that she was still attractive to a man and to show her neglectful husband that she could still make her own decisions, be they right or wrong.

Zach had heard her rationalizations and deep in his heart he knew that she and Witt had never been happy. The house had always been tense while they were married, no safe refuge. He wondered how she'd become involved with Polidori, where she'd met him, who had taken the first step . . . but those were things children weren't supposed to know and he figured he was better off left to his imagination.

"You judge me too quickly, Zach," she said, her voice barely a whisper. "You don't know what it's like to be lonely and ignored, to have your life sorted out and planned for you, to have to pretend to be happy when you're not, to smile when you feel like crying your eyes out."

He cracked a lid and saw that she rested her forehead on the window, her chin nearly touching her neck, her breath fogging the glass. She looked weary and wondered if that aura of exhaustion was from her stormy marriage to Witt or to her guilt over choosing her lover over her children, or because of her new marriage to one of the most well-recognized heart specialists in the country.

She glanced over, as if sensing that he was staring at her. "Don't hate me, Zach," she said, blinking and dabbing the tips of her fingers at the corners of her eyes. "Don't hate me for loving you."

"You don't know what love is."

"Oh, yes I do. I know love and the pain it causes. Unfortunately so will you. No one, not even you, will get through life without it." She wrapped her arms around her middle section and rocked back on her heels. "You want to hate me, Zach, because it's easy. I hurt you because I cheated on your father."

"I don't want to hear this."

"Well, I had to, do you understand? Witt was so . . . inconsiderate and he had other women, plenty of them before . . . anyway I met Anthony at a fund-raiser, he was charming and attentive and even though I knew I shouldn't . . . well, that's what started it," she admitted. "So now you know. I suppose you still want to strike back at me. That's understandable."

"I don't really give a shit."

"Sure you do. Does it make any difference if I tell you I'm sorry?"

He didn't bother responding.

"I'd do anything for you, Zach." She sounded so sincere that he was tempted to trust her, but only for a second.

"What about sticking around? Was that too much to ask?"

"You don't understand."

"I don't want to." His head was beginning to throb again.

She opened her mouth, then snapped it shut. When she spoke again, her tone was icy. "You know where to reach me, Zach. You can pretend all you want, but I know that life with your father isn't easy for you. If you want to come to San Francisco and live with Lyle and me for a while, I'd—"

"No thanks." He didn't need this. If Eunice had some latent maternal feelings, fine, but he didn't want to hear about them. As far as he was concerned she came up to see him only because her guilt was gnawing away at her again, the same as it did during each Christmas and some birthdays. She was a part-time mother at best and content to be no better.

"You might change your mind." She was gathering up her purse and a tan silk jacket that she slung over one arm.

"I won't."

"Whatever you say, Zach, but I only came here because I love you."

She walked out of the room, her high heels clicking softly, the scent of the same expensive perfume that he remembered from his earliest days, trailing after her.

Pain and loneliness engulfed him but he fought the urge to break down. He didn't belong with anyone. His father didn't trust him, his mother—despite her protests—didn't love him and he felt little kinship with his brothers and sisters. He thought of his stepmother in indecent terms and he didn't have many friends— didn't want them. And now London was missing. He was surprised how much it bothered him, thinking that she was small and scared and alone. He blinked rapidly and refused to cry. Not for his mother. Not for London. Not for himself. He'd shed enough tears when Eunice had walked out all those years ago; he wouldn't be foolish enough to do it again.

Sniffing, he decided it was time to move on. As soon as he was well enough, he'd sell his Porsche and . . . God, quit dreaming. He couldn't leave. Not yet. Not until this thing with London was straightened out; otherwise he'd look guilty as hell and half the cops in the state would be after him. But maybe, hopefully, by the time he was released London would be found and home safely. Then no one would notice if he left.

He'd have to be patient, which wasn't going to be easy. Patience had never been his long suit. But right now, he was stuck. There was just no damned way out.

4

Jack Logan didn't like the Polidoris. Never had; never would. It wasn't just that they were Italians, they were uppity Italians. Arrogant dagos with bad attitudes.

The worst of the lot, he thought as he snapped in the cigarette lighter of his pride and joy, a 1969 Ford Galaxy two-door. Cherry red with an ivory top and horsepower that wouldn't quit, the car was a gift from Witt Danvers—an expensive gift. Logan didn't want to think of it as a bribe. Frowning as he caught a glimpse of his weathered face in the rearview mirror, he tried not to dwell on the fact that he, who was basically an honest cop, had been bought by Witt Danvers. Idling at a light near Seventeenth, he slid out a Marlboro from the pack he kept on the dash and stuck it between his lips. Truth to tell, he didn't like Danvers much more than he did Polidori. The lighter clicked and he lit up as the light changed.

Logan didn't trust people with money, especially rich people with political ambitions; at the top of his list of most untrustworthy were Anthony Polidori and Witt Danvers. Polidori was making noise about running for the state senate and the Catholic and Italian voters were on his side; Witt had his eye on becoming mayor or governor, Logan suspected, and the WASPs in Portland would vote for him. Logan's stomach turned at the thought. If things worked the way Witt hoped they would, Witt Danvers would end up as Logan's boss. Hell, what a mess!

He wheeled the Ford through a yellow light on McLoughlin Boulevard and headed south, out of the city, toward Milwaukie, where an entire enclave of Italian truck farmers had thrived for the better part of a century. The Polidoris had been vegetable vendors once, but they'd saved their money, invested in cheap land, sold their produce to the finest restaurants in Portland and quietly amassed a fortune—not as large as the Danvers's wealth, but substantial just the same.

Yep, Logan thought, drawing in a lungful of smoke, he'd love to see Anthony Polidori go down for the Danvers kidnapping. It would be fun to see that little wop squirm in the interrogation room. But it wasn't going to happen. He knew it, Polidori knew it, and Witt Danvers, whether the stubborn old man wanted to admit it or not, knew it, too.

He flipped the ash from his cigarette out the window and stepped on the gas pedal. Ignoring the speed limits, he wheeled through the crooked streets of Milwaukie to the fir-lined drive leading to Waverley Country Club, where mansions and land-scaped grounds surrounded the most elite country club in the city. Acres of lush greens and fairways, which had once been leased by some of Polidori's fruit-selling ancestors, were now part of the exclusive club that sprawled along the eastern banks of the Willamette River.

The Polidoris had lived in the Heights for as long as Logan could remember. Old Stephano, Anthony's father, had been smart enough to save his money and purchase nearly a city block in Portland where he established an open-air market and a little café that grew into an authentic Italian restaurant that was rivaled only by Jake's Crawfish and Chowder House. During the Great Depression, Stephano bought city property at rock-bottom prices and, when the economy turned around, started new res-taurants in different areas of the city as well as purchasing one of the oldest hotels in the city, not three blocks from the Hotel Danvers, the most elegant building in all of Portland.

Stephano wasn't easily satisfied. Now that he had wealth and the prestige that came with it, he needed a new home for his family. Hence, the huge estate near the country club.

The first Italian–American to buy into the exclusive Heights,

Stephano purchased one of the original homes and remodeled the mansion until it was a replica of an Italian villa. Perched on a hill, boasting six fireplaces faced in imported marble, three fountains and tiered grounds that looked over the rolling waters of the Willamette, the pink stucco home was a showplace, the largest in Waverley.

When Stephano, a widower, had died suddenly, Anthony had inherited the house that some of the other residents of the Heights referred to as "Little Italy."

Frowning slightly, Logan turned unerringly into the drive and waited at the gate for a security guard with greasy black hair and a permanent sneer to determine if he should pass. Logan didn't have time for any bullshit. He flipped open his wallet, showing his badge, which was a waste of time, as the guard knew who he was anyway, then stubbed out his cigarette in the tray.

With a whine of electrical gears, the gate slowly opened. Logan pushed on the throttle and the galaxy rolled past rose gardens and fountains to the rambling manor.

Anthony Polidori met him at the front door. A short man with a widening girth, thin mustache, dark eyes that flashed when he was angry and teeth rimmed in gold, he motioned Logan into a vestibule the size of which would hold all of Logan's little bungalow in Sellwood.

"Don't bother explaining why you're here," Polidori said, ushering him through double doors of polished dark wood. "I know it's about the Danvers girl again." With a wave toward a tucked leather chair, he strode to the bar, splashed three fingers of Irish whiskey into each of two cut-crystal glasses and handed a drink to Logan.

The smoky scent of the whiskey tickled Logan's nostrils, but he left the glass on the corner of Polidori's massive desk. He longed for the drink, but managed to hide it. "Your name keeps coming up."

"So I've been told." Polidori didn't bother sitting, just stood near the leaded glass windows and stared at the view of the sluggish river. "Your men have been here daily. You know I'm a patient man, but even I consider this a waste of my time and the taxpayers' money. There's nothing more I can tell them or you. Call them off, Logan. Tell them to go after the real criminals."

Logan didn't bother replying. Let the wop talk. He was on a roll.

"I'm surprised you showed up in person."

"I wasn't satisfied with Taylor's report. It, uh, seemed incomplete."

Polidori clucked his tongue, then tossed back his drink. "I don't know what I have to say to you people to convince you that I had nothing to do with the kidnapping. Please extend the Danvers family my sincerest—"

"Cut the crap," Logan said in a voice so low, he didn't recognize it as his own.

Polidori's dark eyes flashed. "You don't believe me, either." He sighed dramatically.

"Let's just get down to it. Two of your goons attacked Zachary Danvers, messed him up bad enough to send him to the hospital, and, at about the same time little London Danvers and her nanny disappeared. Coincidence?"

"Do I need my lawyer present?"

"You tell me."

"I had nothing to do with either incident," Polidori said, striding to the bar and pouring another stiff shot of whiskey into his empty glass. "Nothing."

Logan didn't believe the little shit. "Maybe you'd like to know why we're riding you so hard. I've got a pretty long memory and I remember you making some pretty rash statements when your old man died."

"That was years ago."

Without blinking, Logan stared him down. "You made no bones about the fact that you blamed Julius Danvers, Witt's father, for that accident at the restaurant."

Anthony's face flushed scarlet.

"You swore vengeance on the whole Danvers clan."

The corners of Polidori's mouth tightened but his eyes shined with a hate so pure it chilled Logan's leather-tough soul. "That was years ago. Julius Danvers—"

"Is dead."

"—was a murdering bastard. He killed my father, Logan. You and I and all of Portland know it. He hired one of his thugs to pour some kerosene in the hotel and the whole damned thing went up in flames." His nostrils flared as he leaned closer to the detective. "That inferno killed seven people. The only reason more didn't lose their lives is because the hotel was closed that weekend. Someone who knew my father would be there gambled. And won."

"Or your old man set it himself to collect the insurance." Logan loved playing devil's advocate.

The slick Italian's nostrils quivered in rage. "He died, Logan. He was knocked over the head and left in his office in the hotel while kerosene was poured all around and over his body and then someone just struck a match and dropped it. I'll never know if my father died unconscious or if he was awake, screaming and writhing, feeling the agony of hot flames eating away his flesh. There isn't a day that goes by that I don't wonder." He sipped his drink and caught Logan's gaze in the mirror over the bar. "Stephano was a decent man. A faithful husband. A good father. And he was turned into a human torch by Julius Danvers. Witt knew all about it."

"Conjecture."

Polidori's smile turned deadly. "How much is he paying you, Jack, hmm? To keep you in his corner. Whatever it is, it isn't enough."

A muscle ticked in Logan's jaw. He thought about reaching for his drink, but settled back in the chair, hoping to appear unruffled. "Let's get back to Witt's little girl. Where is she?"

"I don't know. As I said before, there's nothing I can tell you."

"You didn't decide to finally extract your revenge by stealing the kid?"

"Get serious." Polidori snorted, but his knuckles whitened as he gripped his glass.

"What better way to make Witt twist in the wind than by stealing his daughter? You couldn't do anything that would hurt him more."

"Trust me, I didn't do it. Now, if you're going to continue to badger me, I'm calling my lawyer." He walked to his desk and reached for the phone.

"I don't believe you." Logan's voice was flat and he stared at Polidori so hard he noticed the tiny beads of sweat collecting at the old man's graying sideburns. He was guilty as hell. But of what?

"Doesn't matter what you believe, Jack. It's what you can prove. Now, either you're here for a social visit and if you are, mind your manners and drink the whiskey I so graciously offered you. If you're here on police business, you'd better charge me with something or get the hell out of my house."

Jack didn't budge. Now he was getting somewhere. Polidori had lost his cool. "Joey Siri and Rudy Gianotti worked for you."

"Not recently."

"Then they worked for your boy."

Polidori's calm face flushed red and he leaned across the desk. "Leave Mario out of this," he ordered, his lips barely moving beneath his neatly trimmed mustache.

"He could be in it up to his eyeballs," Logan replied. "Rumor has it he was involved with the Danvers girl—the older one—a few years back. She was underage at the time—sixteen, if memory serves—when the romance went sour."

Polidori's nostrils flared. "My boy was in Hawaii when the little girl turned up missing."

"Convenient."

"He knows nothing about the kidnapping."

"Everyone in town knows about it, Tony. It's been in all the papers, even hit national television. I'll even bet it made it into the news on Waikiki. People keep saying that London's been stolen for ransom like the Lindbergh baby, others seem to think that some terrorist group is gonna turn her into a machine gun-toting robber—kind of like what happened with Patty Hearst, though that's a little implausible considering London's age. But the thing is that she's disappeared, no one's claiming responsibility, and no one's asking for a dime. Strange, isn't it?" He pinned Polidori with one of his hard-ass bad-cop stares. "The way I see it, someone just wanted to fuck Witt Danvers. So I've been checking into things, digging up people who have a grudge against the guy and guess whose name keeps showing up at the top of the list?"

"I don't need to listen to this." Polidori reached for the phone.

"Is Mario around? I'd like to talk to him." Logan finally felt that he had the upper hand. He reached for his drink. So he was on duty. What the hell?

"You have nothing to say to Mario."

"I can talk to him here," Logan said, rimming his glass with his finger. "Or I can cuff him and haul him down to the station." He frowned thoughtfully, as if considering. "Still a lot of reporters hanging around there. Anxious guys. Looking for a story. But it's your choice."

"You're a pig, Logan."

"And you're a dirty wop." He leveled his gaze at the shorter man in the expensive suit. "So what else is new?"

Polidori dropped the receiver and straightened his jacket. Logan could almost see the wheels turning in the Italian's mind. God, it felt good to make the slimy bastard sweat a little.

"If Mario cooperates here, I probably won't have to run him in. If not—" Logan lifted his huge shoulders and watched Polidori over the rim of his glass. The whiskey was expensive. Smooth and warm, it burned a familiar and welcome path to his stomach. "—well, it wouldn't look too good in the society papers if all that old trash about your son was brought up again." He smiled into his glass. "Scandals have a way of raising their ugly heads time and time again. People in this town have long memories."

Polidori's eyes narrowed just a fraction. "You'll keep this quiet?"

"I might be a pig, but I don't lie."

With a snort of disbelief, Polidori dropped into an oxblood chair, pressed a buzzer hidden in the drawer of his desk and a guard appeared. After a rapid-fire exchange of Italian in which Mario's name was repeated several times, the guard slipped away. Logan sipped his drink. Within minutes, Mario appeared in the doorway.

About twenty-six, he was taller than his father by a full head and his eyes were a lighter shade of brown. Curly dark hair, easy smile; the playboy son of the rich father. When he wasn't racing cars, or sailing the Caribbean, Mario ran the family restaurant downtown. And he was edgy. A restless energy kept him moving. Drugs? Adrenaline? Or plain old, kick-you-in-the-gut fear?

Anthony motioned toward Logan's chair. "You know Detective Sergeant Logan."

"We've met," Mario said, his gaze flicking toward Logan for only a second. Logan didn't bother to get up.

"He thinks you might know something about the Danvers kidnapping."

"In your dreams, Jack," Mario said, resting a jean-encased hip against the edge of the desk. His foot never stopped bouncing nervously. "I was in Hawaii."

"You know Joey Siri and Rudy Gianotti."

"They used to work for me."

"Doing what?"

"Whatever I asked," Mario said with a charming smile of even white teeth. "Mainly odd jobs down at the restaurant. I fired Rudy six months ago—he was into drugs, uppers and downers. Caught him dealing and cut him loose. Joey had a fit, claimed he wouldn't stick around if I let Rudy go. So I fired him, too." He shoved away from the desk; moved to the window. Avoided the policeman's gaze.

"That was it? You've never seen them again." Logan finished his drink.

Mario lifted a shoulder. "I've seen them around. Some of the guys who work for me know 'em, but Rudy and Joey stay clear and I like it that way."

"You know Zach Danvers claimed they attacked him?"

Mario's shoulders bunched. "Zach Danvers lies."

"Not this time." Logan pretended interest in his empty glass. "Rumor had it that you and Trisha Danvers were . . . well, involved."

Almost imperceptibly the corners around the younger Polidori's mouth tightened. "I know her."

"The way I heard it, you knocked her up."

"What's your point, Logan?" Mario's eyes snapped with an inner fury that was as dark as hell. Despite all his wealth, the boy carried one helluva chip on his muscular shoulders.

"Somehow Danvers put a stop to it. Wouldn't let his daughter be seen with a dirty Italian. Made sure she never had the kid." Logan set his empty glass on the desk.

"Is that so?"

"I don't know all the details, but I'm looking into them. My guess is you've got plenty of motive to get back at Witt Danvers."

"Lots of people in this town would like to see Danvers go down," Anthony said from his position behind the desk.

Logan lifted a busy eyebrow. "Some more than others."

"I was in Hawaii. On business. At the time of the attack on Zach Danvers, I was—"

"I know, sipping maitais on the beach in Waikiki." Logan set his glass on the desk. "But somehow Joey and Rudy messed up Zach Danvers and at the same time his kid sister and her nanny were abducted."

"My money's still on Zachary." Mario's smile had turned cold. "Come on, Logan, you've covered for that kid from the time he was out of diapers. He'd sell his own mother if it would get a rise out of his old man." Mario shot a look at his own father but Logan couldn't read the message that passed between them. He could only guess that it was about the questions of Zachary's paternity. More than one gossip in town had fingered Anthony as Zachary's sire and come to think of it, Zach looked more like Mario than he did his own brothers.

Mario shifted on the desk. "It's no secret that Zach hates Witt. If you ask me, he staged the whole thing about the attack against him to get back at his father. A few knife wounds and he's got himself an iron-clad alibi. I'll bet he paid off the nanny to get rid of London. Any idiot who knows anything about the Danvers family can figure out that the only way to get to Witt Danvers is to go through his little princess. You're way off base, here, Logan."

"You think Dad would go to this much trouble if any one else had been abducted?" Trisha demanded, her blue eyes cloudy with anger. "No way. He's in a state because it's London!"

Zach didn't want to hear it. Stretched out on a chaise near the pool, he closed his eyes behind the lenses of his sunglasses and wished Trisha would just go away. No such luck. She set up her easel in the shade from the old-growth fir trees that towered along the brick wall rimming the grounds. Sunlight dappled the grass and reflected off the water as Trisha adjusted a three-legged stool, trying to catch the right light.

The day was sweltering. Heat rose in waves that shimmered off the concrete near the pool house. Zach's head throbbed and his shoulder ached. He was recovering, but slowly. He grabbed his can of Coke and smiled to himself because he'd had the foresight to pour "the real thing" out of the can and fill it with Colt 45 Malt liquor from a bottle he'd taken from the refrigerator. He'd probably get caught, but he really didn't care. He took a long swallow of the ale and felt it cool against the back of his throat. In a few minutes, he'd relax. In the meantime he'd ignore his sister.

"Dad's fit to be tied because the police and the FBI can't find out who's behind it," she said, smudging her charcoal drawing with the tip of her finger. "He wants to blame the Polidoris just because those two guys who attacked you worked for them once."

Why was she bothering him? Zach had only been home from the hospital for four days and this was the first time he'd ventured out of his room. He'd decided to rest by the pool because the four walls were closing in on him and he was going out of his mind staring at posters of Jimi Hendrix and Ali McGraw.

"Mom called the other day to see how you were doing . . . but you were sleeping or something."

He didn't want to think about his mother. Eunice. Some mother she'd turned out to be. The bitch had abandoned them all to save her pride. Because she couldn't live with the black moods of Witt Danvers. But she'd left her children to fight their own lousy battles against him so that her reputation—her damned reputation that she'd soiled by sleeping with Anthony Polidori—wouldn't be ruined. Zach hated her. But her words still echoed in his mind. *A mother shouldn't admit this, Zach, but you've always been my favorite.* His chest was suddenly tight and he had trouble saying, "She stopped by the hospital."

"And you wouldn't talk to her."

"Nothin' to say."

"Christ, Zach, you can be so cold and unfeeling sometimes," Trisha said, frowning at the image on her easel.

"Family trait."

"Be serious."

"I am." If she only knew. He reached onto the table and flipped on his transistor radio, hoping that music, hard rock, would drive her away. The radio crackled with static before he found a station blasting an old Rolling Stones hit. The throbbing beat of "Satisfaction" echoed over the aquamarine water.

"I can't get no . . . . no, no, no, no . . ."

"I can't hear myself think with that blaring at me!"

He didn't respond. He didn't give a damn if she was stone deaf, he just hoped she couldn't talk. He needed to be left alone. And he didn't want to think about his mother. Or London. Or anything. He took another gulp of the brew. Most of the time he felt that everyone in the family, including Trisha, was pumping him for information about the kidnapping, as if they could make him slip up and admit that he'd taken the kid. But why? And how? And where?

He didn't trust anyone in the family. Maybe there was some truth about Polidori blood running through his veins, he thought with a sarcastic grimace. Wouldn't that be something—if he really turned out to be Anthony Polidori's son after all these years? It would explain a helluva lot—why he was Eunice's favorite, for crying out loud. But he didn't like the idea. Not a bit. It was true that Witt was a class A-1 bastard, no doubt about it, but Polidori was a slime bucket of the lowest order. For years the police had tried to connect him to organized crime.

"Turn that thing off!" Trisha screamed.

Zach ignored her request. "They have any luck trying to track down Ginny Slade's relatives?" he asked. Jason had told him how they'd torn the nanny's room apart. She seemed to be the key in the kidnapping. Her references had proved false and her family had all but disappeared.

"Not that I know." Trisha angled her head, wrinkling her nose as she eyed her work. "But no one thinks she was in on it, otherwise she would have demanded money. And her checking account hasn't been touched. Still has a couple of hundred dollars in it. She's got a savings, too, over at First National, I think. Nearly a thousand dollars. Still there."

"How do you know so much?"

Trisha glanced at him a second. "I listen. At keyholes and open doors and air shafts."

For the first time Zach was interested in what his sister had learned. For years he'd thought Trisha totally self-absorbed. He assumed that she didn't care about anything other than herself, her manicure, and her latest boyfriend or a new mind-expanding high. Though lately, come to think of it, she hadn't gone out much. After the fiasco with Mario Polidori . . . Zach squinted at his sister. She was pretty, he supposed, with her thick reddish-brown hair and blue eyes. She wore too much makeup and her clothes too tight, but there was something about her, as there was with most of the Danvers children, that was appealing. For the most part, though, she was a pain in the ass.

At twenty, she was still taking art classes, had moved out of the house three or four times and had always returned either with a broken heart, busted for drugs, or flat broke. Sometimes all three. The drug busts—mainly marijuana and once in a while a little hash—were handled discreetly and without arrest by good ol' Detective Jack of the Portland police, and Witt had always covered her bad checks and escalating credit card balances. The broken hearts weren't so easily mended. Trisha had a long track record of picking losers. Including Mario Polidori.

No matter what the circumstances of her latest source of rebellion, Trisha always returned—tail between her legs, fingers stretched toward Daddy's wallet. Zach figured it was because the world with its demand of rent and electricity payments was too difficult for his sister. She was better off having Daddy pay the bills.

He leaned back in the chaise and regarded her. Already, she had a pinched set to her mouth that reminded him of his mother. In the past few years, ever since the Polidori mess, Trisha had changed. Zach didn't know exactly what had happened between Mario and her, but he'd heard arguments that had reverberated through the timbers of the old house and Zach had guessed that Mario Polidori had used his sister to get back at Witt. Trisha had been an innocent, but more than willing, accomplice in the war of hate that had existed between the families for nearly a century. The feud didn't seem to be stopping any time soon. Not that Zach cared. He didn't give a damn about the Polidoris one way or the other.

"You know, Zach," Trisha said, spinning her easel around so

that he could see her work, a caricature of him as a laid-up, unshaven, a generally slovenly teenager, lying on a chaise lounge and swilling Coke. A blaring radio and can of Colt 45 were propped on a nearby table. "You'd better be careful."

"Very funny," he remarked, pointing at her picture.

"I'm not the only one who can see through you, you know." She stuffed her charcoal back in its box. "Kat and Dad, they're on to you. There's a lot of talk about military school or some boarding school in Europe or sending you off to the ranch to, and I quote, 'work his butt off and keep him out of trouble.' "

"No way," he responded, but the ranch was definitely a better choice than options A or B. He gazed up at the thin clouds moving in from the west.

"Any way you look at it, boarding school or shoveling shit at the Lazy M beats MacLaren," she said, mentioning the Oregon school for underage male criminals

"Is that where they think I'll end up?"

"I don't know what they think, but it's my guess, Zach. You haven't exactly been easy to live with since you got out of the hospital and that stunt with the reporters—"

He grinned, rubbing the swollen knuckles of his fist with his other hand.

"—you're not winning friends."

"The guy deserved it." Zach could still hear the damned questions, see the cameras pointed at him as he'd tried to get out of Witt's Lincoln and away from the reporter who had appeared from behind the hedge.

"Can you explain why you were attacked on the night your half-sister—"

He'd reacted and his fist had slammed into the guy's jaw with a bone-jarring crunch. Blood had spurted. Pain had ricocheted up Zach's arm and the man had fallen, groaning to the ground. There was already talk of a lawsuit.

Now, as if reading her brother's thoughts, Trisha sighed and gathered up her easel.

"You think I kidnapped London?" he asked, telling himself he didn't care one way or the other.

Shaking her head and staring pointedly at the scar that still edged his face, she said, "I don't know what you did that night, but you're not telling the truth . . . not all of it and you're going to end up taking the blame for this one unless you come clean."

The muscles in the back of his neck tightened because he'd thought the same thing. "Since when are you the goddess of virtue?" He took another gulp of beer, drained the can and crumpled it in his fist.

Trisha pinned him with eyes that had seen too much pain for so short a life. "You don't know anything about me, Zach. You've never even tried to get to know me, have you? Look, I was just trying to do you a favor, but forget it." She headed back to the house. "I made a mistake. It's your funeral."

Katherine's eyelids stuck together. Her mouth tasted like she'd been licking an ashtray and her head pounded above her temples. She forced one eye open and sunlight streamed through a partially opened window, nearly blinding her. Groaning she rolled over and wondered about the sadness that was a horrible weight on her heart.

She was in her own bedroom and . . . Oh, God . . . the reality came crashing back to her fragile brain. London was gone, abducted nearly two—or was it three?—weeks before. Desperation, like the horrid beast it was, clawed at her from the inside. She needed a cigarette. With numb fingers she reached to the bed table and found an empty pack of Virginia Slims, which she flung onto the floor. Tears flooded her eyes. She couldn't take this, day after day. The bumbling policemen, the useless FBI and the reporters, damn the reporters. The few that had gotten past the guards had asked questions that made her heart bleed and the fire in their eyes, all looking for a story, and insensitive to her pain . . . no wonder Zach had punched out a reporter and broken a photographer's camera as he'd returned to the house from the hospital.

On unsteady legs she stood, then drew the drapes open a little further. Two squad cars and a plain, stripped-down Chevrolet were scattered on the circular drive. Farther away, past the sloping front lawns and tended rose gardens, she caught a glimpse of the front gates where the vultures gathered. Two or three cars were parked in the shade of an ancient oak that spread its branches over the brick wall which kept the scavengers at bay.

"I hope you all rot in hell," she muttered, letting the drapes fall back into place.

What time was it? Bleary eyes focused on the clock. Two in the afternoon. She'd slept seventeen hours, drugged by Doc McHenry's sleeping pills and God only knew what else. Somehow, someway, she'd have to pull herself together. With or without London.

That thought caused her knees to buckle and she grasped the edge of the bureau to steady herself. She'd find her baby. She had to. She couldn't trust the federal government or the police, and Witt, well, he hadn't been much help. The fact that he would no longer sleep with her, insisting that she needed her rest, bothered her. She knew the real reason. He was afraid that she would require more than a pat on the head, that she might need a kiss, a hug, even her husband to make love to her to comfort her.

God, she needed a cigarette.

Running her tongue over filmy teeth, she forced herself into the bathroom where she stripped off the nightgown that she'd worn for days and turned on the shower. Before stepping under the hot spray, she got a glimpse of her reflection and cringed. No makeup, hair lank, her once-curvy body beginning to look gaunt from lack of food. Hazily she remembered Maria, the cook, coming into her room, trying to force soup of some kind down her throat.

In all her life, Katherine had never once let herself go; she believed that her greatest commodity was her body and she spent hours in the gym, with a masseuse, at the hair dresser, having her nails manicured. Her clothes were always flattering, a little sexy, but classy and pressed.

But now she looked like hell.

She stepped into the warm spray and let the hot water run over her hair and skin. Closing her eyes against the dark depression that settled over her whenever she thought of London, she leaned against the slick tiles. She couldn't let this get her down because she was London's only chance. If she gave up on her daughter, everyone else would as well.

Sobs burned deep in her throat and, telling herself that she could allow herself the freedom to cry, to grieve a little by herself, she let the tears drizzle down her cheeks, their salty tracks mingling with the rivulets from the shower as the steam billowed around her.

As long as she was alone, she could wail and scream and gnash her teeth in frustration, but when she was with the others; then she had to pretend to be strong.

An hour later she'd made it downstairs. Her hair was washed, blown dry and brushed until it shined, her teeth were polished, her makeup impeccable, her shorts and halter top a blue that matched her eyes. She grabbed some orange juice from the refrigerator, ignored Maria's pleas that she eat breakfast, and found out that Witt and the police were holed up in the den with strict orders not to be disturbed. Fine. Turning her back to Maria, she splashed a couple of shots of vodka into her juice, swallowed two double-strength Excedrin, reached for a new pack of cigarettes and tucked the *Wall Street Journal* under her arm.

She was ready, or so she thought, but the intensity of the daylight made her reach for the sunglasses she kept in a drawer near the French doors. Outside, there wasn't a breath of breeze and the sun beat mercilessly against the cement and brick that skirted the pool.

She heard a noise, glanced up and realized, as she passed by the ferns and rhododendrons flanking the path that Zachary was swimming laps. He knifed through the water like an athlete and his wounds, still visible against his tanned skin had healed enough to allow him easy, even strokes.

A knot of something akin to desire unwound in Katherine's stomach. Of all of Witt's children, Zachary held the most appeal to her. He didn't look like the rest of the Danvers brood—his skin was a darker shade, he was more muscular in build, and his eyes were a stormy gray rather than the clear blue that seemed to be a Danvers trademark.

Maybe the rumors about him were true, though Katherine couldn't imagine Eunice, that dried-up Amazon of a woman, making it with Anthony Polidori.

Whatever the reason, be it chance of genetics or an unknown father, Zach was different from the rest of the kids. His nose wasn't straight and arrogant like Witt's, but Katherine had decided that was because it had been broken at least three times, once recently on that horrid night when London was abducted, once during a motorcycle accident, and another time during a fistfight when a bully brought up the fact that half of Portland thought that Zach was a dago bastard, his mother an Italian-fucking bitch, and Witt a cuckold. The kid had been twice Zach's size but had left with two black eyes and a swollen cock when Zach's pointed boots had connected with the kid's groin. Zach had gotten the worst of it, not only had his nose been broken but his ribs as well and the boy's father, a snooty lawyer who worked in the First National Bank Tower, had threatened to sue. Fortunately, Witt had bought him off—which was exactly what the lawyer-father had hoped for.

Irreverent and sexy as hell, Zach was attractive on more than one level. Katherine dropped onto a chaise lounge, propped up her feet and watched her stepson glide through the water. Sleek, sinewy muscles, damp and gleaming in the sunlight, moved effortlessly. She wondered if his skin was tanned everywhere or if, beneath the ragged cutoffs, his buttocks were a lighter shade.

Since she'd taken her marriage vows, Katherine had never been unfaithful to Witt. Even in the past few years when he'd all but stopped trying to make love to her, she'd ignored the desire that curled restlessly through her blood when she saw a particularly interesting male. She'd had opportunities, plenty of them over the years—some suggested by Witt's closest friends—but she'd laughed off the passes as if they were bad jokes and never given into the lust that had some nights nearly driven her mad.

But she was tempted by Zachary. No doubt about it. She wasn't alone. He could protest it as loudly as he wanted, but he was attracted to her. The last time they'd been together, when her temper had gotten the better of her and she'd forced him to dance with her at Witt's party, she'd felt the hardness between his legs, saw the stain of embarrassment on his cheeks, knew that he'd responded to her. At that time she'd been a little drunk with champagne and she'd wondered what kind of a lover he'd be. Would he be masterful in bed, or would she have to teach him about loving? Would he come like the kid he was, in seconds, or had he learned patience, waiting for his partner to reach a climax?

Stop it! He's Witt's son, for crying out loud! Your stepson! With shaking fingers she peeled the cellophane from her pack of cigarettes, shook out a Virginia Slim and lit up. He didn't look her way, didn't acknowledge that she was near the pool, just kept swimming as if he would never stop.

Blowing smoke to the sky, she tried to turn her thoughts away from her secret attraction to Zach. However, if she wasn't considering his seduction, her mind turned back to London and the deep depression that enveloped her whenever she thought of her little girl. Where was she? Still alive? Huddled and scared? Or dead already, brutally murdered? Oh, God, she couldn't think about that. She wouldn't! "London," she whispered, her eyes filling with sudden tears again.

She took a long sip from the cool orange juice and hoped the vodka would calm her nerves. If only someone would hold her, place strong arms around her, whisper in her ear that everything would be all right . . . that London was safe and would be returning home. The inside of her chest seemed to cave in on itself.

She needed someone. Anyone. Zach.

Gritting her teeth against the mind-paralyzing fear that had been her constant companion for weeks, she snapped the paper open and pretended interest in the bond market when all the while she watched Zach over the top of the newspaper. Her eyes were hidden by her sunglasses and she was certain that Zach didn't know that as she stared at him, she was beginning to plan his seduction.

Zach's lungs burned and his shoulder was beginning to ache. He'd been in the pool an hour, hoping Kat would finish her drink and leave, but he'd had no such luck. It looked as if she'd parked herself indefinitely. He was relieved she'd finally emerged. It was weird for her to be locked in her room, hardly venturing out.

But then, these days, everything at the house was weird. The cops and FBI, the reporters clustered around the gates, Witt's quiet rage and Kat's isolation. Jason had moved back to the house and paced like a caged animal and Nelson, after following him around for a few days, had holed up in his room with records by Led Zeppelin or something.

Zach didn't trust anyone and thought people were always staring at him, as if he had any idea what had happened to London and the damned nanny.

Surfacing, he tossed the water from his hair and took in a huge gulp of air. He hoisted himself out of the pool and stood dripping because his towel was at the other end, near Kat, and ever since the party he'd wanted to avoid her. He was uncomfortable around her, partly because being near her reminded him of his fear for London, but partly because he was embarrassed about what had happened on the dance floor that night. He was even more humiliated because Kat knew that he'd gone to a hooker. A whore. Like he had to pay for it!

He'd had plenty of chances with girls his age, but he hadn't been interested in some giggling ninny who would let him touch her tits in exchange for his class ring or some such garbage. Girls were always looking to fall in love and he wasn't interested. He didn't believe in love and knew he never would. His parents and his siblings had convinced him that love was a foolish notion. It just plain didn't exist.

The cement was hot against the bottoms of his feet as he jogged the length of the pool and snatched up his towel.

Kat glanced up and offered him a blinding smile that caused his diaphragm to slam into his lungs. "You're feeling better," he said weakly, knowing she expected conversation.

"Yeah."

She lifted her sunglasses to squint up at him. God, she was beautiful. Her lips were a slick, glossy pink and her cheekbones were carved gently. Standing above her, he could see down the column of her throat and lower still to the deep cleft between her breasts. Her tan line, faded somewhat, was still visible and if she moved just the right way, he was certain he'd catch a glimpse of her nipples. "No permanent damage?" she asked, as if she really cared.

"Looks that way." He swiped the towel over his face and through his hair, trying to ignore the raw sensuality that seemed to radiate from her. Hell, why was she looking at him like that?

"That's good. I was worried about you." She stretched and the motion seemed somehow feline in the hot sun. A hot summer breeze kissed the back of his neck.

"Were you?" He didn't believe her and he was suddenly wary. He felt like a rabbit moving closer to a snare.

She swallowed and licked those magnificent lips. Somewhere in the house a door slammed. "Yes . . . there's so much that's happened, some of it so awful." Tears threatened her eyes and for the life of him he felt sorry for her. "Anyway, I know I've treated you badly—that display at the hotel was uncalled for. I was drunk and angry and . . . oh, God, Zach . . . I'm making a mess of this, but I just wanted you to know that I'm sorry."

"Forget it," he said, his face turning a darker shade of red.

"I will. If you'll forgive me."

Jesus, what was going on here? He cleared his throat and glanced at the shadows shifting beneath the trees. "Sure."

"Thanks." Again the blinding smile, though this time there were teardrops drizzling down her cheeks and he realized how devastated she was about the loss of her child.

He felt awkward and stupid for even thinking about her in any way sexual. She was grieving, for Christ's sake. Nervously, he knotted the towel in his hands. "I . . . uh . . . look, don't worry about London. She'll turn up."

"You think so?"

Damn it, she sounded so hopeful. Did he do that—give her a sense of false hope about a poor little girl who might already be dead? He felt absolutely wretched. "I dunno, but . . . everybody's looking for her . . ." It sounded lame, even to his own ears and he noticed the ghost of pain crossing her eyes. Hell, he was just no good at this!

She reached up and grabbed his hand with hers. Heat swirled up his arm. "I hope so, Zach," she whispered, blinking hard as her fingers tightened over his. A jolt of electricity kicked his heart into high gear. She looked so young suddenly, so vulnerable and small. He had to remind himself that this was Kat. "God, I hope so." She used his arm as a brace and climbed to her feet, her body only inches from his.

To his utter amazement, she stood on her tiptoes and brushed a chaste kiss over his cheek. "Thanks for understanding, Zach. I needed a friend." He turned his face, staring into her eyes, feeling her moist, smoky breath against his skin, half expecting her to kiss him again, but she smiled sadly and let go of his arm, then picked up her things and walked back to the house.

He was left standing by the pool, dripping, and wondering what the hell had just gone on.

Pain, as hot as if it erupted straight from the bowels of hell shot through Witt's chest. For a second he couldn't breathe and he felt as if someone had locked their fingers over his throat and was strangling him. Damn, where were the pills? He yanked open the desk drawer and saw the vial in the pencil rack. Agony tore at his heart as he managed to retrieve the nitroglycerin pills and shove one under his tongue. He was nearly gasping now and waiting, his elbows propped on the leather desk pad, his head resting in his palms. Sweat broke out over his forehead and the damned intercom began to buzz impatiently. He didn't answer and knew that Shirley, his secretary of more than twenty years, would get the message.

The buzzer stopped and five minutes later, he was collected again—the damned angina had passed and he straightened his tie. No one save McHenry knew about his condition and he planned on keeping his secret to himself. Witt hated weakness and this heart condition was just that . . . a sign that he wasn't as strong as he once had been.

He reached for his humidor, opened the lid and the heavy scent of Havana tobacco wafted to his nostrils. He grabbed a cigar, wedged it between his teeth, but didn't light up. Not now. Not after the angina attack.

He pushed the intercom button, learned that Roger Phelps was waiting in the reception area of the offices of Danvers International, and growled at Shirley to show him in. Disgusted, he didn't bother lighting up though he longed for a few relaxing lungfuls of smoke.

Within minutes Phelps was seated on the opposite side of Witt's desk. He looked like Joe Average. Tan slacks, brown jacket, off-white shirt, and nondescript, cheap department-store tie. His face wasn't noteworthy, just even features with the beginnings of jowls that matched the paunch developing at his belt line. Witt was more than a little disappointed in the man who had supposedly been an agent with the CIA before dropping out of the government to do independent work.

"What can I do for you, Mr. Danvers?" Phelps said in a nasal voice. He hiked up his pants a bit and Witt noticed that his shoes—cheap Kinney loafers from the looks of them—were scuffed.

"You must've guessed why I wanted you. My daughter, London, was kidnapped. The police and FBI are incompetent jerks. Don't have a clue where my daughter is and it's been damned close to a month."

Phelps didn't comment, just sipped his coffee.

"You come highly recommended."

A lift of a tired shoulder.

Witt was growing irritated. "Tell me why I should pay you when the government and the police seem to be baffled?"

Phelps's expression changed slightly and Witt was reminded of a wolf with his nose to wind, scenting a wounded doe. "Simple. You want her found."

"And you can do that?" Witt settled back in his chair. Maybe there were more layers to Phelps than met the eye.

"If I don't, you owe me nothing besides my retainer."

"Of five thousand dollars."

"Cheap, isn't it?" He sat his untouched coffee on the edge of Witt's desk. "All I ask is that your family comes clean with me. No secrets. No lies. No skeletons tucked into closets."

"Fair enough. You can question everyone here while we're still in Portland, but you may as well know that I'm moving them—even the older kids—to the ranch near Bend. I'm not going to chance losing another one. Zachary—" He scowled when he thought of his middle son. Always the rebel. Always cocksure. Always so damned arrogant. Always in trouble. *Polidori's son.* No! "—he's going first, but he doesn't know it yet. The rest of the family will follow in a couple of weeks. So you'd better start with him."

"He's the one with the phony story about the hooker."

Witt's back went up. "The story was true. The police talked to the girl . . . Sophia, something or other."

"Costanzo. I already spoke with her."

Witt moved the unsmoked cigar from one side of his mouth to the other. "What'd she say?"

"Same thing she said to the police. Not much. Gives your kid his alibi, but I have the feeling she's lying."

"A feeling?" Witt was skeptical.

"Believe me, she's not telling everything she knows." He smiled grimly. "But that won't be a problem. I'll handle her. And as for Zach, I'll talk to him, see what he says; maybe he'll slip up. I'll catch everyone else before you send them packing." He pulled out a notepad from the inner pocket of his jacket, scribbled quickly, then frowned slightly, wrinkles lining his brow. "What about your wife? Can I reach her here or is she going to the ranch with your kids?"

Witt hesitated just a second. He'd been wrestling with this decision, but he couldn't put it off any longer. She needed to get away. "Katherine will be at the ranch." Why sending her to central Oregon was a relief to him, he didn't understand, but he hoped the change of scenery would do her some good.

Phelps cocked his head at an angle. "And you?"

"I've got a business to run, Phelps." Already the man was getting on his nerves. "You can reach me here."

"Good." Phelps folded his hands over his thickening girth. "Now, there's only one thing I want from you, Danvers, and that's honesty, from you and your family."

"You've got it," Witt agreed, anxious for the interview to be over. This blend-into-the-woodwork guy was giving him a case of the creeps, but Witt needed him. He needed someone to help him find London. The police were beginning to look like a bunch of bumbling idiots and the FBI hadn't located Patty Hearst and she'd been missing for months. . . . A darkness settled into his soul and he wondered if he was being punished. He didn't much believe in God, though he attended church, but he'd committed more than his share of sins.

"But maybe you don't 'got it,'" Phelps said, cutting into his thoughts. He leaned forward and pinned Witt with eyes that had suddenly come alive. "If I find out that a member of your family is behind this, then I expect to be paid anyway."

"You will," Witt agreed, though his collar seemed to tighten around his throat like one of those goddamned chains you slipped around the neck of a guard dog.

Phelps managed a phony grin and Witt felt as if he'd pulled on that invisible chain—to remind him where they stood. "Good. Just so we understand each other."

5

A dry wind blew across the stubble of the fields, bringing dust and chaff and the thin smell of diesel from the tractor rumbling along the hillside beyond a ragged copse of pine trees. Digging in the heels of his boots, Zach stretched the barbed wire between the posts, his muscles gleaming with the effort. Sweat stained the red bandanna he'd rolled and tied around his head. The sun was relentless, but Zach didn't care.

"Hang in there," Manny, the ranch foreman called. "Hold tight and I'll tie 'er off."

For the first time in weeks, Zach felt free. His wounds had nearly healed and he loved the ranch, three thousand acres northwest of Bend in central Oregon. Sheltered by the eastern foothills of the Cascade Mountains, the Danvers spread stretched as far as the eye could see. Unlike the brick-walled fortress of the Danvers's home in the west hills of Portland, the Lazy M was wild and open and touched the vagabond spirit of Zach's soul.

He'd been sent here just after being interrogated by Roger Phelps, some sort of private eye his father had hired. The detective was patient, talking slowly, luring Zach into saying things he hadn't intended. Zach had left the interview feeling as if Phelps considered him a prime suspect in London's kidnapping. He'd thought about telling the truth, but couldn't see what good it would have done to rat on Jason about the whore. Who cared? One incident wasn't related to the other. Zach had his own moral code, loose though it may be. One thing he never did was snitch.

After the interview with Phelps, he'd been shipped out here. Witt had figured that long hours working on the ranch, bucking hay, stretching fence-line, herding cattle, and wearing himself out in the saddle was good for him, better than the dreaded military school that had been a constant threat ever since London had disappeared. Witt had told his son that he thought the endless hours of work would keep him out of trouble, and Zach hadn't argued. He'd wanted out of the house, away from the suspicious glances thrown in his direction by everyone in the family, far from the distraction of his stepmother and nowhere near the cops. Jack Logan, like Roger Phelps, seemed to think he was guilty of all kinds of crimes.

If they only knew.

Sure, he'd had his trouble with the law. He'd been caught as a minor in possession of alcohol more times than he'd like to admit, and he'd stolen the hearse from the local funeral home and gone joyriding, leaving the funeral director and a grieving family fit to be tied. Witt had been forced to do some fast talking on that one so that Zach, though underage, hadn't been charged with grand theft auto. He'd been expelled from school for blowing up the faculty room john and he'd been in his share of fights and motorcycle accidents—most before he'd gotten his license.

"Hell on wheels," Jack Logan had called him on more than one occasion.

Jason had stood up for his younger brother. "It's just a phase, a kid sort of thing," he'd told their father. "He's rebelling a little, that's all. No big deal. Let him do his thing."

Kat had seemed amused. "I bet you did your own bit of hell-raising in your time, Witt," she'd said when Witt, in a fury over the hearse incident, looked as if he'd wanted to strangle the boy he'd raised as his second son.

Nelson, each time Zach was returned home in the middle of the night, handcuffed and bleeding from some fight, had wanted all the intimate details and followed Zach around for days after, telling Zach how he hoped his brother had "kicked ass."

Only Trisha had said nothing, smiling as if she were glad Zach was taking the heat instead of her.

Yeah, he'd been trouble for his folks and he didn't really give a shit. That bothered Witt the worst, that Zach had no direction, no drive. At least Trisha had her art and Jason was going to be the best damned lawyer in the entire Northwest, but Zach had no ambition, no focus, didn't seem interested in the hotel business, or the timber business, or anything remotely connected with Danvers International.

But Zach did love the ranch.

And he had nothing to do with the kidnapping. Why didn't anyone believe him?

Sure, London had been a pain and Witt had spoiled her rotten, but, truth to tell, Zach had liked the little kid who could get away with anything just by smiling impishly up at her father while her blue eyes twinkled as if with a private secret. Yep, anyone who could manipulate the old man, was someone Zach respected. Even if she was only a precocious four-year-old.

He was sorry she was gone and had to keep his mind from wandering too far toward the murky thoughts of what had become of her. He, for one, had written her off as dead. Or else whoever kidnapped her wasn't going to let her go; not after so long.

"Okay, that should do it!" Manny tested his post and satisfied that this section of fence would stand, gave Zach the high sign. "It's Friday. Let's call it a day."

Zach checked his watch. Five-fifteen. Since he'd been at the ranch, a little over a week now, Manny hadn't let him off work until eight at night. The routine had been the same. Dog tired, Zach had returned to the house each night, washed, eaten and fallen asleep before nine, so that he would be ready for a new day starting at five the next morning.

He stripped off his bandanna, wiped the sweat and grime from his face and walked to the shady banks of the creek where he'd left his horse after lunch. He could've ridden in the dusty cab of the truck, or even sat on the flatbed as it bounced along the rutted dirt roads of the ranch, but he preferred the horses and this one, Cyclone, was his favorite. A headstrong sorrel colt with four white stockings who was known to kick and bite, Cyclone was the fastest horse on the ranch.

"Come on, boy," he said, hoisting the blanket and saddle onto the colt's back. "It's time."

Ears back, the horse shifted, but Zach was quick enough to dodge the blow and tighten the cinch. "You're a mean son of a bitch, aren't you?" He swung into the saddle and yanked on the reins. "Well, that's all right by me, 'cause I am, too. Hiya!" Heels pressed into the beast's sides, he leaned forward in the saddle and Cyclone took off. Wind streamed through Zach's hair and brought tears to his eyes. Spindly jack pine and red-barked ponderosa pine trees flashed by in a blur and once again Zach felt wild and free—as if he could do anything he damned well pleased.

He didn't miss his siblings. Jason would sell his soul to the devil for a small amount of cash while Trisha was rebelling in the best way she knew how—by getting involved with Mario Polidori, son of Witt's old nemesis, yet again. Obviously she didn't subscribe to the "once burned, twice shy," theory. There were whispers that she was into drugs though Zach had seen no evidence of it. As for Nelson—the kid was a pain—plain and simple. Ever since the kidnapping, Nelson had puppy dogged after Zach, wanting to hear over and over again about the hooker and the thugs with the knife—like Zach was some kind of war hero. It bothered Zach because Nelson was a little on the soft side—his adoration a little too intense.

But London, she was another matter. He closed his mind to all thoughts of her, preferring to be numb rather than think about the horrors his sister might be enduring. "Come on," he yelled at the colt.

Zach kicked the sorrel and the horse responded, gathering speed like a comet streaking across the sky, approaching the ravine where the creek slashed through the field. Without a second's hesitation, the horse responded. Massive muscles bunched then lengthened and horse and rider were soaring across the rock-strewn chasm where only a thin stream of water trickled.

The colt landed with a thud on the pebble-strewn bank and, with renewed energy upon sight of the stables, ran flat out across the yellow stubble of the pasture. Grasshoppers and pheasants, wings flapping in a frenzy, were flushed from the straw.

Zach leaned low over the sorrel's neck and urged the horse even faster. Cyclone took the bit between his teeth, his legs flashing over the cracked earth. Wind screamed past his ears and sweat darkened the horse's coat. Laughing for the first time in weeks, Zach yelled, "Move, you miserable hunk of horseflesh."

Only when they were near the paddock, did Zach pull back on the reins, wresting control from the headstrong beast. "Slow down," he growled, standing in the stirrups. By the time they entered the paddock, the colt had switched from a gallop to a trot and finally into a reluctant walk. Cyclone tossed his head, his bridle jangling as he fought with the demanding demon on his back.

"You did good," Zach said. Cyclone was blowing hard and Zach kept him moving, walking slowly, until the colt's breathing was normal again. "That's better."

Zach didn't see Trisha watching him, didn't notice her lurking in the shadows of the scrub pine until he'd reined up at the fence and she climbed onto the top rail. With a sinking sensation, he knew he'd have to deal with his family again and suddenly his wings seemed clipped. All the old anger and resentment welled up in him again and the ranch that had moments before appeared so vast quickly became confining and small.

"This place is a prison!" Trisha said as she pushed aside a long-needled branch encroaching over the fence.

"What're you doing here?" But he knew. They were all here. For good.

"Family vacation," she said with more than a trace of sarcasm. Her nose wrinkled when she saw the horseflies gathering near the colt's rump. The smells of manure mixed with urine, sweat, and dust, apparently offended her. "Believe me, I tried to talk Dad out of it, but you know how he is when he makes a decision."

"Humph." Zach swung down from the horse's back.

"In a way, I understand. Dad's tired of everyone just sitting around and waiting for the phone to ring at the house in town— even the police and the feds. Doing nothing!"

Zach remembered.

"Dad said we were all getting on his nerves—now, there's something new," she added sarcastically.

Zach didn't respond.

"Anyway, I think he was worried about another kidnapping."

"No way." Zach hauled the saddle off the horse and hung it over the top rail of the fence. "Aren't you the one who pointed out that he wouldn't care if one of us was abducted? Just London."

Trisha pouted.

"You know, if I turned up missing, I think he might buy a bottle of expensive champagne and have himself a celebration."

"He's not that bad," she said without much conviction, then catching Zach's steady gaze, sighed. "Okay, so he is that bad. Anyway, it doesn't matter why he sent us here, the fact of the matter is that we're all stuck in this godforsaken place."

"Is that so?"

"Including Kat."

Zach's stomach dropped a little, but he managed to keep his face from registering the slightest trace of emotion. "She'll hate it here," he said flatly.

"Already does." Plucking a few long needles from a branch near her head, she sighed and twirled the sprig between her fingers. "You should have heard their fight. It reminded me of Mom and Dad before they split up. Kat put up a battle, I'll give her that, but despite her excruciatingly loud protests against being shipped out of Portland, she wound up here, with the rest of us and that really pissed her off. She wanted to stay close to the investigation and I thought she might grab Dad's twenty-two and put a bullet through him before she'd leave town. But, of course, Dad got his way." Her eyes clouded and Zach knew she wasn't thinking about Kat any longer.

"He always gets his way."

Trisha glanced up at her brother. "I think Dad had an ulterior motive for shipping her off."

Zach lifted a disinterested eyebrow.

"Kat'll freak, 'cause I think the investigation's winding down. The cops are out of leads and the FBI isn't doing any better. All a bunch of fools with their thumbs rammed up their asses."

"What about Phelps?"

"The private investigator? He's a joke. Have you ever seen anyone so . . . ordinary in your life?" Dropping the pine needles, she dusted her hands and glared up at Zachary as if the situation were all his fault. "It's all a front, anyway. Dad wants to believe that the Polidoris are behind the kidnapping."

"Are they?"

"They're not stupid, Zach. Anthony has to know that he'd be at the top of the suspect list."

Zach wasn't convinced, but he didn't bother to comment. Let Trisha believe what she wanted.

"It's all such a pain. Ever since London disappeared no one can go anywhere without some damned bodyguard prowling around behind."

Zach tied the reins to the second rail of the fence. He wasn't in the mood to listen to his sister's whining. Trisha was just ticked off because she couldn't sneak around meeting Mario Polidori. Both families disapproved of the romance between Mario and Trisha. The only subject the Polidoris and Danvers had agreed upon in the last hundred years was to forbid Mario and Trisha from seeing each other. They were adults, she'd argued, and Witt had told her that she'd better start acting like one and move out, but as far as he was concerned, while she lived under his roof, she'd abide by his rules.

Trisha had other plans. She seemed to think she was some modern-day Juliet and Mario was her Romeo. The thought made Zach sick and he spat on the dusty ground. She should have learned her lesson about Mario Polidori. With a grunt, he grabbed the saddle and slung it over his shoulder to carry it into the stables.

Following him inside, Trisha said, "I thought you and I could work a deal."

Zach sent her a look telling her silently to get lost. He didn't need Trisha's kind of trouble. He had enough of his own. Though he'd gotten a slight reprieve, the old man was still making noise about military school and Zach was considering walking through the Danvers's gates and never looking over his shoulder.

"C'mon, Zach. I need your help."

Zach swung the saddle over a saw horse, then dropped the blanket over the top rail of a stall. Dust and horsehair rose in a cloud that clogged the air.

Trisha coughed and Zach swallowed a smile. Served her right. She'd never shown any interest in the horses, she was only here because she wanted something. And badly.

"Okay," she said. "Here's the deal: I need to find a way to sneak out of here. At night."

"Why?"

"It's personal."

"To meet Mario, right?"

"The less you know the better."

"No."

"What?" Her face crumpled into a look of wounded pride. "I stood up for you—"

"How?" he demanded.

"I told Kat that you wouldn't hurt a hair on London's head."

"Thanks for the vote of confidence," he muttered as he yanked the bandanna from his pocket and wiped the sweat from his neck.

"That's more than anyone else did for you, and Kat's still not convinced that you weren't involved somehow. If you were any older everyone would think you were behind it, but since you're only sixteen—"

"Why would I kidnap London?"

"For money," Trisha said slowly and Zach couldn't help his reaction. His head snapped up and his eyes narrowed on his sister.

"Then wouldn't I demand ransom?"

"It's only been a little while."

"So how would I do it? How would I grab Ginny and London and stow them away God-only-knows where while I got myself cut up for an alibi. It doesn't make sense, Trisha, and everyone knows it. They're just pointing at me because I was gone that night and there's no one else to blame."

"Tell that to Jack Logan."

"Logan's a jackass. Oh shit, who cares?" Zach stormed outside and unknotted the reins. Cyclone sidestepped and tossed his head, as Zach led him into a stall. Muscles knotted in quiet rage, Zach filled a bucket with water and let the colt drink before rubbing him down. "You're way off base, Trisha," he finally said.

Trisha dusted off the burlap and sat gingerly on a sack of oats. Leaning forward, propping her elbows on her knees, she cradled her chin. Her gaze narrowed through the dusty window and she chewed on her lower lip. "Okay, okay, maybe you really shouldn't be the number-one suspect."

"Thanks."

"So who do you think took her?"

"I don't even want to think about it." And that was the truth.

"Well, someone had to."

"Okay, Ginny, then."

"Yeah, but who was she working for?"

"Don't know. Hell, do we have to do this—dredge it all up again?" Zach hated to admit it, but he missed the little kid. True, she'd bugged the hell out of him and tagged after him. More often than not he'd told her gruffly to "get lost," but he worried about her and had trouble sleeping at night just wondering what had happened and if she were all right.

Trisha plucked a piece of straw from the manger. "One word from me and you'd be shit out of luck."

"How's that?" With the currycomb, Zach worked on a knot in the colt's mane, then sidestepped the blow when the sorrel tried to kick him in the shins.

"I could say that Mario told me you were involved in the kidnapping."

Zach tensed. Where was this going? Slowly, he resumed brushing the horse. "It would be a lie."

"Everyone would believe it. You know, there are still a few rumors floating around about you."

"Can it, Trisha." He'd heard all the gossip and didn't want to be reminded that while he'd been conceived his mother was having an affair with Polidori. His teeth ground together but he just kept working, ignoring Trisha's innuendos and veiled threats. Christ, what did she want from him?

"It's just that I hate it here, Zach. This is . . . nowhere. I want to go back to Portland."

"You just got here."

"Doesn't matter."

"You want to be close to Mario."

"So what?"

Zach slid her a look that called her stupid. "Get smart, Trisha. It's never gonna work between you and Polidori. Dad'll never approve."

"Since when do you care?"

"I don't. I'm just giving you some free advice."

"Save it."

"Fine." He opened the door at the back of the stables, then let the colt trot outside. With a snort and toss of his head, the horse ran free, bucking and kicking up his heels before laying in the thick dust and rolling. Clouds of dry earth roiled to the sky and the colt grunted in pleasure. Soon all Zach could see of the animal were four white-stockinged legs thrashing madly.

Trisha made a face. "You're not going to help me?"

Zach shook his head. "No way."

She arched a delicate brow and set an expression somewhere between a sneer and smile on her pouty lips. "You'll be sorry."

"Tell me something I don't know." Irritated, he strode out of the stables and wished that the rest of his family would just leave him alone.

It was hours later when Kat found him. The sun had set and Jason had taken Trisha and Nelson into town. Zach, avoiding his family as much as he could, had stolen two beers from the refrigerator and had climbed onto the roof of the tack shed that butted up to the stables. The dark sky was alive with shooting stars and Zach sat alone, his back propped against the rough outer wall of the second story of the stables, his legs stretched out on the sloping cedar shingles. Through the tar paper and split shakes, he heard the muffled sounds of horses, snorting, rustling in the straw, letting out an occasional whinny.

The moon was small, just a sliver, but gave off enough light so that he could see the stands of trees flanking the rambling ranch house and out buildings. The house was lit like a Christmas tree, patches of warm light glowing through the windows. Kat was still awake, prowling the rooms. He caught glimpses of her now and again, moving restlessly from one window to the next and he decided he wouldn't slip through the French doors to his room until all the lights had been turned down and he knew that she was asleep. So far, he'd avoided her, but he wouldn't be able to sidestep her forever.

He bent one knee, glanced up at the vast sky and tried to regain the sense of freedom he'd experienced before the family had appeared. Even gazing to the flat endless land stretching to the west, he felt cooped up again. All because of them. Gritting his teeth, he opened a can of Coors and beer foamed over the side. He took a gulp, catching most of the overflow when he heard the old dog let out a quiet bark, then the unmistakable sounds of tread, small footsteps walking unerringly to the stables. His heart nearly stopped. Seconds later the rungs of the ladder to the hayloft clicked as someone climbed to the top. Now what?

He smelled the scent of her perfume before he saw her in the open window of the hayloft, her face white, her black hair the color of midnight. His chest felt as if it were suddenly constricted with iron bands.

"Manny said you might be here," she said as casually as if she'd spent all her life creeping around barns and climbing into haymows.

His gut tightened as she slid through the window and stepped onto the roof. Balancing herself with a hand on the roof of the stables she walked the short distance to his side and slid onto her rear.

The scent of her perfume was stronger as it drifted to his nostrils and her arm was so close to his that he could feel the heat of her body. He remembered how she'd felt in his arms, supple and pliable and willing . . . oh, God . . . "What do you want?"

"Company." She offered him a smile. "I thought we were friends."

Off in the distance a coyote howled.

"I don't know if that's possible."

"We could try to be. Especially if you offered me a beer."

Throat so dry it felt like sand, he handed the second can to her and she, with a smile that flashed in the dark night, popped the tab and giggled when the foam erupted and spilled across her fingers. She lapped it up with her tongue and Zach tried not to notice how sexy she looked with the white flecks on her lips.

"It's beautiful tonight," she said, staring up at the heavens and sighing loudly. "If you like this kind of thing."

"You don't?"

"I'm a city girl." She drank from the beer, then drew her legs up and wrapped her arms over her bare knees. Her shorts barely covered her butt, but Zach tried to keep his eyes and mind on anything but how damnably sensual she was. "Grew up in Ottawa."

He didn't reply, couldn't.

They sat in silence for what seemed forever. Zach's heart was drumming so loudly, he wondered if she heard it and though he pretended disinterested insolence, he suspected she saw right through him.

"I didn't want to come here," she admitted. "I don't like being this far away if there's any news about London . . ." Her throat caught on her daughter's name, but she didn't break down. Instead she sighed and ran her fingers through the thick black curls that framed her perfect face. "You don't like me much, do you, Zach?" she asked suddenly.

"You're . . . my stepmother."

"As in *wicked* stepmother?"

He lifted a shoulder and took the last gulp of his beer. His fingers were still around the empty can when she turned her eyes up to him and they sparked with an inner light. Zach could barely breathe as she, staring at him boldly, placed her hands on his shoulders and brushed her lips across his.

"Jesus, Katherine—" he breathed, his heart knocking crazily. "Don't!"

"Ssh." She placed those supple lips against his again, just for a second—a second he was certain would change the course of his life forever. Her mouth was teasing and warm, filled with promise.

Zach groaned low in his throat. "Don't do this, Kat."

"You want it, too," she murmured in a sigh as soft as the summer night.

He told himself that he couldn't kiss her or touch her or even think about her and yet he was too weak to tear away from her embrace. Her lips fastened over his and her breasts, beneath the fragile barrier of her T-shirt, brushed across his bare chest.

A thousand reasons to stop screamed through his head but

when her tongue skimmed his lips, then pressed urgently, demanding entrance, he gave up and he kissed her back, closing his mind to the warnings screaming through his mind.

Her tongue was wet and slick and wonderful. It touched the roof of his mouth, flicked against his lips and teeth and promised untold delights.

Heat swirled through his blood and his cock was so hard it strained against the zipper of his cutoffs. *Don't do this! Don't!* an inner voice cried, but instead of protesting, he reached up and his fingers wound in her thick hair. She slid down him and kissed his naked chest, her tongue licking its way against his skin.

A shudder that felt like fire ripped through him. He dropped his beer and the empty can rolled noisily down the roof. His body convulsed and hot desire pumped through him. Grabbing her with strength born of desperation, he kissed her hard on the lips and all he could think about was kissing her and touching her and riding her all night.

She's your father's wife, Danvers! his mind yelled and for once he listened to it. He found the strength to push her away. "This isn't gonna work," he said, breathing hard, wishing he could call back the words. He was so hard he was sure he would explode and his fingers clamped around her shoulders, keeping her at arm's length.

Katherine chuckled deep in her throat and the sound seemed to echo off the distant hills. "What is this, Zach?"

"Wrong. That's what it is!" He dropped his arms, scooted farther away from her and ran sweaty, trembling fingers through his long hair.

She pouted a little in the darkness. "Since when did you care about right and wrong?"

"Don't play with me, Kat," he warned and was surprised at the conviction in his voice.

"I just felt we had an understanding." With a lift of her shoulder, she tucked her feet under her and stared down at him. "I don't get it Zach. I thought—no, I knew—you wanted this."

"I don't."

She snorted. "As a matter of fact, I was certain this is what you needed."

"I don't need you, Katherine," he said, wishing he could put more distance between her sensual body and his own. "I don't need anybody."

"Oh, baby, that's where you're wrong." To his mortification she slid closer and patted his head as if he were a naughty little boy finally forgiven. Zach jerked away from her touch as if she repulsed him.

"Leave me alone, Kat," he muttered between his teeth. His groin still ached and he was on fire inside, but he stared off into the distance, refusing to look at her. He focused instead on the ridge of dark mountains that loomed on the horizon and heard her sigh before she climbed to her feet, walked the short distance along the roof, slipped through the window and disappeared into the hayloft.

When she was gone he flopped back on the weathered cedar shakes, angrily gazed up at the stars and wondered why he was such a fool. He could have had her; she was there for the asking and he, because of some latent sense of nobility, had shrugged off her advances. He could still smell her perfume mingled with the lingering smoke from her cigarettes and he remembered her touch—that warm, bone-melting touch.

Jesus, you're an idiot!

For the next few days, Zach managed to keep his distance. Up hours before Katherine ever thought about arising, he worked long hours in the fields and returned at sundown. Kat, invariably, was locked in her room, the television blasting. He never ran into her. As for his siblings, they were all a royal pain in the ass, each and every one. Jason kept crowding him, offering to take him into Bend to meet women, but Zach declined and Jason went off prowling on his own. Trisha was pining for Mario and probably plotting her escape from the family compound. Sometimes she reeked of marijuana smoke and her eyes were often glassy. Zach had less trouble dealing with her stoned than when she was straight and plotting ways to escape. As for Nelson, the kid was still in the throes of hero worship, tagging after Zach as he went about his chores, trying to find ways to talk about his night with the prostitute. It didn't seem to matter how many ways Zach explained that nothing really had happened except that he'd managed to get a few new scars, Nelson was still enthralled, certain that Zach had really "scored" with the whore but was protecting her honor, or some such shit.

The kid was sick, Zach thought as he stepped out of the shower and threw on a pair of cut-offs. Nelson's fascination with all things sexual seemed bent. He wanted to know all about bondage and S&M and all that shit that Zach didn't really know about and didn't want to know. Men and women in leather and chains—like some kinky group of Hell's Angels or something. It kind of made his skin crawl.

Pushing all thoughts of Nelson aside, Zach found leftovers in the kitchen, and since the maid had already retired for the night, he heated up the pork chops in a cast-iron skillet, snatched himself a beer out of the fridge and took his meal onto the back porch where the old collie was curled near the porch swing. Shep perked up at the smell of the meat and whined as Zach sat down and started in on the chops.

"Don't give me that," he said to the dog. "You're too fat as it is." Shep thumped his tail on the floorboards. Somewhere in the distance an owl hooted softly and the sound of bats' wings disturbed the silence. The air smelled of horses, dust, and sagebrush. Zach thought he could find peace out here in the middle of nowhere. If it weren't for his family. He scowled to himself. It seemed as if not only in looks but in temperament as well, he'd been destined to be different from his brothers and sister, who all still professed to love their mother though she'd abandoned each and every one of them, and who all clung to Witt, either out of love or greed, he couldn't tell which.

Zach finished his dinner, tossed the bones to the dog and

wiped his fingers on the frayed edges of his cutoff Levi's. He finished his Budweiser in two swallows, then walked back to the kitchen for another. Downing the second can quickly, he began to feel a slight buzz as he crushed the aluminum in his fist. He made his way back to his room, where he flipped on his stereo and flopped onto this bed. The song was an old one by the Doors.

". . . Come on baby, light my fire . . ."

Like Kat. Boy, could she light dangerous fires. Zach closed his eyes and let the music surround him.

". . . Try and set the night on FIre!"

The French doors were cracked and the hint of a breeze stirred the curtains. His eyes opened and he stared up at the ceiling. He was hard, as hard as he'd been when Kat had kissed him on the roof of the tack room. Just thinking about being with her had given him wet dreams for three nights running. The ache in his loins was so bad that he'd even considered driving into Bend with his brother and looking for some woman who would ease his pain, but the memory of his last visit to a whore had kept him at the ranch. He didn't need any more trouble, but, Lord, did he need some release. The pressure. Pounding, pounding . . .

Deep down, in the darkest oblivion of his soul, he knew that he didn't want just any woman, that though he would go through the motions with any willing female, he was certain that anyone but Kat wouldn't do and Kat, his *stepmother,* was the worst choice of all. He rolled over to his side and considered jacking off. It sure as hell wouldn't be the first time, but it left him so . . . empty or lonely or feeling stupid. *Face it, Danvers, you want her. All you have to do is walk down the hall, turn the corner and tap on her bedroom door and the sweetest bit of pussy this side of the Rockies will be waiting to give you any fantasy you can dream up!*

His throat was so dry he couldn't draw up any spit and he squeezed his eyes shut, resigned to his fate as he reached for the fly of his pants.

He heard the creak of the door, felt the wind turn and his heart jolted. His eyes flew open. At first he thought she was a vision, the beautiful woman on the other side of the glass. Moonlight spangled Kat's black hair silver and her silk pajama top shimmered. His heart began to pump so loudly that he was certain she could hear it.

The doors opened further and dry leaves blew into the room. The wind tossed her hair away from her face and as she entered the room, he saw the tears glistening in her eyes. Her lips trembled and her nose ran.

"What—what are you—?"

"Just hold me, Zach," she whispered in a voice strangled by grief.

"What is it?"

Walking numbly to the edge of his bed, she sniffed loudly, then stood in front of him, as if hesitating.

He drew himself into a sitting position. "You shouldn't be here, Kat—"

"I know, but . . . Oh, God . . ." She rolled her eyes toward the ceiling and tears trickled down her cheeks. Between the broken sobs she said, "Witt just called and the police have run out of leads . . . the investigation is still open but they all think, the police and the FBI, that London . . . that London is dead." The last word was barely a squeak and Zach couldn't help himself. He stood and took her into his arms, trying to comfort her as sob after heart-wrenching sob shook her body.

"Oh, God. Oh, God." Burying his face in the crook of her neck, holding her close, he willed himself to think of her not as a woman, but as a person to whom fate had handed a crushing blow. She clung to him and cried like a child, her tears raining down his chest. He told her it would be all right, that of course London was alive, that someday they would all see her again, but even as he said the words, he believed them to be lies.

When at last the wracking sobs quieted, he lifted his head. "You should go back to the room, take some sleeping pills—"

"I can't. I don't want to be alone. Please, Zach, don't make me

go. Let me stay with you. Just hold me. Please." Her words held
the echo of doom, but he couldn't deny her and when she turned
her face up to his, he kissed her trembling lips, knowing that he
was about to cross a threshold from which there was no return.
Life would never be the same. The truth would be blurred with
lies, but he kissed her and she responded, her body quivering in
fear and desire.

His brain thundered and his blood turned to liquid heat as she
let her fingers slide down his scarred back, along the slope of his
spine and lower still to his buttocks. He felt his already stiff cock
rise to the occasion, knew there was no turning back as she
tugged and the buttons holding his cutoffs together popped in a
ripple and her hands were upon him. Warm and soft, her fingers
brought a magic that he never dreamed existed.

They tumbled on the bed together, lips searching, tongues
eager and before he could consider all the consequences of his
actions, Zachary stripped her of her nightshirt, ripping the buttons from their holes as the seams of the soft fabric gave way.
Then he gazed at her divine breasts, felt the gentle pressure of
her fingers on his spine and watched as she licked her lips. He
could barely breathe when she ran her tongue across his nipples
and anxiously parted her legs, lifting her hips to rub her dewy
nest of curls to his crotch.

He thought he might come all over her. "Kat—"

"Just do it, Zach. Please." Her fingers dug deep into his muscles.

Closing his eyes, he entered into that moist, dark warmth. A
primal cry rumbled from his throat and he couldn't stop himself.
In three long strokes it was over; Zachary came fast and hot and
fell against her, realizing dimly that he'd just doomed himself to
a living hell. No son dared lose his virginity to his father's wife
and expect to survive.

But he didn't care. He wrapped himself in her warmth and
kissed her again, more sure of himself. He'd take it slower with
her this time, learn from her and be the best damned lover she
ever had.

* * *

Zach couldn't remember when he'd slept so soundly. He moved slightly and felt another body, warm and soft and naked. With a smile, he remembered the night of lovemaking and he rolled over to find Kat, her eyes half open, staring at him. Dawn was breaking over the horizon and soon the ranch hands would be up; she had to leave.

"I wondered how it would be with you," she said as she slid a finger along the scar that was still visible near his hairline. Though she smiled, a sadness lingered in her eyes.

"How was it?" He nuzzled her cheek. Though it was dangerous to be with her, he couldn't give up. He'd made love to her three times last night, and he'd woken up with a hard-on. Maybe there was still enough time for a quick . . .

"It was the best, Zach," she said, though her face remained troubled.

He grinned, and touched her hair, brushing soft curls off her face and wishing he could stop the agony that pinched the corners of her mouth. As if reading his thoughts, she began to weep, tears suddenly starred her lashes and he pulled her closer to him, holding her naked body next to his. "Don't worry."

"I can't help it, I—"

"Shh. We'll find London." He felt suddenly strong, as if he could change the world. "I'll find her."

"Oh, Zach, what can you do—"

"You'd be surprised." His hands found her breasts and he toyed with a nipple that stiffened expectantly under the gentle teasing of his fingers. "Let me show you—"

She broke off suddenly, her eyes wide. "Do you hear anything?"

"No—"

"I do." She scrambled away from him. "I hear something—"

Zach listened and groaned at the sound of an engine whining as some kind of vehicle—most likely a truck—approached.

"Probably Pete coming early. He does that sometimes," Zach

said, already aroused again. God, he couldn't get enough of her. He let one hand rest on the curve of her waist.

"You sure?" she asked.

"Mmm." He listened again and felt his heart knock a bit. The engine wasn't the deep rumble of a truck, but the smooth purr of an expensive car's engine as it sped down the lane. An expensive car like a Lincoln Continental. "Oh, God."

Gravel crunched and brakes squealed.

"Witt," Katherine mouthed.

"No—" But even as he denied it, he heard the car door open and brisk footsteps sounded on the path. Footsteps he'd recognize anywhere. Authoritative footsteps belonging to his father. Footsteps of doom. "Damn it, Kat! You've got to get out of here."

But it was too late, the front door opened and the footsteps continued the short distance to the master bedroom. Kat froze at the muted rap of fingers against wood.

"Oh, God," she whispered. "Oh, God, oh, God."

"Leave. Through here." He was pushing her now, toward the open French doors. She rolled out of bed, grabbed her torn nightshirt and was stepping outside when Witt's voice reverberated through the rooms. "Katherine? Are you here?" There was a worried edge to his voice.

"Go!" Zach reached for his cutoffs as he heard the first door in the hallway open then close. Only a few more seconds.

The door to his room opened just as Kat disappeared through the doors.

His father looked gigantic. Zach didn't bother feigning sleep and Witt didn't say a word, just looked at the rumpled sheets and sniffed at the lingering odor of Katherine's perfume. His mouth flattened to a white line of fury and an ugly tic developed under his eye. "Get out," he said under his breath. Zach rolled off the bed as his father's fist collided with his face. Pain exploded in his jaw. "You no-good bastard!"

"Witt!" Kat stood in the doorway, her fingers curling over the brass door handle. "Don't. It . . . was my fault."

"Your fault? You forced him to screw you?" He slammed Zach against the wall. Zach's head smacked against the plaster and pieces of stucco crumbled to the floor. Pain ripped all the way down his spine. "You fucking son of a bitch!" Witt snarled, shaking the life from him as the mirror over the bureau rattled. "I always suspected you were no son of mine and now I'm sure of it. Get out before I kill you!"

Zach staggered toward the door. His eyes barely focused and he felt something sticky and wet running down the back of his head.

"You can't do this!" Katherine cried and Zach heard a slap that made his stomach turn over. He turned and saw the welt forming on Katherine's cheek and Witt's stunned expression, as if he couldn't believe that he'd struck her.

"Don't you ever touch me again!" she said, backing outside.

"I'm sorry. Christ, Katherine, I swear, I'd never do anything to hurt you—"

He took one step toward her but she kept backing up. "Stay away from me, Witt. I mean it," she said, before turning and running into the grayish dawn. Witt's great shoulders slumped and he sagged against the wall. He turned damning eyes up at his son. "Now, look what you've done, Zach," he said, barely able to breathe. With an expression straight from hell, he loosened his tie and Zach remembered the times he'd been whipped by his father's belt. Not again. He wouldn't suffer like he had when he was eight, leaning over the bed and biting his lower lip until it bled to keep from crying out as his father flayed him with the stinging leather. No way.

"Leave now and don't ever . . ." Witt, suddenly ashen, reached into his pocket, fumbled for a vial of pills and popped the top. He stuck one of the tablets under his tongue. "Don't ever come back here."

"I won't," Zach promised, jaw clenched in determination. Injustice burned through his veins and he held his father with his remorseless stare. "You'll never see me again."

120   *Lisa Jackson*

Witt's blue eyes were cold, his fury evident in the white lines
of strain near his mouth. "That's the way I want it, boy." He took
one menacing step toward his son. "However, if I find out that
you had anything to do with your sister's kidnapping, I swear I'll
personally hunt you down like the lying dog you are and rip you
apart with my bare hands."

Zach stumbled back toward the door. His head throbbed, his
jaw ached and he glared at the man he'd called father all his life.
He had to leave. Now. Run as far and fast as he could. And if he
never saw Witt Danvers alive again, it would be much too soon.

PART TWO

Portland, Oregon

1993
The Family

6

The memory was vivid.

"The Lord thy God is a vengeful God, Adria—"

"He's not my God," Adria, then eighteen had said. "He's your God, Mom. Yours. But he's not mine!"

The slap had been one of the few blows Sharon Nash had ever inflicted upon her adopted daughter and it had stung deeper than Adria's skin; the pain had reached the thick hide that covered her soul.

"Don't you ever, *ever* talk like that again." Sharon's breath, bitter from the coffee and tinged with the underlying odor of gin had drifted over Adria's face. "Now, go wash up, and you forget about ever seein' that Kennedy boy again. He's trash, y'hear. Trash. Just like his ma. Bad blood flows through his veins, girl."

"And what kind of blood flows through mine?" Adria had demanded.

"We don't know; you don't need to."

"Of course I do!"

"The Lord works in mysterious ways, he brought you to us for a reason. You're not to question His wisdom, y'hear?"

Adria had turned on her heel and fled to her little bedroom tucked under the eves of the second story.

Years ago. But it seemed like yesterday and the argument seemed to ring through the tiny motel room on Eighty-second Avenue.

She'd remembered the fight because of Zachary Danvers, another rogue, another man she should avoid. Though she'd only talked with him for a few minutes, she'd read all about him and his family, *her* family, and she hadn't been disappointed.

He was the black sheep of the family—kicked out of the house and cut out of his father's will more often than not. He did things his own way, didn't give a hang that he was born rich and he was cursed with an irreverent spirit that just might want to help her find the truth.

Or maybe not. In the year before his father's death, Zach and Witt had seemed to bury the hatchet. Nonetheless, she knew instinctively that he would be her only ally in the family; the others appeared to be ready to pick at the old man's bones and take his fortune.

Maybe Zachary was like the rest.

If so, her battle would be harder than she'd thought.

She stared at her reflection in the cracked mirror and bit her lip. Was she on a fool's mission? How could she ever hope to battle the powerful Danvers family? And why was Zachary Danvers, her half-brother for crying out loud, so attractive?

Adria had always been drawn to the kind of men her mother despised—the rebels and misfits and loners whom Sharon Nash found repulsive. The Zach Danverses of the world.

Yet Zach was the one member of the Danvers family she instinctively turned to, the only one of her siblings she felt she could trust. *Trust!* She snorted a laugh at her own foolishness. Zachary Danvers was about as trustworthy as a hungry rattler with a trapped mouse. She found a copy of the videotape that had led her to Portland and tucked it into her beaded bag. As she snapped the purse closed, she wondered why she never seemed to learn that very important lesson about men.

Just because Zach might be her half-brother didn't mean he was safe. He was a predatory man, a man who would take any challenge, a man with a wild streak that he hadn't yet tamed, a man who wouldn't care one bit if she were his half-sister. There was an animal side of him—pure male and extremely lethal— that defied the bounds of kinship. He was sexy and rough and seemed about as stable as a blasting cap.

No wonder she was attracted to him. It had been the flaw in

her character to be attracted to rough-and-tumble irreverent boys and men all her life.

"You're an idiot," she told her reflection as she stood barefoot on the stained orange shag carpet that had worn thin near the door.

So if she couldn't trust Zachary, who in the family could she trust? No one. Just as they couldn't trust her.

Half dressed in her lacy slip, she walked into the tiny bathroom where her dress hung on a hook in the door. She'd found the dress in a boutique that handled "previously worn" items. A white, silky confection with a designer label, the gown fit her perfectly. She'd never owned such a creation before, never spent so much money on one dress and a used one at that!

Her adoptive mother had been a frugal God-fearing woman who didn't believe in women wearing ornaments of any kind; no jewelry save a gold wedding band or a gold cross suspended from a necklace and clothes that were practical, shoes that were sensible and sturdy.

Not so her father. Unlike his wife, Victor had been a dreamer, always expecting a larger crop than the land would yield, always certain that the next year life would become easier.

And she'd believed him. When she'd discovered his secret, that he thought her to be London Danvers, she'd grabbed that gold-plated carrot he'd swung before her nose and held on with a death grip.

She'd done her research, read every clipping on the Danvers family and the kidnapping, searched through all the old papers in her father's desk, called her deceased Uncle Ezra's secretary, searching, digging through every scrap of information, praying she'd find some irrefutable scrap of evidence that either proved or disproved that she was the little lost princess. Ezra Nash, a lawyer known to bend the law, had handled the adoption. Either he hadn't bothered with records, or they'd long-since been destroyed, or there was a secret surrounding her birth that he'd wanted to keep hidden.

She'd fought the anticipation that had raced through her bloodstream when she'd learned that she might be London Danvers, that she might finally discover her true identity. She told herself the chances that she was London Danvers were a billion to one, but in the end, she'd followed her heart—her father's dream—and driven her beat-up Chevy Nova steadily westward to Portland, London's hometown. She'd nearly convinced herself that she was London Danvers, believed that she would finally find her family, and after the initial shock had worn off, they would welcome her with open arms. Now, as she tilted her head and screwed on the back of her zirconium earrings, she bit her lower lip. The teardrop earrings sparkled in the light, as if they were diamonds, but they were fakes, made to look like expensive jewels when they were really cheap and common.

Like you.

No! She wouldn't believe the speculation she'd heard all her life from the people in the small town where she'd grown up.

She swallowed as a memory from her far distant past assailed her. She'd been only eleven at the time and Tommy Sinclair, a bully two years older, had cornered her on the playground, grabbed her and tried to pants her on a dare from some of his friends.

She'd fought like a wounded mountain lion, kicking and clawing and scratching and shrieking until he'd placed a fat, dirty hand over her mouth and dragged her away from the playground, away from the running, laughing and screaming children, past a row of tamarack trees, across a dry creek bed, to the dusty ground on the other side of the trash bins. Brush grew in the hard ground and the stench of rotting garbage filtered through the dry air. The lot was empty. Not a soul in sight and the playground seemed suddenly a million miles away, the sounds of squeals of delight and laughter far in the distance. "Stop!" she'd silently screamed against his hand.

"Shut up and enjoy this, you dirty cunt!" Tommy snarled, his pig-eyes bright as he threw her on the ground and her head cracked on the dry earth. The world spun crazily. Tommy straddled her, pinning her with his weight. Sweat ran down his nose to drop in a tiny puddle on her blouse, just over her breastbone.

"Let me go!" she yelled against the filthy hand.

"I just want to see what you've got down there, or maybe up here." His crotch was planted firmly over her ribs and she slapped at him, her arms flying, her fingers clawing at his hair.

"Hold her down!" Tommy yelled to his friends, Ben Whittaker and Billy Ackerman who were emerging from the row of tamarack trees. The sounds of the playground sounded so far away . . .

Ben's voice had already changed. "No, Tommy, I don't think—"

"Hold her down!"

"Oh, shit!" Ben complied, grabbing both her wrists and sitting on her hands. She tried to curl her fingers and pinch him, but he was too heavy and strong. "Don't hurt her, Tommy, this was just a joke—"

"Shut the fuck up! This was your idea."

"No! No! No! Help!" she cried, though no sound escaped. Her eyes rolled back and she silently appealed for Ben to help her, but he looked away, his face suddenly pinched, his long blond hair falling over his eyes. Rage and terror stormed through her, but she wouldn't give into the horrible dark thoughts that she was helpless. Tommy ripped open her blouse and her little breasts, just beginning to grow, peaked up through her thin nylon training bra. Her nipples were large, out of proportion to the rest of the tiny mounds.

"Shit, you don't have nothin'."

"Stop it!" she cried through his fingers.

"Hey, Tommy, go for it!" The other pimply-faced friend, Billy, said in his high-pitched voice. "See what she's got!"

Adria wished she were dead. Hot tears of shame filled her eyes. Still she bucked, trying to rid herself of the horrible weight and her fingers dug against the soft denim covering the inside of Ben's thighs.

"Hey, she's a wildcat!" Billy said, cackling.

Tommy ripped her bra and looked at her sorry little nubbins of breasts. "Flat as a fritter," he pronounced.

Billy laughed.

"That's enough, Tommy," Ben said, loosening his grip on her hands.

"No way, the fun's just startin'," Tommy replied, spittle showing beneath the fine mustache he hadn't started shaving quite yet.

Adria kicked, hating them, hating herself, hating Mrs. Elliot, the teacher on duty, for not coming to her rescue. Her head ground in the dust, sending up thick clouds, but Tommy just chuckled deep in his throat at her vain attempts.

Tommy's nose wrinkled at her sorry nubbins and he reached lower, scooting his crotch down her rib cage so that she couldn't kick him as he found her zipper and it slid down with a quick, horrifying hiss.

"Don't!" she cried against the horrible fingers. Writhing and tossing her head and bucking upward she fought the dead weight holding her down.

But Tommy had two years and fifty pounds on her and all he did was laugh at her feeble attempts to dislodge him. "You're a girlie bastard, y'know that, Adria? Some whore got knocked up and had you. Probably didn't even know who your father was."

"No!" she shrieked but the sound was cut off by his hand.

His fingers wriggled under her panties and an evil smile showed up a row of tiny sharp teeth. "Yep. Your ma was a whore—she gave it away for a few bucks. Probably went down on all the boys. Bet you'll do the same when you finally get some tits."

His fingers slipped beneath her panties and he touched the new-sprouted curls at the junction of her legs.

God, if you exist, strike him dead now! Please! I promise I'll be good!

"Maybe you'd better stop," Ben said nervously.

"Not yet! Let's see if she's tight between those long legs of hers. Just what kind of a piece of ass are you—"

Adria bit down as hard as she could. Only a little piece of the calloused, dirty flesh of his palm caught between her teeth, but Tommy let out a howl and she moved quickly, bringing up her knee, trying to hit him in the balls.

"You bitch!" he said and his tiny eyes turned livid. "I should do it to you. Right here!" He reached for his fly and in horror, she saw that his jeans were bulging.

She started to scream, and he smacked her. Lights flashed behind her eyes.

"Stop it, Tommy!" Ben yelled, jumping to his feet and setting her hands free. "Leave her alone."

"No way. She's a fucking cunt, just like her mother. She wants it."

"No!" she yelled, hitting and squirming and kicking.

Ben's voice was shaky. "Come on, man, let's go—"

"He's right," Billy agreed. "Let's get out of here. Oh shit!"

From the corner of her eye, Adria saw a movement and then a boy torpedoed through the air, hitting Tommy on the fly, sending him rolling off her and into the dust. Adria scrambled to her feet and watched in horror as Mark Kennedy, fists clenched, began pounding on Tommy. "You fat bastard, leave her alone!" Mark spat as Tommy twisted and landed a punch to Mark's jaw that sent the smaller boy sprawling onto his back. He was up on the balls of his feet in an instant, placing himself between Adria and the boy who had attacked her.

"Stay out of this, Kennedy." Tommy was breathing hard and he sniffed against the trickle of blood that dripped from his nose. From the playground on the other side of the trees a sharp whistle shrieked.

"Oh, shit! It's old lady Elliot." Billy vaulted the fence on the other side of the lot with Ben in hot pursuit.

Tommy staggered a little. Blood was trailing from the corner of his mouth, but he fixed Adria with his evil glare. "Everyone in town knows that your mother didn't want you, Adria. She gave you to that dried-up old farmer and his wife because she didn't give a shit about you."

"No!"

"She was a whore, Adria. She loved humping everyone in town. She didn't even know who your father was!"

"Shut up!"

Tommy's gaze slid to Mark who began circling the older boy. "And you. Your pa's a lush and your ma gives it away."

Mark's fingers tightened into fists, his face twisted into a hideous mask of hatred and he lunged at the bigger boy, but Tommy took off, jumping over the fence just as the bell signifying that recess was over jangled. In frustration, Mark kicked the fence. He took several deep breaths, then turned to face her. One eye was bloody and beginning to swell shut. "You okay?"

She nodded mutely, but she couldn't help sobbing.

"Don't pay any attention to Tommy. He's an ass. He don't know what he's talkin' about."

Adria swallowed back her tears. "Is . . . is it true? Does everyone know who my mother was?"

Mark ran his forearm under his nose. "No way. He's just full of shit. You know that—"

"I hate him!"

"I know." Mark managed a crooked smile as the second bell rang. "Me, too."

Hot injustice swirled through her veins. "I'm going to prove him wrong!"

"Sure you are. Right after I kill him."

"I—" she was suddenly tongue-tied. "I, um . . . thanks. You—"

He snorted and shook his head. "Don't thank me. I've been wanting to beat the crap out of Tommy Sinclair all year."

Tommy, Ben, and Billy had been suspended for a week, but that was just the beginning of Adria's love for Mark Kennedy and her personal quest to find out who she was.

She'd always wondered where she'd come from, who her natural parents were but until Tommy Sinclair had humiliated her, she hadn't really made any attempt to find out. Tommy had given her a purpose and now, years later, she was close to finding out the truth.

She slipped the white dress from its plastic sheath and slid the shimmering fabric over her body. The silk felt smooth against her skin and fit over her curves as if it had been tailored for her.

She smiled to herself. *Tonight. Tonight was the beginning.* She'd waited so long and now she was close, so close to the truth.

After being humiliated by Tommy Sinclair, Adria hadn't been able to let the subject of her biological parents rest, and Sharon Nash had refused to divulge anything to her wayward daughter.

The fact that Adria was asking questions about her natural parents was a constant source of friction in the old farmhouse. Sometimes it seemed as if Victor wanted to confide in his daughter, but one sharp glance from his wife always forced him to hold his tongue and whatever secrets surrounded Adria's past were kept hidden from her.

Adria felt as if a part of her was missing. Not knowing where she came from or what had happened to her natural parents was like a slow-rising wind, small little gusts that tickled at her mind and then, as the years rolled by, more and more forceful until she often lay on her bed wondering how she'd ended up here. If only she knew . . .

She'd checked all the old papers locked in the bottom drawer of the desk, hoping for some glimmer of information as to her parentage, but in the wills and insurance papers and meager savings certificates, she hadn't found a clue. Everything in her life those days had been frustrating: not knowing where she came from, her sexual awakening in her relationship with Mark, a relationship she was trying and failing to keep under tight reins, and the constant bickering with her mother.

Sharon, it seemed, had a personal hatred of Mark as well as his entire family. She'd forbidden Adria to see him though Adria didn't know why.

One night, when the little family was seated at the maple table with the oilcloth cover and coffee had been poured, Adria worked up the nerve to ask. She added a thin stream of fresh cream to her cup, then lifted her gaze to meet her mother's. "What is it you have against Mark anyway?" she asked.

Sharon's color turned high and her eyes blinked rapidly. She nearly dropped her cup as she glanced nervously at her husband. "I don't have anything against him."

Adria was tired of playing games. "Sure you do, Mom," she said, somehow managing to hold onto her runaway temper. "You called his dad, told him to keep Mark away from me."

"I did no such—" Her shoulders stiffened and she scooted back her chair. "I don't have to explain myself to you, Adria. I've spent the past dozen years trying to raise you properly and I've done a fine job. Sacrificed when I had to, even let you run wilder than I thought you should. You rode horses and roped steers and went mountain climbing, for the love of God, but I didn't mind, so now, you have no right"—her eyes blazed with indignant fury and her hands trembled—"*no right,* to question my authority!"

"And you have no right to keep secrets from me."

"I don't—"

"Then why do you hate Mark!"

"I don't—"

"And who were my natural parents? You know, don't you?"

"Dear God," Sharon whispered, the cords in her neck beginning to strain. "I've given you love and—"

"This isn't about love, Mom. This is about the truth. You're always talking about the truth and the light and Jesus, well, I think He'd want me to know."

With a chocked sob, Sharon stormed out of the back door and down the kitchen steps.

"Oh, hell," her father muttered and slammed his napkin down before taking off after her.

Adria thought about following them and apologizing for working her mother up so, but she couldn't. She was too angry. A deep rage boiled up in her, the same kind of rage she'd felt on the day that Tommy Sinclair had dragged her behind the garbage bins. She ran upstairs to her room and sat on the window ledge where she could look at the stars and feel the warm summer breeze on her face.

Her parents were in the garden, her mother sobbing softly between the rows of corn and their conversation drifted up through the stalks.

". . . tried my best," Sharon said, sniffing loudly. "Lord knows I was delighted when Virginia showed up with the girl. The answer to my prayers."

Virginia? Adria's heart missed a beat. Who was Virginia?

"I know, honey, it's all right," her father said.

"For years I was afraid she'd come back and try and take Adria away. I've been so frightened, oh, Victor, I've had to pray so hard—"

Adria's stomach wrenched. Virginia was her mother! Her birth mother! Victor and Sharon were talking about her and her real mother. Her throat grew tight and she didn't dare breathe. She'd known she was adopted, that Uncle Ezra had handled the legal work, but she'd never heard her mother's name spoken. Virginia. Virginia *who?*

"No one's going to take her away," her father consoled.

"You don't know that!"

"Ah, Sharon, don't worry yourself into a frazzle. No one in the family knows what happened to Virginia. She up and disappeared."

Sharon sniffed loudly. "It doesn't matter if it's Virginia, or someone else like that . . . that horrid boy will try and take her away. I have such dreams for Adria, Victor. I know she'll get married, raise her own family and that's what I want, but—"

"But you don't want her to marry Mark."

"No!" Her voice had lowered.

Then her father was mumbling placating words. "Don't worry, honey, they're just kids, full of life and—"

"I think she's . . . well, you know . . . sleeping with him!"

The words hung on the hot summer air and Adria gulped. Although she and Mark hadn't yet gone all the way, they'd come close. Mark was pressuring her and Adria would soon give in. Because she loved him.

"You don't know any such thing—"

"That boy's randy, just like his ma! All he wants is to . . . oh, I shouldn't have to explain it. If they aren't sleeping together yet, they will be soon—!"

"Christ, Sharon, listen to what you're saying!"

"Oh!" Adria's mother cried as if stricken. "Don't you ever take the name of the Lord in vain with me, Victor!"

There was a pause and all Adria heard was the rustle of wind through the stiff stalks.

Her father's voice was calm. "Come here, hon," he said to his wife. "This isn't all that bad. Adria's a good kid. You've just got to trust her, that's all."

"And pray for her. She's always been a little wild, Victor, you know that. Probably in her blood. You encourage it, let her run around like a wild Indian, treating her as if she were your son and not your daughter! And stubborn, Lord, I've never seen such a stubborn girl, not like that nice Alice Weber."

Adria thought she might be sick. Alice was such a two-faced suck-up. Alice was the last person Adria would want to act like.

"Alice Weber puts on a show for adults," her father said.

"Well, at least she doesn't embarrass her parents by running around with some young thug. I wouldn't be surprised if that boy didn't steal the gas from Pritchart's station two weeks ago, or break into the McAllister house in June when they were off visiting Nora's folks in Kansas City!"

Adria bit her tongue to keep from yelling down at her mother and her vicious lies.

"No one knows who did those things, Sharon."

"Lots of people suspect that Kennedy boy."

"It hasn't been proven, though, has it, now?"

"Doesn't matter. We both know he's trouble and he's interested in Adria and oh, Victor, we've got to pray hard. Real hard."

Adria swallowed back the lump in her throat at the memories. Her mother had been so adamant about her not being involved with Mark. "He's too wild . . . a hothead . . . got bad blood running through his veins . . . can't be trusted . . . a hellion!"

But Adria wouldn't stop seeing Mark, nor would she quit trying to find out who she was. The little tidbits of conversation she overheard, the snatches whispered behind closed doors, the lowered voices on the phone, the guilty looks exchanged between her parents whenever the subject came up, only whetted her greedy appetite. Finally, she could stand the suspense no longer.

It had been early morning and she was already late for school. She hurried down the stairs and slid into her chair at the kitchen table.

" 'Bout time," her mother said, eyeing Adria's jeans with disapproval though, for once, Sharon held her tongue and didn't comment on her daughter's inappropriate wardrobe. "Sit down and Dad will say grace."

Adria squirmed as her father fumbled his way through the prayer and her mother corrected him several times.

"Just let him do it his way," Adria suggested and Sharon shot her a stern glare until the prayer was over.

Buttering a slice of toast, Adria simmered at the unfairness of her life. "How come you've never told me about my real parents?" she blurted out.

Sharon was lifting a piece of egg to her mouth, but she stopped short and runny yellow yolk slid through the tines of her fork to land back on her plate. "We told you a long while ago that you came from a family that couldn't afford to keep you."

"What were their names?"

Adria's mother's tongue rimmed her lips nervously. "We never knew."

Adria looked at her father who suddenly found his plate fascinating. "Dad?"

"Your Uncle Ezra handled everything."

"Then there are records."

"I don't know—"

"I want to know where I came from," she said stubbornly, though she was feeling no bigger than a gnat. She'd wanted to hurt them as she had been hurt. The silence settling like doom around the table weighed heavy in her heart. She'd been selfish and cruel to people who had done nothing more than love her.

Victor cleared his throat. "I'll see what I can find out."

"But all the records were destroyed in a fire . . ." Sharon whispered, her face as pale as skim milk.

"I'd just like to know." Even though she'd hurt them, Adria wouldn't back down. It was time she knew the truth. For years she'd wondered about her real parents, either fantasizing that they were a loving couple who just couldn't afford a child and would return for her or worrying that her mother had been a prostitute who didn't even know which man had fathered her—the image that had been branded into her mind by Tommy Sinclair on the playground years ago. "I thought maybe you knew my mother's name. I overheard you talking about someone named Virginia."

"Oh, Lord." Sharon held her napkin to her mouth.

"Who is she?"

"Adria, don't," her mother pleaded and a silent look of agony passed between her parents.

Her father set his fork down and cleared his throat. "Virginia is . . . was . . . a relative of mine—distant cousin. She couldn't raise you alone."

"And my father?"

"I really don't know."

"Did she—did she know who he was?" Adria asked, barely able to breathe. The room seemed to close around her and she could almost feel her mother's pain.

"We never asked," he said.

"How can I get in touch with her?"

"You can't," Sharon said, swallowing with difficultly. "You just can't."

Victor said, "I've tried to locate Virginia, Adria, but I've had no luck. Really."

"But I have a right to know!" Adria felt a fury storming through her blood. "You've never told me about this woman, in fact, you let me believe both my parents were dead."

"We're your parents," Sharon said as if she'd been stricken.

"My natural parents," Adria clarified ruthlessly.

Victor touched her arm. "It wasn't a lie. Since we haven't been able to locate Virginia and we've never heard from your father—your real father—it was natural to assume that they were dead. At least to you."

"Didn't you think I might want to know?" she said, her voice low, but filled with accusations.

"I suppose. As I said, I'll look into it, Addie. It's the best I can do."

She didn't argue with him, didn't have time and there was no reason to hurt them any further. She'd made her stand about Mark as well as about her birth. With one eye on the clock, she bolted down a biscuit and piece of bacon and was aware that her mother hadn't taken another bite.

"You come straight home," Sharon said softly as Adria scooped up her books and dashed out the back door. The screen slapped closed behind her and she didn't look over her shoulder, didn't want to see her mother's anguish.

Now, years later, she might be able to answer the questions that had nagged at her for years. She ran a brush through her hair and started working with the long, black curls. Wild, "witchy hair," Sharon had referred to it as it fell past her shoulders in riotous waves that Adria didn't bother taming.

She planned to crash the party celebrating the grand opening of the Hotel Danvers. It was time to face the family. She'd tried to call Zachary Danvers after their first meeting in the ballroom, but hadn't been able to get past the hotel reception desk and though she'd left messages, Zachary hadn't seen fit to call her back. She hadn't bothered trying to reach anyone else in the family. She knew too much about them to try and trust any of them. Zachary was the one with the least to lose, the only one of Witt's children to make something of himself on his own; the others, Jason, Trisha, and Nelson had, from what she'd read, been content to stay in Witt's shadow, doing his bidding, waiting, like vultures, for him to die.

But Zach was different and had been from the beginning when there had been speculation about his paternity. He'd been in trouble with the law and he and the old man had been rumored to be at each other's throats. When Zach was still in school, there had been a major blowup and rift, though she never found out why, and Zach had been thrown out of the house and disowned. Only recently, before Witt's death, had he been back with the family.

Adria figured that someone who had been on the outside so long would be her most likely ally. So far, she'd been wrong. So tonight, she'd make public her claims and if nothing else, get the Danvers family's attention.

She was a fraud.
Zach could smell a fake a mile away, and this woman, this black-haired woman with the mysterious blue eyes and hint of irreverence in her smile when she claimed to be London, was as phony as the proverbial three-dollar bill.

But he couldn't get her out of his mind. He'd tried, but she kept swimming to the surface of his consciousness, toying with his thoughts.

Already in a foul mood because of the grand opening, he poured himself a drink from the bar in the suite he'd called home for the past few months, the very same set of rooms he was to have shared with Jason on the night London had been kidnapped. The suite on the seventh floor looked different now, as the decor reflected the turn of the century rather than the nineteen seventies, but it was still eerie remembering that night. Witt had raged, Kat had wept, and the rest of the children . . . the survivors . . . had cast suspicious glances at one another and the police.

He ran a finger along the smooth surface of the window, then pocketed his hotel-room key. He didn't have time to reminisce and he resented Adria for bringing back the pain of his checkered past.

Right now, Zach just wanted out. He'd held up his part of the bargain, which was to renovate the hotel and now he wanted his due—the price he'd extracted from the old man before Witt had died.

It had been a painful scene. His father had tried to break the ice and admit that he'd been wrong about his faithless wife, but the words had gotten all tangled up and once again they'd ended up arguing. Zach had nearly walked out, but Witt had enticed him back.

"The ranch is yours, if you want it, boy," Witt had declared.

Zach's hand rested on the doorknob of the den. "The ranch?"

"When I die."

"Forget it."

"You want it, don't you?"

Zach had turned and skewered his father with a stare intended to cut through steel.

"You always take what you want, if I remember right."

"I'm outta here."

"Wait," the old man had pleaded. "The ranch is worth several million."

"I don't give a shit about the money."

"Oh, right. My *noble* son." Witt was standing near the window, one hand in his pocket, the other wrapped around a short glass of Irish whiskey. "But you still want it. What for?" His white eyebrows had raised a bit. "Nostalgia, perhaps?"

The jab cut deep, but Zach didn't so much as flinch. "It doesn't matter."

Witt snorted. "It's yours."

Zach wasn't easily suckered by the old man. He was smart enough to know the ranch had a price—a high one. "What do I have to do?"

"Nothing all that hard. Restore the old hotel."

"Do what?"

"Don't act like I've asked you to fly, damn it. You have your own construction crew in Bend. Move them over here or hire new people. Money's no object. I just want the hotel to look as good as it did when it was built."

"You're out of your mind. It would cost a fortune to—"

"Indulge me. It's all I'm asking," Witt said, his voice low. "You love the ranch, I'm fond of the hotel. The logging operations, the investments, they don't mean much, not to me. But that hotel has class. It was the best of its kind in its day. I'd like to see that again."

"Hire someone else."

Witt's eyes narrowed on his son and he swallowed the last of his whiskey. "I want you to do it, boy. And I want you to do it for me."

"Go to hell."

"Already been there. Seems as if you had something to do with that."

Zach's throat tightened. He'd never seen eye-to-eye with the old man, but knew an olive branch when it was thrust under his nose. And this particular branch was attached by a silver chain to the deed to the ranch.

"Don't let your pride stand in the way of what you want."

"It won't," he lied.

Witt extended his big hand. "What d'ya say?"

Zach hesitated just a fraction of a second. "It's a deal," he'd finally said and the two men had clasped hands.

Zach had started work on the hotel and Witt had changed his will. The project to reclaim the Hotel Danvers and refurbish the old building to its earlier grandeur had lasted two years, and Witt had died long before it was finished, never realizing his dream. Zach had been able to spend most of his time at the ranch, until about March of this year. Then the job had become so involved that he'd been forced to move to Portland to ensure that all the finishing touches were just right.

Now, he tightened the knot of his tie around his throat. He had to get through the grand opening, check a few last bugs and then get the hell out of Dodge.

What about Adria?

Christ, why couldn't he stop thinking about her? It seemed that she was always there, close to the surface of his thoughts, just as Kat had been. A curse, that's what it was. For, like it or not, she did resemble his deceased stepmother. That black hair, her clear blue eyes, her pointy chin and high cheekbones, replicas of Katherine LaRouche Danvers. Adria wasn't quite as small as his stepmother had been, but she was every bit as beautiful and had the same feline grace that he hadn't seen in a woman since Kat.

His gut twisted as he remembered his ill-fated, one-night affair with his stepmother. The passion, the danger, the thrill that he'd never found with another woman. At the memory of his stepmother, a forbidden heat curled through his blood. She'd seduced him, taken his virginity, showed him a glimpse of heaven, then heaved him through the gates of a hell that was to be the remainder of his life. Not that he would've changed a thing.

So why did his one meeting with Adria Nash conjure up such vivid memories of what he'd tried to hide for twenty years?

He hadn't seen Adria since she'd appeared in the ballroom all starry eyed as she'd tried to convince him that she was his long-lost half-sister, but he knew she'd turn up again. Like the proverbial bad penny. They always did. She'd tried phoning him and he hadn't bothered returning her calls. He wouldn't give her the satisfaction or the false hope. She wasn't the first imposter trying to claim to be darling little London and she sure as hell wouldn't be the last.

Sticking two fingers under the stiff collar of his tuxedo, he growled at his reflection and wondered why he bothered with the stupid monkey suit at all. Formality. And he hated it. Just as he hated the party he was about to attend.

He glanced at his duffel bag. Packed and ready to go. He'd be out of here by noon tomorrow.

"Good riddance," he muttered as he locked the door behind him and strode along the corridor to the elevators. He hadn't told the rest of the family about Adria's visit. No reason. They'd all just wind themselves in tighter knots than they had tied themselves into already. The old man's estate hadn't been settled yet and if the principal heirs got wind of the fact that another London impersonator had shown up . . . One side of his mouth lifted at the thought. He ran his thumbnail along the edge of the brass rail in the elevator car and considered dropping the bomb, then discarded the idea. He was well past toying with his siblings just to get a reaction.

The car stopped on the second floor and Zachary stared into the open doors of the ballroom. Guests, like flocking birds, had already collected. A sense of déjà vu crept over him as he heard the rustle of silk, the clink of crystal, and the murmur of soft laughter. There hadn't been an event in this room for almost twenty years; the last party had been Witt's fiftieth birthday.

Beneath his tuxedo jacket and shirt, his shoulder muscles bunched, as if he expected trouble. From the corner, a pianist in long tails was playing on a concert grand that gleamed like polished ebony. Zachary recognized the tune, the theme from a recent movie, but he didn't pay much attention.

Champagne flowed from a fountain that gurgled to a pool at the base of an ice sculpture of a rearing horse, the symbol for the Hotel Danvers. Pink roses floated in crystal vases and petals were strewn across linen table cloths. A fist knotted in Zach's stomach. This was too much the same.

He'd let Trisha handle the arrangements for the event, barely listening as she'd rattled off the guest list, the caterers, the musicians, the artists or anything else to do with the damned celebration. He'd told her to do what she wanted; he'd done his part in fixing up the old hotel and he'd stick around for the party, but that was it. He had no interest in the grand opening itself.

Now he wondered if he'd let loose a demon. This celebration was certain to evoke memories of the surprise party Kat had thrown for Witt on his fiftieth birthday. The twinkling white lights in the trees, the polished dance floor, the prestigious guest list, even the champagne, served in long throated glasses that held strawberries and raspberries and slices of peaches were reminiscent of the fated celebration.

He swept past a table laden with hors d'oeuvres from Portland's finest restaurants. Making a beeline toward the bar he ignored his brother who was waving for him to join a group of his friends. The men with him looked a lot like Jason. Neatly trimmed hair, impeccable and expensive tuxedos, polished shoes, bodies built at exclusive athletic clubs. Zachary was willing to bet they were all junior partners in some stuffy law firm in the city. Who needed them?

Insolently, Zach leaned an elbow on the bar. The bartender, barely twenty-one and sporting a thin mustache, trimmed beard, and gold earring, smiled. "What'll it be?"

"A beer."

"Pardon?"

"Henry's. Coors. Miller. On tap or in a bottle, I don't care. Anything you've got."

The bartender offered a patronizing smile. "I'm sorry, sir, we don't have—"

"Get some," Zachary growled and the bartender, though perturbed, spoke quickly to a passing busboy who scurried off in the direction of the service elevators.

"Hey, Zach, great job. The place looks fabulous," a female voice enthused from somewhere behind him. Zach didn't bother to respond.

Another woman, someone from the press, he thought, caught hold of his arm. "Just a few questions, Mr. Danvers, about the hotel—"

"I think my sister sent out a press release."

"I know, but I have some questions."

Zach was barely civil. "Speak to Trisha. Trisha McKittrick. She's the interior decorator."

"But you were the general contractor."

"She handled all the interior design." Turning on his heel,

Zach left the woman with her questions and glanced pointedly at his watch. Jason was going to make some sort of speech and be congratulated by the mayor, the governor, and someone from the historical society. Zach would stick around, get his face photographed a couple of times, then make good his escape.

Still waiting for his beer, Zach paced to the windows, frowning, wishing the evening were over. He shouldn't have agreed to stay. Damn, he was getting soft. There was a time when he would've told Jason explicitly what he could do to himself if his brother had asked that Zach be a part of this farce. As it was, probably because of some sort of egotistical pride in what he'd accomplished here at the hotel, Zach had reluctantly agreed. *You're as bad as the rest of them, Danvers, always hoping for a little glory.*

"Mr. Danvers?"

Zach blinked and found the busboy carrying a silver platter with a long-necked bottle of Henry Weinhard's Private Reserve, and a frosted glass. With a crooked smile, Zach grabbed the beer. "Don't need that." He pointed to the glass as he twisted off the cap and dropped it onto the tray. "But I will want more than just this one."

"At the bar, sir. When you're ready."

"Thanks." Zach took a long tug on his bottle and felt better. He glanced out the window and saw the stream of glossy white limousines waiting to pull up to the striped awning and deposit their guests, the elite of Portland, to the front doors. Men in dark tuxedos, women in jewels, furs, and silk emerged from their modern-day royal coaches and dashed into the hotel.

It was a goddamned joke.

He itched for a smoke and told himself to forget it. He'd given up that particular vice nearly five years ago. Leaning a shoulder against the windowpanes he glared out at the night. Then he saw her. Like a ghost from his past, Adria Nash appeared on the opposite street corner. His insides twisted as he watched her weave through the clogged traffic, dashing between cabs, limos, and cars idling near the front door of the hotel. Wrapped in the same black cape she'd worn before, she sidestepped puddles and swept past the doorman.

So she'd had the guts to show up here.

With a final swallow, he finished his drink, left the empty bottle on the corner of the table and moved quickly through the crowd. Several people tried to stop him; women offered him encouraging smiles and men looked up as he passed. He was probably the subject of more than one conversation, but he didn't really care that he was labeled the black sheep of the family or that people thought he'd reconciled with the old man just before Witt had died to get himself back in the will.

As he dashed through the double doors, he saw her, smiling at the hotel manager, assuring him she had an invitation.

"You said your name was Nash—?" the manager asked with a friendly smile as he scanned his list.

"Actually it's Danvers."

The manager's smile didn't waver. "Danvers? Then you're related."

"Yes—"

"It's all right, Rich. She's with me." Zachary grabbed hold of Adria's chilled fingers but didn't bother to smile.

She looked at him with those clear blue eyes that seemed to cut straight to his soul. "Thanks, Zach," she said, as if she'd known him all her life.

The tightening in his chest warned him that he was making a colossal mistake, he could feel it in his bones, but he helped her leave her coat with an attendant guarding the closet and walked with her into the ballroom. He felt almost as much a traitor as he had on the night he'd slept with his stepmother; that same sense of doom, of stepping onto a path that had no beginning or end was with him, and yet he let her link her arm through his.

More than one head turned in her direction. She was as beautiful as the woman whom she claimed was her mother. Her black hair gleamed, caught in a long loose braid that wound past her shoulders to brush against the bare skin of her back. Her dress, white and shimmery, fell off one shoulder, draped across her breasts, nipped in at her waist and flared again over her hips to sweep the floor.

"What're you doing here?" he demanded when they were out of earshot of most of the guests.

"If you would have called me back I would have explained."

"Sure." He didn't believe her.

"I belong here."

"Like hell!"

She smiled tightly. "Why'd you come to my rescue?"

"I didn't."

"Sure you did. Otherwise old Richard would have tossed me out on my ear." A waiter stopped to offer them each a drink and Adria took a fluted glass from the silver tray. Zach shook his head and the waiter disappeared through the crowd. "Face it, Zach, you saved me."

"I just avoided a scene."

Her smile was bewitching. "That's what you thought I'd do— create a scene?"

"I know it."

"You don't know anything about me."

"Except that you're a gold-digging fraud."

"You don't believe that."

"Sure I do."

"Then why not let me make my 'scene' and let me hang myself." She sipped from her drink, somehow managing a smile for the eyes of the curious.

"Bad publicity."

"Since when would you care?"

"This family has had enough scandals," he said.

"And I thought you didn't give a damn about the family name." Her eyebrows arched in a sensual manner that caused a tightening in his groin.

"I don't." He watched her closely. She wasn't as confident as she pretended to be. There were questions in her eyes, but also a challenging light that dared him to defy her. As beautiful as Kat, with full lips and high cheekbones and eyebrows that arched over those mysterious blue eyes, she was sensual and earthy. Yet there was an innocence about her that had never been a part of Katherine LaRouche Danvers. Even at her most vulnerable, Kat had seemed to play a part and that role was always sexy and manipulative.

"You can prove you're London?" he asked, deciding to get to the point.

"Can and will."

"Impossible."

She lifted a bare shoulder and sipped slowly from her glass as the pianist found the notes of an old Beatles tune and managed to strip the melody of any hint of nostalgia. Laughter and smoke drifted to the ceiling where the chandeliers sparkled with a million tiny lights—just as they had nearly twenty years before.

Zach ignored the sense of dèjá vu that threatened to swallow him whole.

"I think you should introduce me to the rest of the family."

"Is that why you came here tonight?"

She smiled slowly and Zach's heart nearly stopped. "I came back to see you, Zach."

Just like Kat. His chest squeezed tight, but he wouldn't be fooled. "I doubt it. Don't try and pander to my male ego, all right? It won't work."

Smiling as if she knew he was joking, she said, "You're the only one I could approach; the only family member who might believe me, give me a chance."

"You've got that wrong, *sister*. I don't believe you at all. I don't care who you are or what your game is, but I don't believe that you're London. Now, you can sell your story to the press if you want to, and you can tell it to the rest of my family, but even if you turned out to be the Queen of England, I won't give a damn."

"You're a liar, Zachary," she said in a tone that chilled him a little because she was at an advantage. Obviously she'd done her homework and she knew a helluva lot more about him than he did about her.

"Fine. Meet the rest of the clan. They're charming." He grabbed her by the arm and pulled her through the knots of guests, raising eyebrows and causing whispers to follow in their wake.

Much as it bothered her, Adria let Zach propel her through the crowd. She knew that showing up tonight would be the best way to capture every member of the Danvers family's attention. She held out a slim hope that she'd find an ally within the family, someone who would be honest with her. She'd thought that person might be Zachary because of everything she'd read about him; how, soon after his sister's kidnapping, he'd been disinherited. How he was always at odds with his father. How he'd struck out on his own and made a small fortune out of a bankrupt construction company that he'd managed to turn around. There was a time when he'd been thrown out of the family, but somehow he'd weaseled his way back in. Street-smart with a ruthless edge, Zach always seemed to land on his feet.

She recognized Jason from the photographs she'd studied. He was tall and raw-boned with red-brown hair flecked with gray. His expression was serious. Caught in conversation with a reed-thin woman about half his age, he glanced up at the commotion, took one look at Adria and hesitated for just a second, his eyes narrowing as if to focus. The skin beneath his tan paled and he swallowed with sudden difficulty before he recovered to look the part of a poised, successful attorney.

Adria wasn't surprised by his reaction. She knew of her uncanny resemblance to the woman who was supposed to have been her mother; saw in the fear flashing through Jason's blue eyes that he recognized it, too.

"I think you might want to meet someone," Zach said, as they approached.

"Excuse me a minute," Jason whispered to his thin blond

friend. The girl's gaze slid to Adria and small wrinkles appeared between her perfectly arched brows. "I'll be just a little while, I promise, Kim."

With a thrust of her lower lip, Kim didn't move; obviously ready to meet Adria's challenge.

Zach's fingers clenched around Adria's arm, as if he expected her to bolt. "This is Adria Nash; my brother, Jason."

"Have we met?" Jason asked.

"In another lifetime," Zach intervened. "Adria thinks she's London."

Kim's mouth rounded a little, but Jason managed to smile. "Another London. How perfect, considering the circumstances." His voice was cold as his eyes. "Let me guess, you showed up tonight to make a big splash, be sure that the reporters and photographers saw you?" He took a swallow from his glass and observed her over the rim. "Am I right?"

"Actually she showed up last week," Zach said as he released her arm.

Jason turned on his brother. "And you didn't say anything?"

"I thought she might go away."

"Just go away." Under his breath Jason muttered something about thickheaded fools. A ruddy stain began to crawl up the back of his neck as he pinned Adria under a harsh, uncompromising glare. "How'd you get in here?"

"I said she was with me," Zach intervened.

Jason's lips flattened over his perfect teeth. "You let her in and you don't know what she plans to do? Or are you in on it, too? Is that it?"

Zach didn't bother to answer, just lifted a shoulder.

"You just like to see the rest of the family squirm, don't you?"

"She's a fake," Zach said flatly. "Let her do what she wants."

"Not here. Not now." Jason lowered his voice, suddenly aware of more than a few curious glances cast in his direction. "Don't you know what the law firm for the estate will do if—" His blue eyes suddenly sharpened on Adria and it was all she could do to keep from shrinking away from that hate-filled glare. "Take her upstairs. To your suite—no, better yet, to my house. You've got a key."

"No one's *taking* me anywhere," she said.

"You started this," Zach reminded her.

"Which means we'll do things my way," she countered, knowing she had to appear strong—any sign of weakness in front of the Danvers clan would be suicide.

One side of Zach's mouth lifted in a crooked, amused grin. "Maybe you are London after all. She was a stubborn thing, too."

"Just get her out of here. I'll meet you at the house."

"What about Nicole?" Zach asked and watched his brother's mouth tighten at the mention of his wife. Theirs was a rocky marriage at best.

"She's out of town. Visiting relatives in Santa Fe."

Zach didn't ask any questions. Why Jason's wife was away on one of the most important nights of her husband's life didn't concern him.

"I'm not going anywhere," Adria stated. "And don't talk about me as if I'm not here. As far as I'm concerned, I have as much right to be here as the rest of you."

"She has a point."

"Get her out of here, Zach."

"As I said, Jason, I'm not budging," Adria insisted, unmoved by the older Danvers brother's anger. She hadn't grown up on the Montana range without learning a thing or two about arrogant, self-important men. She could be just as headstrong as any man when it came to something she believed in and she was certain . . . well, nearly . . . that she was London Danvers.

Adria noticed the glint in Zach's eyes and she realized that he was enjoying watching his brother lose his cool. Jason, the attorney. Jason who had married well. Jason who seemed to be the one in charge of the family fortune.

"This is not the time or the place—"

"Then name them," she said firmly and caught a movement

from the corner of her eye. Kim, the waif-thin blonde, inched closer, listening to every word.

"What?"

"The time and place, name them." She wasn't backing down, not after she'd come this far, swallowed all her doubts, and found her nerve.

"My God!" another male voice whispered behind her and Adria turned to find a man, tall, dark blond and lanky, with startling blue eyes that widened when he caught sight of her face. "She looks just like—"

"We know, Nelson," Jason said, obviously irritated.

"Nelson, this is Adria Nash," Zachary drawled as if enjoying his family's discomfiture. "She's here claiming to be London."

Nelson looked quickly from his oldest brother to Zach. "But she couldn't be. Not really. Everyone knows that London was killed . . ."

"Everyone assumed," Adria cut in.

Jason's temper snapped. He glared at Zach. "You got her in here, you get her out."

"Maybe I'm not ready to go."

"If you want anyone in this family to listen to your story with an open mind, you'll haul your sweet ass out of here," Jason ordered.

"I'll take care of her." Zach's hands were coiling around her arm again but she jerked away from him.

"I don't need anyone to take care of me," she said, suddenly defiant.

"Then why are you here?" Jason asked. "If not for a piece of the pie, for someone to take care of you, why didn't you stay wherever it is you came from?"

"Because I need to know."

"So this isn't about money?"

She didn't answer and Jason smiled without a trace of warmth. His companion, the woman he'd called Kim, watched her with interested eyes.

"It's always about money, Adria," Jason said as the pianist took a break and the music suddenly stopped. "No reason to lie about it."

Before she could respond, Zachary had grabbed her and this time he didn't let go. No amount of wriggling could pull her arm free and rather than make a scene, she allowed herself to be shepherded from the familiar ballroom. She knew she'd been here years before; everything was nearly the same. The lights, the music, no . . . there had been a band instead of a solitary pianist and the champagne glasses had been stemmed and circular rather than tall and fluted. And there were other changes as well, there had been a huge green cake ablaze with fifty candles and the ice sculpture had been of a running horse rather than a rearing stallion. And the rose petals had been cast upon the floor creating a fragrant pink carpet.

Surely she was remembering Witt's fiftieth birthday, her last night with her parents—or was she only dreaming, caught in the fantasy that was London Danvers? In the past few months she'd read every newspaper article, studied every photograph, read every word written she could find about the Danvers family. She recognized her half-brothers from the pictures she'd seen of them and would have recognized her parents, had they still lived.

Witt had never given up believing that his favorite daughter would return to reclaim her heritage and he'd left a million-dollar reward for anyone who could find her; he'd also provided for London in his will and his estate was rumored to be valued at well over a hundred million.

The money wasn't important, she told herself as Zachary retrieved her cape, but she was determined to find out the truth, and damn the consequences.

7

"What makes you think you're London?" Zachary shifted down for a light that reflected red on the rain-washed streets. The engine of his Jeep idled and the wipers slapped drops of water from the windshield.

"I have proof." Well, that was a little bit of a lie, but not a big one.

"Proof," he repeated, easing up on the clutch as the light changed. He punched the throttle and the Jeep started climbing through the steep, twisting streets of the west hills. As she gazed out the window, staring past the thick branches of fir and maple, Adria saw the city lights winking far below. "What kind of proof?"

"A tape."

"Of what?"

"My father."

"Your father— meaning Witt?" He took a curve a little too fast and the Jeep's tires skidded before holding firm.

"My adoptive father. Victor Nash. We lived in Montana."

"Oh," he said derisively, "that clears things up."

"You don't have to be sarcastic."

He slid her a glance that silently called her a fool as they crested a hill and he turned sharply into a drive complete with electronic gates that whirred open when he pressed a numerical code into a key pad.

He parked near the garage of a rambling Tudor home. Three stories of stone and brick with dark cross beams and a gabled roof, the house seemed to grow from the very ground on which it had been built. Exterior lamps, hidden in dripping azaleas, rhododendrons, and ferns, lined the drive and washed the stone and mortar walls with soft light. Ivy clung tenaciously to one of several chimneys and tall fir trees rose above a stone fence that guarded the grounds.

"Come on," Zach instructed, leaning across her to open the door of the Jeep. He climbed out and led the way up a brick path and through a breezeway to the back door. "Bring back any memories?" he asked as he flipped on the lights of a huge kitchen.

She shook her head and he lifted a brow, as if surprised that she would admit that she couldn't remember. "This is it—home sweet home."

Swallowing hard, she looked around, hoping for a trace of remembrance, but the gleaming tile floor meant nothing to her, the glass doors of the cabinets, the hallways that angled in different directions, the plush Oriental carpets, nothing sparked any old, long-dead memories. "We can wait in the den," Zachary said, watching her reaction. "Jason will be here soon."

Adria's stomach knotted at the thought of squaring off with the Danvers family, but she hid her uneasiness. The den, located in a back corner of the house, smelled of tobacco and smoke. Coals glowed from a stone fireplace and Zach tossed a piece of mossy oak onto the embers before straightening and dusting his hands. He shed his jacket and dropped it over the back of a leather chair. "What about this, hmm? Dad's private room. You—well, London—used to romp in here for a good-night kiss." His eyes were challenging, his chin thrust forward.

"I—I don't think so," she admitted, trailing fingers on the timeworn desk.

"Gee, isn't that a surprise," he mocked. "The first of many, no doubt." He propped a foot on the edge of the raised hearth. "Now, you want to get this over with and tell me your little story or wait for the rest of the clan?"

"Is there a reason you need to be so offensive?"

"This is just the start. Believe me, I'm the prince of the family."

"That's not what I read," she said, holding her ground. "Rebel son, black sheep, no-good, juvenile delinquent." He wasn't pulling any punches, so neither would she.

"That's right, the best of the lot," he said through clenched teeth. "Now what's it going to be, Miss Nash?"

"I don't see any reason to repeat myself. We can wait for the rest of the family."

"Your choice." His gray eyes were glacial, as warm as an arctic sky as he gave her a cursory glance, then walked to the bar. "Drink?"

"I don't think it would be such a good idea."

"Might take the edge off." He found a bottle of Scotch and poured a stiff shot into a short crystal glass. "Believe me, you'll need it before they're done with you."

"If you're trying to scare me, it's a waste of time."

He shook his head as he raised the glass to his lips. "Just warning you."

"Thanks, but I think I can handle whatever it is they have to say."

"You'll be the first."

"Good."

Shrugging, he drained the drink and set the empty glass on the bar. "Have a seat." Waving to a tweed couch, he pulled off his tie, unbuttoned the top button of his shirt and rolled up his sleeves. Dark hair dusted his forearms, and despite the season, his skin was tanned. "Just for the sake of argument," he said, "how much would it take to have you close your mouth and go home?"

"Pardon?"

He rested his hands on the bar and pinned her with an uncompromising glare. "I don't believe in bullshit, okay? It's a waste of time. So let's cut right to the chase. You plan on making a big stink, start talking to the press and lawyers and claim that you're London, right?" He poured another drink, but let it sit untouched on the bar.

"I am London. At least I think I am."

"Of course you are," he said, his voice dripping with sarcasm.

"You don't need to patronize me."

"All right. Then we're back to square one. How much money would it cost to change your mind and decide that you are, after all, just Adria Nash?"

"I am Adria."

"So you want it both ways."

"For now."

"Until we accept you as London." The fire popped loudly.

"I didn't expect you to believe me," she said, refusing to leap at his bait. Her stomach was jumping. Sweat collected at the base of her neck and dampened her palms, but she told herself to remain outwardly calm. *Don't let him get to you. That's exactly what he wants.* "I wouldn't have come all this way if I didn't think I was—am—your sister."

"Half-sister," he said with a smile that didn't touch his eyes. "Get it right. If you're gonna do this thing, Adria, get all the facts and do it right."

Rankled, she said, "I have the facts and I know all about your family."

"So you decided to take advantage of your resemblance to my stepmother."

"Maybe you should just see the tape."

"The tape?" he challenged.

"Yes, the videotape that brought me here." The tape that had been the catalyst but certainly not the proof—not all of it. Suddenly it seemed frail, as fragile as her father's dreams and beliefs that she was some sort of modern-day princess. "I found it after my father died. He left it for me."

"Can't wait," he muttered sarcastically. Glancing at her for a moment, he poured a second glass. "But we'll wait to start the show." He set her drink on the corner of a glass-topped coffee table, then snatched his off the bar and claimed his position at the window. He stood like a sentry, staring through the rain-drizzled glass.

Standing, she said, "If you don't mind, I'd like to use the powder room."

"Powder room?" he said with a snort. "Kind of a fancy term for a farm girl from Montana."

She stared at her hands for a second, then lifted her eyes to meet his. "You love this, don't you"

"I don't *love* anything." His gaze raked down the length of her body.

"Oh, but you enjoy baiting me. You get a perverse pleasure in taunting me, trying to trip me up."

"You started this." His lip curled slightly. "Find the damned 'powder room' yourself. See if you can conjure it up from all those hidden memories."

Gritting her teeth in frustration, she grabbed her beaded bag and swept out of the room. The hallway was unfamiliar, but she turned to the right, rounded a corner and stopped dead in her tracks when she saw what could only be described as a shrine to the family of Witt Danvers. Pictures, plaques, and trophies resting in a glass case cut into the wall, were displayed prominently.

She swallowed with difficulty when she spied a large portrait of the three of them: Witt, Katherine, and London. Could this be . . . ? Adria's heart caught and she touched the glass, her finger displacing a tiny sheen of dust. Seated in a wicker chair, Katherine was dressed in a wine-colored dress with a scooped neck and long sleeves. Diamonds encircled her throat and winked from her fingers. She held a grinning London, who appeared near the age of three. London's wild hair fell in ringlets and she wore a pink velvet dress with a lacy collar and cuffs on the short, puffed sleeves. Witt stood behind them both, one hand placed possessively over his wife's shoulder. He was smiling at the camera and his eyes seemed to twinkle mischievously.

"Dad," she mouthed, though the word wouldn't come. Could this have been her family? Her natural family. Her chest seemed to cave in on itself. "Oh, God." Tears stung the back of her eyes and she felt her teeth sink into her lower lip. After all the years of not knowing, could she be looking at her family? Her throat grew hot and she blinked as she traced the line of Katherine's jaw, so like her own, with a finger and then looked into the child's smiling face. True, there was a resemblance, though Victor and Sharon Nash had taken very few pictures when she was young.

Were you my mother? she silently asked the woman in the portrait and again she lifted her finger to the glass.

"Touching, isn't it?"

Startled, she jumped backward. She hadn't heard Zach approach, didn't realize he was standing behind her, one shoulder propped on the opposite wall, watching her reaction. Her heart drummed wildly in her chest. "I—I didn't hear you."

He lifted his shoulder. "What do you think of the family memorial? Nice, isn't it?" Sipping his drink slowly, he gazed at the wall of pictures. "The Danvers family et al. Kind of reminds you of Ozzie and Harriet, doesn't it?"

Adria stared at the glass case. There were diplomas and football trophies, an art school award for Trisha, an outstanding student certificate for Nelson, a swimming medal with Jason's name engraved on it, and key to the city issued to Witt Danvers. Surrounding the case were the pictures: shots of Witt with dignitaries, Witt with one or more of his children, Witt as a young man with his father, Jason in a football uniform, Nelson in a cap and gown, Jason's wedding, even Trisha dressed in a long formal with a scrawny, wide-shouldered beau.

But there wasn't one snapshot, not one single faded black-and-white Polaroid of Zachary. She couldn't believe what her eyes told her and she searched again.

"I didn't win too many popularity contests," he explained, as if reading her mind. "The old man wasn't into mounting mug shots."

"I—uh—I didn't expect to see this." She motioned toward the wall.

"Who would?"

He gazed at the framed portrait of Witt and his second wife

and daughter and Zach's eyes seemed to lock with those of Katherine. A muscle worked in his jaw and Adria felt as if she were suddenly intruding, that this place was somehow sacred and intimate and she was, indeed, the interloper. The air seemed suddenly hard to breathe as Zach stared at Katherine.

"I couldn't find—"

He snapped out of his reverie and the darkness in his eyes disappeared "Around the corner. Second door on the left."

She didn't wait for other directions but hurried down the hall. Her steps were quick, as if she were running from something, something so private and dark that she felt a jab of dread.

In the bathroom she splashed cold water over her face. *Don't let them get to you,* she told herself as she saw her pale reflection in the mirror. *Don't let him get to you.*

When she returned to the den, he was back at the window, staring out at the gloomy night.

Reminding herself that she needed at least one ally in a family that was certain to try and discredit her, she picked up the drink he'd left for her and took a sip that burned all the way down her throat. "Do you know why I came to you first?" she asked, hoping to break down the barriers that he erected around himself.

He didn't answer; just glared out at the night as if the blackness were hostile.

"I thought you might understand."

"I don't understand anything fake."

She plunged on. "You know what it's like being on the outside."

His shoulder muscles bunched and he took another swallow of his Scotch. "Don't let a few pictures on the wall make you think that you and I have anything in common. So I was on the outside."

"But you wanted back in."

His back stiffened. "Get this straight, *sister,* I never wanted in. It was the old man's idea."

"Was it?" she asked, then decided that she wouldn't learn

anything if she didn't push a little bit. "What did you do to him to have him disown you?"

"Why did it have to be something I did? Why not him?" He slid her a cold glance that cut to her bone, then looked back through the window.

"I'm just guessing," she admitted, but her hands were shaking a little and she gripped the glass more tightly. Just being around him was unnerving, sitting calmly under his harsh stare was nearly impossible.

"Then figure it out yourself."

"What happened, Zach?"

He turned on her then and his eyes, once so cold, had shifted subtly and she felt as if the temperature in the room had suddenly elevated. From the fire, the flames reflected on the hard contours of his face, the flickering shadows making the angles and planes appear harsher, rougher, but she felt another sensation as well, one that started deep within her and caused her heart to pound, a sensation she didn't want to analyze too closely. She licked her lips.

"It's really none of your goddamned business."

Despite the knots in her stomach, she said, "I tried to find out what happened between you and Witt, but couldn't dig up anything substantial. I thought it was because you were considered a suspect in the kidnapping, that somehow what had happened to you that night was confirmation that you were involved."

He snorted. "That was probably part of it."

"And the other?"

Zach's jaw tightened and for a second she thought he might confide in her. Instead he turned back to the window and continued to glower. "Doesn't matter."

"Of course it does—"

"Leave it alone, Adria." She heard the warning in his voice and decided it was better to back off. For now. But she was determined to find out Zach's secret. More than ever, she wanted to find out what made Witt's rebellious son tick. Maybe there was some truth to the rumors that he wasn't really Witt's boy; that his father was Anthony Polidori. She took another drink and slowly settled back into the cushions of the couch to wait.

Jason Danvers threw caution to the wind as he put his Jaguar through its paces. Speeding up the narrow, rain-slickened streets of the west hills, he tried to think rationally. He'd left the celebration early, after giving his well-rehearsed speech and spending enough time to dance with the mayor, a woman recently elected and surprisingly popular. He'd made small talk, accepted congratulations from the president of the historical society for refurbishing the old building, smiled at the appropriate times and even managed a clever quote or two for the reporters of the *Oregonian* and *Willamette Week*. Finally after two hours, he managed to stuff Kim into a cab and leave the celebration behind.

He felt sweat beading along his collar line and he remembered Adria's beautiful face, so much like Kat's. Could she be the real thing—after all these years? Jason's biggest fear—his worst nightmare—was that someone impersonating his long-lost sister would turn up and look so much like her that people might believe she was truly London. For nearly twenty years he'd sweated it out, suspecting that someday the imposter would waltz into Danvers Manor, calmly say she was the little lost princess, make a statement to the press and start a legal battle over the fortune that would be tied up in court for decades.

Jason had thought his father, while alive, would be foolish enough to believe any beautiful black-haired, blue-eyed woman who would smile at him and call him "Daddy." But Witt had proved to be made of tougher stuff than Jason had given him credit for.

Soon after London's disappearance, when the police, the FBI, and even Witt's private eye, Phelps, had given up hope of ever locating the little girl again, Witt had determined he had to find her himself.

He'd bought some airtime on television and offered a million-dollar reward, no questions asked, if anyone could lead him to his little girl.

The television appeal had created chaos. Thousands of phone calls and letters had poured in not only from this country but from as far away as Japan, Germany, and India. All of the would-be heiresses had been fakes, of course, screened by Witt's team of specialists and defrauded quickly, but the search had cost millions of dollars only to turn up fruitless.

Even Kat had given up and when she had lost her faith that her daughter would return, she had seemed to lose interest in life. She'd died in 1980, eleven years before her husband, a young, beautiful, guilt-riddled woman, estranged from Witt. From everyone. Except Jason. He hadn't been able to stay away. And he'd borne the guilt of her suicide silently.

The Jag hugged the asphalt as he rounded the final hairpin curve.

Jason should have seen Kat's death coming, should have warned someone that she was in a deep depression, but he hadn't. He'd known that she'd never gotten over the loss of London, that she'd hidden her feelings by drinking. He'd seen her in tears, held her when she was hysterical. She'd told him over and over again how much she loved her little girl and how there would never be another one; she'd even hinted that he could father another child for her. She'd been losing all touch with reality for a long time.

Witt had never trusted her after discovering her with Zach. It had been a case of dèjá vu and nearly destroyed his father's confidence in himself as a man. First Eunice had cheated on him and then Kat . . . with his son no less.

But Jason hadn't told anyone that Kat was in serious trouble. Because, deep down, he was a coward. He'd managed to keep all his feelings for Kat hidden, but seeing Adria tonight had brought all kinds of thoughts about his stepmother to the surface of his troubled mind.

The resemblance was so damned creepy. It scared the shit out of him.

What if she's really London?

That thought settled like lead in his gut, but he knew, damn it, he *knew* she had to be a phony.

The beams of headlights splashed against the window and Zachary felt a sense of relief knowing that his brother had finally arrived. Good. Jason could deal with Adria and Zach could get the hell out of town. He didn't want or need to be so close to a woman who reminded him of Kat. "Looks like we've got company."

"About time." She was seated in a corner of the couch, her shoes kicked off, her knees drawn up beneath the silky folds of her gown.

As if she belonged. As if she were really a Danvers. As if she were Kat. Shit. He watched his brother's car screech to a stop near the garage. "He's not gonna be happy."

"Neither are you."

Zach caught the irony in her voice and felt the corners of his lips curve upward. She was something. Trouble was, he didn't know what. But she'd rattled Jason and that, in and of itself, was a trait Zach respected.

The Jaguar's powerful engine shut down and a door slammed. "Still time to back out of this."

"No way."

Jason, like many lawyers, was one of the most consummate actors Zachary had ever met. Always aware of presence, drama, and effect, Jason never appeared surprised, unless it was to his advantage. Except tonight, when he'd been forced to face his deepest nightmare—that London, his half-sister—was back and ready to claim her portion of the estate, which just happened to be the lion's share.

Jason's expression was grim as he strode into the room, but he seemed composed. Not a hair out of place, his tuxedo as crisp as when he'd taken it from his garment bag, he'd managed to regain control of his emotions. With a smile as cool as November, he walked to the bar and poured himself a drink.

"Let's just get down to it, shall we?" he said as he recapped a bottle of expensive Scotch.

Zach rested a hip against the fireplace.

"What is it you want, Miss Nash?" Jason asked.

She was ready for him. "Recognition."

"That you're London?"

"Yes."

Jason's smile was so cold Zachary felt a moment's concern for Adria. "You know we don't believe you."

"I expected it, yes."

"And you know that there have been hundreds of young women who have claimed to be our half-sister."

She didn't bother answering, but her eyes never left Jason's face.

"She says she has proof," Zach interjected, uncomfortable with Jason's arrogant attitude.

"Proof?" Jason's eyebrows raised and a muscle tightened in his jaw.

"I have a tape."

"A tape of—?"

"It's from my adoptive father. It explains what happened."

Jason looked at his brother. "You've seen it?"

"Not yet."

"Well, what're we waiting for? I assume you have it with you, Miss Nash."

"In my purse." She reached for the small beaded bag near her feet.

Zach stuffed his hands in his pockets. "Don't you think we should wait until Nelson and Trisha are here?"

"Why?"

"We're all involved, Jason," Zach said as Adria handed Jason the tape.

Opening the plastic cover, Jason asked, "Is this the only copy?"

Adria slanted him a glance that told him to quit acting as if she didn't have a brain in her head. "Of course not."

"Didn't think so." Jason stared at the videocassette, flipped it over and slipped it onto the corner of the desk. "Everything on this tape can be verified, right? If there's any question of legality, there would be documents to back it up."

"Such as?"

"Adoption papers, that sort of thing."

"The papers were destroyed."

Jason's lips twitched. "Destroyed?"

"By a fire."

"Convenient."

"I don't think so."

For a reason he couldn't explain, Zach stepped in. "There must be copies, filed with the state."

Adria shook her head. "I think the adoption was illegal."

Jason's mouth swept into a grin. "This just gets better and better."

Zach felt his stomach curl at the way Jason stepped closer to Adria—moving in for the kill. "Back off," he warned his brother.

"Oh, no, she started this." Jason was suddenly enjoying the evening.

But Adria didn't back down. "Look," she said, still reclining on the couch, as if she didn't have a care in the world, as if she hadn't dropped the bomb that she believed she was London, as if she didn't think Jason would strike hard and fast, going for her jugular if given the chance. "I know you're going to do everything you can to disprove me. I expect you to put me through hell. I did a lot of soul-searching before I came here, because, to put it frankly, I'm not sure I'm London Danvers."

Jason looked smug, as if he thought she was already hedging her bets. "You've changed your mind."

"No," she said emphatically. "I just want you to know where I stand. My father thought I was London."

"Your father?"

"Victor Nash. He died last year. I didn't find out the truth until I discovered the tape."

"That makes things easy, doesn't it?" Jason asked. "Your father—and I presume your mother, as well—aren't around to be questioned. But, happily for you, he leaves you a mystery tape telling you that you're going to inherit millions. Have I got it right so far?"

"Dad thought I should know," she said, a slight defensive edge to her voice.

"So he gave you some sort of death-bed swan song about you being the lost princess of the Danvers kingdom, is that it?"

She lifted her head and pinned him with eyes that darkened with the pain of her past. "That's it."

"And you must believe it or you wouldn't be here."

"Of course. But I'm not sure."

"How much would it cost to convince you that you're no blood relation?"

"As I said before, it's not a matter of money. If I find out I'm not London, I'll leave."

"And you won't go running to the press?"

Suddenly she was on her feet and she crossed the short distance between Jason and the couch so quickly, Zach's breath caught. Without the added inches of her heels, she was a full head shorter than Jason yet she craned her neck upward and glared at him. Two spots of color stained her cheeks. "You may find this impossible to believe," she said in a voice so low it was nearly inaudible over the hiss of the fire, "but I don't give a damn about money. I've seen what it's done to your family as well as a few others, but it is important to me to find out the truth." Her lips flattened in distaste and her eyes narrowed just a fraction. "Be honest, Jason, wouldn't you like to know if I'm really London?"

"I already know," Zach said.

Jason glanced at his brother.

"She's a fake." Zach finished his drink.

So like Zach to make a snap judgment, Jason thought. He was so damned cocksure. To Zach, everything was black or white, right or wrong, good or bad. Once again, Jason's hotheaded brother wasn't reading the situation the way it was. The reason this woman worried Jason wasn't because of her incredible resemblance to Kat. Hell, any decent plastic surgeon could alter her face, her black hair could come out of a bottle and she could be wearing sky-blue contact lenses for all he knew. Her looks weren't the real problem, though they did worry him more than a little, but it was her attitude that bothered him. Adria was the first person to claim she wasn't sure of her birthright. Whereas every other imposter, the pretenders to the Danvers's crown, were sure of themselves and threatening lawsuits, adverse publicity and stories in newspapers coast to coast, Adria was different . . . chillingly so.

"Sit down, Miss Nash," he suggested in a voice that most witnesses in a court of law obeyed instantly.

Unmoving, she stood her ground and from the corner of his eye, Jason saw Zachary's mouth twitch in amusement. He was enjoying this, because he didn't have much of a stake in the inheritance. The old man had written him out of his will once and then, as he'd aged and discovered the truth about his young wife, Witt had mellowed, tried to patch things up with Zach and offered him the ranch, the only asset that Zach cared about.

Zachary had been reluctant, but finally capitulated. The old man and his rebellious middle son had struck a deal of sorts, something no one ever brought into conversation. There were no signed papers, no evidence that Zach had blackmailed his father, and yet somehow he'd ended up doing Witt's bidding and refurbishing the Hotel Danvers. In return, Zach inherited the ranch in Bend—acres and acres of rich farm land, a drop in the bucket as far as the family fortune was concerned, but worth something nonetheless. The fact that Zach wanted it gave Jason a bargaining point with his headstrong younger brother. Jason couldn't prove that Zach had strong-armed the old man, but he suspected that his indifferent younger brother was just as greedy as the rest of the clan.

If London suddenly were to appear, Zach's share of the estate wouldn't alter too much. He had no percentage of the assets, just the damned ranch, which would shrink by a few hundred acres if he had to pay off London for her share. But Jason, Trisha, and Nelson would suffer seriously because Witt, damn him, had talked his lawyers into leaving fifty percent of his holdings, including the value of the ranch, to his youngest daughter. Fifty goddamned percent. There was no provision for the fact that she couldn't be found. Only after fifty years—*fifty* years—would the assets revert back to the rest of the estate. By that time, Jason would have a foot planted firmly in the grave.

Hell, what a mess!

Fortunately, most people didn't know the terms of the will, thank God, or there would be London Danvers after London Danvers crawling out of the woodwork trying to get their hands on the fortune.

And the first one was glaring defiantly up at him and looking so much like Kat that he felt the same hot urges he had when he was in his early twenties and his stepmother had been the most gorgeous and sexy woman on this earth. He'd had dreams about her, fantasized about making love to her, but she'd had the hots for Zachary, who had only been a boy at the time.

Zach, for God's sake!

Zach's attitude reeked of insolence and he had no respect for the good things in life, yet women seemed to flock to him. Kat had been the first in a long succession of women who would have given their eye teeth, or their diamond earrings, just to get him into their beds and between their legs. The fact that Zach had always appeared uninterested had seemed to drive them into wild and hot pursuit.

Jason didn't understand it; never would. All he knew was that Zach had always been more trouble than he was worth.

"Look," Adria was saying, her chin lifted several notches. "Why don't you just play the tape?"

"I will," Jason assured her as he glanced at his watch. "But we can wait a few more minutes, until Nelson and Trisha get here."

"So it's a family party after all," Zach said, cynicism edging his words. "Should be a barrel of laughs."

"I tell you, Trisha, it was downright eerie," Nelson said as he braked in front of the garage. Zach's old Jeep and Jason's Jag were already parked in the drive. "I mean, I felt like I'd traveled back in time about twenty years. She looks just like Kat."

Trisha wasn't impressed. She'd been through this routine too many times before. Nelson was quick to jump off the deep end. "So what does she want?"

"No one knows. Money, I imagine."

"Where does she come from?"

"I'm telling you no one knows a damned thing about her."

"Don't you think it would have been smarter to check her out before we confront her?"

"Jason didn't want her to cause a scene at the party. Too many reporters were there."

"So he hustled her out here. Great." Trisha climbed out of Nelson's Cadillac and slammed the door shut. She didn't have time for these kind of games. There had always been women who claimed they were London Danvers, and there always would be. Why was this one any different? Either intimidate the bitch into leaving the family alone, or buy her off. The impostors could usually be purchased cheaply. Offer them a check for five or ten thousand and they were only too happy to do anything anyone asked. They all signed sworn statements that they would never pretend to be London Danvers or bother the family again and in some cases, Trisha suspected, they'd slept with Jason. He seemed to get off on fucking any woman who remotely resembled Kat. Some sort of weird Oedipal thing. Trisha didn't care, just as long as the women took off. Paying off the little whores saved a whole lot of time and law-yers' fees and everyone was happy. So why not do the same with this one? Hell, it would be fun to watch Jason try to ma-neuver her into his bed.

Nelson was still babbling. "Right now we can't afford any adverse publicity. My job—"

"Isn't worth diddly squat. You work for the public defender's office," she reminded him. "If you didn't get checks from the trust fund, you'd be scrounging every month to pay the rent."

Nelson's eyes thinned on his sister. "You know why I work where I do. It's a stepping-stone, Trisha."

"Politics," she said with a sneer. "You're as bad as Dad was. Delusions of grandeur."

"Politics is power, Trisha, and we both know how you feel about powerful men."

"Kind of the same way you do," she cooed though she felt like slapping him. He'd hit a raw nerve, but then Nelson had the uncanny ability to find a person's weak spot and expose it. Sometimes Trisha wondered if there were any secrets in the family that Nelson didn't know and wouldn't use for his own personal gain. Well, he had a few skeletons in his closet as well.

As they walked through the front door, she checked her watch. It was after midnight and she was tired. The hotel opening had been a success and she would have much rather bathed in the accolades of the guests than return here, to the house where she'd been raised, a house filled with ghosts and bad blood, treachery and lies. There had been little laughter echoing through the hallways of the Danvers Manor. In truth, she remembered nothing but the continual arguments and explosive outbursts as Witt Danvers tried to force his five bullheaded children into becoming exactly what he wanted them to be.

Trisha reached into her purse and found her cigarette case. Pausing in the foyer, she clicked her lighter to the tip of her Salem Light and drew in a calming breath of smoke. She needed something stronger. A drink or a hit of cocaine would help, but she settled for nicotine and ambled farther down the hall, trying not to remember the emotional fights, the hate that had filled this house when her father had found out that she'd been sleeping with Mario Polidori.

"You did this to spite me!" Witt had screamed, his face flushed scarlet, the veins in his temples throbbing.

"No, Daddy, I love him—"

"Love?" Witt had cried, his blue eyes electrified with disgust. *"Love?"*

"I want to marry him."

"For the love of Jesus! You're not going to marry him, or any other stinking Italian! Don't you know what the Polidoris are? What they've done to this family?"

"I love him," she said firmly, tears standing in her eyes.

"Then you're a fool, Trisha, and of all the things I've ever thought about you, I've never thought you were stupid."

She began to shake inside, but she squared her shoulders. "You hate Mario because of Mom. Because she slept with Anthony—"

The slap sent her reeling backward and she fell against the wall of Witt's den, her head bouncing off the corner of the mantel. "Don't you ever speak of that woman again, do you hear me? She was a whore. A wop-loving whore and she left me as well as every one of you kids so that she could carry on her dirty little affair with Polidori. So don't you be lecturing me about how you're in love with that Italian bastard's son!"

"You don't understand—"

"No, Trisha, you don't understand! You're never to see him again! Got it?"

Cowering against the wall, faced with her father's horrid rage, she refused to agree. She loved Mario. She did. Her fists curled into tight balls and tears rained from her eyes and it became blindingly clear that her father was an ogre, an ugly, ruthless monster who cared about only one thing: his precious daughter, London. Trisha rubbed the welt on the side of her cheek and bit her lip to keep from crying. At that moment she hated Witt Danvers and she'd do anything she could to hurt him!

Now, years later, she still felt the same. Her father had been a bastard while alive and he was still controlling his children from the grave, putting reins on his money, making them jump through hoops. She drew on her cigarette and walked unerringly to the den. Her father had never loved her, not at all. He'd only loved his youngest daughter and now she, or more probably some imposter, was back, trying to get her greedy little fingers into the old man's fortune. Well, Trisha was bound and determined to fight the gold digger tooth and nail. London had escaped when the rest of them had been forced to suffer and face their father day after day, to cower and shudder and kiss the old man's ass so that he wouldn't cut them out of his will.

Except for Zach. He'd managed to tell his father to go to hell and then slip back into Witt's good graces. Much as she hated to admit it, Trisha admired her brother for his grit.

As for Adria Nash, even if she could prove that she was London, Trisha silently vowed she'd never get a penny of the Danvers's fortune. She hadn't paid her dues, hadn't lived with the heartless tyrant who was Witt Danvers. London didn't deserve half the old man's estate and besides, this woman was probably just another fortune hunter.

"What're you thinking about?" Nelson asked, his eyebrows pulled together anxiously as he glanced at his sister.

"Nothing."

He didn't believe her. "Just be on your best behavior, Trisha, and hear what she has to say. Brace yourself. She looks like our dear departed stepmother did twenty years ago."

They entered the den and Trisha nearly missed a step as her gaze fastened on the woman—a beautiful woman. The resemblance was uncanny, and although this girl didn't have the innate feline sensuality of the woman she claimed was her mother, she was nearly a dead ringer for Kat.

Someone, Nelson probably, thrust a drink in Trisha's hand and she took a sip. Zach made introductions, but Trisha didn't pay much attention; she was too wrapped up in memories of her stepmother. Her throat tightened and she forgot her cigarette. Ash tumbled to the carpet. God, could it be? Was this woman really her half-sister? She took another calming drink. Jason was talking . . .

". . . so we waited for you two before we looked it over. Adria assures us this is the proof we'll need." He slapped a black video into the VCR and turned on the power and Trisha pulled her attention away from the woman with the uncanny resemblance to Kat and watched the screen.

Zachary took his position at the window. The room was tense, but he found a grain of amusement in the tight smiles of his brothers and sister. Adria had gotten to them. All of them. They were worried. For the first time in nearly twenty years.

He heard a voice and turned his attention to the television screen where an emaciated bald man was lying on a hospital bed and speaking with obvious difficulty.

"I suppose I should have told you this before, but for reasons I'll get to later, selfish reasons, Adria, I kept the story of your birth a secret. When you asked me about it, I swear to God, I didn't know the truth and later . . . well, I couldn't bear to tell you.

"Your mother and I, rest her soul, always wanted children, but, as you know, Sharon couldn't conceive. This was a constant torment to her and she somehow thought that God was punishing her, though why I'll never understand. So when we found you . . . when you were handed to us, it was the blessing she'd been praying for.

"We adopted you through my brother, Ezra. You probably don't remember him much as he died in seventy-seven. But he was the one who brought you to us. He was a lawyer, practicing out of Bozeman. He knew that your mother and I were desperate for children. Already in our fifties and with debts that were burying us and the farm, we were considered too old and too poor to adopt through the usual legal means."

The man paused, took a sip of water from a glass on a nearby table, then cleared his throat and looked at the camera again.

"Ezra told me that one of our distant cousin's daughters had herself in a fix. The girl, Virginia Watson, was divorced and penniless and had a five-year-old daughter whom she couldn't care for decently. All she wanted was to see that Adria, her girl, was placed with a loving family. Ezra was a bachelor. He didn't want a child but he knew that Sharon and I would do anything for a baby.

"And we did. The adoption was secret and the papers . . . well, there weren't many, let me tell you. We didn't want the state involved, you see. So, anyway, Virginia came with you and dropped you off and from that day forward we thought of you as our own."

He paused, the next words difficult. "I suspected everything wasn't on the up and up, but I didn't care. Your mom, she was happy for the first time in years, and I had no idea who you really were. I told myself someone didn't want you and we did and that was that.

"Only years later, after Sharon had passed on, did I start to figure it out. I swear, until that time, I didn't have a clue that you could be someone's missing daughter. Hell, Adria, truth to tell, even if I had known, I'm not sure I could've given you up. But the long and the short of it is that I was cleaning some old newspapers out of the barn and I saw one with the story of the Danvers girl being kidnapped. The police were searching for her nursemaid, a woman by the name of Ginny Slade. That didn't mean anything to me, either, but about two weeks later I sat down in my chair by the fire to read a little from the Bible and the page opened up to the family tree and right there I see the name, big as life: Virginia Watson Slade. According to the tree, at one time Ginny Watson was married to Bobby Slade from Memphis."

He licked his lips nervously. "I'm not a stupid person and even I can put two and two together and come up with four. It looked like you could be the missing Danvers girl, but I wanted to be sure so I tried to contact Virginia, but no one had heard of her for years. From the time she dropped you off at the house, she seemed to have disappeared. No phone calls, no letters, no address. Her parents didn't know if she was dead or alive and had no idea where Bobby Slade was. It was damned near as if she'd fallen off the face of the earth and I hate to admit it, but I was relieved. I didn't want to lose you." Victor blinked rapidly and took another sip of water.

The man sounded and looked sincere, as if he were really a dying father, but Zach wasn't going to let this dog-and-pony show get to him. In his mind Adria was a fake.

"I know this sounds callous," Victor said in a hoarse whisper, "but I couldn't stand the thought of losing you, Adria. You were all I had in the world. As for the Danvers, I figured the damage was already done. I couldn't undo the kidnapping. And I had to consider the adoption. At the time we'd taken you in, we knew that all the proper papers weren't filed, that the adoption wasn't by the book. Hell, it was probably illegal. I was afraid that somehow I'd be implicated in the crime, even though I had no idea where you'd come from. So, I've decided to die with this secret intact and leave this video in the safe by my bed. If anyone questions the tape's authenticity, so be it. Saul Anders lent me his equipment, set up the tripod and saw to it that I had some privacy. He has no idea what's on this tape and has sworn to me that he wouldn't view it."

The old eyes turned glassy for a second. "Okay, kiddo, that's all I know. I hope it helps. I guess maybe I just loved you too much to tell you the truth. I'll miss you, baby . . ." He forced a smile and the tape went black.

Nelson whistled low under his breath.

Jason scowled into his empty glass.

Trisha clapped her hands as if she were at a theater production. "Well, if that wasn't an all-time low in the history of video-taping! Did you really think we'd believe that schmaltzy story?"

"I don't know," Adria said huskily and her eyes shined a little brighter than they had before.

Zach told himself that this was all part of an elaborate con, that the man in the video was probably an actor, or her father trying to run a scam on the wealthy Danvers family.

"Touching," Trisha said, unable or unwilling to hide her sarcasm.

Jason pressed the eject button and pulled the video cartridge from the machine. "This is your 'proof'?" he asked.

"Yes."

"All of it?"

Adria nodded and the quiet rage drawing Jason's features into a knot of anxiety seemed to fade. "Well, Miss Nash, it's not much, is it?"

"What it is, Jason, is a start," she replied, standing and slipping into her shoes. "You don't have to believe me. God knows I didn't expect you to, but take this as a warning. I'm going to find out who I really am. If I'm not London Danvers, trust me, I'll walk. But if I am," she said, her small chin thrust in determination, "I'll fight you and every lawyer you sic on me to prove it." She grabbed her purse and slung her cape over her arm. "It's late and I know you have a lot to discuss, so I'll just call a cab and—"

"I'll drive you," Zachary said, unwilling to let her leave just yet, though why he couldn't name. He was better off without her, but there was a part of him that was intrigued with her story. Who was she really?

"Don't bother."

"I want to."

"It's not necessary."

"Sure it is." He caught a speculative glance from Trisha and a harder-edged, more pointed glare from Jason. "Danvers hospitality," he drawled.

"Look, Zach, don't do me any favors, okay?" She started out of the room and he caught her by the elbow.

"I thought you said you needed a friend." His fingers clamped over her arm and she felt his breath, warm and smelling faintly of Scotch brushing the nape of her neck.

She reminded herself that this was the man like her, the man who had no past if the family portraits could be believed. "Maybe I changed my mind," she said and her voice sounded ragged.

"Wouldn't be wise, lady. Looks like you need all the friends you can get." Hesitating a heartbeat, she glanced over his shoulder to the rest of the Danvers family. *Her* family. Or was it? In a show of independence, she yanked back her arm and stepped away from him.

"Thanks, anyway."

Obviously, Zach wasn't about to let her make a fool of him. He followed her out of the den and through the kitchen where she reached for the phone and he plucked the receiver deftly out of her fingers. "I'd think you'd jump at the chance to be alone with me."

"Don't flatter yourself."

His lips twisted into a self-deprecating grin. "No, I mean, to get more information on the family. That is what you want, isn't it?"

A little wrinkle of concentration formed between her eyebrows. "Whose side are you on?"

"No sides," he said, opening the back door. The night seeped into the room. "I only look out for myself." A solitary man. A man who needed no one. Or so he wanted her to believe.

"Humble of you."

"I didn't think you were looking for humility; just the truth."

"I am."

His expression was hard and unyielding. "Then you may as well know that I really don't give a damn about the family or the money."

"But you do care about the ranch," she said, slipping her cape over her shoulders.

His eyes flashed in the darkness. "My weakness."

They stepped into the breezeway and the cold midnight wind whistled through the fir trees lining the drive. She was struck by the width of his shoulders, the angle of his jaw. Raw-boned and sexy. "Do you have many—weaknesses, that is?"

"Not anymore." He opened the door to his Jeep. "I gave up on my family when I was sixteen, I quit trusting women when I was twenty-eight, and I'd give up drinking, too, but I think a man should have at least one vice."

"At least."

"At least I'm not a pathological liar." He slid behind the steering wheel and his features seemed more rugged and dangerous in the encroaching darkness.

"So why would you want anything to do with me?"

He switched on the ignition and flipped on the headlights.

"Let's get one thing straight, okay? I don't *want* anything from you." Pumping the accelerator, he jammed the Jeep into reverse. "But I have a feeling you're going to shake things up a little, Miss Nash."

"That doesn't worry you?"

"Nope." He cranked on the wheel and the Jeep turned easily on the slick asphalt. His eyes were dark as obsidian. "Because I still believe you're a fake. A good one, maybe, but still just a cheap fake."

8

What the hell was he going to do with her? He drove through the gates and shot a quick glance in her direction. She was huddled against the door, staring through the windshield and her profile was so like Kat's it caused his gut to clench into a painful fist. If she wasn't London Danvers, she was one helluva look-alike, a damned dead ringer for London's mother. The curve of her jaw, the thick black hair, even the way she slid a glance through the fringe of curling lashes, half seductive, half innocent. So much like Kat.

He clutched the wheel in a viselike grip, his knuckles showing white. He didn't need to be reminded of his self-destructive, sexy stepmother. It had taken years to purge Kat from his system. Then, just when he'd convinced himself he was over her, she'd taken an overdose of pills and all the demons of his guilt had awakened and screamed through his mind.

Now, this woman, this mirror-image of Kat, had appeared like a ghost and had come back to haunt him. He should run like hell. But he couldn't and there was a magnetism about Adria that pulled at him and seeped under his skin, burning like dry ice promising heat but searing with a frigid intensity that scarred deep. Just like Kat.

"Tell me about my mother," she said, as if reading his thoughts.

"If she was your mother." Zach flipped on the wipers.

Adria ignored the jab. "What was she like?"

Squinting into the darkness, Zach asked, "What do you want to know about her?"

"Why she committed suicide."

A tic developed under his eye. "No one knows if she tried to kill herself or she just took a few too many pills."

"What do you think about it?"

"I don't. Won't do any good. Won't bring her back." His jaw was hard as granite.

"Would you want that? Her alive?"

He flicked her a disdainful glance. "Let's get something straight, okay? I didn't like Kat. In my book, she was a manipulative bitch." He slowed for a corner and added, "But I didn't wish her dead."

She'd obviously hit a nerve, but she didn't believe he was being completely honest with her. Too much tension coiled in his muscles, too much anger grooved in the lines of his face. There was more he wasn't telling her. "What about the rest of your family—how did they feel?"

He snorted. "You'll have to ask them." The Jeep reached the bottom of the hill and Zach merged into the traffic heading east. "Where are you staying?"

She was ready with her lie. "The Benson."

He lifted an interested brow and Adria knew why. The Benson, like the Hotel Danvers, was one of Portland's oldest and most prestigious hotels. Its lobby was reminiscent of an English club with warm wood walls, a huge fireplace, and sweeping stairs to an upper floor. Visiting dignitaries, ambassadors, Hollywood stars, and politicians stayed at the Benson as well as the Hotel Danvers. The price of a room wasn't cheap.

Yet, she needed some privacy; a little space away from the watchful eyes of the Danvers family, so she lied. What did it matter if she was really spending her time in a fleabag on Eighty-second? None of the Danvers clan needed to know anything more about her. At least not yet. Until she was ready. She wasn't going to fabricate her life. She would tell them all the truth, when she deemed it necessary, but right now she was tired, the fight was out of her and she wasn't ready for round two of the battle.

"Where do you live—when you're not staying at the Benson?"

Fair enough question. A smile touched her lips. His cynical humor touched her. "Montana—I already told you—I grew up in a small town near the Bitterroots called Belamy."

"Never heard of it."

"Not many people have."

"Lived there all your life?"

She eyed him carefully. "For as long as I can remember."

"With your folks?"

"Yes." His questions put her on edge. He was looking for lies. She stuck close to the truth. Though she'd never been really close to her mother, Victor had been kind and loving to her and she was beginning to suspect that he was a far more patient parent than Witt Danvers had ever thought of being.

"Did your mother think you were London as well?"

Adria shook her head. "I don't think so."

Accelerating through a yellow light, he asked, "Don't you remember the first time you met your folks? If you were London you would have been around five. As you pointed out, even five-year-olds have memories."

She watched as the skyscrapers fingered upward into the night-black sky. "I don't have memories, not real ones. Just images."

"Images? Of what?"

He nosed the Jeep into a side street, near the Benson. "Of the party. It was loud and exciting and . . ."

"You read about it."

"I remember Witt. With his white hair, he reminded me of a polar bear . . . so huge . . ."

"Again the newspapers." He pulled into the lane reserved for guests of the Benson and she turned her startling blue eyes at him. "You're right of course," she said, reaching for the door handle, "but there's something that doesn't quite fit. In all the faded images that I have stored in my mind, there's one that's so clear, it's frightening."

"What's that?" he scoffed, though he felt as if a vise had clamped over his chest and his heart began to thud.

She stared him full in his face. "I remember you, Zach."

"I doubt it." The clamp twisted tighter.

"As clearly as if it were yesterday, I remember a sullen, dark-haired boy whom I adored." She pushed open the door and stepped onto the curb. Zach reached for her, but she was gone. Like a faint puff of white smoke, she disappeared into the hotel.

He considered chasing her down—calling after her and making her explain herself. What did she remember about him? But he didn't move. The last throwaway line was obviously planned, a comment intended to get under his skin.

A horn blasted behind him and he stepped on the gas, but he didn't leave her words behind; they hung on the air and followed him all the way back to the Hotel Danvers where, to avoid any guests still lingering in the bar after the party had wound down, he took the service elevator to the seventh floor and walked into his room. The red message light on his phone was flashing. He wasn't surprised to learn Jason had called.

"Great." Zachary looked at his bags. They were packed and ready to go but he knew with sudden clarity that he wasn't going anywhere. At least not tonight. Kicking off his shoes, he sat on the edge of the bed and dialed. Jason picked it up on the second ring.

"About time. Where were you?"

"I dropped her off at the Benson."

"That's where she's staying?" Jason sounded suspicious.

"A nice touch, don't you think? Claims she's the long-lost Danvers heir and stays at the competition."

Jason's voice was muffled but Zach heard him ordering Nelson to call the Benson on the other line, talk to Bob Everhart, who had once worked for Witt and find out Adria's room number. His voice was stronger when he turned back to Zach. "You know if I had the number of your damned cell phone, I could've called you and told you to wait around her hotel."

"Why?"

"Why?" To follow her of course."

"Of course," Zach mouthed. "Why didn't I think of it?"

"She represents a threat, Zach."

"I don't think so." Flopping back on the bed, he wondered why he was even bothering with the conversation. "Look, it's late, I'm taking off—"

"Now? You're leaving *now?*"

"Yeah."

"When we're in the middle of a fucking family crisis?"

"I don't give a shit."

"Sure you do," Jason said and Zach stared up at the ceiling. He was lying a little. He did care. About the ranch. And he was curious about Adria. Just what was her game?

Jason wasn't giving up. "You think your ranch is protected, right? Because it was a specific bequest? Well, things change if this woman proves she's London. A lot of the extra acres were bought after the will was originally signed and all those wouldn't be considered part of the ranch, per se. And if everyone else has to cough up to make sure she gets her fifty percent, you will, too."

Zach frowned into the receiver. "You've been busy."

"Now listen. Adria seems to trust you. She came to you first. Get close to her. Find out what makes her tick—what?" His voice faded as he turned his head and the words were muffled, but Zach heard them all. "I knew it! Okay, so start calling cab companies . . . I don't know. Just do it. The police do it all the time—right, call Logan; he's still on our payroll and he has connections even though he's retired. Oh, for Christ's sake, don't give me that conflict-of-interest crap." There was further argument and Zach was about to hang up, but Jason turned back to the receiver. "Big fucking surprise. No Adria Nash or London Danvers, or London Nash or Adria Danvers at the Benson. She probably just ducked into the ladies' room and satisfied that you were gone, took a cab to God-only-knows-where."

"She'll show up. Her kind always does."

"You're forgetting something, Zach. She's different. She's not here claiming she's London, screaming that she's our darling long-lost sister, no, she's got a different story and one the press would love. 'Is she or isn't she?' And she looks so much like Kat, there's bound to be speculation. We've got to keep her mouth closed."

"How?"

"First, you've got to follow her—"

"You've got to be kidding!"

"I'm not."

Zach's jaw was so tight it ached. He didn't like being manipulated and for as long as he could remember, someone in his family, either Witt, or Kat, or Jason, was trying to pull his strings.

"My guess is that she's working with an accomplice."

"Come on—"

"Why not? We're talking a lot of money here. *A lot.* People would do just about anything to get their hands on it—even impersonate a dead girl. Think about it, Zach, our biggest worry has been that someone would show up now, after Witt and Kat are both dead, claiming to be an heir and there's no way to take DNA tests or anything of the sort."

"I'm not worried about it."

"You should be—whether you like it or not, you're a member of this family and . . . hang on a minute." His voice was muffled for a second, then clear again. "Look, Logan's checking with the cab companies. I'll call you when we hear something."

"Don't bother." Zach slammed the phone back in its cradle. He was tired of Portland, tired of his family, tired of all the mess. He stripped out of his tuxedo—a rental—stuffed it back in its bag and left it hanging in the closet. By the time he'd changed into jeans and a sweater, the phone was ringing insistently. He wanted to ignore it, but snapped up the receiver again. He didn't have to guess who was calling.

"She's at the Riverview Inn on Eighty-second, somewhere

near Flavel," Jason said, pleased with himself. "Seems our little gold digger isn't so well off, is she?"

"It doesn't matter."

"Of course it does. She can't afford the best lawyers if she can't even pay for a decent room. Why don't you go out there, Zach, check out what the situation is? If she's working alone, take her to the ranch with you."

"No way."

"She'd be safe there. Isolated."

"The lady won't want to come."

"Convince her."

"How? Tell her that maybe she'll get a piece of the estate? Forget it."

"Come on, Zach. Do it. Who knows? She might even be London."

"Not in a million years," he said and ignored the funny feeling in his stomach when he remembered her clear blue eyes and her low, seductive voice. *I remember you, Zach. As clearly as if it were yesterday, I remember a sullen, dark-haired boy whom I adored.* His palms began to sweat around the receiver.

"I hope you're right, but I sure would like to find out."

"Drive over there yourself."

"As I said, she trusts you."

"She doesn't even know me." He tapped a foot in frustration and thought of Adria. She was beautiful and seductive and he was attracted to her. That fascination, in and of itself, was dangerous. He didn't want or need a woman in his life, especially one who had her eye on the family fortune. He'd already learned that lesson.

"This'll all blow over soon. But we need to get a handle on her. All you have to do is convince her to come to the ranch with you for a couple of days."

"No way."

"Well, at least go talk to her. Ask her to stay at the Hotel Danvers, compliments of the family."

Zach barked out a laugh. "As if she'd believe you. She went to a lot of trouble to hide herself; I don't think she'll want to stay in a hotel where she could be watched day and night."

"My guess is she'll like the higher rent district. She's after money, remember, and it must gall her to stay in some dump of a motel."

"Maybe she likes her privacy."

"Then she should never have started this, because before it's over she won't know what the word means." He paused for a second and Zachary imagined Jason running a nervous hand around his neck. "Damn it, Zach, we have to keep our eye on her."

"You invite her to stay at the damned hotel."

"She trusts you."

Zach snorted. "If she's smart, she won't trust anyone in the family." He thought about the way she gazed at the picture of Witt and Katherine and London. As if she really cared. She either believed her farfetched story herself or was the best damned actress he'd ever met.

"Talk to her," Jason insisted.

"Oh, hell." He hung up not agreeing and not disagreeing. Grabbing his bag, he mentally kicked himself all the way to the parking garage. Adria Nash was trouble. Big-time trouble. Trouble he didn't need or want.

"Shit!" He threw his single piece of luggage into the back of the Jeep and drove away from the hotel, heading east, through the drizzle and across the murky Willamette River and along the grid of streets on the east side. Traffic was light and he pushed the speed limit, suddenly anxious to find her. Damn, he was as bad as the rest of the family. He'd never heard of the Riverview Inn, but found it easily, a low-rent cinder block building painted stark white. The flickering lighted sign advertised free cable television. All the units were connected in a U shape. The panoramic view from the windows of the units was a pockmarked asphalt lot and an all-night bar across the street. Riverview stretched the imagination. No river. No view. But cheap daily rates.

Zach studied the cars in the lot and spied a battered Chevy Nova with Montana plates parked in front of unit eight. "So you are here," he said, backing the Jeep into an unmarked spot near a solitary oak tree. He turned off the ignition and stared at the bank of rooms facing each other.

The manager's unit was dark and he hoped no one peeked out the window and wondered what he was doing. He slid lower in the seat, glanced at his watch and frowned. It was nearly four in the morning and still traffic whizzed by, throwing up rainwater and creating a low, constant hum. He wondered if Adria was an early riser and told himself he'd soon find out.

Jason ran a nervous hand around the back of his neck. He had to think. He was the brains of the family, the only person who knew how to run his father's vast holdings. Trisha dabbled with her art and redecorating, Nelson practiced some archaic form of law as a public defender, Zach had earned his trade as a builder and now owned a construction firm in Bend while he managed the ranch in central Oregon, but Jason was the one who held the whole fraying fabric of the family businesses together.

He stripped off his tuxedo, threw it over the back of a chair for the maid to deal with in the morning and frowned when he looked at his bed. Ever since Adria Nash had crashed the grand opening of the hotel, Jason's plans for the night had been thrown into a tailspin. Right now, if things had progressed as he'd hoped, he would be in bed with Kim, rolling in the sheets, arms and legs entwined, mouths pressed to body parts, groans and moans of pleasure filling the room. Instead he was standing here half dressed, wishing he had another drink and worried that somehow a woman—a cunning and gorgeous woman he'd never seen before tonight—might find a way to steal the family's fortune.

After Zach and Adria had left he'd been forced to deal with his neurotic younger brother and sister, both of whom, in Jason's opinion, needed to spend a few more hours a week on psychiatrists' couches.

Zach was a pain, but at least he didn't have any hangups, not like Trisha and Nelson. Trisha, though she'd been through a dozen lovers and one marriage, had never been happy and Jason suspected that she'd never really gotten over Mario Polidori. As for Nelson, different demons attacked that boy. Working for the public defender's office was bad enough, but there was more about the youngest Danvers son to worry Jason. Nelson had a high set of moral standards, which he expounded for endless hours, and yet, there was a darker side to Nelson, a secretive side that only surfaced when Nelson was angry or worried.

He poured himself another drink and kicked off his jockey shorts, so that he was completely naked. From his bedroom he stood at the sliding glass door, backlit by the light from the hall, as he stared over the tops of trees and across the lights of the city. He was a man of action, a man who made quick decisions and lived with them, a person who got things done.

Without a qualm he reached for the phone and dialed a number he'd memorized and used years before. An answering machine clicked on and Jason sighed. His message was brief. "Yeah, it's me. Danvers. It's time to call in all my markers and you owe me one. A big one. I've got a job for you. I'll call back tomorrow."

His conscience twinged a bit, but he took a long swallow and felt the familiar warmth of Scotch as it burned down his throat, curled in his stomach and warmed his bloodstream.

A few hours of rest and he'd be ready to face anything. And that included exposing Adria Nash as a fraud.

Adria's head was pounding as she turned out the light. The room smelled musty and stale with the lingering odors of old cigarettes and years of filth. But the motel was cheap and anonymous. At least for now.

She fell back on the bed and closed her eyes but images of the night played like a kaleidoscope through her head. Zachary was always in the forefront, and she tried to shut him out. She needed him as a link to the family. Nothing more.

His restless energy and defiant gaze brought back memories that she'd tried to keep buried, long-ago images that she didn't want to think about. But she knew, if she was going to step forward into her future, she had to face her past. Gritting her teeth, she unlocked the doors and tried to remember Mark's face.

Mark Kennedy.

From the wrong side of the tracks.

Who had saved her from Tommy Sinclair.

To whom she'd felt forever indebted.

Her first love and her last love.

So much like Zachary Danvers.

Her throat thickened and she let out a long, tremulous breath. Despite her mother's strenuous objections, Adria had kept seeing Mark, certain that their love would conquer everything. How wrong she'd been. How young. How foolish. How naive. She'd convinced her parents to let her go to the prom with him and it was the worst mistake of her life. If she hadn't been so stubborn, if she hadn't insisted, if she'd gone with someone else, maybe that night would have turned out differently. A little sound of protest formed in her throat as she remembered.

"You can't be goin' to the prom dressed like that!" Sharon Nash had said as Adria had walked down the stairs in the silver dress that she'd bought with her own money.

Sharon clucked her tongue when she saw the hint of cleavage at the neckline. "This dress is beggin' for trouble, honey, and you'll get it with that boy—"

"Mom—" Adria cut in.

"That's right." Victor was seated in the living room, his stocking feet propped on the worn ottoman, his half glasses on the end of his nose as he read the paper. "I thought we agreed it wasn't the Christian thing to do—talkin' about people behind their backs."

Sharon's mouth compressed, but she didn't argue. Against her better judgment, she and Victor had allowed Adria to go out with Mark as long as she kept her grades up and honored her curfew. "You go wear that pretty yellow frock I made you last spring."

Adria groaned inwardly. The buttercup yellow dress had a white collar and puffed sleeves and looked like something a girl of eight would wear to church on Easter Sunday. "But—"

"If you want to go, you'll wear it. And you'll behave yourself. Otherwise people will talk."

Adria blew her bangs out of her eyes. "People will always talk, Mom."

" 'Specially when you give them reason. And you've given them enough, takin' up with Janet Kennedy's boy." Sharon fingered the gold cross hanging from the chain around her throat. "Janet's always waggin' her tail in men's faces, right in front of her own husband."

"Mark's not like that," Adria said, her heart warming at thoughts of the boy she loved. If her mother had ever guessed how far they'd gone, she'd faint dead away.

"He's no good. Just you remember that."

Adria swallowed hard but wouldn't back down. Defiantly she stood in the hallway as the old grandfather's clock ticked off the seconds. "Mark's the most decent person I know."

"Ha!" A spark of hatred flared in her mother's eyes. "Believe you me, the apple doesn't fall far from the tree. And his old man isn't much better than his wife. Cy's been pouring himself into a bottle for years. He can't even stagger into church on Sunday morning after getting stinking drunk on Saturday night. Not that I blame him, mind you, he had to put up with Janet for so many years, runnin' around and makin' him look like a fool. No wonder he can't face the congregation and Reverend Phillips."

"Sharon—" Victor cut in.

"Well, it's true and I'm not condemning the man. I, too, have a drink now and again, but not to hide from my problems. Now, if you were goin' out with someone like Steven McFarland . . ."

"I'd rather rot in hell," Adria muttered under her breath.

"We don't talk like that in this house," Sharon hissed and the scent of gin wafted through the air. "You may as well know what's what. That Kennedy boy's a hot one, he is, just like his mama. All randy and ready." Sharon frowned as if the words were distasteful. "You keep your legs together, Adria. Won't no man want to marry you, if you're givin' it away for free. We're God-fearin' people here and I won't have the townspeople whispering about my daughter because she can't keep her pants on."

"Sharon! Enough!" Victor snapped his newspaper shut and pushed himself upright.

"You don't have to worry," Adria said, feeling a wash of embarrassment climb up her cheeks.

"Well, I do, Adria. You're not my blood-kin, though, Lord knows I've loved you as much as if I'd borne you myself." She placed her work-roughened hands on Adria's shoulders and held her at arm's length. Her gaze was suddenly loving again. "But you're too beautiful for your own good, believe me. Men will always be tryin' to get into your panties. Don't you let them. Not ever. Now, I'm not tryin' to be crude, I'm just tellin' you how it is."

"You can't run my life!"

"Oh yes I can. And I will!" Sharon's eyes glittered like hard stones and her fingers dug deep into her daughter's bare arms. "You do as I say, missy. If you want to go to that prom, you'll wear the yellow dress."

"I worked for weeks to buy this one."

"Like I told you before, a fool and her money are soon parted. I'll put the tags back on it and you can take it back to the store on Monday. Now, go on . . . elsewise you can spend the night here with us. There's a John Wayne movie on television Dad's been wantin' to see . . ."

She'd let her voice trail off as she'd left the room and Adria, tears filling her eyes, ran upstairs, stripped herself of the silver sheath and reached into the closet just as the idea hit her. It was daring; she was taking a big chance, but she found her long winter coat, ripped open the lining and carefully pinned the silver dress inside.

Then, she made quick adjustments to her makeup, hoping to hide her tears. She heard his pickup approach and swallowed back her fear.

As the doorbell rang, she flew from her room, her coat wrapped over her arm. Her mother was waiting, eyeing her critically. "Be good," she said as Adria opened the door and Mark stood nervously under the porch light. With shaggy light brown hair and gold eyes and a suit that was a little too small for him, he grinned and her heart melted.

He'd given her a corsage and she'd pinned a boutonniere to his lapel and then they were off and free. And she would do anything she damn well pleased, she thought, as the truck bounced down the potholes of the gravel drive. She'd change her clothes, and she'd dance, and she'd drink from the bottle of champagne that Mark had managed to buy.

The night was everything she'd hoped for. She and Mark had talked and laughed as they'd eaten dinner at a nice restaurant in town and then, in his pickup, drank part of the bottle of champagne. At the prom, they'd danced to the music, kissed in the corners, and barely noticed anyone else. She loved him. She was sure of it. She hadn't even minded when Alice Weber had tried to gain Mark's attention.

Contrary to her mother's belief, Alice was a fast girl who bounced from boy to boy and tonight seemed interested in Mark. "Be sure to come to the river after midnight," Alice had said to them both, though her green gaze had locked with Mark's. "Jeff's got a keg. It'll be a great time."

"I don't know—" Adria said.

"We'll be there." Mark swept her into his arms and kissed her neck. "It'll be fun.".

As the music wound down, Mark held Adria close and whispered in her ear. "Let's ditch this. Everybody's already gone."

For the first time she realized that most of the couples had already disappeared.

"We'll check out the party."

"I can't," she protested.

"Why not?"

"Curfew. Mom and Dad will kill me."

"It's prom night."

"And I'm lucky I got to come with you." They walked outside and Mark slung his arm around her shoulders, shielding her from the gusts of wind and the rain that was starting to fall from the sky.

"Come on . . ." he said as he helped her into the truck.

"Mom would call the police, really." She snuggled up beside him on the bench seat.

"You could sneak out."

Her insides froze.

"Just pretend to go to bed and sneak out the window."

She swallowed hard as he poured them each another glass and clicked the rim of his to hers. "We could have fun," he said, nuzzling her neck, making her warm inside. She nearly slopped her champagne on the silver dress.

"Come on, Addie," he said, finishing his drink and letting his glass slide to the floor. He kissed her on the lips and she felt the tip of her nose tingle. "We can have a few beers, then sneak off to the woods alone. I'll get a sleeping bag." One of his hands cupped her breast. "I love you. Come with me."

She groaned inwardly. "I want to, you know I do—"

"Do you?" He looked at her and his hair fell over his eyes. His lips found hers and her heart began to knock wildly. She was lost in the smell and feel of him. "Come on, then."

He drove her home and they made out in the lane. His hands were warm and touched her everywhere. "Let me," he whispered when they were half dressed. "I love you."

"Not now. It's five minutes after my curfew."

He groaned and pushed away from her. "When, then?"

"I want it to be special," she said, feeling like a silly romantic.

"It will be."

"In the cab of a pickup?"

"Anywhere with you," he said, looking at her again. "I love you, Adria. I want to marry you, don't you know that?"

Her heart squeezed. "I want to marry you, too."

"Then we will."

"Just like that?" she said, laughing.

"As soon as you're eighteen and I get a job. After school's out."

"Oh, Mark!" She threw her arms around him and kissed him hard on the lips. She wanted so much from life, to graduate from college, to have a career, to find her real parents, but, above it all, she wanted to marry Mark Kennedy. It sounded like heaven.

"Come on, baby." he said when he finally lifted his head. "Meet me at the river. I'll wait for you." He finished the champagne, drinking straight from the bottle.

"I can't!" she whispered, changing into the yellow dress again and hiding the silver one in the lining of her coat.

"You mean you won't." Angrily, he put the truck into gear.

"I love you, Mark."

"Sure."

The bliss of the moment before shattered.

Because she was afraid of defying her parents.

He drove to the yard and she was out of the pickup like a shot, racing up the porch steps, praying that her parents were already asleep. The back door opened with a creak and she found her mother in the kitchen. Gray hair wound in rollers, her old flannel bathrobe cinched around her thick waist, she sat at the table, her Bible spread open in front of her, a neglected cup of coffee growing cold near her hand. Sharon glanced up at her daughter, then pointed at the clock. "You're late."

"I'm sorry."

"I was worried."

"I'm fine, Mom."

"Did you have a good time?"

"The best," she said, knowing that her eyes were shining, her cheeks flushed. She hurried out of the room, then nearly missed a step as she dashed up the stairs. The champagne made her mind fuzzy and she lay on the bed, the room seeming to spin. Kicking off her shoes, she closed her eyes and drifted off to sleep.

She dreamed that she was with Mark, that she'd finally agreed to let him make love to her, that they were going to be married.

She was kissing him when she heard the first scream of a siren, far away but wailing plaintively. At first the sound was part of her dream, but then she opened her eyes and the piercing squeal was louder, coming closer.

An icy knife of dread cut right to her bones.

Still groggy, she found her slippers, then hurried down the stairs and, despite the amber glow from a night-light in the hallway, nearly ran into her father who was making his way to the kitchen. Wearing only a flannel nightshirt, he listened to the keen of sirens echoing through the hills. "Sounds like trouble." He reached into the pocket of his nightshirt for a handkerchief. "Headin' west."

Toward the river! Oh, God, please, don't let it be Mark!

Her mother stepped into the kitchen and snapped on the lights. Yawning, she walked to the window and stared into the distance. "I hope it's not a fire . . ." But there were no flames visible against the dark sky.

"Or some fool hasn't drowned," her father said.

Adria couldn't stand the suspense a minute longer. She grabbed the ring of keys hanging by the back door. "I have to leave."

"Why?" Sharon asked, stiffening. "Adria, it's the middle of the night."

"It's Mark. He's at the river! I . . . I have to go!" She was already flying out the door.

"You'll do no such thing! Adria, do you hear me?"

But Adria was already down the steps. She dashed through the rain to her mother's beat-up old wagon. Jabbing the keys in the ignition, she prayed over and over again that Mark was all right. Just because she heard sirens screaming toward the river didn't mean that he was hurt . . . or in trouble.

Gravel spun beneath the balding tires of the old Plymouth as she roared down the lane and braked at the county road. The wagon shuddered and slid, then picked up speed as she floored the accelerator.

The wipers slapped away the rain and the night-darkened fields flashed by, but Adria didn't see anything but the road ahead where the twin beams of her headlights slashed across the drenched asphalt.

"Please, God, no," she whispered over and over again as if it were a litany. "Don't let him be hurt."

The lane leading to the river was littered with cars; some she recognized, others she didn't. She slowed, searching for Mark's pickup. Her heart sank to her stomach when she saw the dented yellow truck. It was empty.

"Please, please, please . . ."

Lights strobed the woods by the river, flashing angrily against the trunks and branches of the cluster of trees near the water's edge. Blue. Red. White.

Two cruisers from the sheriff's department were parked at the edge of the lane near a fire truck and ambulance. Cars and pickups lined the road, illuminating the area with their headlights and Adria's heart was in her throat. She climbed out of the station wagon as it ground to a stop. Her slippers slid on the slick grass and rain poured from the sky. Racing toward the crowd that had gathered, she watched in horror as the paramedics slammed the back doors of an ambulance shut. "Let's go," the driver yelled.

"Wait a minute, what happened?" Adria screamed, but the siren shrieked to life and the ambulance sped down the gravel road, splashing through puddles.

"Oh, God," Adria whispered, rain pummeling her head. She searched the grim faces gathered around, barely heard the disappearing scream of the siren over the rising wind and the rush of the river as it raged, swollen by spring rains.

"So much tragedy in that family," one woman said, sniffing loudly.

"His mother will never get over this . . ."

People whispered, shaking their heads, while the sheriff's deputies talked over static-riddled walkie-talkies.

"Dumb kids."

"Most of 'em never had a lick of sense. 'Specially that one."

They couldn't be talking about Mark! Her heart was pounding, her insides shaking, her teeth chattering with fear and the cold. Frantically, she searched for him. Gathered between two deputies, a group of teenagers was huddled. Blankets had been thrown over their shoulders as they stood between the trees, their teeth clicking, their faces white with fear, their fancy tuxedos and dresses ruined by the rain. Surely Mark was with them. She recognized Mark's friend, Jeff Hinson, his lips blue, his eyes swollen and red. He caught sight of her and turned his gaze to his feet. Rain and tears dripped off his nose.

"Where is he?" she asked, scanning the boys.

No. Oh, God! NO! She wouldn't believe the horror that was growing in her mind. She thought she might throw up as she ran across the wet ground.

One of the deputies was talking to the somber group. "—we'll call your folks and take you home, but I'll need to talk to each of you again, at the—"

"Where's Mark?" Adria broke in, her gaze searching each boy and girl's gaze. Her insides churned when she found herself staring into the red-rimmed eyes of Alice Weber. In the grim glare of the police lights, Alice's usually tanned skin was an ugly shade of blue, her red hair was bedraggled and wet and leaves stuck in the thick strands. Her dress clung to her, dirty and wet.

"Who are you?" one of the deputies asked.

"Adria Nash. I'm . . . I'm a friend of Mark Kennedy's. He was supposed to be here . . ."

She saw the tears raining from Alice's eyes and Jeff Hinson blinked rapidly and sniffed.

"No," Adria said, guessing that Mark had been hurt. She whipped around, stared at the lane where the ambulance had disappeared. He was going to the hospital. Dread pounded through her head.

The deputy glanced at his partner.

"What's happened to him?" she demanded.

Silence. Thunderous silence.

"I'm his girlfriend!" Adria screamed when she realized that they might not tell her the truth. She clutched the shorter man in uniform's arm. "Tell me."

"I'm sorry, miss," the deputy said and there was honest regret in his eyes.

"Sorry?" she said blankly.

The deputy's lips curled in on themselves. "We couldn't save him."

"You couldn't what—?" she said. She must've heard him wrong. Something was missing, her brain refused to understand, but the deputy's grim countenance caused her heart to nearly stop beating. This had to be some kind of horrid, ugly joke. Or a dream, that's what it was, a hellish nightmare that would go away as soon as her bedside alarm sounded. That was it. She was dreaming.

"We tried, miss," the deputy said. "But he was too far gone. He drowned while he was trying to save—"

"Drowned?" she whispered.

"I'm sorry—"

"No!" she screamed, the ground pitching beneath her feet. "No! No! No!" Desperation tore at her soul. Whirling, again she faced the road where the ambulance had raced screaming away. She saw only the anguished faces of the people who had gathered around the accident scene. "There must be some mistake. You're wrong," she said as she pushed the deputy aside and glared at Jeff who bit his lip as his chin wobbled and tears glazed his face. "Where is he? Where is he!"

"It's like the deputy said, Adria. He jumped into the river to save Alice and the undertow caught him. He was drunk and oh, Christ—"

"No!"

"It's true, Adria," Jeff said, grief wrenching his face. "Mark's dead! We tried to save him after they pulled him from the river, but he's gone!"

"Nooooo!" Her own voice sounded far away. The earth buckled. Darkness swam behind her eyes and she started to fall. In slow motion she saw the ground coming up at her and she was certain she would awaken before she hit the wet leaves and mud and her mother would tell her this was all just a horrible, horrible dream.

She didn't remember the rest. She was told later, that someone, a neighbor she thought, had carried her to one of the cruisers and two deputies had driven her home. She woke up in her own bed, teeth chattering, fear tearing at her and her mother's stern visage ever present. A weight pulled her down and she felt as if she were sinking, deeper and deeper into a black abyss that had no bottom. Though her parents, and friends, even preacher Phillips talked to her, speaking of God's wisdom, the power of faith, that everything in life was according to some greater plan, Adria wrapped herself in her grief and wouldn't listen.

Mark was gone.

Forever.

Numb, she attended the funeral in a fog, barely remembering the snow melting on the ground or the plain pine casket being lowered into the dark earth. People cried and whispered, Mark's mother sobbed and wailed but Adria could hardly recall how she'd gotten through the ordeal. She managed to speak and move around but her mind was disengaged and she seemed to be watching everything, herself included, from a distance.

When she returned home that day, her mother told her it was time to quit moping around.

"You can't change things, Adria," Sharon said, brushing the snow from the shoulder of her wool coat and trying to sound calm, though Adria as she'd begun to surface from her grief had noticed her new prescription for tranquilizers in the medicine cabinet downstairs. "You have to learn to accept God's will." Sharon hung her coat in the hall closet.

"Don't talk to me about God's will," Adria said with tears streaming from her eyes. "God didn't want Mark to die!"

"It's useless to argue about it. The Lord works in mysterious ways."

"That's bullshit, Ma! God doesn't put people on this earth just to kill them off."

"Don't use that kind of language in this house! And don't tell me about God's ways. We can't begin to understand—"

"Of course we can't!" Adria said, sobbing. "Because it doesn't make any sense. And I'm not going to believe in a God that would kill someone for trying to save someone else's life! Jesus, Ma, listen to you—Oh!"

With a resounding smack, her mother struck her, slapping her so hard her head spun. "Don't you *ever* speak to me like this again! You will worship God and His son and you will never take Their names in vain! God brought you to me, Adria, and He could take you away, just like that!" She snapped her fingers in front of her twisted, angry face.

"Like He took Mark?" Adria cried.

"Yes, like Mark."

"Then who needs God?"

Sharon's color was high. "We all need the good Lord, baby. You more than ever. If you would only get down on your knees and pray for that poor boy's soul—"

"Never!" Adria said, standing firm, defying her mother to strike her. "I'll never pray again."

All the compassion in her mother's eyes fled. "Then you'll be punished."

"I already am! Don't you see! Mark's dead, Ma, *dead!* He'll never come back. Your precious God stole him from me."

Sharon's mouth pinched into a tiny knot of fury. "You're grounded, Adria. For two weeks and if you don't repent, then it'll be two weeks longer."

"I'm not going to repent, Mother. I haven't sinned."

"You don't call lying a sin?"

"Who lied, Mom? Huh? How about all the lies you made up about me? What about keeping me in the dark about my real mother?"

"I'm your real mother."

"Why won't you tell me about her!"

Hysterical, Adria ran up the stairs to her room. She slammed the door shut and flung herself on her bed. Sobbing bitterly into her pillow, she thought about running away. But why? She couldn't run away with Mark. He was gone. And he wasn't coming back. She'd never see him again. Never marry him, never bear his children. Great wracking sobs convulsed in her body and she squeezed her eyes shut against the pain. In her mind's eye, she saw Mark's face, handsome and brooding and she wondered if he'd still be alive if she'd gone with him to the river, if she'd chanced her parents wrath and met him by the water's edge, if, as he wanted so desperately, she'd made love to him.

She'd never know, but what she was certain of was that she could never let herself love so freely again. It hurt too much. With love came doubts, with love came fear, with love came guilt and with love came pain. Horrid, sorrowful, soul-wrenching pain that might never go away.

She'd never know what would have happened if she'd gone with Mark, just like she didn't know who she really was. Biting her lip in determination, she decided that no matter what, she'd find out her true identity.

Now that Mark was gone, what else was left?

From that night on, she'd never faltered in her quest. She'd written letters, met with lawyers, people from government agencies and kept a diary, trying vainly to find Virginia Watson. Only now, after her father's death, did she have an inkling as to who she was.

And she was going to go through hell and back trying to find out if, as her father insisted, she was really London Danvers.

9

Adria woke up to the squeal of hydraulic brakes and the thrum of a huge engine as a truck idled in the parking lot. With a groan she rolled out of the bed and surveyed her shabby surroundings. It certainly wasn't the Ritz, or the Benson, or the Hotel Danvers, for that matter. But it would have to do.

The pipes were rusty, the drain of the tub stained, but she closed her eyes to the flaws of the Riverview and quickly showered under tepid water. She towel-dried her hair, tamed it by snapping a rubber band around a ponytail, and ignored her makeup bag. She didn't need to look glamorous when she planned to spend the day in the library, the offices of the *Oregonian,* the historical society, and the Portland Police Bureau if need be. But as she glanced in the mirror, she remembered the family portrait and her heart began to thud. All night long she'd tossed and turned, thinking of the portrait and of Zach as he'd stared so intensely at Katherine, as if he wanted her approval.

"Dysfunctional," she told herself. "The whole damned family. And you want to be a part of it. Stupid, stupid girl."

With an eye on the silk dress in its plastic casing, she yanked on a sweatshirt, a pair of worn jeans, and slipped into ancient Reebok running shoes. She grabbed an oversized purse that doubled as a briefcase and was out the door.

Reading an old city map, she wheeled through the drive-in window of a McDonald's and while waiting for her coffee, reacquainted herself with Portland.

Basically the city was cleaved by the river and the east side spread away from the banks of the Willamette in a careful grid that was infrequently interspersed with winding streets or slashed by a freeway. The west side, however, was more difficult. Though the streets ran north-south and east-west, they were older, more narrow, and tended to follow the contour of the Willamette River, or meander through the hills that rose steeply from the water's shore.

She paid for the coffee, took a sip and drove steadily westward, through the low-rising office buildings and shops toward the river and the twin spires of the Convention Center. Smiling to herself, she wondered what her half-brothers and -sister were doing.

At that thought, she glanced in the mirror. Worried blue eyes stared back at her. Was she really London Danvers, or was this all a fierce joke that her father had played upon her? Well, it was too late to start second-guessing herself. For now, she was London Danvers and Jason, Nelson, Trisha, and even Zachary were not only her enemies, but her closest blood kin.

Tires singing on the metal grid, her Nova sped across the Hawthorne Bridge. Unfortunately, she had to drive downtown again, close to the Hotel Danvers and the building only three blocks down the street where the offices of Danvers International were housed.

She parked her car in a corner lot, finished the coffee and grabbed her bag. Though the sun was making a valiant effort to warm the wet streets, the wind was cold as it blew down the Columbia River Gorge, rolled across the Willamette and whistled through the narrow streets of the city.

She hurried up the steps to the library doors and felt a chill against the back of her neck, as if someone were watching her. "You're just being paranoid," she told herself, but couldn't shake the feeling.

"Something happened last night at the grand opening." Eunice Danvers Smythe had the uncanny ability to read Nelson like a book. He was edgy and restless and chewed at the corner of his thumbnail. Dressed in a sloppy T-shirt and jeans that had seen better days, he hadn't shaved or bothered to comb his unruly blond hair and his lips were pinched. "Something went wrong," she guessed again, shooing her Persian cat off one of the chairs.

"You could say that." Nelson was slouched in a chair across the table from her in the morning room of her home in Lake Oswego. He'd called from his condo and been on her doorstep in less than the fifteen minutes it took to make the drive within the speed limit.

"What is it?"

"Another imposter." Nelson ignored the newspaper sitting next to his plate.

"London?"

"So she claims."

Sighing, Eunice sipped from her coffee cup and stared past Nelson and through the bay window over his shoulder. The lake, reflecting the clouds that had moved quickly in front the west, was a desolate steely gray. A rough winter wind caused a few white caps to surface. On the opposite shore, like bony fingers, empty boat slips jutted into the cold water.

"She's a fake," Eunice surmised.

"Of course she's a fake, but she's trouble just the same. When the press gets wind of this, the shit's really going to hit the fan. It'll start all over again . . . the speculation and dredging up of the kidnapping. Reporters, photographers . . . just like before." He plowed both hands through his thick blond hair.

"It's always going to be a problem," Eunice said with a little smile that she reserved for her children. "But it's something you have to deal with. And it might help you. If you're really interested in running for mayor someday—"

"Governor."

"Governor." She clucked her tongue and shook her head. "My, my, but aren't we ambitious?" She didn't mean to sound scathing, just concerned.

His eyes crinkled a bit at the corners, but he wasn't laughing. "I suppose *we* are. We'd both go through hell and back to get what we wanted, wouldn't we?"

She ignored that little dig. "You could use the adverse publicity to your advantage, if you're smart."

"How?"

"Welcome her with open arms," she said and Nelson stared at her as if she'd suddenly lost her mind. "I'm serious, Nelson, think about it. You, defender of the downtrodden, you, seeker of truth, you the one-day politician, listen to her story, try to help her and then . . . well, when she's proved a fraud . . . you don't even denounce her, not really, just explain to the press that she was an opportunist."

"You're not serious."

"Something to think about." She added cream to her coffee—not too much as she prided herself for having the body of a thirty-year old—and watched the clouds swirl to the surface. "Come on now," she encouraged, blowing across her cup before she took a sip. "Tell me about her."

Cradling the warm porcelain between her fingers, Eunice waited. Nelson would tell her everything. He always did. It was his way of trying to be special to her. After her divorce from Witt, all the children suffered and she felt an incredible sense of guilt for their pain. She'd never wanted to hurt the children—they were her most precious possessions. Never would she intentionally wound any of them. It had been Witt she had hoped to cripple, but he seemed to have survived the divorce, even thrived as a businessman and had taken that slut of a young girl for his second wife. Suddenly her special blend of French roast seemed to curdle in her stomach.

Nelson scraped his chair back and stood near the windows. Throwing out a hip, he gazed through the glass. Though he'd called her, begged to come by and unburden himself, she sensed that he regretted his decision to open up to her. He'd always been volatile—not so openly hostile as Zach had been—but energized by a pent-up anger just under the surface, a blasting cap primed to explode. She wondered if he even had a clue about how he'd been conceived, but held her tongue.

Nelson was the child who should never have been born. She and Witt were estranged when she'd gotten pregnant. Witt had finally found out about her affair with Anthony Polidori and all hell had broken loose.

"You dirty, wop-fucking cunt!" Witt had roared when he'd discovered the truth. He'd sensed that Anthony had been in his house, his room, his bed, though Anthony had slipped away minutes before.

Witt had slapped her so hard her head had snapped back on her neck and she'd stumbled to fall back on her bed. He was on her in an instant, pinning her to the mattress with his enormous bulk. "How could you?" he'd yelled, straddling her and crushing her face between his meaty hands. She was a big woman, a strong woman, but no match for him. "You lying, cheating bitch, how could you?"

She was crying, tears streaming down her cheeks and through his fingers and she knew that he might kill her. His palms squashed her cheeks and she stared up at eyes bright with rage and hatred. Saliva collected in the corners of his mouth and his lips were pulled into a snarl of malice.

"I . . . It just happened," she choked out.

"Like hell! You're my *wife*, Eunice, my *wife!* The wife of Witt Danvers. Do you know what that means?" He gave her head a little shake and she mewed a protest. She could barely breathe. "You may not like me—"

"I detest you!" she spat.

"So you go crawling to Polidori. Taking off your panties and spreading your legs and screwing his brains out. Why? To get back at me?"

"Yes!" she screamed, not daring to utter that she loved Anthony as she'd never loved Witt and the hands around her face pushed harder. Pain jolted through her brain.

"You bitch! You lying, Jezebel of a bitch!"

"At least he's a man, Witt! He knows how to satisfy a woman!"

He roared back and this time the hand that came down against her cheek landed so hard she heard bones crack. A moan escaped her throat.

"A man, eh?" Witt thundered. "I'll show you a man."

She'd shivered as he'd held her down with one hand and undid his belt with the other. He'd never beaten her before, but now she was certain he was going to flay her until her skin was raw. Swallowing all of her pride, she whispered, "Don't Witt . . . please . . ."

"You deserve it."

"No." She got one hand free and held it up to protect her face. "Don't—"

He hesitated, his shirt undone, his breathing hard and fast.

"You're a whore, Eunice."

"No—"

"And you deserve to be treated like one."

Still straddling her, he took her hand and guided it to his fly. "Undo it."

"No, I—" She withdrew her hand and then held back a little scream as she saw his muscles flex beneath his shirt. He slid his leather belt out of the loops and for a second she saw the flash of a silver buckle—a running horse with sharp little hooves, made of metal that could cut and scar. Oh, God. Pain jolted through her body. She bit her lip to keep from crying out.

"Take the zipper down."

"Witt, no—"

"Just do it, Eunice. You're still my wife."

"Please, Witt, don't make me do this," she whispered and watched as his nostrils flared and his eyes bulged. How had they ever come to this? How had she ever thought she loved him?

"Now!"

Her hands were shaking and she felt revulsion when she noticed the bulge beneath his fly. He was enjoying torturing her

and had become hard, after months of impotence, months of
silent fury. He'd blamed the business, then her and now he was
wreaking his vengeance.

The zipper slid down with a sickening hiss.

"You know what to do. Do for me what you do for Polidori.
Show me what it takes to make that filthy bastard come."

"Witt, no, I don't want—" He grabbed her by her hair and his
eyes glowed with evil rancor. Thick fingers knotted in her French
braid as it fell loose.

"We're going to do what I want, Eunice, and we're going to do
it all night long. I'm going to fuck you until I can't stand the sight
of you. Over and over again. You're going to make me feel good,
Eunice, no matter what it takes, no matter how it hurts." The
fingers pulled hard on her hair. "And when I'm finished with
you, you'll never run back to that Italian bastard again!"

Sick to her stomach, she had closed her eyes and given herself
up to her husband and all his perversity.

"Mom?" Nelson's voice broke into her painful reverie.

Startled, she cleared her throat and quickly reached for her
napkin, to dab at her eyes.

Nelson was staring at her. Her baby. The last of her children.
The boy conceived during that night of hell. Never once had
there been any question of Nelson's paternity. Even now, staring
at her, his carved features set with worry, he was the spitting
image of his father as a young man, a man Eunice had thought
she'd loved, a man she could barely remember. Witt Danvers
with all his energy, his ambitions, his vision for Portland had
seemed the perfect match. Though she wasn't a dainty woman,
he hadn't minded, probably because she was from the "right"
family, had a small fortune of her own and he felt that she would
help and support him.

"It will be ours one day," he'd said, smiling from a penthouse
apartment and looking down at the city. "Every block will have
a building with the Danvers name!" She'd believed in him then,
trusted him. Until the other women. And the fact that after two
children his sex drive at home had dwindled.

Anthony had been the balm for her ego and she'd stupidly fallen in love with him.

"Are you all right?" Nelson asked, snapping her back to the present. His handsome face was etched in concern, his blond brows beetling to form one line. So like Witt. Poor child. Despite the rough, humiliating way Nelson had been conceived, Eunice had loved him, as she'd loved all her children.

"I'm fine," she lied, forcing a smile. As she stared up at her son now, she thought all the agony and humiliation was worth it. Clearing her throat, she took her boy's hand. "Now, tell me what you know about this girl—the one who claims she's London."

"There's not much to say. No one knows anything, except what we heard last night."

Eunice stirred her coffee as Nelson unburdened himself and she heard the sketchy details of the woman pretending to be London Danvers. Nelson was worried, but that was nothing new; he'd been born worried. As a child he'd had a wild imagination, dreamed of fantasy worlds and as an adult he was always trying to prove himself—as if he silently knew that he hadn't been wanted, that he'd been created during an act of violence. His job with the public defender's office was just to show the populace that although he had been born with a silver spoon wedged firmly between his Danvers gums, he still cared about the little people.

She would help him of course—as she would help all her children. To make up for the years when she hadn't been there, when she'd been banished to the role of unfit mother and Jezebel. Witt's power and money had seen that she had been forced to watch from the outside as he molded her children into little carbon copies of himself.

Of course it hadn't worked. Her offspring were too strong-willed on one hand, and too weak on the other. Jason was the most like Witt in personality and he, too, seemed to care little about anything other than the Danvers name, the Danvers money and the Danvers corporation and Trisha would never really be her own woman. Witt had taken care of that a long time ago. Zach . . . She smiled as she thought of her second son. He was special. He'd been a thorn in Witt's side from the minute he was born and Eunice had reveled in her son's rebellious nature. Nelson was more of a conformist, but he'd only gone along with Witt for his own purposes.

The divorce had been ugly, most of it replayed in the newspapers. Eunice was portrayed as a bored, rich woman who had partaken of numerous affairs, including sleeping with her husband's sworn enemy. She hadn't had the energy or the resources to fight Witt's power, so she'd agreed to a nice little settlement and left her children with their beast of a father. Even now, as she thought about how Witt had manipulated her into losing her darlings, her teeth clenched in silent rage. She should have known better than to have pushed him so far, she should have sacrificed herself and lived with his mood swings and impotence and rage, so that she would never be separated from the children, but she'd been cowardly and accepted his token alimony—blood money—and left.

Her life had never been complete. Even when she'd remarried, she'd been restless and there hadn't been a night she hadn't gone to bed feeling guilty as sin and lonely for the chubby little arms and adoring eyes of her babies.

As for her affair with Polidori it had cooled and cracked as quickly as hot glass dipped in ice water once Witt got wind of the situation. She often wondered if Anthony had used her. If he'd seduced her for the express purpose of tormenting Witt. She blinked rapidly and once again fought the threat of hot tears.

"You're sure you're all right?" Nelson said, touching her lightly on the shoulder.

"Right as rain," she replied, refusing to break down. "Now, come on. Surely we can find out more about this imposter who's posing as London."

Adria zipped her huge purse shut, then closed her eyes and rotated her head, straightening the kink that had tightened between her shoulder blades. She'd learned a lot about the history of the Danvers family. They were powerful and influential and had been for over a hundred years. Some of the scandals had been reported to the press, others had only been hinted at, but she felt as if she'd made progress. She had names and dates and more information than she'd ever found in Montana.

She'd started her search in 1974 at the time of the kidnapping and worked backward and forward, learning as much as she could. She wasn't finished; the Danvers name littered the newspapers before and since the kidnapping, but she needed a break. Gathering her papers, she left her table by the window on the second floor.

Outside, the sun had won the weather battle. Beams reflected off the puddles on the sidewalk and the breeze had died. A few clouds drifted over the sky, but the day, for winter in the Pacific Northwest, was mild. She decided to walk south to the Galleria, an old department store that had been converted to several stories of shops.

She found a café on the first floor.

She'd just picked up the menu, when she spied Zachary and her breath caught at the base of her throat. Without a word or an invitation, Zachary picked up the chair opposite hers, turned it around, set it back down and straddled it.

In the few hours they'd been apart, she'd forgotten how imposing he was. Dressed down in faded Levi's, flannel shirt, and buckskin jacket, he was formidable nonetheless. He hadn't bothered to shave and his features bordered on harsh. He seemed distinctly displeased as he folded his arms over the back of the chair and glared at her.

"You lied to me."

"Did I?" she asked as she ignored the sexy slope of his jaw.

"Big time. You didn't stay at the Benson."

"Is that a crime?"

"I really don't give a damn where you stay, but the rest of the family seems to think it's important."

"Then I must worry them."

"Appears so," he drawled, his gray eyes cloudy.

"What about you? If you don't 'give a damn,' then why are you here?"

"I got elected."

She wasn't buying it. She didn't think that Zachary was the kind of man who let anyone talk him into doing something he opposed.

"How did you find me?"

"It wasn't hard."

She had to hold onto her temper. "You followed me."

He shrugged and the tense little smile that touched the corners of his mouth infuriated her.

"How?"

"Doesn't matter. I'm here to extend you an invitation."

She eyed him suspiciously, but a waitress, dressed in a white blouse, black skirt, and bow tie appeared to take their order and the conversation lagged for a few minutes.

"You weren't invited here," she told him once the waitress turned her attention to the next table.

"Just like you weren't invited last night."

"Why are you following me?"

"You make some members of the family nervous."

"You—do I make you nervous?"

He hesitated and stared at her with such scrutiny that she wanted to squirm out of his range of vision. Cold, assessing gray eyes searched her face. "You bother me," he admitted, tilting his head back, "but you don't worry me."

"You still don't believe me."

"You don't believe it yourself, not really."

There was just no winning this argument. Zach Danvers was obviously like a terrier with a bone and he believed what was convenient. Fine, she told herself, let him think what he wants, but the cynical disbelief in his eyes made her uncomfortable. She took a sip from her water glass and decided she should try to make some peace with this man. He was her only link to the family.

"You said something about an invitation," Adria reminded him as she buttered a slice of sourdough bread.

"The family thinks it would be a good idea if you would stay in the Hotel Danvers."

She should have expected as much, but she hadn't. "So it's easier for them to spy on me."

"Probably."

"Well, you can tell *the family* to go to hell."

One side of his mouth lifted. "Already have."

"Look, Zach. I don't like being manipulated, I hate being followed, and I detest the feeling that Big Brother is watching me." She broke off a piece of bread and chewed it.

"You came looking for us, remember?"

That much was true. With a sigh, she blew her bangs out of her eyes. She shouldn't have let her temper get the better of her. She was tired from too little sleep on a sagging mattress, grumpy from lack of food, and her nerves were strung tight as piano wires at the thought of facing the Danvers family, *her* family again.

"I just want you to help me find the truth."

"I know the truth," he said.

"If you're so sure, why are you following me?"

Zach studied her another long minute. "I think you're going to stir up a hornet's nest the likes of which you've never seen before and I think you'll regret it."

"My mistake to make."

"I'm just warning you."

"About what?" She leaned her elbows on the table and pushed her face closer to his. "I've had months to think this through, Zachary. I had doubts, of course I did, but I can't spend the rest of my life wondering who I am."

"What if you find out you're not London?"

Her smile was slow and sexy and caused Zach's diaphragm to

cram hard against his lungs. "I believe in crossing bridges when I come to them."

The waitress brought their orders and Adria dived into her crab Louis with a vengeance.

"Jason thought you might be more comfortable at a suite in the hotel." Zach took a bite of his sandwich.

"Concerned for my health and safety is he?" she mocked.

Zach lifted a shoulder.

"Tell him 'thanks' but 'no thanks.' The cost's a little too high."

"The room is gratis."

"I wasn't talking about money." Her eyes met his for an instant and again Zach felt an unwanted tug on his gut. She was getting to him, with her clear blue eyes, sexy smile, and quick wit. He didn't say another word until they were finished with their meal and he insisted on paying. She argued, of course, but he wouldn't take no for an answer and in the end, she gave up, deciding that she'd forgo the small battles for the larger ones to come, or so she'd said.

The streets were crawling with people by the time they started walking back to the library. Cars, trucks, bicycles, and pedestrians clogged the alleys and sidewalks. Adria yanked the rubber band holding her hair away from her face and shook the loose curls free. Zach's mouth went dry as the wild blue-black strands shimmered in the sunlight. She looked so damned much like Kat it was eerie.

"So what was it that caused the rift between you and your father?" she asked as she shifted her shoulder bag from one arm to the other.

"I was a pain in the neck."

She let out a little laugh. "That, I believe."

"Always getting into trouble with the law."

"Oh."

"Witt didn't approve. He wanted all of us to graduate at the top of our class from an Ivy League school . . . or if we couldn't get in, then Reed College would do since it's kind of a family tradition . . . afterward we were to finish law school and join a prestigious firm."

"You're a lawyer?" She knew better, of course, but wanted to see his response.

"Not hardly," he said with a distasteful snort.

"But you just said—"

"I didn't really count, though, remember?" His face was set in a hard expression she was beginning to recognize, though he didn't look contrite, nor did he seem to want to elicit her sympathy. His eyes were hard, his chin thrust forward as if he were about to prove his worth.

But to whom?

"Just what is it you do, when you're not renovating hotels?"

"Come on, Adria, don't play stupid. It doesn't wash. You already know that I'm a builder; I spent a lot of years remodeling houses, then ended up fixing the ranch. I guess I just stayed on."

"The family's ranch?"

He shot her a look. "Yep."

"You run it, now?"

"You already know this."

"What about building?"

"Still have a construction company. In Bend."

"A jack-of-all-trades?"

"I do what I have to." They reached the park surrounding the library. Cocking his head toward the building, he asked, "So did you dig up all the dirt on the family?"

"Not yet, but I will."

"And then you'll know if you're really London."

"I hope so."

His lips compressed. "I can save you a whole lot of time and money and effort: you're not."

A breeze feathered through her hair. "How can you be so sure?"

"Practice," he said.

She lifted a finely arched brow in a gesture that mimicked his stepmother's so perfectly that his stomach squeezed. "So are you going to follow me around for the rest of my life?"

"I'm just waiting for an answer."

"An answer?" she asked, squinting a little as the sun was behind his shoulder.

"That's right. What's it going to be, Adria?" he asked, unable to camouflage the contempt in his voice. "Are you content to stay in that dump on Eighty-second or are you going to gamble and move into a higher rent district and take the all-expense-paid suite at the Hotel Danvers?"

10

He wasn't cut out to be a detective. Zach shoved his hands deep into his pockets and watched Adria run up the steps to the library. Though she hadn't agreed to take the family's offer of a free room at the hotel, Zach figured it was only a matter of time before she caved in and gladly accepted the first of what would be a string of gifts—bribes, really—to get rid of her. He'd thought, well, at least he'd hoped that she was smarter and had more integrity than that.

Of course she hadn't. She was a gold digger, for Christ's sake—a gold digger who looked a helluva lot like his dead stepmother.

Clouds were beginning to gather again when he jogged back to the street where he'd left his Jeep. He had more important things to do than chase after Adria Nash and yet a part of him was reluctant to leave her. She was an interesting creature—sly and beautiful, shrewd and fascinating. He wondered just how much like Kat she was. For an instant he imagined what she would feel like writhing beneath him in bed.

"Stop it!" He was as bad as the rest of the family. Slamming the door on those dangerous thoughts, he drove toward the river, pulled into the parking garage under the hotel and told himself that he'd stay a couple more days. That was all. Just until things with Adria were settled. It shouldn't take long. A little game of cat and mouse, money offered and declined until the family reached a number she liked or until someone dug up the dirt on her and threatened to expose her for a fraud.

Either way, the end result would be the same. She'd be gone.

Lisa Jackson

He sat in the Jeep for a second and listened to the engine tick as it cooled. Sightlessly he stared into the middle distance but was unaware of other cars or people emerging from the elevator. Adria was getting to him and he didn't like a woman—any woman—starting to turn his thinking around.

Snapping back to the present, he hoisted his bag from the back of the Jeep, then walked to the service elevator and rode to the main lobby. Three clerks in green jackets were working at computer terminals at the front desk and bellboys ducked in and out the front door. Several people loitered in the lobby and one woman was angrily arguing with a clerk about the telephone charges on her bill. Though the Hotel Danvers had passed final inspection and was up and running, there were a few bugs left to iron out. Cable television trouble on the upper three floors, plumbing leaks in the basement, faulty locks on the doors on the sixth floor, a chlorine problem with the pool, and a touchy stove in the kitchen were just a few of the minor headaches that his crew was fine tuning.

He found Frank Gillette in the kitchen, with one of the ovens pulled away from the wall. A cigarette hung out of the corner of his mouth as he frowned against the curling smoke and checked the wiring. Glancing up, he spied Zach. "Whatever we paid for this, it was too damned much."

"You ordered it."

"So I made a mistake," Frank grumbled. "Give me a minute—" He twisted to look over his shoulder, the cigarette clamped between his teeth. "Okay, Casey, let's give this bitch some juice!"

Within seconds there was a whir and more lights in the kitchen blinked on. Frank stood and, with Zach's help, shouldered the oven back into place. "It's a heavy bastard," he said. "Fire it up!" he told the cook, who was a thin Chinese man with a small goatee. With a skeptical glance at Frank, the cook did as he was told. The lights on the face of the oven winked on and when the cook switched on the gas, after a series of clicks and a whoosh, blue flames eagerly licked upward. "Son of a bitch. Looks like it's fixed," Frank said. "Sometimes I amaze even myself." He took a long drag on his cigarette.

"Why don't you tell me everything else that's gone wrong?" Zach asked.

"Got a few hours?"

"All the time in the world," Zach said as they walked out of the kitchen, along a short hallway that opened to a small office located behind the lobby desk. "Good," Frank said in a cloud of smoke. "Let's start with the fucking security system—"

Oswald Sweeny prided himself in being everything Jason Danvers was not—well almost everything. Short, with a thickening waist, and dark eyes that could see nearly a hundred-and-eighty degrees without moving, Oswald had spent a decade with army intelligence before being dishonorably discharged over a small matter of beating up an enlisted man who'd made the mistake of trying to pick him up. Oswald had called the kid a fucking homo and knocked out his two front teeth and the kid had taken offense. He'd had enough balls to file charges against Oswald. In the end, they were both kicked out of the service.

Which was fine with Oswald. Just as it was fine that he wasn't a stuffed shirt like Danvers. They were as opposite as two men could be.

Jason was rich, Oswald was always sweating out his next paycheck. Jason was educated, Oswald thought academics were for idiots. Jason was married and kept a mistress. Oswald took his pleasure in thirty-dollar streetwalkers and never asked their names.

His only vices were unfiltered cigarettes, cheap women, and fast horses. Sometimes, unfortunately, the women were faster than the nags he picked.

Despite their differences, however, Oswald and Jason had a common trait; they both were willing to do whatever it took to get what they wanted.

Right now, Jason wanted the dirt on some woman named
Adria Nash, a woman who claimed she was London Danvers and
Jason was willing to spare no expense. It seemed that this woman
was the spittin' image of his stepmother—a beautiful woman
who managed to kill herself with booze and pills. Few people
understood the reason Katherine LaRouche Danvers decided to
end it all; Sweeny was one of the privileged who knew that
particular piece of information. He should write a book. He could
make a fucking fortune in a "tell-all" about the Danvers family.

"I don't care what it takes," Jason said as he paced restlessly
on the cracked linoleum in Oswald's hole-in-the-wall of an office. The single room contained a few army-surplus file cabinets,
an answering machine hooked up to a phone he never picked
up, a desk in which every drawer stuck, and two chairs.

Oswald didn't trust anyone; he did his own books and typed his
own letters. He paid his rent month to month for the little cubicle
overlooking Stark Street—in case he had to blow town quick. No
need to be tied into a yearly lease. Oswald needed to keep mobile
and though this old concrete building didn't have an uptown
address, it served his needs just fine. He kept his money in a
safe-deposit box and figured he had nearly twenty thousand
tucked away. Not a fortune, but a nice little nest egg. He squashed
out the stub of his cigarette in an overflowing ashtray.

"Find out everything you can about her and here"—Jason
snapped open his leather briefcase and withdrew a videotape—"
this is a copy of her 'proof,' which is some guy who's supposed
to be her father making a tear-jerking confession that he thinks
she could be Witt Danvers's long-lost daughter. It's schmaltzy
enough to turn your stomach."

"You think she's in this alone?"

"Hell, I don't know." Jason slid the tape across the desk. "All
I know is she's trouble. If she runs to the press with this, it could
hang up probate another couple of years."

"You give a copy to the police?"

Jason frowned. "Not yet. Too many leaks in the department."

So Danvers was trying to avoid the press. Oswald fingered the black plastic case holding the videotape: "Couldn't you get Watson to handle this?" Oswald needled and was rewarded with a look that would melt steel. Bob Watson was the private investigator sometimes used by Danvers International. Bob wore three-piece suits and eighty-dollar ties and had more secretaries and flunkies than Kellogg's had cornflakes.

"You know why I want you."

Oswald knew all right. He was willing to push the limits of the law, go a little further than anyone else, including Watson. Oswald Sweeny was only called in when Jason was desperate and needed more than a simple surveillance job.

"I want you to follow Ms. Nash. Find out if she's working alone or if she has any accomplices. Also, dig up everything you can about her. She says she's from some hick town in Montana, Belamy, I believe, and that uncle of hers, Ezra, practiced law in Bozeman. See what you can find on him and everyone else in the family."

"How much do you want?" Sweeny asked, resisting the urge to rub his hands together in anticipation of his payment.

"Everything. All the dirt on this woman, enough so we can discredit her and force her out of town. Everyone has a secret or a weakness. Just find out what hers is. I'll handle the rest."

Sweeny couldn't help but smile as he flipped the cassette over and studied it. He enjoyed seeing Danvers sweat and right now Jason Danvers seemed more desperate than ever. Good news for Oswald Sweeny. "Any chance there's some truth to this?" He tapped the case with a nicotine-stained finger.

"Of course not. But she worries me. She's working this differently from anyone else." With a scathing look at the cracked seat, Jason settled into the single worn chair for visitors and clients. "Instead of making harsh demands, threatening to go to the police and the press, she's playing it cool. Too cool." He tented his hands and stared at Sweeny, but the detective guessed his mind was miles away. With Adria Nash.

"She still wants to score. She's just in it for more bucks," Oswald said.

Jason seemed to snap back to the present. His lips pinched together. "It's up to you to prove it. Unfortunately, this may take some time."

Sweeny grinned, showing off a gap between his yellowed front teeth. "You're in luck. I got nothing pressing." He grabbed a legal pad from under the desk and a pencil that had been chewed repeatedly, then plopped a recorder onto the desk, as a backup. "Let's go over it. From the top. Your old man, he hired a PI when London was kidnapped."

"Phelps—but he came up with nothing. He was supposed to be the best and he couldn't find anything. You can talk to him if you want, but he's retired. Lives with his daughter up in Tacoma."

"I'll talk to him and put a tail on Ms. Nash," Oswald said. Though he didn't like the idea of having someone else follow her, he couldn't be two places at once and he felt he should shag out to Montana, find out what he could about her while she was away from her hometown. He had a couple of men he could trust to stick to her like glue and report back to him.

"I just don't want any fuck-ups."

"There won't be." Sweeny smelled money and he wasn't about to let it slip between his fingers.

As Jason gave him the particulars, Sweeny scribbled the information and decided if nothing else, this Adria Nash had balls. Hard to find on a woman.

Two hours later, Jason stood, brushed a little lint off the sleeve of his jacket and left Sweeny with a retainer of three thousand dollars. Oswald stuffed the check into his shirt pocket and moved to the window, tipping the blinds. He watched Jason, bareheaded in the rain, slide into the expensive interior of his Jaguar before firing the engine and nosing the sleek car into traffic.

Bastard. Filthy rich bastard.

Noticing the dead insects and cobwebs on the window ledge, he frowned and let the blind snap back to cover the brittle little carcasses. Yes, this place was a dump, but it suited him just fine. He reached into a lower drawer of his desk, pulled out a bottle of Jack Daniel's and screwed off the cap. Wiping the greasy cuff of his jacket over the top of the bottle, he grunted, then took a slug. The whiskey hit the back of his throat and seared all the way to his belly.

He loved it when Jason Danvers came crawling to him. It wasn't just the money, but the satisfaction of having that rich, arrogant son of a bitch begging for his services. He'd seen the disdain in Jason's eyes as his gaze traveled over the bleak furnishings, the unswept floors, the full ashtrays, and the grimy window. Oswald remembered the flare of Jason's aristocratic nose at the smells of sweat and stale cigarette smoke.

Chuckling to himself, Oswald slid a Camel from the pack he kept on the desk and lit up. Still holding the cigarette in the corner of his mouth, he took another tug on the bottle. Yep, things were definitely looking up.

Zach hung up the phone in his suite and swore under his breath. Despite assurances from Manny the ranch foreman that everything was running smoothly and that his presence wasn't needed, Zach felt restless and short-tempered. All because of that damned woman.

He'd tried to reach Jason and tell him to do his own legwork, but he'd been informed by a secretary with no inflection that Mr. Danvers was in a meeting and would be unavailable all day. She assured Zach that Mr. Danvers would get back to him.

The phone rang and he snatched up the receiver.

Adria's voice drifted like smoke over the wires. "You said you wanted an answer."

"Right."

"I've decided to accept the Danvers hospitality."

His hand clenched tighter over the receiver and he felt a shot of disappointment, though he'd known this was the way things would turn out. She'd take the handouts, one by one, until she had what she wanted, or a neat little compromise thereof.

Zach checked his watch. "Meet me here at six."

She hung up and Zach told himself it didn't matter what she did. So she was taking a room in the hotel. Why not? He wondered what she'd discovered in the library, checking old newspaper clippings and magazine articles about the family. While Witt was alive, he managed to keep most of the Danvers secrets locked tightly away from the press. After the old man's death, Jason had taken over that responsibility. But Adria would dig deep, she wouldn't be content to just scratch the surface; she was too damned thorough.

So how had she been fooled into thinking she was London? Or was that all an act? There was a chance, and a damned good one, that she was lying through her beautiful teeth.

They must really be worried, Adria thought as Zach unlocked the door to the suite on the top floor of the hotel. With a sitting room complete with a fireplace, two bedrooms, two baths, tub, French doors opening onto a flagstone veranda, and view of the city that stretched for miles, the suite was spacious and decorated in hues of soft peach and beige. The furniture looked to be antique, though Adria guessed the highboy, Queen Anne canopied bed, tea table, and Chippendale side chairs were all modern imitations of authentic pieces. The carpet was a thick ivory, the bar stocked with the best labels and a vase filled with pink roses rested on a glass topped coffee table.

"Is this a bribe?" she asked as Zach hung her garment bag in one of the closets.

He lifted a shoulder. "Call it anything you want."

She'd only agreed to stay in the hotel as a gesture of good faith. Though she suspected that the family just wanted to watch her closely, she decided to accept their offer. "Any strings attached?" she asked.

"Not to me." His eyes narrowed on her. "You'll have to ask Jason what he expects of you."

"If he thinks he can buy me off—"

"He does." Zach cast her a look that silently called her naive. "But it's just his nature. Don't take it personally. And don't be fooled. This little bit of generosity isn't because the family has all of the sudden decided to welcome you with open arms."

"I know that."

"Good."

She tossed her jacket onto the foot of the bed. "You don't much like your family, do you?"

He snorted and didn't bother hiding his sarcasm. "What's not to like?" Reaching into his pocket, he withdrew the hotel key and flipped it through the air. "You're now a guest of the Danvers family. I'm not really sure what, exactly, that entails, but I'm sure my brother will let you know."

He started for the twin doors of the suite, but she laid a hand on the crook of his arm. "Look . . . is there a reason we have to be at each other's throats?"

He turned and stared into eyes as blue as a summer's day. Glancing at the throat in question, he felt his gut tighten and sultry memories clouded his mind. He'd too often been mesmerized by Kat's treacherous and seductive eyes. Just as he could be with this woman. "You want to be what . . . well, I mean besides brother and sister, you want to be friends?" he asked, unable to hide the cynicism in his words.

"Why not?" she asked. Her smile was sincere and cracked open a dark corner of his heart, a corner he preferred to keep locked. "I don't know a lot of people in town."

He waited, his face a mask, not daring to move a muscle but singularly aware of the smooth hand upon his forearm. "Christ."

"I thought maybe you'd let me buy you dinner."

"Why?"

"Because it would be easier on both of us if we weren't always looking to kill the other."

"You think that's possible?"

"Sure it is," she said and her breath seemed to catch for a second. "Trust me."

He knew he should just walk away. Yank the door open and slip through. Instead he stared at that vulnerable face and wondered how anyone who looked so guileless could be considered dangerous.

"This isn't a good idea," he said and saw the edge of her teeth dig into the soft flesh of her lower lip. Desire curled in his guts. It was suddenly hard to breathe and between his legs he felt the stirrings of an erection.

"What are you afraid of?"

He could barely speak. The room seemed suddenly hot. He had to get away. "It's not a matter of fear."

"Then what?"

He hoped to sound callous. "I don't think I should be consorting with the enemy."

Her laughter was low, like the seductive roll of an ocean tide. It thundered through his ears. "Didn't your brother send you out to spy on me? Didn't you camp out by my motel, then follow me to the library? Sorry if it wasn't all that interesting, not the usual cloak-and-dagger stuff. Anyway, you're in this as deep as I am, Zach, and you can protest as loud as you like, but deep down, you want to know as much as I do whether I'm your sister or not."

"*Half*-sister," he clarified.

"Right." She removed her hand and tossed her thick, wild hair off her shoulders. "Half-sister. Give me a minute to change."

He should tell her no and get out. Now. But he didn't. Instead, his gaze skated down her worn sweatshirt and jeans. "You look fine."

"I look like I just stepped off the farm in Belamy, Montana. I'll only be a minute."

She didn't wait for him to answer and hurried through the door to the master bedroom. She wondered if he'd second-guess himself and leave, but, by the time she'd slipped into a white cowl-necked sweater and black jeans, slid a tube of lipstick over her lips and tugged a brush through her hair, he was where she'd left him, in the sitting room, one shoulder resting against the window casing, a drink in one hand as he stared out the window. His hip was thrown out and she noticed the way his jeans had faded across his buttocks and the movement of muscular thighs beneath the timeworn denim.

He caught sight of her reflection in the mirror, turned, and didn't move. His lips thinned at the sight of her, as if he were suddenly angry and his gaze raked her down and up again.

"Ready?"

He tossed back his drink. "As ready as I'll ever be."

All the way to the lower level he was broodingly silent and his eyes had darkened with accusations she didn't begin to understand. The elevator car seemed close, the air thick with the scents of whiskey and leather and though he'd made a point of standing as far from her as the small car allowed, she could feel the heat radiating from his body.

His boots rang on the concrete floor of the parking garage and Adria half ran to keep up with him, stepping around puddles of condensation that splattered the ground from the low-hanging pipes webbing across the ceiling.

"Where do you want to go?" he asked as he unlocked the passenger door of his Jeep.

"You're the native," she said as she climbed into the seat.

"Well, hell, I thought you were, too." He slammed her door shut and strode to the driver's side of the Cherokee.

"I just meant—"

"I know what you meant, lady." He climbed in, jammed the key into the ignition, threw the rig into reverse, then shoved it into first. Within seconds the Jeep had emerged from beneath the hotel and joined the traffic of the clogged Portland streets. A light mist was falling, catching in the headlights and adding a silvery sheen to the streets.

"I thought we were going to be civil to each other."

He slid her a noncommittal glance.

"Why do you hate me?"

His lips compressed as he headed east across the river.

"Zach?"

"I don't hate you. I don't even know you."

"You act as if I'm poison."

His jaw clenched visibly as he stopped for a light. "Maybe you are."

"Why won't you give me a chance?"

He practically stood on the brakes as the light changed at a crosswalk and an elderly couple crossed the street. Zach's fingers drummed impatiently against the steering wheel and the instant the light changed, he tromped on the accelerator. "I'm not giving you a chance, because I don't buy your story, Adria."

"Why not have an open mind?"

"What good would it do?"

"Nothing. For you, I suppose." She crossed her arms over her chest and glared out the windshield. There was no use trying to force him to believe in her when she didn't really believe in herself. But she'd hoped that he would become her ally. She looked at him from the corner of her eye and felt an impending sense of doom. Of course he couldn't be her friend. If he weren't her half-brother, she would find him attractive. Long and lean, rugged and cynical, quick to anger but with a killer smile that could warm even the most frigid heart. Intense. Cocky. Irreverent. Just plain bad news.

He caught her looking at him. Shifting down, he shot her another murderous glance. "You look a helluva lot like Kat, I'll give you that."

"Is that a crime?"

"It should be," he growled.

"Kat . . . is that what you called Katherine?"

"Behind her back."

She leaned against the door and rubbed the kinks from her neck. "What did you call her to her face?"

He snorted. "Mommy dearest."

"What?"

"That was a joke, Adria." Zach's expression hardened. "To be honest I tried to avoid her."

"Why?" She watched as his fingers curled around the steering wheel in a death grip.

"She was trouble," he said as he flipped on the radio and Garth Brooks's voice filled the interior. So he didn't want to talk about Katherine. Adria wasn't surprised. Throughout her research, she'd learned very little of the woman she suspected had borne her. It seemed as if Katherine had been content to let her husband bask in the spotlight; she'd always hidden in the wings, hauntingly beautiful and supportive. Adria wondered if Katherine truly avoided the limelight or if her powerful husband had found ways to keep his family, including his beautiful wife, in the shadows.

Adria didn't know much about London's mother; the information had been spotty, but she'd thought Katherine and Witt had met in Canada. After a whirlwind romance, they'd been married, to the shock and horror of Witt's entire family. That was to be expected, Adria supposed. After all, rumor had it that Witt's divorce from his first wife, Eunice, had been messy and harsh. Accusations had been hurled and in the end, Witt, ever powerful, had ended up with his kids. No wonder Katherine wasn't greeted with open arms.

But Adria couldn't help making comparisons between herself and the second Mrs. Witt Danvers. As Katherine had been an outsider to the family twenty-odd years before, Adria was the outsider now. For the first time Adria felt a kinship with the woman who was supposed to be her mother, and yet she also suspected that Zach wasn't being completely honest with her. There was something he was hiding, something dark and mysterious about Katherine. He didn't admit to it, but obviously, whenever the subject of Katherine LaRouche Danvers was bridged, he grew silent and brooding.

As he drove, the skyscrapers gave way to shorter complexes, the city lights became less frequent, the traffic thinned and eventually the offices gave way to homes lining the streets. Adria wondered about his childhood. Witt Danvers was a powerful, dominating man. His first wife was weak and his second . . . how little she knew of the woman who had become Zachary's stepmother.

"What kind of trouble was Katherine?" she asked, when Zach didn't elaborate.

"The worst."

"Meaning—"

"Meaning that she came on like gangbusters. If she saw something she wanted, she'd use every means possible to get it. She never stopped until she got it."

"What did she want?"

Hesitating, he stared through the windshield and he seemed lost in a whirlpool of murky memories. His mouth compressed into a hard, unyielding line, the cords in his neck seemed more pronounced, as if he were angry and waging an inner battle with himself. Seconds passed without an answer as the Jeep sped out of the city and through rolling pasture land surrounded by black looming hills. He braked for a corner as the mist thickened into rain.

"What did Katherine want?" she repeated as the road angled upward through the hills.

Again, he slid her an insolent glance. The tires whined on the wet streets. "Everything."

Adria felt that he was talking in circles and yet at least he was speaking. After hours in the library, reading dry accounts of the Danvers family, she finally had someone who was willing—albeit reluctantly—to give her information. She cautioned herself to tread softly.

The road had narrowed into two twisting lanes winding

through the foothills. Adria barely noticed, she was too intent on finding out about the woman whom she thought was her mother. "Did she get it? Everything?"

He snorted in disgust. "Don't you know?" he asked sarcastically.

"No, I—"

"After all those hours in the library, digging through the dirt. Kat's dead, Adria. She killed herself."

Stunned, she could barely speak. The temperature in the Jeep seemed to drop ten degrees and she shivered. "I thought it was an accident," she whispered. "The accounts I read said she inadvertently overdosed on sleeping pills."

"It wasn't an accident," Zach said as he yanked on the steering wheel and turned into the gravel parking lot of some kind of tavern or inn. "Kat took her life. She opened up a bottle of sleeping pills and downed them all with half a bottle of eighty-proof whiskey."

"You don't know—"

He slammed on the brakes, cut the engine and grabbed her with both hands. His fingers dug into her shoulders as he gave her a little shake. "She committed suicide, Adria. It was white-washed in the papers, but Katherine Danvers was a victim of her own fantasies, her own dreams."

His eyes had narrowed at the memory, his nostrils flared in the close interior of the cab. Raindrops beat against the roof of the car and music, floating out of the door of the inn whenever a customer entered or left, drifted through the closed windows of the Jeep. Adria licked her lips and stared up at him, this man who could be her half-brother.

His breath was warm against her face, his hands strong and forceful, his eyes as dark as the night. Adria's throat caught and she couldn't look away. Spellbound, she held his gaze and knew in an instant that he was going to kiss her. Her heart squeezed. Unwanted desire—wicked and wanton—crept stealthily through her blood.

"Damn you," he whispered hoarsely, his face so close to hers she could see smoky desire in his eyes.

"Zachary—"

"Go home, Adria," he said, letting go of her so suddenly she nearly fell against him. His expression turned harsh. "Go home, before you get hurt."

11

"Who's going to hurt me?" she demanded, pushing away from him and creating as much distance as possible in the Jeep. Her heart was pounding so loudly she could barely breathe. She'd thought he would kiss her, knew it was on his mind, and he'd run scared. She *couldn't* get involved with him. The windows of the rig had fogged, seeming to cut off the rest of the world and as she stared at him, she felt as if they were the only two people on earth.

"You're going to hurt yourself."

"How?"

His eyes glittered in the darkness. "You're playing with fire."

"And you're talking in circles."

"Am I?" He reached for her again and this time when he drew her close she could feel the heat of his body, found her own heart beating with desire. His breath was warm and ragged, his eyes defiant. "Why are you doing this?" he asked before he lowered his head and his lips crashed over hers in a kiss that was almost brutal and his fingers wound in the thick strands of her hair. Anger and passion sizzled through her blood. She tried not to respond, to push him away, but her hands were useless against his broad chest and he ground his mouth over hers in a way that was wickedly possessive and seared her to her very soul. His tongue prodded insistently at her teeth, gaining entrance to and plundering the dark recess of her mouth.

A low moan escaped her and she wanted to die from embarrassment, yet she kissed him back. Her pulse throbbed and for the first time in years a hot yawning desire uncoiled deep within her. She couldn't think, couldn't move, couldn't deny. She wound her arms around his neck, feeling him yank her closer, knowing that her breasts, already full, were crushed against his leather jacket.

As suddenly as he'd taken her into his arms, he released her. "Jesus H. Christ," he swore, breathing hard. Closing his eyes, he let his head drop back against the seat cushions and gritted his teeth, as if suddenly struck by the magnitude of what he'd done. It seemed as if he was mentally willing his desire away. "Damn it, Adria, what is it you want from me?"

"I—"

"And don't give me any crap about wanting to be friends. I think I just proved we're way past that."

She swallowed with difficulty. Desire pulsed through her veins. "Zachary, I can't—this isn't—"

"What isn't?" His eyes flew open and he searched her face as if he intended to kiss her until she finally shut up. For several heartbeats she felt his indecision. "Hell," he ground out before reaching for her again and roughly folding her into his arms. He kissed her without restraint, his lips anxious and hungry, his body hard and straining against hers as he forced her back against the seat, his weight pinning her. Again, his tongue delved deep and she felt the hardness between his legs. She should stop him, but she couldn't. Delicious little flames of desire lapped at her, caused her lungs to constrict. He kissed her lips, her face, her eyes, his hands restless, but not moving from her back. When he finally lifted his head, he glared down at her and there was hatred in his eyes—intense, self-loathing hatred. "Don't tell me you can't," he said through clenched teeth. "You can and would. But I won't give you the satisfaction! You're as bad as she was." He struggled into a sitting position and reached for the door handle.

"As . . . who?" she asked, but knew that he was talking about Kat.

"She came on to anything in pants."

"No—".

"You didn't know her."

"But I didn't mean—"

"Neither did I."

"I'm sorry."

"Sorry?" He raked stiff fingers through his hair. "Sorry?" His smile was cold in the darkness. "Don't play the innocent virgin with me, Adria. You wanted it. You were hot."

She itched to slap him, to deny what had so obviously been the truth, but curled her hands into tight little fists. "I didn't . . ." If only she could lie and tell him that she didn't feel any attraction to him, but she held her tongue. Her heart was still racing, her hands shaking.

The look he sent her seared her to the most forbidden recesses of her mind and she knew then that what they felt for each other— this pure animal lust—was part of her destiny. A horrid attraction that she would have to fight. Her throat went dry and she wanted to deny the desire that pumped through her veins.

"I just wondered how much you were like Kat," he said, his gaze raking over her uncombed hair, messed sweater, and swollen lips. "How far you'd go."

She didn't believe him and her anger sparked. "So you expect me to believe that you kissed me out of curiosity?"

He shrugged. "I don't give a shit what you believe."

"Don't lie, Zach. I didn't. You kissed me because you want me. Hide it any way you like, but you felt what I did."

"Christ, now you even sound like her!"

A sickening thought rolled through her mind as she pictured Zach, only fifteen or sixteen and Katherine, her mother, locked in a compromising embrace, bodies shining with sweat and hard with desire. Oh, God. "What are you trying to say?" she whispered as the horrid thought congealed in her mind. "That she came on to you—that she was your—"

"She was nothing to me!" He sliced her a glance that cut her to the bone.

"I don't believe—"

"Believe what you want, Adria. As I said before, it's no skin off my ass how you want to delude yourself." He opened the door of the Jeep and cool air swept inside. She scrambled out and half ran to keep up with his long, furious strides. Rain peppered the ground and washed down her neck but she didn't care.

"Wait—" Her fingers grabbed for the crook of his arm, but he tossed her hand aside and whirled upon her. His face was twisted into a mask of rage and he seemed larger than ever in the darkness. Rain caught in his dark hair before trickling down the contours of his face and disappearing beneath his collar.

His lips curled into a sneer and the neon lights from the restaurant reflected red and blue in his eyes. "I don't know what you want from me, Adria, but you'd better be careful. You might just get it!"

He turned on his boot once again and walked up two long, low steps to the porch of the log cabin.

Adria had no choice but to follow him. Slowly counting to ten, she followed his path, shouldered open the door, walked through a pine-paneled vestibule and found him standing at the bar, one boot resting on a tarnished brass rail, his elbows propped on the battle-scarred surface of glossy cherry wood.

"I already ordered for you," he said as the bartender, a slim woman with kinky blond hair and red lipstick, slid two frosted glasses of beer to him, then deftly snatched up the bills he'd left on the counter. His eyes met Adria's in the mirror over the bar and his gaze had become cloudy again. "Come on. Let's grab a table." He cocked his head to an empty booth situated beneath a wagon wheel suspended from the ceiling. Lanterns, made to look as if they burned oil but were powered by electricity, stood on the rim of the wheel and gave off low-wattage illumination.

Adria tried to put a lid on her simmering temper. Though she was boiling inside, she slid onto the worn plastic cushions and accepted the beer—his notion of a peace offering.

Zach gulped half his beer in one swallow. "Anything else

you'd like to know about the Danvers family?" he asked with a scornful lift of his eyebrow.

"Whatever you want to tell me."

"That's the problem. I don't want to tell you anything. I think it would be better if you just packed it all in and drove off to Bozeman—"

"Belamy."

"Whatever."

"Now you're sounding like the rest of your family."

"God forbid," he muttered and drained his glass. He signaled for another drink, which a waitress, a heavier version of the blond bartender, brought over along with menus.

She winked at Zachary as if they were longtime friends, then smiled at Adria. "Refill?"

"Not right now."

"I'll give you a few minutes to decide." She moved to a nearby table and Adria kept her voice low.

"You know," she said, not really believing her own words, "despite what you said earlier, we could be friends if we tried."

He made a sound of disgust. "Friends." His lips curved into a smile without any warmth. "Is that how you treat all your 'friends'?"

"Don't do this—"

"You don't do it! We can never, *never* be friends," he growled, leaning over the table and grabbing her shoulders. "Got that?"

She threw off his hands and glared furiously at him. "Why are you trying so hard to hate me?"

"It's easier that way!" Dropping back onto his bench, he studied the head of his beer and his jaw clenched. "For both of us."

"You're afraid I might end up with the Danvers fortune," she said, realizing he was more like his family than he wanted to admit.

He snorted and rolled his glass between his fingers. "I don't care if you end up with the whole damned lot of the inheritance—the logging company, the saw mills, the hotel, the house in Tahoe, even the ranch—and I'd say good riddance. I'm not afraid of you."

"I don't believe you."

"Your prerogative," he said with a shrug.

"You can be a real bastard, Danvers. You know that, don't you?"

One side of his mouth lifted insolently. "I work at it."

"A true Danvers."

His smile faded. "Let's order."

They didn't say another word to each other and Adria watched as the waitress flirted outrageously with Zachary as she spouted off the specials of the day. In the end, they both ordered flank steak, grilled onions, and Caesar salad.

Some country song about lost love and broken hearts was overshadowed by the clink of glasses, rap of pool balls, and murmur of differing conversations. More tavern than restaurant, the old log cabin seemed home to a dozen or so few blue-collar types. Hard hats had been exchanged for baseball caps and cowboy hats, but it seemed as if the men sitting on stools in the bar were at home. It reminded Adria of Belamy.

"Why'd you bring me here?" she asked as the waitress slid a basket of hot bread between them.

"It was your idea, remember."

"But out here—in the middle of nowhere?"

"You'd rather go to some restaurant downtown?"

"Not really." She grabbed a slice of bread and tore off a corner.

"Thought you wanted to know the real me." His eyes glinted sensually. "Now you do."

"I don't think so. I think you're hiding something, Zach. Trying to scare me off." She took a bite from the bread and stared him down. "It won't work." Leaning back against the tufted plastic upholstery, she said, "You were raised in Portland."

"I try to forget about that."

"Why?"

He hesitated and gazed to a point over her shoulder where, she suspected, he saw his own youth. "I was always in trouble. Gave the old man nothing but grief."

"And you're still cultivating that bad-ass attitude, aren't you?"

He relaxed against the back of the booth and took a long drink from his glass. "Maybe."

"No maybes about it."

Lifting a shoulder, he said, "So what've you found out about my illustrious family?"

"Not enough."

He pinned her with a look and she thought twice about answering. Finally, as the meals were delivered, she said, "Okay. The library was pretty much a bust. Sure it had information on the kidnapping and on the family, but there wasn't much . . . much substance to it all."

"So you came up empty."

"Almost. But I'm not done digging." She started in on her salad and Zach muttered something about mule-headed women under his breath. She let the comment slide.

"Where are you going to look next?"

She smiled and took a sip from her glass, her eyes meeting his over the rim. "Lots of places. *The Oregonian*, the historical society, the police. Believe me, I've only just begun."

"You're going to wind up empty-handed."

"Is that right? Why?"

"You've got one helluva hole in your father's story. It's about as big as all of Montana."

"I'm all ears," she invited, anxious to hear what he thought. Somehow it was important, as if his opinion would help.

He sliced a portion from his steak. "If everything you say is true—why did Ginny Slade take London in the first place?"

"Who knows?"

"No one, I guess," he said thoughtfully. "But it wasn't because she wanted a child or she wouldn't have left you with the Nashes."

"I know, but—"

"And it wasn't for the money because she left some cash in her bank accounts in Portland and never demanded ransom."

"Maybe she was paid off."

"My father offered a million dollars, no questions asked, for the return of his daughter. In 1974 that was a helluva lot of money."

"It's a helluva lot of money today."

"But Ginny didn't claim it."

"She could've been worried about prosecution. Your father—our father—wasn't known to be as good as his word. He had a reputation for retribution."

"The plain truth of the matter is you might not be London."

"There is still one motive left," she said as she finished her beer and set the empty glass on the table.

"Which is?"

"Revenge. Witt had made more than his share of enemies, Zach. He'd walked all over people, didn't care who he stepped on to get what he wanted. Seems to me there were plenty of people who would have loved to see him hurt. I just have to figure out who it is. I was hoping you would help me."

"Why would I bother?" he asked.

"Because London was your half-sister and a lot of people in town thought you were somehow behind her disappearance."

"I was a kid at the time."

"A kid who was always in trouble. A kid who had more than his share of run-ins with the law, a kid a lot of people thought was fathered by Anthony Polidori, a kid who suffered big time at Witt Danvers's hand, and a kid who was involved in some kind of mugging that night."

"I didn't have anything to do with what happened to London," he growled, the skin over his cheekbones stretching tight.

"Okay, Danvers, now's your chance to prove it. All you have to do is help me find out who I really am. If I'm London, then your name is in the clear, the little girl didn't really die, she was raised in Montana."

"And if you're not?"

"You're no worse off than you were before. At least your family and the people who care will know that you tried to find out the truth."

"Except—" he said, nudging his plate aside.

"Except?"

"Except I don't give a shit what the 'people who care' think." He settled back in his chair and regarded her with eyes suddenly smoky with desire. "Your offer's not good enough, Adria." His gaze drilled into hers. "I'm not interested."

Oswald Sweeny shivered in the breeze that roared off the mountains and cut through his coat. He drew one last warm lungful of smoke from his Camel and ground the butt into the gravel lot surrounding the rooming house. In his opinion, Belamy, Montana, was about as far from civilization as he ever wanted to be. He locked the car door and shuffled up the steps to the wide front porch.

Inside, heat and the smell of something cooking—soup or stew, maybe—enveloped him.

He heard the landlady rattling around in the kitchen, but didn't bother with any chitchat just now. He hurried upstairs, snapped on the light and yanked off his jacket. He hadn't found more than he'd expected in Belamy, Montana, and that bothered him because he was already tired of this little town and its straight-arrow, salt-of-the-earth type of citizens.

He'd suspected Adria Nash was broke, and it looked like she was drowning in red ink—hospital debts, a large mortgage on the farm she owned, college loans, doctor bills. Even leasing the farm wasn't enough to cover everything. He had to do a little more checking to find out just how desperate she was for money—Danvers money.

For the last twenty-four hours he'd trudged around this podunk town and nearly frozen his butt clean off trying to pick apart Adria's story. There were discrepancies, but not many and the part about her growing up as the adopted daughter of Victor and Sharon Nash was absolutely true.

But there was more dirt yet to dig. He'd seen it in a few of the good citizens' eyes when he started asking questions about the Nash family in general and Adria in particular. Sweeny was certain she was hiding something, he just didn't know what.

The pieces as he'd put them together from the few people in Belamy who were willing to talk to him linked into a straightforward picture. Sharon Nash had once been a pretty girl who had married Victor, a decent farmer a few years older than she. All she'd wanted in life was to be a wife and mother, but her dreams had been stolen away when she wasn't able to get pregnant and medical research in the fifties and sixties was more interested in preventing births than helping sterile couples conceive. She'd gone from doctor to doctor, becoming more desperate as the years passed. When medical technology had swung around and fertility pills were available, she was too old. Fertility pills didn't work. She reluctantly accepted the fact that she was barren and she convinced herself that God, in keeping her from having children, was punishing her for not believing more strongly in Him.

The farming years had been lean and no adoption agency would offer the land-poor couple a child they couldn't afford. A private adoption, because of the cost, was out of the question. It seemed as if Sharon was destined to be childless.

As the years passed, Sharon threw all her energy into the church. Though her husband rarely attended services, Sharon never missed a Sunday or a weekly prayer meeting. As everyone here on earth—her husband, the doctors and the lawyers—had failed her, she decided to trust in God completely and became nearly fanatic in serving Him.

Suddenly her prayers were answered, though not through the church, but through Victor's brother's law firm. A little girl—a relative most people thought—had become available and, if Sharon and Victor asked few questions, the adoption could be handled. Sharon didn't need to have any answers. There were no questions. In her mind this girl was sent from heaven. Victor was more hesitant as he and his wife were getting up in years, but as much to help out the struggling mother of the girl—a shirttail relative, Sweeny had gleaned—as keep his wife happy, Victor agreed. In the end, Adria became the apple of her father's eye.

Sweeny pulled a small flask from his jacket pocket and took a warming swallow. Everything he'd found out so far was all just town gossip and speculation, the idle talk of neighbors and friends. There were no public records of the adoption and Ezra Nash, the lawyer who had handled the case was dead, the paperwork in his office in Bozeman destroyed in a fire. It was frustrating as hell. All the information fit neatly into Adria's story and matched the testimony of the pathetic man in the video, but Sweeny could smell a rat. Something didn't quite mesh.

And it had to do with money. Money she didn't have.

Ms. Nash could have all the good intentions in the world, but Sweeny was certain that she was after the Danvers family fortune. Somehow she'd managed to put herself through college and graduated at the top of her class with a double major in architecture and business, but she'd only worked for a construction company after graduation.

Tomorrow he'd ask for a simple credit report that would confirm the town gossip, then he'd request some information from the Department of Motor Vehicles that would give him some personal insight into the woman, help him find out what it was that made her tick.

He took another swallow from his flask and without removing his shoes, dropped onto the bed. For the next couple of days he was stuck in Belamy, which was little more than a stoplight stuck in the middle of no-goddamned-where. The sooner he was out of here, the better.

His only lead was Ginny Slade aka Virginia Watson Slade and he'd have to track her down, but it wouldn't be easy. It would take time and money. Lots and lots of Danvers money.

                              *   *   *

Zachary slung his bag over his shoulder. It was time to leave
this town. Being in the same hotel with Adria, on the same
damned floor no less, was asking for trouble big time.

It had been two nights since he'd last seen her and he'd been
unable to close her out of his mind. He had plenty to keep him
busy, still working out the kinks of this damned hotel, but he'd
been tense, his muscles tightening when he thought he caught a
glimpse of her or heard her voice. He was slowly but surely,
losing it. He'd never considered himself a fool; nor had he ever
had any kind of death wish. He'd always thought clearly and
known what he wanted.

Until he'd met Adria.

Whenever he was around her, his senses were on overload
and his normally clear mind became muddied. She was beautiful,
damned beautiful and she looked so much like Kat he felt an icy
drizzle of déjà vu whenever he looked at her. Yet, mingled with
that cold drip of memory was a flame of desire, melting away his
inhibitions, heating his blood and causing him to lose sight of
reality.

Which was what?

That she was really his half-sister?

Or that she was a beautiful, treacherous woman whose greed
had blinded her to the truth? Had she used her uncanny resemblance to Kat for her personal gain, or did she really believe that
she was London?

Christ, what a mess! He hitched his bag up a notch and headed
for the elevator. This time he was leaving, if only for a little while.
He welcomed the three-hour drive over the mountains, was
anxious to get back to the ranch. He needed time and space
alone. Away from the enigma that was Adria Nash. Jason
wouldn't like it, but it didn't really matter.

In the parking lot, he threw his bag into the backseat and
drove to Jason's house in the west hills. His older brother had
requested that he show up for a family meeting and Zach had

decided he'd make an appearance, then drop the bomb that he was taking off. If only for a few days. He just needed a little time and space to get his head on straight again.

The garage doors were open and Jason's Jag was parked near his wife Nicole's white Mercedes. In the third bay, a vintage Rolls-Royce gleamed glossy black under the lights. One of the men who did yard work and basic mechanics for the family was running a soft white rag along a sleek, spotless fender.

Toys. Jason loved toys. From racehorses to classic cars, to rich wives and sexy young mistresses, Jason had always loved toys.

Zach eyed the house where he'd grown up, tamped down any unwanted memories, rapped on the door with his knuckles and waited. Within seconds Nicole opened the door and smiled wanly at her brother-in-law. A waif-thin woman with tanned skin and white-blond hair, she stepped out of the way. "Zachary."

"Is Jason here?"

"In the basement."

"Good. I'll see myself down," he added, when she seemed intent on leading him down the stairs he'd played on as a kid.

He and Nelson had slid down the staircase in cardboard boxes, raced each other up and down the steep steps, and been hauled downstairs whenever Witt wanted to discipline them. Witt, one hand on the back of Zach's collar, the other clenched firmly around his belt, had dragged his second son down the stairs more times than Zach wanted to remember. Witt had seemed determined to break Zach's spirit and despite Eunice's pleading, to "go easy on the boy, Witt, he's just a child," Zach had felt the razor-sharp sting of Witt's leather belt against the skin on his back time after time.

"Shit," he muttered as the memories and pain thundered through his brain. The beatings had been brutal, but had never broken Zach's spirit. Clenching his teeth until his jaw ached, he shoved those hideous memories to the dark corners of his brain as he rounded the corner of the staircase.

He found his older brother, shirtsleeves rolled over his fore-

arms, throwing darts at a target mounted on the wall near the
mirrored bar. A pool table dominated the room and a flagstone
fireplace climbed up one wall. Through steamy French doors, a
sauna and Jacuzzi waited, and on every wall hung trophies, the
heads of bear, antelope, tiger and bison, contributions from his
grandfather, Julius Danvers, who prided himself in being a big-
game hunter. A polar bear, claws extended, stood in one corner,
and a zebra hide was stretched beside that of a kangaroo. Glassy
eyes and snarling teeth greeted all who entered.

"What did you find out?" Jason didn't even look his way, just
threw another dart toward the bull's-eye.

"From Adria? Not much." Zach grabbed the cue ball and
rolled it in his hands. His conversations with Adria had been
minimal, but he did know a few facts. However, he wasn't particularly interested in sharing them with Jason. "She grew up a poor
farm girl in Montana. Her mother was kind of a religious nut and
her father put up with it but wasn't a fanatic." He leaned a hip
against the table. "She's bound and determined to see this
through no matter what the outcome."

"So it's her personal quest."

Zach frowned and stared at the fire—blue and yellow gas-fed
flames that hissed as they licked a ceramic log. "I think she's just
trying to find the truth."

Jason glanced at him, then threw a dart, hitting the target
dead-on. "Sounds like you're weakening where our new little lost
sister is concerned."

"I still think she's a fake."

"Of course she is." He threw another dart and just missed the
red bull's-eye. "We'll watch her and she'll trip up."

"I'm going back to the ranch."

"Not now."

"Tonight."

A tic developed beneath Jason's eye. "Can't it wait? Manny
seems to be more than capable—"

"I'll be back in a couple of days. I just need to do a few things.
Check what's going on at the ranch and in the office."

Jason looked about to argue, but held his tongue at the sound of footsteps on the stairs. Trisha didn't bother saying a word to either of her brothers, just ambled over to the bar and poured herself a straight shot of tequila. "Where's Nelson?" she asked as she hoisted a hip onto the stool and sipped her drink.

"He'll be here."

"I heard Mother was invited, too."

"Hell," Zach muttered, placing the cue ball back on the table.

"She was included in the will," Jason said.

"Part of her deal with Dad when they divorced."

"Nonetheless, she counts."

"Christ."

Trisha motioned to the bar. "Maybe you need a drink, Zach?"

"Not tonight."

She glanced at Jason. "And the girl's coming, too?"

Zach's neck muscles bunched. "Adria? You invited her here?"

Jason checked his watch. "She should be arriving any minute. Didn't want to leave her out, you know. I thought maybe we could hammer out a deal and send her packing back to the farm."

"I don't think so." Zach was irritated. He didn't want to see Adria again, didn't want to smell her perfume or get lost in her eyes.

"Look, even if she is a fraud, she looks too much like Kat to let it pass. The press will go crazy. There will be pictures in the paper—old photos of Kat put up against new ones of Adria. Comparisons are going to be made whether we like it or not and unfortunately, we all have to admit that the girl does look a lot like our late stepmother."

"I'm not admitting anything." Trisha tossed back her drink and poured herself another. "I don't want to hear this."

"The newspapers and television reports are just the beginning. Then she'll get herself a lawyer, a good lawyer who wants some notoriety, someone who's willing to take a risk just to score big and get his face in the papers. A lot of attorneys are more interested in fame than money."

Trisha snorted.

"Well, nearly as interested."

"So what do you plan to do?" Zach asked, his gut twisting a little. Talking about Adria behind her back, plotting against her, bothered him more than it should have. Maybe Trisha was right, maybe he needed a beer.

Jason's lips curved into a smooth smile. "What's the saying from *The Godfather*—I'm going to 'make her an offer she can't refuse'?"

"There is none."

"I think a hundred grand will do it."

Trisha's mouth fell open. "You'd give her that much?"

"Not to begin with, of course. We'll start low and try to intimidate her, but a hundred thousand isn't much when you think of the cost of attorneys if we have to go to court. And think of all the time the estate will be tangled up in probate. It's bad enough as it is—an estate this size takes forever."

"I bet the old man is sitting down in hell somewhere and laughing at us," Trisha said, lighting a cigarette and blowing smoke rings. "Imagine, leaving nearly fifty percent of his estate to a daughter he couldn't find or didn't even know if she was dead or alive. What a joke!"

"Unless we have proof of her death," Jason reminded them both, "then her share of the inheritance can be divided among the rest of us."

Zach's blood turned to ice as he noticed the cold hint of a smile curving Jason's lips. Just how far would any of his siblings go to get their hands on Witt's fortune? They all had their personal axes to grind. Jason loved money; Trisha had always wanted revenge against the family, and Nelson was ambitious to a fault.

And what about you? You're not exactly lily-white.

As for his brothers and sister, he was certain they would lie to get what they wanted, and they would surely steal. But would they kill? His back teeth gnashed silently and involuntarily his fingers clenched into fists.

Trisha gulped from her drink and sighed. "Our father who art in hell. Truly one of the world's great bastards." She looked up sharply and her gaze met Zach's. "No offense, Zach."

Zach let the comment slide. The questions about his paternity no longer rattled him. Who really gave a damn?

"Just because he made a provision for London, doesn't mean we can't fight it," Jason pointed out. "Haven't you heard that wills are meant to be contested? We just have to prove that the old man was senile at the time he had the will drawn up. That shouldn't be too hard. After all, who in his right mind would leave millions of dollars to a girl who had been missing for nearly twenty years?"

"So why haven't you done anything about it?" Trisha said, squinting through her smoke. "You're the hotshot lawyer."

"Because Dad's attorney will swear that the old man was as sane as you and I. Claims he's got proof that Witt hadn't lost any of his marbles."

"So it's his word against ours."

Zach hated discussing the old man's estate. It was necessary, of course, he wasn't foolish enough or rich enough not to care, but he really wished he could just wash his hands of the whole damned family. Greedy vultures, that's what they'd all become.

And what about you? You're here, aren't you? Hoping to keep the ranch. Hell, what a mess. Then there was Adria. At the thought of her, his blood heated and he rubbed his chin in frustration. He didn't like the idea of trying to buy Adria out, but he didn't have a better plan.

"So, the first order of business is getting rid of our latest London," Jason said. "Send her packing and try to break the will."

"I don't think she'll go for it," Zach said, his voice sounding a lot steadier than he felt. "It's more of a question of pride and truth than money with her."

Jason shook his head and rubbed his chin. "It's always money, Zach. Haven't you learned yet that everyone has a price? Even Ms. Nash. We just have to find what it is."

Zach heard noises on the stairs and his nerves tightened. He could feel Adria's presence before she followed Nicole into the room. "Have you all met Adria?" Nicole said, forcing a smile on her tanned face.

Adria didn't seem the least bit intimidated. In fact, she looked as if she really did belong. Her hands were stuffed into pockets of a jean jacket trimmed in leather and she didn't bother to smile. She slid a glance in Zach's direction and he stiffened. For a second they stared at each other before she forced her eyes to meet Jason's steady gaze. "I got a message that you wanted to see me."

"I did. Come in and have a seat—" He pointed to the grouping of leather furniture positioned near the fireplace. "Would you like a drink?"

She hesitated for a heartbeat, but then she managed a thin smile. "Why not? Have you got any white wine? Chardonnay."

Jason moved to the bar, as if he were willing to do whatever she wanted. Zach considered leaving but before he could make his way to the door, footsteps sounded on the stairs and his mother and Nelson strolled into the room. Eunice took one look at Adria and for a split second her face drained of color, but she recovered herself. "So you're Ms. Nash," she said, extending her hand, though she appeared anything but friendly. Her eyes were cool, her mouth pinched at the corners, her skin stretched tightly over the bones of her face. "I'm Eunice Smythe."

Adria knew quite a bit about the woman whose fingers felt like dry parchment, but mostly she'd pieced together rumors. She would love to know the truth. There had been gossip that Witt had divorced Eunice because of infidelity with Polidori; though, of course, no one but Eunice knew the truth. Whatever had happened between Witt and his wife, it had cost Eunice. She'd been denied custody of her children in a time when father's rights were virtually ignored.

"Well, Adria. Nelson tells me you think you're Witt's long-lost daughter." Eunice's smile was as cold as steel as she let go of Adria's fingers.

Jason handed Adria the glass of wine she really hadn't wanted. She held the stem in a death grip. Her throat was suddenly dry, her fingers damp with sweat. "That's why I'm here, yes," Adria replied. "To find out the truth."

"The truth," Eunice murmured as she studied Adria. "Sometimes so elusive." Without so much as a sip, Adria set her drink on a nearby table. "So let's get down to it, shall we?" Eunice settled into a cream-colored chair. "Nicole, would you be a dear and fix me a gin and tonic?" she asked her daughter-in-law and when Nicole poured the drink and handed it to her, Eunice patted the younger woman's slim arm. "That's a good girl."

"Always," Nicole replied in a brittle voice as she shot her husband a glance that would have cut through granite.

Every muscle in Adria's body was strung tight; the tension between her "family" was thick in the air and she didn't know which was worse, being stared at by the dead animal heads mounted on the walls, or by the very living beasts that congregated around her. *You asked for this,* she reminded herself. *You knew it would be tough, so just hang in there!* Giving herself a mental shake, she sat on the edge of the couch, directly across the glass-topped coffee table from Eunice and refused to give into the impulse to stare at Zachary, to silently ask for his help.

Jason slid onto the couch next to her.

Zachary looked bored. He leaned against the stones of the fireplace, his features composed, his gaze fixed on her, his jaw looking as if it hadn't seen a razor for a couple of days.

Adria shifted a little and watched as Nelson slung a leg over his mother's chair, positioning himself near her. Nicole, after delivering the drink to her mother-in-law, caught her husband's commanding gaze and hastily said something about checking on her daughter before hurrying up the stairs. Trisha didn't join the rest of the group, but preferred to sit on a stool at the bar, where she smoked and drank and observed everyone from a distance.

"No one here believes you," Eunice stated flatly.

"I expected as much."

"So you came ready to accept defeat."

"I came for—"

"I know, I know," Eunice waved in the air, as if swatting a bothersome insect. "The truth. Listen," she leaned closer, "let's get past all this talk about the truth, all right? It's tedious. Noble, I suppose, but tedious just the same, and we all know it's a lie. What you really want is to be taken seriously enough so that the family scrambles around and offers you a decent amount of money to go back to wherever it is you came from."

"I didn't—"

"Cut the crap," Nelson said quietly. "We're prepared to pay you, but you'd have to sign a document—"

"Aren't any of you interested in the fact that I could, just could, be your sister?" Adria asked. "I know you're worried about the estate, but think about it, what if I really am London?"

"Doesn't make any difference," Trisha said through a cloud of smoke. "To us, you're a stranger and if you fell off the earth, we wouldn't care." Her lips curved up just a little. "In fact, a few of us might celebrate."

"Trisha!" Eunice said sharply, then turned her attention from her daughter to Adria. "She's a little harsh."

"Look, I don't need this. I thought you called me here to talk to me, to ask me questions, to help me find out the truth, but I guess I was wrong." She stood and slung the strap of her purse over her shoulder. "Believe it or not, I didn't drive to Portland to wreak havoc on your lives, or steal your fortune, or hurt anyone in any way."

"Of course you did," Trisha said.

Adria's back stiffened. "I won't give up."

Trisha, with her cigarette dangling from the corner of her mouth, clapped her hands. "Bravo! What a fine performance!"

"Stop it, Trisha!" Zachary said so vehemently that Eunice's eyes narrowed on her second son.

Jason ignored the outburst. "We could make it worth your while."

"You still want to pay me off?" She picked up her glass and sipped.

"Mmm. Say twenty-five thousand?"

She almost choked on a swallow of wine. She had expected a bribe, but the amount staggered her. "I—I don't think so."

Jason's smile tightened. "We'd be willing to go up to fifty."

Nelson visibly blanched and when Adria shot a glance in Zach's direction, he returned her stare impassively. He was in on it! He wanted to buy her out, too. Her blood boiled silently because she'd told herself that he was different, that he would help her, that he, the rebel, *cared*. Obviously she'd been mistaken.

"If you'll excuse me," she said, setting her drink on the table with trembling fingers, "I think I'll go pack."

Jason was on his feet. "You don't have to move out of the hotel—"

"Of course I do. Staying there was a mistake. Only one of many." Her gaze swiveled once again to Zachary's and this time she saw a little spark of the fire in his gray eyes. She thought about their kisses in his Jeep, the anger and passion that had radiated from him. Had it all been part of the plan to break down her defenses? Would he stoop low enough to try and seduce her, just to scare her off? Sick at the thought, she squared her shoulders, turned on her heel and marched up the stairs. As far as she was concerned the battle lines had been drawn. The Danvers family could rot in hell for all she cared.

12

Adria moved out of the Hotel Danvers. It was just as well, she told herself, as she found a room in the Orion Hotel just a few blocks away. The Orion intrigued her because it was the hotel where Zachary was supposed to have been beaten up and left for dead on the night London had been abducted.

The Orion had changed hands several times in the last few years and had been updated. Whereas the Hotel Danvers had been refurbished to offer a charming glimpse of Victorian Portland, the Orion was modern with plush beige carpeting, recessed lighting, and walls tinged a subtle shade of mauve. What it lacked in character, the Orion made up for in convenience with three restaurants, a pool, weight room, and sauna.

She pored over her notes until two in the morning and tried to shove all thoughts of her meeting with the family out of her mind. At least she knew where she stood and she didn't have an ally in the lot of them.

Even Zachary. Some rebel he'd turned out to be. When it came to the Danvers fortune, he was as greedy and suspicious as the rest. He seemed anxious to be out of town and rid of her and away from the problems of the estate.

As she curled up on the queen-size bed, she wondered about him. He'd kissed her as if he meant it, and yet it had been nothing more than a test. She'd nearly been duped into thinking that he cared for her, but that notion was foolish. If she were London Danvers, then he was her half-brother and a romance was out of the question. If she wasn't London, then he'd expose her as a fraud and a romance would be out of the question.

Not that she wanted a romance, she told herself. She'd learned that lesson the hard way and she wasn't going to fall for Zachary. Not even if he wasn't related to her.

No, all she wanted was to find out who she was and she'd fight tooth and nail to discover the truth, no matter how deeply the Danvers kin had buried it.

As his Jeep crested the Santiam Pass, Zachary reached into his pocket for a cigarette, then frowned at himself and scowled at the twin beams his headlights threw on the asphalt slipping beneath the rig's tires. He'd stopped smoking years ago, but since he'd first set eyes on Adria, he'd felt a gnawing restlessness deep in his gut—a restlessness nicotine wouldn't satisfy. Nothing could drive away the feeling except one thing—sex with Adria Nash. His lips tightened at the thought and his jeans felt suddenly tight.

She was definitely off limits.

For Christ's sake, she could be your half-sister!

He gnashed his teeth and shifted into fourth.

The truth of the matter was that Adria or London or whoever the hell she was just happened to be the most attractive woman he'd seen in a long, long while. Beautiful, sexy as hell, with a quiet confidence and sharp tongue that should have repelled him, he found her more fascinating than any of the women he'd known. Even Kat. There had been a predatory edge to his stepmother that he hadn't liked and during the time she'd set out to seduce him, Zachary had felt manipulated. While in Kat's bed he'd felt as primal and manly as humanly possible, but after the hot sex was over, he'd been empty, emotionally drained and left with the uneasy sensation that he was being used.

He'd tried to avoid women after Kat, but it had been difficult as the more aloof he'd become, the more female attention he attracted. The hell of it was, he loved sex. It was just that simple. He just didn't need the emotional entanglements that came with a night in a woman's bed, so he'd made a stab at celibacy. It hadn't worked and he'd eventually married.

He'd met Joanna Whitby shortly after Kat's death. In retro-
spect, the relationship had been doomed from the beginning.
Zach, carrying a truckload of guilt around with him had been
devastated when Kat had committed suicide and Joanna had
been there, with her magical hands, soothing words, and compli-
ant body, she'd helped him forget and he'd married her. He
hadn't even suspected that she was after her slice of the Danvers
family pie, but of course that had been her motive. When he'd
told her he wasn't interested in the fortune, she hadn't believed
him. "You can't be serious," she'd said with one of her beautiful
smiles. "Zach, that's crazy!"

"No more crazy than it is to sit around here and kiss up to the
old man just hoping that he cuts me into the will."

When she'd finally figured out that Zach wasn't going to beg
Witt to leave him so much as a dime, she'd found a reason to
divorce him and had moved on. Word had it that she'd remarried an older man in Seattle, a widower with no children and now
she was fixed for life.

Zach hoped so. He'd learned his lesson about what women
really wanted out of life and it seemed to revolve around dollar
signs. Adria wasn't any different.

Jack Logan wouldn't give Adria the time of day. Retired from
the police department, he lived in Sellwood, a small community
wedged between southeast Portland and Milwaukie. His cottage
was one block off Thirteenth, behind a warehouse that had been
converted into one of the antique shops for which Sellwood was
famous.

Adria had called and left messages on his answering machine
and, when he hadn't called her back, she'd decided to visit him.
But she couldn't get past the gate at the front walk where a
snarling German shepherd stood guard.

Obviously the ex-police detective wanted his privacy.

She didn't have any better luck with Roger Phelps, a private
investigator Witt had used in trying to locate his daughter twenty
years ago. Phelps was retired, living in Tacoma and when Adria

had reached him by phone, he told her he never discussed his clients' cases. She'd explained who she was and he'd laughed, telling her to "join the club." Apparently he'd seen more than his share of would-be London Danverses when Witt had posted the million-dollar reward.

"Strike two," she told herself as she hung up the phone in her hotel room. Another reason she'd stayed at the Orion was in the hopes that there might be someone working in the old building who would remember back to the night when London Danvers had been kidnapped and Zachary Danvers had been nearly killed.

Most of the people who had worked at the hotel then had long since left the employ of the hotel. Only a middle-aged Thai woman and a man who ran the magazine shop in the lobby remained. The maid wouldn't talk to her, explaining in halting English that she didn't understand, but the man who sold candy, cigarettes, and magazines enjoyed reminiscing.

"Sure I remember," he said when she approached him. "Hell, I was right here in this very booth when I saw Witt's kid stumble out of the elevator. I knew right away somethin' was wrong with him. 'Course I didn't realize who he was at the time, not until the next day, when the first edition came in." With a gnarled hand, he slapped a stack of newspapers under the counter. "That night several of the guests had shown up, all excited they were talking about trouble at the Hotel Danvers, but no one seemed to know exactly what had happened. The talk was fast and wild about a kidnapping or a murder or some big heist, but no one knew the real scoop.

"Well, I poked my head out for a look-see and couldn't help noticin' the police cars with their lights aflashin' all over the place. I couldn't leave my chair too long, though, 'cause some of those bellboys back then had sticky fingers, if ya know what I mean. Even though I had the key to my cash box in my trouser pocket, they could rob me blind in a couple of minutes. So I had to sit on this here stool and wait for news.

"It didn't take too long. The kid, he stumbles out into the street and within fifteen, maybe twenty minutes, cops are crawlin' all over this place, runnin' up to the third floor where he said he'd been with some call girl. Room 317, no that ain't right. 307. That was it; 307. The manager takes the police up there and I guess they found booze and drugs and a pool of blood stainin' the carpet, but no whore and no sign of the two guys who were supposed to have roughed the Danvers kid up."

"Who was the room registered to?" she asked, leaning over the counter.

"That was the hell of it. Get this. The name on the guest register was Danvers. Witt Danvers."

"Witt?" she said, stunned. "But—"

"Isn't that a hoot?" He cackled. "While Witt's up at his own hotel havin' the time of his life, someone steals his name and uses the room as a damned whorehouse." He scratched his head above one ear and turned his attention to a man in a dark suit who wanted a copy of the *Wall Street Journal*. After handing the guy his change, he turned back to Adria. "If ya ask me, Anthony Polidori was behind the whole setup. There was always bad blood between the Polidoris and the Danvers. Had been for generations. It just seemed to explode about the time Witt lost his little girl, and Zach Danvers, if you can believe what he says, claims the guys who roughed him up were Italians. Same with the whore."

"Just because they were Italian didn't mean they were working for the Polidoris."

"On the same night Witt's kid is taken?" The man's silvery eyebrows lifted behind the thick rims of his glasses. "What'd'ya think? It was just coincidence?"

A good question. She knew there had been some sort of feud between the wealthy Italian family and the Danvers clan, but didn't understand how the feud affected the kidnapping. After asking a few more questions and getting nowhere, she purchased a couple of candy bars and two magazines about Portland, then checked with the clerk at the desk for messages before heading up to her room.

On impulse, she stopped at the third floor and walked the corridor, pausing at room 307. So this was Zach's alibi. A tryst with an Italian prostitute. Adria smiled. He'd been little more than a kid at the time—sixteen. What was he doing with a whore?

Stupidly, she felt a touch of jealousy for the woman he had planned to meet. What could it possibly matter to her—she'd been only five at the time! *And his half-sister!* Damn it all, this was more complicated than she'd thought. She hadn't planned on being attracted to Zachary. She'd hoped he would become her friend, perhaps even her accomplice, and eventually proved to be her blood kin . . . but nothing romantic, nothing dangerous, nothing so sinful. For a second she thought of her mother and what she would have said had she known the path Adria had taken. *The wages of sin are—* "Stop it!" she whispered harshly to herself. She'd already convinced herself to forget Zachary. Aside from the fact that he might be her half-brother, he wasn't the kind of man to get involved with, a rawhide tough man who dared cross the line to the wrong side of the law, who didn't give a damn about what other people thought, who ran the world the way he thought it should be run, rather than the way it was. A good man to avoid.

Except that she needed him. If she were ever going to get to the truth.

Refusing to dwell on Zachary, she twisted the doorknob and turned, but the bolt was drawn and she couldn't peek inside. Not that it would help. The room had probably been redecorated three times over since the night Zach was beaten to a pulp. How much of his story was true? How much fabrication? How much exaggerated by the old man in the lobby?

Zach seemed to hold the key to what happened that night, but he'd been evasive with her, suspicious of her motives. Somehow she had to gain his trust. Not an easy task, she thought, as she stepped into the Orion's mirrored elevator car and slapped the button for the door to close.

* * *

As agreed, Jack Logan sat in the darkened booth of the Red Eye Café, a small dive near the airport. It was a smoky bar that he'd used before when he didn't want to be recognized. He spied Jason Danvers and swore under his breath. The man was dressed in a double-breasted suit for crying out loud and he'd pulled up in his Jag.

"Why didn't you just put a neon sign on your back?" Logan growled, nursing his glass of McNaughton's.

"What?"

"You stick out like a fucking sore thumb."

Danvers frowned. "I don't intend to be here very long."

"Neither do I."

Jason ordered a whiskey on the rocks and waited until the waitress left the drink and picked up the bills. Ignoring the drink, he reached into his jacket and pulled out the tape, which he slid across the table to Logan.

"What's this?"

"I hope nothing." Jason filled Logan in on all the details.

"How many copies of this are floating around?"

"God only knows. She gave me one, and I gave a copy to Sweeny."

"None to the police."

"Not yet. I thought you could check it out."

"Should go to the station."

"Too many leaks. I turn it in and it'll be on the six o'clock news."

Logan grunted. He couldn't argue with that logic. "I'll see what I can do, but she's been nosing around."

Jason froze. "What do you mean?"

"She's called my house a dozen times and even come up the front walk."

"You talked to her."

"Not yet."

"Shit!" He ran a hand through his hair. "This is worse than I thought."

"You worried about her?"

Jason's gaze darted around the bar. "Hell, yes, I'm worried."

"Think she's London?"

"No!"

"But you're not sure."

"Nothing's sure, Logan."

"Looks just like your stepmother." The two men glared at each other for a second, sharing a secret neither wanted revealed, then Jason finished his drink.

"Just don't talk to her and find out what you can. If she goes public, we'll give the tape to the police."

"But not before."

"Nope."

"You say Sweeny's in on this?"

"In Montana right now. Checking out her story. He called yesterday."

"He's an asshole."

"Work with him on this, okay? Keep your ear to the ground and your mouth shut. If the police get wind of the story, let me know." Jason left a twenty on the table and swaggered outside.

"Bastard," Logan muttered under his breath as he quickly changed the twenty for a five.

Manny was right. The ranch could run itself. Zach didn't need to be here. Once again he wasn't needed. The story of his life. He smiled grimly to himself as he walked across the dusting of new-fallen snow to the shed where Manny was repairing a tractor. Tools lined the walls, a stained workbench stretched along a far wall and the smell of oil and dust hung in the air.

Light flickered from fluorescent tubes and Manny, cursing to himself, was half lying under the tractor's engine. "Damned fool thing," he muttered, working on the fuel line.

"How's it going?" Zach asked.

"Like hell." He gave the wrench another tug, then grunted. Satisfied with his work he crawled out from under the tractor and pulled himself upright.

A full-blooded Paiute, Manny was a tall man with smooth

burnished skin, long braids beginning to gray, and a face usually devoid of expression. He found his black cowboy hat on the seat of the tractor and plopped it onto his head. "I thought I told you to stay in the city where you belong." Manny wiped a rag over his greasy hands.

"Couldn't stand it."

Manny flashed a grin that showed teeth rimmed in gold. "Don't blame you. The only reasons to go into town are women and whiskey. You can get those here."

He thought of Adria. Right now women were dangerous. Especially a woman claiming to be his half-sister. Whiskey was definitely safer.

Together they walked out of the shed. The sky was a gray shade of blue, the air crisp, and dark-bellied clouds collected to the west, hanging along the rigid skyline of the Cascades.

"Family business all taken care of?" Manny asked.

Somewhere in the distance a horse neighed.

"It'll never be," Zach said. If not Adria, then another imposter would show up. For the rest of his life Zach would meet women pretending to be London Danvers. He just hoped they didn't get to him the way this one did. He knew that one of the reasons he'd driven like a madman over the mountains was to put some distance between him and her, to run back here where he could clear his head.

"Got a buyer for the two-year-old steers."

"All of them?" Zach asked, trying to forget about the woman who claimed to be his half-sister.

"Couple hundred head."

"A good start."

"Mmm."

"Come on inside, I'll buy you breakfast and you can bring me up to date."

He spent the day at the ranch, reviewing the books, checking offers to buy and sell livestock as well as land, then rode through some of the fields. The water pump for the house and out-buildings was going out, the roof of one of the sheds was leaking like a sieve, there was a fight with the government over harvesting some of the ancient pine, and one of their regular customers who bought hundreds of head of cattle every year, was delinquent on his payments. There had been an outbreak of a cattle virus in the next county and several ranchers in the area were concerned. Zach was supposed to attend a local meeting of the Cattlemen's Association in Bend, and order the feed and supplies to get the ranch through the winter.

"Same old, same old," Manny said as they drove through the fields and spotted a break in the fence where cattle could escape. It was true. Though there were problems at the ranch, they weren't insurmountable. Manny and the hands could keep the place going should Zach have to return to Portland.

He stopped by his office in Bend and found that work was slow, as it had been ever since he'd turned his attention to refurbishing the old hotel. He made a few phone calls, met with a couple of realtors interested in starting a new resort development around a golf course, and conferred with his secretary, Terry, a petite, red-haired woman of thirty who was expecting her third child come February. Efficient to the point that she could run the office blindfolded, she knew Zach as well as anyone.

"So how's city life?" she asked when he walked back into the office. She was seated behind the desk, a pencil tucked over her ear, a neglected cup of coffee near the typewriter. She was studying a bank statement and little lines of worry crinkled her freckled forehead.

"Not great."

"Jason called." She sat back in her desk chair and it protested with a groan.

"Here?"

"He tried the ranch. You weren't in. Manny told him you'd come into town, so he tried tracking you down here. Said it was urgent that he talk to you."

"With Jason it's always urgent."

"He was more insistent than usual." She set her glasses on the desk, grabbed her half-full cup and stood. Rubbing a kink in her back, she walked to the coffeepot warming on the hot plate and lifted the glass carafe. "Want a cup? It's just decaf."

Zach shook his head. "Thanks just the same."

Pouring some of the weak coffee into her mug, she asked, "So why does Jason think he needs you back in Portland—the hotel?"

"Yeah, that's probably it," Zach said, but he guessed that the problem was Adria Nash. No doubt he'd have to drive back to the city. Resentment boiled through his blood. He didn't want to see Adria again; didn't want to deal with all the conflicting emotions she inspired.

He grabbed the handle of the coffeepot and poured himself some of the tasteless decaf as the telephone rang and Terry answered.

With a sweet smile, she said, "He'll be with you in a second," and snapped the hold button. "It's your brother dear again and he's fit to be tied."

"Why?"

"Something about the shit hitting the fan." She went back to the bank statement and Zach walked into his office. Kicking the door shut, he reached for the phone and sat on a corner of the desk.

"Hello?"

"Where the hell have you been?" Jason demanded and Zach couldn't miss the agitation in his voice.

"What's the problem?"

"You know what the problem is. It's Adria! I think she's going to run to the papers with her story."

"She told you this?"

"In so many words."

Zach felt his shoulder muscles pull together into hard, tight knots. "What happened?"

"I called her. Offered her a little more money."

"And she got pissed."

"Beyond pissed."

"Christ, Jason, you never back down, do you?" He was on his feet without even thinking about it.

"Just get back here."

"And clean up your mess."

"Do whatever it takes, Zach. You're in this as deep as the rest of us!"

Anthony Polidori didn't like his breakfast disturbed. In his later years, he felt as if an intrusion upon his meals or his sleep was a personal affront and he left strict instructions with everyone in the household that he was not to be interrupted. Even by his son.

He sat in the bay window of the morning room overlooking the river and picked at his croissant with idle fingers as he scanned the newspaper for sports scores from the day before. The day was bright for late October, and he wore sunglasses to protect his eyes.

Mario sauntered into the room carrying a chipped ceramic mug. His hair was disheveled and he hadn't yet shaved. He looked like hell as he poured himself a cup of coffee from the silver carafe on the table. Mario was uncivilized—he had no manners.

Anthony didn't bother hiding his irritation. He folded the sports section of the *Oregonian* and set it by his glass of juice. "What is it?" His son wasn't usually up by noon.

"Big news." Mario flashed his killer smile—the one that got him into all the trouble with the women. He walked to the glass wall facing west and watched a barge being pushed upriver by a tugboat.

"It must be to get you out of bed while the sun's still up."

Mario snorted, then plopped into the wrought-iron chair opposite his father. "I think you want to hear this."

"I'm waiting."

"Looks like there's a new lady in town."

"This is news?"

Mario slowly poured a thin stream of cream into his coffee. "Could be. Claims she's London Danvers."

Behind his sunglasses, Anthony's eyes narrowed thoughtfully. "This isn't news. It's predictable. Damned predictable."

Mario's dark eyes twinkled and he reached over and stole the fruit cup his father always savored for the last part of the meal. Annoyed, Anthony motioned to the maid, who had already anticipated his request and was scurrying off to the kitchen.

"There's always someone claiming to be London."

Mario rubbed the stubble on his jaw. "But you should see this one. She's the fuckin' spittin' image of her old lady. Katherine—wasn't that her name?"

Anthony's spine stiffened a bit. He didn't like foul language—not at the table and he wasn't in the mood to be jerked around by his son. It was hard to read Mario these days. "So she resembles—"

"Not only resembles, the way I hear it she's the goddamned mirror image!"

Anthony set down his fork as the maid brought a second cup of fruit and a plate for Mario. He was enjoying himself, grinning as he sliced into a greasy sausage, ignoring all sense of decorum as he set his elbows on the table.

"Maybe I should meet—what's-her-name?"

"Adria Nash. Hails from some hick town in Montana; I've got a couple of guys working on it."

"How'd you find out about her? I haven't seen a word in the paper or heard anything on the news."

"She hasn't gone public yet, but probably will. One of our men spotted her at the grand opening of the hotel. She came in with Zach Danvers, then made the rounds meeting the 'family.' " Mario took a sip from his cup. "Jason nearly shit bricks."

"I'll bet," Anthony said dryly. "How authentic is she?"

"Could be the real thing." Mario skewered his father with a hard look. "You know, lots of people think you kidnapped the girl."

Anthony picked up the remainder of his croissant. "If I'd taken her, do you think she'd be walking up to the Danvers family right now and announcing that she was their long-lost sister?" He saw his son blanch and felt a glimmer of satisfaction. "What does Trisha think? Is she worried?" he asked coldly.

A small muscle worked in the side of Mario's cheek. "How should I know?"

"Aren't you still seeing her?"

"You took care of that a long time ago," his son said with more than a trace of bitterness.

"Trisha Danvers is a slut."

Mario's eyes sparked with a deadly rage.

"She used you to get back at her father. That's all there was to it." Anthony snapped his newspaper open and wondered about the woman who called herself London Danvers. He'd have to find out everything there was to know about her. "Maybe we should invite Miss Nash over," he said, flicking a gaze over the top of the paper. Mario had elbowed his plate aside and was brooding.

"Why?"

"For old time's sake."

"Witt's dead. What could it mean to you?"

Anthony didn't bother answering. How could he explain to his son that feuds never ended? No matter how many of the players died, the vengeance continued. As long as there was anyone named Danvers left in Portland, Anthony wouldn't be satisfied.

He was pleased with the news that another London Danvers had shown up.

Adria knocked on the door of the small apartment in Tigard, a suburb just over the west hills of Portland. Within minutes she saw a dark eye in the peephole and quickly the bolt was thrown.

The door opened and a small Chicano woman with graying black hair twisted into a bun and incredibly white teeth stood over the threshold.

"Mrs. Santiago?"

"For the love of Mary," the woman whispered, crossing her ample bosom. "You are the image of the missus."

"Could I come in?" Adria asked. She'd already called the woman, Maria Santiago, who had worked for the Danvers family until her retirement shortly after Witt's death. She'd explained her business and Maria had reluctantly agreed to see her.

"Please, please—" Maria stepped out of the way and waved her inside the tiny rooms. "Sit down."

Adria perched on the edge of a floral couch that was worn around the edges and Maria settled into a rocker by the window and put her feet onto a stool.

Adria had already explained on the phone why she was in Portland. She'd sketched out her story, explaining that she was adopted, that she wanted to find her roots, that all the records were destroyed and Maria, obviously lonely, had offered to speak with her.

"I don't mean to ask you to break confidences," Adria said, "but there's just so much I don't know about the Danvers family. I thought you could help me."

Maria rubbed her chin and stared out the window to the parking lot. "A few years ago, I would not have said a word," she admitted, "but then, the mister, he died and Jason, he fired me. Now—" She rubbed her hands anxiously together. "What is it you want to know?"

"Everything."

"Ahh. That would take some time. There is so much."

Adria couldn't believe her good luck. She smiled at the pleasant little woman. "I've got the rest of my life," she said and sat back to listen.

It was nearly ten o'clock by the time she returned to the Orion and her head, as well as her tiny tape recorder, was filled with facts about the Danvers family, secrets, and the answer to some mysteries, including the feud with the Polidoris.

She considered celebrating with a glass of wine and a hot bath in the hotel room because tomorrow she'd have to move to a cheaper, and less high-profile apartment. After settling in, she had other important business to attend to. Since the Danvers family wouldn't recognize her, it was time to go to the police and press. As soon as she found a more permanent address, she'd contact the authorities and grant an interview with someone from the local newspaper to start the ball rolling. Then, of course, she'd have to speak with the lawyers for Witt's estate. She wasn't looking forward to any of the interviews, but she'd get through them.

She'd be called a gold digger, a fraud, an opportunist, and an imposter. The Danvers family would go after her with all the money they had behind them. They would try to dig up any rumors that might discredit her and they would look into her past, digging, always digging and looking for any glitch in her story, any inaccuracies in their attempts to disprove that she was London.

That's what she wanted.

And what about Zachary?

Oh, Lord, yes. What about Zachary?

In her room, she stripped off her clothes, poured herself a glass of Chablis, then slid into a tub of hot water. She sipped her wine slowly and considered her half-brother.

Sexy.

Smart.

Rough.

Big trouble.

Like Mark Kennedy, Zach Danvers was a man to avoid unless she wanted to lose her heart.

13

The water in the tub was cold and somehow she'd finished her glass of Chablis, but she'd lost track of the time, her thoughts had been so jumbled, the past and present blurred. Her life in Belamy seemed distant and try as she would, she couldn't remember the lines of Mark's face, though her memory of that horrid night at the river was never completely repressed, always lingered just below the surface of her conscious thoughts.

Her mother's stroke and eventual death had foreshadowed her father's steady decline. Victor Nash's death had come after so much agony that it had been a blessing when life had slipped away from him; however, losing them all had stripped her emotionally and taken away her sense of family, of belonging.

Now, as she eased out of the tub and buffed her skin dry with one of the Orion's thick towels, she wondered about her mission—her quest to find her true identity. Was she London Danvers? Did it matter if she was? Did she really want to be related to any of those people—the Danvers kin? None of them appealed to her.

Except Zachary.

Not that she trusted him. He was no better than the rest, but she couldn't wedge his image out of her mind. Rugged whereas his brothers took pride in being polished; outwardly irreverent while Nelson took pains to look as if he played by the rules. Zachary was arrogant because he didn't give a damn, Jason was arrogant because he thought he deserved the money and power into which he'd been born.

Zachary was different.

Because of the blood flowing through his veins? Because he could be a Polidori? She grimaced at the thought, but found it intriguing. Her relationship with him would be easier to understand if he wasn't part of the Danvers family. She rubbed the mist from the mirror with the edge of the towel and wondered about Zachary, what kind of man he was, what it would feel like to have him take her to his bed. . . .

The thought was like a cold slap in her face. What was she doing fantasizing about a man who detested her, a man who could be her half-brother? Giving herself a swift mental kick, she stared into her reflection and told herself that she had to think of him as her brother: her irritable, woman-hating, problem of a half-brother who was, without a doubt, her sworn enemy.

Just like the rest of the clan.

She slipped into a oversized T-shirt and climbed into the bed. The sheets were crisp and clean, but didn't have the same country-fresh scent of those that were dried on the line at home. In Belamy. Funny, for years she'd wanted to escape. City lights had beckoned her young heart, but duty had kept her tied to the only town she'd ever called home. Not that it mattered, but the harsh Montana grassland didn't seem so loathsome anymore and for the first time in years she thought of her hometown and felt the pull of her heartstrings.

But she wasn't running back to the safety and boredom of Belamy. Not when she'd come so far. "When the going gets tough, the tough get going," she reminded herself as she plumped a pillow.

Closing her eyes, she heard the hum of traffic, an occasional shout and, every so often, the distant cry of sirens. She wondered where Zachary was, and then, irritated that she allowed him into her mind, she rolled over. Within twenty minutes she fell into a deep sleep and she didn't hear the footsteps that paused in the hallway during the middle of the night, nor did she awaken as a note was slipped under her door.

It was only the next morning when she was still rubbing the

sleep from her eyes as she walked toward the door intending to
pick up the newspaper left in the hallway, that she spied the
single sheet of white paper, creased neatly in half laying on the
carpet in front of her closet. She picked it up and unfolded it. The
message was simple and concise: GO HOME BITCH.

Her mouth turned to dust.

She read the words again and fear crept up her arm in the form
of goose bumps.

She felt a tingle of dread before wadding the paper in her fist.
"Great," she mumbled to herself. She should be frightened, she
supposed, for this was just the first warning of what would
probably be many, but along with a tiny drop of fear, she felt a
small amount of satisfaction.

Someone was worried.

Worried enough to try and warn her off.

Smiling for the first time that morning she decided that maybe,
just maybe, she was on the right track.

Wedged between the pool tables and the rest rooms, the
phone booth was located in the back corner of the tavern.
Sweeny charged the call to his credit card and waited as the
phone rang in Portland. He needed to report to Danvers, but first
things first.

Foster's voice boomed over the line. "You have reached the
offices of Michael Foster. I'm away from the phone right now, but
if you leave your name and number and the time you called, I'll
get back to you—"

"Bullshit!" Sweeny growled. Foster was a damned paraplegic.
Where the hell could he go? Sure he had one of those special
vans with hand brakes and all, but really, how could the guy get
around? It beat the hell out of Sweeny and the fact that Foster was
involved with a beautiful, intelligent woman bothered him. What
would a babe like that do with a cripple? The beep shrilled in his
ear. "Foster? You there? It's me, Sweeny. Pick up the goddamned
phone." He waited, but no one answered. "Hell," he ground out.

"Look, I know you're there, so pick up. I've got a job for you. One that pays well. If you're interested . . ." He waited but still no answer. Drumming his fingers on the edge of a tattered copy of the yellow pages, he finally decided to give up. "I'll call later." As he slammed down the receiver, he tried to shake off his bad mood, but it lingered, like the snow-blowing wind that seemed to forever cut through this bitch of a town.

He settled into the bar, drank his beer and listened to some country-western ballad where the guy was all choked up over some dead woman. Christ, what a miserable place. A few of the locals came in, smiled and chatted with the bartender and climbed onto their usual stools. Just like goddamned "Cheers" on television. Sweeny could name them all—Norm, Cliff, Sam . . . Rather than gawk at the hicks, he turned his attention to a television positioned over the bar where a baseball game was in progress. He didn't even check the score.

His bones ached from the job he'd done the night before. After he'd driven to the farm where Adria Nash had been raised, he'd talked with the people who'd leased the place, but he hadn't learned much. Either the couple was tight-lipped by nature or they'd seen through his story of being an insurance agent interested in selling fire insurance on the house and out-buildings. He'd never even gotten inside. The woman had kept the screen door closed and locked and had spoken tersely through the torn steel webbing. After striking out at the farm, he'd driven to the only bank of storage units in town, bribed the kid who was the night watchman and broken into Ms. Nash's unit. Sweeny, sensing a bonanza, had spent hours in the cramped space, moving boxes, climbing over old, tasteless furniture, and digging through pile after pile of crates until he'd hit pay dirt and come up with the family Bible as well as copies of tax returns that proved how broke Adria Nash really was. No wonder she was after the Danvers's money. The tax files and the Bible were now sitting securely back in the storage unit. He'd taken copies of the returns and the family tree section of the Bible including any pages with notations on them, then slipped the kid watching the storage place a fifty, and replaced Adria's property in the packing crates. She'd never be the wiser.

But he was still stuck in this frigid hellhole. He downed another beer and checked his watch. Hauling his briefcase, he strolled back to the phone booth. This time, Foster was there. The computer nut picked up on the second ring.

" 'Bout time," Sweeny grumbled.

"Oswald. Always a pleasure." Foster didn't bother hiding the sarcasm in his voice.

"Yeah, right."

"Okay, so I got your message. What's up?"

"It's a piece of cake. I want you to find some people for me. The first one has several names. She goes by Ginny Slade, Virginia Watson, or Virginia Watson Slade. She's somewhere around fifty, give or take a few years, I think, and was married to Bobby or Robert Slade."

"That's it?" Foster asked.

"What more do you need?"

"Watson and Slade aren't uncommon names. How about a location to start with—you know, something like east of the Mississippi?"

"Just a minute." Impatiently Oswald opened his briefcase and pulled out his copies of the family tree from the Bible. "Okay, let's see," he said, running his finger down the page. "Looks like Virginia was born in Memphis, Tennessee. She and Bobby were married in the First Christian Church in June of 1967. Other than those specific dates, all I know is that she cruised through Montana at one time and gave up her daughter, probably named Adria or something like it for adoption. An old couple—Victor Nash and his wife Sharon—adopted the kid some time in late 1974, I think, though I can't find any reference to a specific date and no official papers were filed."

"That all?"

"Not quite," Sweeny said, loving to spread news meant to

shock. "Get a load of this: we suspect this Virginia Watson Slade might have been the governess for London Danvers."

There was a long, low whistle on the other end of the line. "Ginny Slade."

"Bingo."

"So why're you involved? No, let me guess. The kid's shown up and is demanding her part of the fortune."

"You got it."

"Could be interesting."

"See what you can come up with."

"Where can I reach you?"

"I'll call you. Need anything else?"

"How about a Social Security number?"

"Right." Sweeny sorted through his notes on Ginny Slade. "Got it," he said and rattled off the series of numbers she'd used when she was London's governess. He explained a little more about the case and hung up, satisfied that Foster would come up with something. He was a computer hacker from the eighties who'd found a way to put his skills to work. Sweeny didn't really know how he operated, if he broke into the IRS's files or had someone in the government working for him, but Foster was part of a national service where people who had been lost were found—even people who didn't want to be located. He'd get the job done one way or the other.

Satisfied, Sweeny snapped his briefcase shut, then found his seat on the bar again. He felt better. Another drink and he'd call Jason Danvers.

Adria glanced over her shoulder but she didn't see a familiar face in the stream of people that passed by the front door of the Orion. She told herself that she was being paranoid, that no one was following her, but she couldn't shake the feeling that someone was watching her. All day while she scouted around town looking for a more permanent residence, she'd felt as if a pair of eyes had been boring into her back, watching her every move.

Probably because of the note she'd found on her floor this morning.

She'd half expected to run into Zachary again, but he hadn't shown up and it wasn't his style to stay in the shadows. He might follow her, as he'd done before, but he'd end up confronting her again.

So who?

No one, she decided as she swept her gaze along the street again. She didn't see anyone hunched over a newspaper, or lounging near a telephone booth, or quickly ducking into store-fronts when she glanced behind her. The Danvers family had just put her on edge, that was all. She was jumping at shadows.

Waving to the old man behind the magazine counter, she dashed into the hotel and asked for messages at the front desk. She was handed one note from the switchboard and a stiff white envelope with her name scrolled across the linen surface. Rather than read the messages where anyone lounging in the lobby could see her, she took the elevator to her floor.

In her room, she kicked off her shoes and dropped onto the foot of one of the two queen-size beds, then scanned the notes. The telephone call was from Nelson Danvers, who wanted to speak with her "urgently." Good. Progress, she thought. But she could let Nelson wait a little longer.

The invitation in the linen envelope wasn't expected. She pulled out the handwritten card and read the offer: Mr. Anthony Polidori requests the honor of your presence tonight at dinner, seven o'clock at Antonio's. A driver will pick you up in front of the hotel.

No telephone number. No address. Just a note left at the front desk of the Orion.

Adria read the words over again. Why would Polidori want to see her? Obviously he'd heard that she was in town claiming to be London Danvers, but how? And how did he know where she was staying? She felt goose bumps crawl up her back and she walked to the window and stared out at the street, wondering again if she were being followed or if anyone was watching her room.

She saw no one leaning against a lamppost and smoking a cigarette while staring up at her window, no malicious figure darting into the shadows.

"Just a case of nerves," she told herself as she tapped the edge of the card to her lips and walked to her closet where she eyed her meager wardrobe. What would it hurt to meet Polidori? Should she take him up on his offer or would that be playing into his hands?

She smiled to herself because she was starting to think like a Danvers. She had no reason to fear the Polidoris, in fact, talking with Witt Danvers's sworn enemy could be enlightening. According to everyone in the family, he was the most likely suspect in the kidnapping of London. So why would he want to see her?

She changed into a simple black skirt and white silk blouse, twisted her hair onto her head and slipped her arms through the sleeves of a royal blue jacket.

By the time she hurried out of the elevator in the main lobby, the limo had arrived and a driver helped her into the shadowed interior. She wasn't alone. Two men sat across from each other. The short older man in an elegant gray suit and dark glasses greeted her. "Ms. Nash," he said taking her hand as she slid onto the seat beside him. "Welcome. Welcome. I'm Anthony Polidori. My son, Mario."

"My pleasure," Mario said smoothly. He was dark-skinned with even features, curling black hair cut longer than fashionable and eyes the color of obsidian.

"I was surprised to hear from you," she said, deciding not to play games.

Anthony smiled and tapped his son on the knee with his cane. "She was surprised." He patted her arm as the limousine pulled away from the curb. "You've not heard of the feud between the Danvers family and my own?" His voice was skeptical.

"A little," she hedged, not wanting to give anything away.

"A little, ah, well, there is much. Such a waste . . ." For a few seconds he seemed lost in thought and only the soft sound of classical music filled the plush interior of the car. "Mario, where are your manners? Ask Ms. Nash if she cares for a drink."

"Later, maybe," she said, but Mario ignored her and poured a glass of wine from a bottle chilling in an ice bucket.

"Please, be our guest," Mario insisted. Probably in his late thirties or early forties, Mario was a smoothly handsome man who wore his good looks like an expensive suit. He seemed to pose as he sat across from her and as he handed her the stemmed glass of chilled wine, his fingers brushed hers for just a fraction of an instant but his gaze touched hers briefly before he removed his hand.

Staring out the tinted windows, Anthony clucked his tongue. "It's sad, this feud," he admitted, "but it can't be helped. It goes back for generations, you see. Starting with Julius Danvers and my father."

That much Adria understood. Maria, who had worked for the Danvers family for years, had told her of Stefano Polidori and how he became the rival to the Danvers family.

The original patriarch of the Danvers family Julius Danvers made his money and the beginning of the family fortune in the late 1800s. An immigrant logger who had the foresight to acquire all the timber-rich land he could beg, borrow, buy, or, in some cases, steal, he not only founded a company to harvest the raw timber that was abundant in the state, but also built a chain of sawmills that eventually stretched from northern California to the Canadian border north of Seattle.

It had been rumored, but never proven, that Julius was a mean son of a bitch who was willing to kill any man who tried to thwart him in his quest for unrivaled power in the timber-rich Pacific Northwest. His guilt in several "logging accidents," which took the lives of some of the men not particularly loyal to him, was always assumed, but never proved.

Already a wealthy man by the turn of the century, Julius

diversified into shipping and hotels, spreading the family fortune into new industries. He opened he elegant Hotel Danvers in downtown Portland in time for the Lewis and Clark Exposition of 1905. The hotel, rumored to be the most lavish in Portland, became home to the elite who traveled to the city on the Willamette River.

Though Julius never finished the ninth grade, he was also instrumental in establishing Reed College, the first college in Portland, where his children attended school and earned diplomas as well as social standing.

Julius was famous for his hard, cruel streak and it was generally thought that he'd won favors from politicians, judges, and policemen, thereby having more than his share of important men hidden deep within his gold-filled pockets. Julius was careful to align with the powers-that-be in the city and state in order to assure that nothing would ever stand in the way of his ambitions or threaten his family.

His biggest competitor was Stefano Polidori, an Italian immigrant, one of the few in Portland, who had started his career by working on a truck farm in southeast Portland. Stefano had sold vegetables from a cart and later a truck, saving every penny and eventually buying several farms as he could afford them. As the city and his business grew, he opened a highly successful open-air vegetable market and later a restaurant. Eventually he had accumulated enough money to build a hotel that rivaled the Hotel Danvers in turn-of-the-century charm.

The Polidori family, too, became rich and as Stefano added to his fortune and diversified his investments, he stepped on Julius's toes by outbidding him on prime real estate along the river or by convincing conventioneers that his hotel was better able to serve their needs than the Hotel Danvers.

Stefano and Julius became bitter rivals.

Julius couldn't believe a dago could do anything more than sell tomatoes and lettuce from a cart. But Stefano was as shrewd and tough as his fiercest competitor. Like Julius, Stefano used his

wealth to purchase rungs in the gold-plated social ladder of
Portland.

The rivalry and hatred between the two men and their families
deepened as the years passed.

"I've heard about Julius as well as your father," Adria ventured
as the limo turned into the parking lot of the riverfront restaurant.

"Stubborn men, both of them." Anthony sighed loudly. "We
all blamed Julius for my father's death, you know."

She'd read of the fire, of course. It had been a major news story
in 1935. The cause of the blaze had been a grease fire that had
started in the kitchen, but some journalists wondered if Stefano's
death had truly been an accident, or if Julius Danvers had somehow masterminded the blaze that had burned the hotel and
surrounding buildings to the ground.

Upon his father's grave, and in full view of the press, Anthony
Polidori, the new patriarch of the family, had sworn vengeance
against the murdering Danvers family.

"Here we are," he said, motioning to the restaurant. "A friend
of mine owns it." The door of the limo was opened by the driver
and Anthony, barely using his cane, walked briskly down the
plank docking leading to the front doors.

As they entered they were greeted loudly by the maître d'.
Voices from the kitchen staff and waiters shouted out greetings
as well. In this Italian restaurant, Anthony had no enemies.

"So good to see you," the maître d' enthused. "Your table's
ready. Please come this way." They were led up a steep flight of
stairs to a private glassed-in room on the second story that
offered a 360-degree view of the bridges spanning the murky
Willamette River.

"Beautiful, is it not?" Anthony asked.

"Very." Adria nodded as the maître d' pulled out a chair for
her.

"This river, it's the life blood of the city." Anthony gazed
through the windows as if he could never get enough of the

panorama of the Willamette River and the skyscrapers rising off the western shore.

Without waiting for him to order a slim waiter brought wine and crusty Italian bread. "The usual?" he asked as he poured three glasses.

"For all of us," Polidori responded.

"Why did you want to see me?" she asked as the waiter disappeared.

"Haven't you guessed?" Anthony's dark eyes twinkled devilishly and he chuckled.

Mario came to the rescue. "It's because we know you've come to Portland for your birth right. That you're claiming to be London Danvers."

Adria took a sip of the Chianti. "Why would you care?"

"Try the bread," Anthony ordered, ignoring her question for the moment. "It's the best in the city. Probably in all of the Northwest." He reached for a slice himself.

"Does the Danvers family still bother you?"

She was rewarded with one of his smiles. "I always care what happens to the family of my old rival." He glanced up at her and dusted the crumbs from his fingers. "It was a shock to me when the little girl was abducted and yet I was considered a suspect." Shaking his head at the folly of it all, he added, "Despite my protests and alibi, Witt and his henchman, Jack Logan, seemed to think I had something to do with the girl's disappearance. Even Mario, though he was in Hawaii at the time, was regarded as a suspect. The fact that the second son, Zachary, claimed he was roughed up by some Italians immediately put my family at the top of the list of possible kidnappers. Never mind that the two men whom he claimed to have attacked him had airtight alibis and were seen at several restaurants around the city." He wagged a finger in the air. "Didn't matter. A *Danvers* had made the accusation and in this town that makes a difference—a big difference." He raised his palms to the ceiling. "So, I would like to clear the Polidori name. And, if you are indeed London, I would like to help you." He bit into his bread and sighed happily, as if he'd forgotten the conversation, but Adria knew differently. When she didn't respond, he said, "Surely the Danvers family is not anxious for you to be their half-sister. Am I right?"

She hedged. "There's been a little resistance."

Mario snorted a laugh at her understatement and pronged a slice of bread with his knife. "I'll bet."

Waving off his son's sarcasm, Anthony said, "Of course I know nothing of your financial situation, but it's no secret that the Danvers are exceedingly wealthy and influential. If they decide to fight you on this—and believe me, they will fight you like wounded wolves, with everything they've got—I'm willing to help you."

"Help me?" she said, not sure she understood correctly.

"Yes, yes."

Mario leaned back in his chair, his dark eyes squinting thoughtfully in her direction. He steepled his fingers beneath his chin. "Our family, too, has some power in this town. In fact we think our lawyers are the best in the city. If you need legal help, or a loan—"

"I don't think that would be such a good idea." It was beginning to sound as if they wanted her in their camp and she suddenly felt anxious.

"Do you want to prove you're London or not?" Anthony asked and his dark eyes gleamed with a frosty inner light that was as cold as death.

"Of course."

"Then you should take my offer. I feel it is the least I can do to make up for the earlier injustices served to my family as well as to you."

She wanted to turn him down flat. Though he and Mario were both trying their best to be charming, she felt as if he was attempting to orchestrate the conversation and push her into a position where she'd be in debt to him forever. However, she wasn't foolish enough to reject his offer outright. Not yet. She'd learned that patience was a virtue, though sometimes hard to attain. The fact of the matter was that she was in no position to turn away help of any kind. Though the Polidoris had axes to grind with the Danvers family and there was a feud as dark as the depths of hell, she needed allies in her search—any allies she could get. "You're very generous."

"Then it's settled."

"Not quite." She swirled her wine in her glass. "You know, most of the family still thinks you were behind London's kidnapping."

With a smile as broad as his face, Polidori studied the red wine in his glass, watching the play of candlelight in the red depths. Finally, he took a long sip from his glass. "The belief that I was involved in the little girl's disappearance has been the bane of my existence as well as one of the greatest joys of my life," he admitted. "At the time, of course, it wasn't so pleasant. The police coming all the time. That Logan, he was the worst. Very upsetting. But over the years"—he gave a little shrug—"it has come to amuse me that the Danvers people think I am so powerful as to arrange the abduction right under their noses." Again his dark eyes glittered.

Adria felt her stomach clench, but she wasn't going to let this man or his reputation make her back down. There were rumors, probably generated by the Danvers family, that the Polidoris were linked with organized crime. "Did you do it?" she asked.

Again he chuckled. "To tell you the truth, Ms. Nash, I wish I would've thought of it, though, of course, I wouldn't have hurt the girl. But I would have loved to watch Witt squirm. It would have been . . . well, ironic, for lack of a better word. As I said before I'm certain old Julius Danvers was behind my father's death."

"Stefano's death has nothing to do with Witt."

Anthony settled back in his chair and cradled his wine glass. "The children must pay for the sins of their fathers."

She glanced at Mario whose expression had turned harsh. His

gaze found hers for a moment, then he stared out the window and watched the lights of a barge as it moved slowly up river.

"Is that why Robert Danvers had to die?" she asked the old man.

Polidori's smile faded. "Julius's oldest son had a boating accident, if I recall."

"Some people think you arranged it."

"People like to make something of nothing."

She plunged onward. "Julius had three children. Only one— Witt—survived."

With a long sigh, Anthony said, "Julius's second boy, Peter, was killed in the war." He frowned. "I had nothing to do with that, either, you know. Though I'm sure the Danvers family would like to think I was in league with Mussolini and Hitler, I didn't hire the Nazis to shoot Peter's plane down. Nor did I do anything to the boat that Robert was driving on the river the summer he was killed. The way I heard the story was that he'd been drinking heavily and came too close to some rocks in the Columbia. His boat crashed and exploded, breaking his neck and killing him instantly. A tragedy. But an accident."

"An accident that left Witt as the only Danvers heir."

"Precisely. If I was so vile as to have arranged all these deaths, why not kill Witt as well?"

Adria considered, then decided to gamble. She ran her finger around the rim of her glass and said, "Maybe you wanted him to twist in the wind a little. There are rumors about your rivalry with Witt. It isn't out of the question to think that you might want to watch one of Julius's sons face a little pain in his life." She didn't mention Anthony's affair with Witt's first wife, Eunice, but it hung on the air between them—suspended by invisible threads of innuendo.

Anthony's lips twisted into a cold smile. "You think I'm some big Mafia don, is that it?" he asked and exchanged looks with his son.

"I don't know you at all," Adria pointed out. "In fact, I wasn't sure I should come here."

"And why is that?"

Leaning closer to him, she said, "Because, Mr. Polidori—"

"Please. Anthony." He smiled, revealing short, gold-capped teeth. "We are all friends here, are we not?"

She didn't miss a beat and her gaze was level with his. "—I thought you might have wanted to talk to me to get information on the Danvers family for your own purposes."

"You don't trust me."

"As I said, I don't know you."

He smiled at that.

"The Danvers's stories are exaggerated," Mario interjected. Again his eyes, dark and sensual, found hers. His gaze lingered on her face as if searching for flaws or insight into her character. "I won't lie and say there wasn't a feud at one time and that there was a lot of bad blood between the families, but it's over."

"What would be the point?" Anthony said. "Witt is dead."

"That he is," Adria said.

"And he is the man you believe is your father." His voice was without feeling.

Adria saw a new side to the Italian, a hard, ruthless edge that he kept hidden beneath a spit-polished exterior. "Why do you care, Mr. Polidori?"

"As I said—"

"And I don't believe you," she said boldly. Tired of the cat-and-mouse game, she saw no reason to prolong it. "There's a reason you asked me to dinner and I don't think it's because you think that I've had a lack of Italian cuisine while growing up in Montana."

One graying brow lifted. "I'm just curious, that's all."

"Why?"

"It is rumored that if London Danvers does appear, she'll inherit a good portion of Danvers International."

Here it comes.

"Many of our business interests are in direct competition with the Danvers corporation and I was hoping, should you come to inherit part of the fortune, that you might be willing to sell off some of the smaller industries." Resting his elbows on the table, he propped up his chin. "I'm specifically interested in the Hotel Danvers."

Her heart dropped to the floor. The hotel? She thought of the ballroom with its glorious chandeliers, the old elevator, the time and money put into renovating the old building to its original state.

"You brought me here to . . . what? Bribe me?" She shook her head and laughed at the pomposity of this man, who, though he was loathe to admit it, was very much like several members of the Danvers clan. "I'm afraid you'll have to take a number and stand in line. A few people in the Danvers family are already in a bidding war. They seem to think that I can be bought off."

"Can you?" he asked.

"No."

"Ahh . . . an *honorable* woman. With *noble* intentions." His eyes flickered dangerously.

"I just want to find out the truth."

"Sure you do," he said, motioning to the waiter for another bottle of wine.

"And you want the hotel to rub it into the face of Witt's children that you've finally beaten him."

Before he could make another comment the waiter brought the Chianti along with a large bowl of minestrone soup. After refilling the wineglasses, he silently ladled the rich broth and vegetables into smaller bowls, then set one in front of each patron. When he retreated, Anthony motioned to the soup, urging her to eat. "Since our hotel burned in thirty-five, the Polidoris have never again been able to reconstruct anything so elegant. The insurance money wasn't sufficient to rebuild and it has been a personal dream of mine to restore the Polidori name to one of the older hotels in town."

"There are lots of hotels for sale," she said. "Why the Danvers?"

"Why? He picked up his spoon and offered her his winning smile. "Good question. It just seems fitting somehow. A coup even Witt would admire. Don't you think?"

14

Zach smelled trouble. It sizzled in the air, like electricity before a lightning storm and drew him back to Portland.

Jason's panicked phone calls hadn't caused him to climb into his Jeep and head west over the mountains. Pressing business worries weren't the reason. Nor had his concern that he'd lose the ranch if Adria proved to be London been his impetus. No, the reason he'd driven like a madman across the mountains had been something more basic, more primal, an urge deep in his guts that he couldn't suppress and didn't want to name.

"Idiot," he ground out as he glowered through the raindrops drizzling down the windshield. The lights of Portland shone like tiny beacons, leading him closer.

To what?

Adria.

He ground his teeth together and his fingers clenched around the steering wheel, gripping hard. He didn't even know where she was staying.

It was after ten by the time she returned to her hotel room. She kicked off her shoes. Rubbing one foot, she sat on the bed and picked up the receiver with her free hand. As she dialed the number Nelson had left with someone at the front desk she cradled the receiver between her shoulder and ear. The phone rang five times and she was about to hang up when he answered.

"Nelson Danvers."

"This is Adria," she said. "You called?"

There was a pause on the other end of the line. "Yes, I, uh, thought we should meet. You know, to talk, to get to know each other. I was hoping maybe tonight if you can make it. I'd be willing to come downtown and meet you in the bar of your hotel."

She glanced at the clock. Why not? It was early and she wasn't the least bit tired. In fact, her dinner with Polidori had set her nerves on edge and she needed to calm down. She told him she'd meet him in twenty minutes and hung up before she noticed the note—a single piece of paper folded, with her name scratched on the back—lying on the bureau. No one had slipped this piece of paper under the door.

Dread settled in the back of her throat. Her privacy, it seemed, was nonexistent.

She snatched up the note and opened it.

BACK OFF BITCH.

Like a snake scurrying away, a chill slithered down her spine, leaving her skin to crawl in apprehension. Her lungs were suddenly tight and she nearly dropped the paper onto the floor.

Pull yourself together!

Taking in a deep breath, she decided that the message didn't bother her as much as the frightening fact that someone had delivered the simple piece of paper to her locked room. Her stomach turned at the thought. Someone—someone who wasn't happy with her—knew where she was staying and could come and go as he pleased, while she was away or while she was sleeping.

Panic, that same blind fear she'd felt years ago in the school yard with Tommy Sinclair, gurgled upward threatening to control her, but she tamped it down. She couldn't let some chicken-shit letter writer get to her. She reminded herself that she didn't scare easily. She'd grown up on the farm and her father had taken her hunting, fishing, and even rock climbing in the Bitterroots. She'd skinny-dipped in Flathead Lake and branded cattle, smelling the searing flesh, hearing the cows bawl, as she learned to be tough. She'd shot the rapids as well as her .22 and she'd watched as her favorite horse had to be destroyed after shattering his leg.

She'd faced the threat of losing her home and the death of all her loved ones and, by God, she wasn't going to let anyone get the better of her. Not by writing silly little notes. Damned coward. She folded the stupid threat and tucked it into her purse with the other one that she'd crumpled, then smoothed flat and decided to keep. Maybe she'd show them both to Nelson and see what he had to say.

Within ten minutes, she was downstairs in the bar, at a private table near windows that looked onto the street. She watched the steady stream of traffic moving slowly between red lights. Pedestrians carrying umbrellas and wrapped in winter coats with the collars turned against the wind dashed along the sidewalks, like so many rats in a maze—scurrying down one dead-end ally only to turn at the next blind corner. Always in a hurry.

She hadn't planned to order a drink, but receiving the note had changed her mind and she was sipping a rum and Coke when Nelson appeared. She nearly didn't recognize him as she'd always seen him impeccably dressed in suits that must've cost him a month's salary. Tonight his hair was uncombed, windblown and damp from the rain and he wore a wool sweater, black jeans, and a black leather bomber jacket that looked brand new, as if he'd bought it for the occasion.

Whereas Zachary was rough and tumble and wore his I-don't-give-a-shit attitude comfortably, Nelson seemed out of place in clothes a little too fashionable to be casual. An enigma.

Nelson glanced nervously around the room before he spied her. Relief crossed his face as he threaded his way quickly through the tables scattered on the patterned carpet. He seemed paler than she remembered, less self-assured and there was a little-boy quality to him that she hadn't seen before.

"Adria!" His face broke into a warm smile as he dropped into the chair opposite her. The waiter was there immediately and he ordered a bourbon on the rocks. "You must think it's strange that I called you," he said, rain dripping off his jacket.

"I expected it."

"Did you?"

"You're just the first. I'd guess that everybody in your family will want to have his say. Try and convince me that it's in my best interests to leave town."

His smile didn't even falter, though she thought she saw a flicker of ice in his warm blue eyes. "Well, I hate to say it, but it would make it a helluva lot easier on you."

"Mmm. So I should just turn tail and run?"

"Not exactly."

"And then I'd be back to square one."

"Is that so bad?"

"Yes!" she said, her temper frazzling. "Do you know, have you any idea, how many years I've been trying to find out who I am? Where I came from?"

The waiter brought his drink and Nelson fingered the glass.

"So it doesn't matter if you're London, as long as you find out who you are."

"I *am* London."

He shoved a lank lock of hair off his face. "What is it you want from us?"

"I already told you: recognition."

"And, with the recognition, your inheritance." He said it pleasantly, as if stating a fact, without the malice or cynicism of his brothers and sister. He seemed almost as if he were resigned to help her, but she didn't trust him.

She watched a slice of lemon dance between the ice cubes melting in her glass. "Look, Nelson, I don't expect you or the rest of your family to roll over and take me in with no questions asked. That wouldn't make sense."

"No . . ."

"And I realize I'm not the first one to make the claim that I'm you're half-sister."

"Not by a long shot." He offered her a warmer smile—still boyish and charming.

Adria spread her hands over the table, as if in supplication.

"All I want is a chance. I don't know what your family's doing, but I imagine everyone is trying his damnedest to prove me a fake. I imagine you've got a team of lawyers and investigators working on this day and night." His eyes shifted away from hers and she knew she'd been right. She was being followed, by some detective hired by the family. A knot tightened in her stomach, but she managed to appear calm. "Well, that suits me just fine. But, if you get any information that conclusively says I'm *not* London Danvers, let me know and I'll back off. I'll take blood tests, lie detector tests, DNA tests, anything, to help sort this out. So, just let me know when your PI reports back to you."

He swallowed convulsively. "How do you know about—?"

"Only makes sense." She sat back against her chair and regarded him with a coolly assessing gaze. "It's what I would do if the situation were reversed."

"You could go away from this empty-handed."

"I know." She stared at him steadily and he blinked before finding interest in his half-empty glass. "I just have to know the truth, Nelson. Maybe you aren't interested in that, but I'd say it's a shame if the public defender wasn't looking for it around each and every corner."

He took a quick swallow of bourbon and Adria thought that he of all the children looked the most like his father. Witt had been a bigger man, but he had the same startling blue eyes, aristocratic, straight nose, thick hair and square jaw. Aside from the similar facial features, the resemblance ended, however. Nelson was decidedly different from Witt—or at least what she imagined Witt to have been from all the articles and newspaper reports she'd read of him; the pictures she'd seen. Witt Danvers had been imposing and ruthless and cruel. Nelson seemed to have a gentler side to his character and Adria guessed there had been little, if any, gentleness in Witt Danvers. Whatever tenderness had been trapped in his black soul had been given only to his youngest child: to London. His little treasure.

She felt suddenly sick and surprisingly empathetic for this

man sitting across from her. All Witt's children bore emotional scars that might never heal. But she wouldn't learn anything if she showed any sign of weakness, if she let her emotions get the better of her. "What if I do turn out to be London," she said, lifting an eye brow. "What would you do then?"

"I don't know . . . it's impossible to even consider it. She's been dead too long . . . at least dead to me. Us. The family."

"If I do turn out to be dear little London, you'll have to see me day after day and have to deal with me regarding all the family business, won't you?"

"I don't really work for the company."

"You're on the board of directors. You aren't high-profile, but you're involved. Sure, Jason pulls all the strings, but you and your sister are always hovering in the wings." When he didn't respond, she plunged on, determined to make her point. "I could be helpful to you, you know. I read somewhere that you'd like to go into political office. If you assisted me in uncovering the truth, it would look very good on your record, wouldn't it?" She winked at him, as if they were coconspirators. "The headlines could be a veritable bonanza of goodwill—which wouldn't hurt you in the final ballot count. I can see them now: DANVERS BROTHER FINDS LONG-LOST SISTER. Or NELSON DANVERS PROVES WOMAN IS HIS HALF-SISTER. CANDIDATE FINDS LONG-LOST RELATIVE. It could go on and on."

Nelson's eyes grew wary.

"Then again," she said, with a lift of her shoulder. "If I really do turn out to be London, I could really throw a monkey wrench in all your ambitions. You're probably banking on getting your share of the fortune." She clucked her tongue and wondered what it was about him that brought out the bitchy side of her character one minute, and kindness the next.

"You know, Adria," he said, staring at her as if he still couldn't believe she was real. "I came here hoping that we could settle things. I don't need to be threatened."

"Glad you brought it up, 'cause neither do I." Reaching into her purse, she retrieved the nasty little notes she'd received. His mouth fell open for an instant, then he snapped his teeth together and reached across the table, but she yanked the letters back. "Look what has been finding their way into my room—no, fingers to yourself. In case the police want to do whatever it is they do. You should know. Is it 'dust them for prints' or is that just some fancy movie talk?" She held the notes outstretched, so he could read them if he wanted.

The color seeped from his face. "Who gave these to you?"

"Don't know. Notice that they're not signed. The mark of a true coward."

"How'd you get them? They were delivered?" he asked, a muscle ticking near the corner of his jaw.

"One was shoved under the door. The other turned up on my bureau. Not many people know that I'm a guest here, Nelson, but obviously you did, so I assume the rest of your family does as well. My guess is that the guy you've got following me reports back to you and you all know when I'm out of the room." She tossed her hair over her shoulder and glared at him. "Give the family a message: it won't work. You can send me a thousand notes, much worse than these, but I won't back off. I've been told that I've got a stubborn streak that is downright obstinate when people try to force me into doing what they want." She leaned across the table, pressing her face closer to his. "The bottom line is this: the more you push, the harder I'll push right back. These"—she gave the letters a shake—"are a waste of my time."

"I have no idea where those letters came from," he said, blinking hard, as if trying to put his thoughts in some sort of order.

"No? Funny, I could hazard a damned good guess. I'll bet you could, too." She dropped the vile notes on the table in front of him. "Give your wonderful siblings a message from me. Tell them to knock it off. I'm about ready to go to the press as it is and this is just one way of pushing me right through the open doors of the *Oregonian*. I know of several columnists who would have a ball with this story and probably a dozen free-lance reporters who would cut off their right arms if they could create a little controversy in this town. They'd love to shake up the social strata a bit by writing an exposé of some sort on the Danvers family." She took a long drink from her glass. "What do you think?"

"What I think, Adria," Nelson said, his voice surprisingly low and calm, "is that you're just like all the rest. A fraud."

"And what I think is someone in the family is running scared." She tapped a fingernail on the letters. "Really scared."

"You don't even know that they're from the family."

"Who else?"

She folded the notes and put them in her purse. She didn't like acting out the part of the bitch, but she had no choice. Someone in the family had decided it was time to play hard ball. Was it Nelson? She didn't think so, but she didn't know much about him. If Nelson were really her half-brother, she'd feel sorry for him wearing his expensive suits during the day, and his new black leather jacket at night, while holding onto his crummy job—just because he was a part of the political game started long ago by his father. She suspected that even though good old Witt was in the grave, Nelson was still trying to prove himself to his father—or to himself—that he was truly worth something after all.

"Is there anything else you wanted to know?" she asked.

"Why don't you just leave us alone?"

"I can't."

"This is your damned mission, right?"

"You got it, Nelson." Since the conversation wasn't going anywhere, she stood. "Look, this doesn't have to be a battle," she said.

"Of course it does." He stared up at her and his eyes seemed suddenly lifeless. She wanted to wiggle away from his dead gaze, but she didn't. "If you know anything about our family, you know it does."

"As long as we understand each other." She motioned toward the bar. "Don't worry about the bill. I charged it to my room."

Nelson watched as she walked briskly out the double glass doors of the bar. Damn, he'd made a mess of things. He'd hoped to befriend her and weasel a little information from her, but she'd turned the conversation around and he'd been nearly tongue-tied. He was usually calm around women, immune to them for the most part, but occasionally he found one that could rattle him and Adria Nash, whoever the hell she was, had done more than her share of rattling.

He had the horrible premonition that she was London. Not only her looks, but her manner spoke of arrogance and power. He'd expected a shy little hick from Montana, a girl interested in scamming a few bucks and beating a hasty retreat, but there was more to her than met the eye and that scared him shitless.

Straightening his collar, he caught his reflection in the beveled mirror over the bar. Another murky gaze met his and locked and Nelson felt the back of his throat turn to cotton. There was passion in that stare, unreined, raw sexual energy that hit him with an intensity that knocked the breath from his lungs. He felt the same dark stirrings he'd tried to deny for years, held the stranger's gaze for just an instant, and turned quickly on his heel. He didn't have time for any one-night stands. Besides, they were much too dangerous. He had his career to think about and he couldn't, for the sake of one wet tongue sliding down his spine, give into the dark desire that had been his curse for as long as he'd been interested in sex. One night could put his entire future in jeopardy. Especially now.

Ignoring the heat that crept into his loins and brought a sheen of perspiration to his upper lip, he left the bar and hunched his shoulders against the cool October breeze. Briskly, before he gave into the sexual demons still burning through his mind and he turned around to meet with the sensual stranger, he walked the few blocks to the Hotel Danvers where his car was parked. Without a second's hesitation, he called Jason from the cellular

phone in his Cadillac. "I just met with Adria," he said, looking
over his shoulder as if he expected someone—the potential
one-night stand perhaps—to be staring through the windows.
"I'm on my way to your house."

"Great!" Jason slammed the phone down and rotated the
kinks from his neck. It had been one hell of a day. He'd been
fighting all day with lobbyists for the timber industry, trying to
persuade the bastards that they'd have to do something more in
Washington to get rid of the protection of the old growth timber
and all the while he'd negotiated on the phone, or lunched with
the junior senator, or played racquet ball with a land developer
interested in converting some old warehouses into a mall, he
hadn't been able to stop thinking of Adria Nash—the proverbial
fly in the fucking ointment.
    How could the family get rid of her? There was something
about her that got his blood up and he imagined himself either
knocking her senseless or making love to her or both. He got
hard just thinking of shoving her onto the bed and giving her the
fuck of her life. "Get a grip," he muttered. Even thinking about
a sexual involvement with her was a ridiculous, treacherous
notion and had probably started because she reminded him of
Kat. He gritted his teeth as he thought of his hot stepmother and
his part in her death. Guilt gnawed a painful hole in his brain.
    God, he had problems! Too many problems!
    He was waiting for a call from Sweeny and he'd already had
a run-in with Kim who was making demands upon him, begging
him to get the divorce he'd so foolishly promised her. He didn't
need the added aggravation and now Nelson was losing it. The
kid was about to go around the bend with this Adria/London
thing. Usually even-tempered, Nelson was coming damned close
to becoming unhinged. And this wasn't a good time for it. He
checked his watch and frowned. "Come on, Sweeny," he said
before pouring himself another drink and tossing it back.
    Ten minutes later the phone rang. Jason picked up the re-

ceiver on the second ring and heard Sweeny's nasal drawl. "I've done as much checkin' in this shit hole as I can," Oswald announced without so much as a greeting. "Our friend Ms. Nash has been a busy woman. After discovering the tape from her father, she checked out every library book in the county on the timber business and the hotel business as well as shipping and real estate."

Jason's bones seemed to freeze. Danvers International. All the assets and same sources of revenue of the company. "So she's done her homework."

"Hell, yes, she's done her homework, even got herself some goddamned extra credit, if you ask me. She ordered books from other libraries all across the Northwest: Seattle, Portland, Spokane, Oregon City and newspapers, too. Contacted all the majors in three or four states. As I said, the lady's been busy."

Jason's insides seemed to congeal. He'd hoped she was a bimbo, a low-class gold digger out for a quick buck.

Sweeny was still saturating him with the bad news. "Now you have to remember that she graduated with honors from the college she attended. Summa cum laude."

"Christ!"

"This gal isn't another one of your look-alike airheads. She's got brains and it appears as if she wanted to know everything she could about you, the family and how you go about making your money."

Jason sagged against the wall and stared out at the night. He felt as if the floorboards were shifting from beneath his feet.

"If you look through your list of stockholders, you might find that she owns some stock in Danvers International, not much, mind you, just a hundred shares, enough to get all the information you send to your investors."

Jesus! Jason resisted the urge to clear his throat. "Anything else?" he asked, his jaw clenched so tight it began to throb.

"Oh, yeah. A lot. And nothing you're going to want to hear. She's got the right kind of blood. A negative. Not all that uncom-

mon, but since Witt was O negative and Katherine was A positive, their daughter could very well have been A negative. I never
found any records where London was typed, but A negative
would certainly have been in the ball park. It's just too damned
bad that old Witt or Katherine aren't around so that we could do
a DNA test. Kind of a break for her that she had to wait until both
London's natural parents were cremated, don't you think?"

"Damned convenient for her."

"So far, it looks like she's got you by the short hairs," Sweeny
said and Jason heard the note of satisfaction in the oily man's
speech.

Jason took in a deep, calming breath. "So tell me the good
news," he said, praying there was a chink in Adria's story.

"She's broke."

"How broke?"

"Broke as in drowning in red ink. Even though she's leased
her farm, looks like she'll have to sell it and she's still got hospital
bills hammered up her ass. A chunk of Danvers change would
definitely keep the wolf from the door."

That news was encouraging. In a legal fight, Ms. Nash would
lose unless she came up with some egomaniac of a lawyer, some
renegade who wanted a piece of the Danvers fortune himself and
was willing to work on a contingency with no money up front.
Jason had a lot of friends in town, attorneys who wouldn't dare
go up against the Danvers family in a court of law, but there were
plenty who would—on a contingency basis, just for the challenge and fame of it all. "Okay, what else?"

"That's it for now, but I plan to come up with something when
I get to Memphis."

"What's there?"

"Hopefully Bobby Slade."

"Virginia's husband?" Jason began to feel a little ray of hope.
"You found him?"

"I think so, and a word of advice to you. You'd better get down
on your knees and pray he's got A negative blood running

through his veins. Would help cast a big shadow over her story. Oh, and there's one more thing you might like to know. Earlier tonight, our Ms. Nash was picked up at the Orion Hotel in a stretch limo."

"By whom?"

Sweeny hesitated a beat and Jason had the sickening feeling that he was being strung along. "Well, that's the kicker," Oswald Sweeny finally drawled. "Seems as if your good friend Anthony Polidori took her out to dinner."

"Listen," Nelson said, tossing his jacket over the back of a high-backed chair. "I'm telling you she's a wild card. There's just no knowing what she's going to do next. She's said she'll go to the press, do whatever it takes to get what she wants and I believe her. She wasn't just jacking me around."

Zach stood near the fireplace, resting his hip on the Italian marble, feeling uncomfortable in the formal living room—the room he'd never been allowed to walk through as a child. Decorated in white, with touches of black and gold, it was a cold room and he would've preferred to be anywhere else in the world, rather than cornered here at the old family home with his brothers and sister.

Now, his eyes narrowed on Nelson. The youngest Danvers brother was known to exaggerate and for that reason he'd probably make a good politician. The fact that he took bribes and lied convincingly through his perfect white teeth wouldn't hurt much, either.

Nelson had been pacing the length of the living room, nervously eyeing Zach ever since his middle brother had shown up unannounced at the hastily convened family meeting. Zach knew his presence bothered his brothers and sister and, truth to tell, he didn't want to be a party to whatever they were cooking up, but he stuck around, partly to annoy them, partly because he wanted to know everything there was to know about Adria.

"What do you think we should do?" Zach asked, unable to

read his younger brother. Nelson was a mystery. Always had been. Kind one second, cruel the next, almost as if he were two different people trapped inside the same skin. Zach had never understood him, not even when Nelson was just a kid.

"Shit, I don't know what we should do! That's why I'm here."

"You'll make a helluva mayor, Nelson," Zach remarked before lifting his bottle of Coors to his lips.

"Governor," Nelson clarified.

Trisha flicked a lighter to the end of her cigarette. "So what would you do, Zach?"

"Leave her alone. Let her play out her hand."

Through a cloud of smoke, Trisha laughed. "Just because you don't give a rat's ass, doesn't mean the rest of us don't."

"You've got a better idea?"

"Hire a hit man." Trisha crossed her legs and settled back into the plump white pillows of the couch.

"Don't even say it!" Nelson bit out.

"Christ, don't you know when I'm joking?" Trisha rolled her eyes.

Nelson spun and faced his sister. "No one knows when you're joking, Trisha. Not even you."

"Clever, Nelson. Clever." She took a long drag from her Salem Light.

Nelson was more agitated than usual. He shoved both hands through his hair. "We'd all better be careful. She's already received a couple of threatening letters."

"How nice," Trisha purred but Zach felt every muscle in his body grow instantly taut.

"What do you mean?"

As Nelson related his conversation with Adria, Zach's insides grew colder than the bottom of a mine shaft. Someone was threatening Adria? But who? Only the people in this room, his mother, and the Polidori family knew she was in town. No, that wasn't right, there were all the people who worked for the family, servants who could have overheard phone calls and then there was the private investigator and anyone else he'd put on the payroll.

Trisha, her expression bored, crushed her cigarette in a crystal ashtray. "Have any of you thought about the fact that Adria could just be who she claims she is? Maybe she is London and if she is, we're all up shit creek without our proverbial paddle."

"London's dead," Jason said, cutting off further speculation

"How do you know? How does any of us know?" Trisha asked.

"We all know it. She obviously died years ago or maybe, there's a one-in-a-million chance that she's living somewhere oblivious to the fact that she's a Danvers."

"Or maybe she just found out who she is," Zach drawled, narrowing his eyes on his family.

"It's all just a pain in the ass," Trisha said as she climbed off the couch. "You know, I despise it when this happens, when someone comes in with all that crap about being London: Witt Danvers's little princess. That's what he called her, you know." She turned her shadowed eyes on Zach. "You remember, don't you? She was all he cared about. The rest of us could have dropped off the face of the earth and he wouldn't have blinked an eye. But because it was London— because it was goddamned London—it was a fucking big deal!" Her voice had risen as she'd spoken and her throat worked now in silent agony— the ignored daughter to whom her father never said a kind word. The old man had only noticed her when she was rebelling.

The whole damned family was a basket case.

"She's got to be dead," Jason said.

Zach couldn't help rising to the bait. "Maybe one of us killed her."

"Jesus, Zach, listen to you. Don't even think it." Nelson shoved the sleeves of his sweater to his elbows as he looked from one of his siblings to the other. "Look, arguing among ourselves isn't doing any of us any good. What we've got to do is find a way to discredit her. She assured me that if we found out the truth and proved to her that she *wasn't* London, she'd take a hike."

"And you believe that?" Trisha asked with a low-throated chuckle. "Jesus, Nels, you really are a dumb shit, aren't you? The more I think about it, the more I think you're the perfect public servant."

"Knock it off," Jason ordered. "I've got Sweeny checking out her story and he's got a man following her. If she's got an accomplice, we'll hear of it."

"Sweeny?" Zach said, disgusted. He'd suspected that Jason would have Adria followed, but Oswald Sweeny was low-life trash who would sell his own mother if the price were right.

"He'll get the job done."

"He's a fucking creep," Trisha said.

For once Zach agreed with his sister, but he didn't have time to argue with Jason's choice of private investigators. Like a starving terrier with a bone, Sweeny wouldn't stop until he got all the facts, and just like the damned dog, if he had to, he'd sink his teeth into anyone who made the mistake of getting in his way.

Zach turned his attention to his younger brother. Nelson seemed incredibly nervous—like he was on speed. "Are the notes legitimate threats?" he asked, forcing himself to think logically. On one level he wanted to tear his siblings limb from limb for all their disparaging remarks about Adria, and yet, he was a fool to think he could trust her one little bit. She was a user. Out for number one.

A kindred spirit.

Nelson eyed him curiously. "What're you getting at?"

"Could she have written them herself?"

"What for?" Nelson asked.

Zach peeled the label off his beer. "Public sympathy."

"You are perverted, aren't you?" Trisha said.

"Wait a minute. Why not?" Jason asked, warming to the subject. "She's clever enough to have written the threats herself. Shit, yes, that's probably just what she did." There was genuine admiration in his eyes.

"Or else she might be in serious danger," Zach said aloud and that thought chilled him to the bone. "Why don't you tell me where she is?"

"She's got a room at the Orion," Nelson supplied. "Don't know the room number."

Zach's breath caught in his throat and time seemed to stand still. *The Orion.* He hadn't been in that hotel since the night of the kidnapping, had never been able to drive past its cold concrete exterior without feeling a time warp that dragged him back to the horrid night when he'd been beaten, left for dead, and ended up a suspect in his kid sister's abduction. "Who knows she's there?"

Nelson bit his lower lip. "Probably half the people in Portland by now. Hell, Zach, didn't you hear me? She's talking about going to the press! Do you know what will happen? It'll be a damned circus—"

"Why do you care?" Trisha asked Zach as she reached for another cigarette. "As I said, you've never given a good goddamn about the family."

"Still don't."

"But you've got a bug up your butt, don't you?" She flicked her lighter to the end of her cigarette and shot a stream of smoke from the corner of her mouth. "You know, Zach, if I didn't know better, I'd think you were interested in Adria. Romantically speaking."

He didn't bother answering.

"Just like Kat. Couldn't keep your hands off her, even though you knew it was suicide." Trisha studied the glowing tip of her cigarette as if it held all the answers to the universe. "I'd hate to think this copy-Kat's got her claws into you already."

Zach forced a cold smile. "Hell, Trisha, and here I thought you were the only one with claws."

She glowered at him through the curling smoke that wound in a foggy coil to the ceiling.

Jason said, "I still think the best idea would be to hide her away somewhere like the ranch."

"Forget it." Zach told himself he wasn't interested.

"Could give you a chance to be alone with her," Trisha taunted. "At the ranch. Just like Kat."

Zach's fingers tightened around his Coors and Jason, his mouth set and grim, held up a hand. "Time for a truce, you two. Get a hold of yourself Zach. You know who the enemy is here."

Yeah, Zach knew. But he didn't like it. Jason was still suggesting that he convince Adria to leave Portland and go to the ranch with him.

Zach didn't listen to all the bullshit lawyer rationalizations about why Adria should be on the other side of the mountains and away from the family. He had to get out of the room and away from the hatred that simmered in the air. Beginning to believe that Adria wasn't lying about the threats, he jogged up the stairs and out the front door into the driving rain. Come hell or high water, he was on his way to the Orion.

15

From the outside, the Orion Hotel looked the same as it had years ago when Zach, determined to lose his virginity, had crossed the threshold. Inside, things had changed. The old glass and oak counter where a grizzled old man sold magazines, cigarettes, and candy hadn't been updated over the years but the main lobby had been remodeled. Glass tables and fat floral couches were positioned away from the desk and spiky-leaved palms seemed to grow out of the terra-cotta floor.

Ignoring a sense of déjà vu that made his skin crawl, Zach walked straight to the desk where two clerks—a man and a woman both in their early twenties—were manning the night shift. "Would you ring Ms. Nash's room?" Zach asked. "Tell her she has a guest in the lobby." The two exchanged glances and the woman, a redhead with faded coral lipstick, checked her watch.

"Is she expecting you?"

"No."

"It's late—"

"She won't mind."

Polished fingernails flew over the keyboard of her computer. "Let me see if she's asked not to be disturbed . . ." She studied the monitor, gave a little shrug and lifted the phone receiver to her ear. "What's your name?"

"Zachary Danvers."

"She knows you?"

"Yeah."

"It'll be just a minute."

"I'll wait in the bar."

* * *

As the telephone jangled for the third time, Adria reached blindly for the phone and glanced at the clock. Twelve-thirty. She'd been asleep for less than an hour, but the clouds of slumber had been heavy and hard to part. Fumbling for the receiver with one hand, she pushed her bangs out of her eyes with the other. "Hello?"

"Ms. Nash, this is Laurie at the front desk. I'm sorry to disturb you, but you have a visitor. Mr. Danvers is here to see you."

"Who?"

"Zachary Danvers."

"Zach?" The fog cleared from her mind as the apologetic clerk conveyed Zach's message. Her heart skipped a tiny little beat before she realized that he'd been called in by the troops. It was time to circle the Danvers's family wagons as Adria, the enemy, had threatened to go to the press. She wondered how he'd try to convince her to take a hike.

She threw on a pair of jeans and a bulky sweater. Unable to control the wild black curls, she clipped a barrette over her hair at the base of her neck and grabbed her purse.

"Ready for round three," she told herself as she thought of Polidori and Nelson Danvers. Suddenly she'd become popular. Too popular. And too many people knew where she lived. It was time to move to cheaper, more private quarters.

She saw Zach the minute she entered the bar. Despite the soft lights and the dark interior, she noticed him at a table in the corner. He was the only man without a tie—or a suit for that matter.

His jean-clad legs were stretched out in front of him and he rested on the small of his back. His blue work shirt was pushed high on his forearms and he was watching the door with hawk-like eyes that followed her as she made her way to the table.

She'd forgotten how formidable he was: the cruel set of his mouth, the thick black brows, his face—all sharp angles and planes—and eyes that seemed to see past all her facades.

Nursing a beer, he didn't say a word as she approached, didn't offer the hint of a smile or indicate in any way that he was glad to see her. In fact, he almost scowled as if irritated by the sight of her.

"Do you know what time it is?" she asked, dropping her purse onto the table and jangling her keys.

He shrugged. "After midnight."

"If you're here to offer me a bribe, forget it."

"Sit down, Adria." He kicked a chair in her direction and she, feeling a streak of defiance, wanted to stand but reluctantly dropped onto the soft cushions.

"I'm tired, Zach."

"Heard you've been getting some nasty mail."

"Bad news travels fast."

The waiter came and she started to decline, then decided she could use a drink. Zach's presence always unnerved her. It was his attitude, she supposed, all male ego and raw sexuality, as if he knew he was attractive to females, the kind of cynical man most women considered a challenge and itched to tame, the kind of man she should stay away from—a lonesome cowboy who was up to no damned good. "I'll have a glass of Chardonnay, please."

"Tell me about the letters."

She drew both notes out of her purse and he didn't try to touch them, instead just read the words and scowled more deeply, his eyebrows slamming together. Beneath a thatch of jet-black hair, deep furrows etched across Zach's forehead as he skimmed the notes. "You sure have a way of making new friends," he drawled.

She scooped up the notes and stuffed them back into her purse. "These weren't written by anyone I'd call a friend."

He took a swallow from his beer, then lifted his eyes to hers. "You'd better go to the police. Whoever sent those definitely has a screw loose. He could be dangerous."

"Whoever sent these is a coward and probably named Danvers."

"Maybe," he said, opting not to argue.

"But he won't stop me. Instead of running scared, I've decided to take my story to the newspapers," she said, testing the waters.

He lifted a disinterested shoulder. "You can do whatever you damn well please." After another long pull on his bottle, he set his beer back on the table.

"Don't you care?"

His eyes held steady on hers and her breath caught at the base of her throat. "Not much. No."

"But you're here," she pointed out. "Why?"

"Because you, Ms. Nash, probably aren't going to believe this, but you need a bodyguard."

"A *what?*"

"You heard me."

She nearly laughed. "Give me a break." The nerve of the man, acting like she was some fragile porcelain doll destined to break. But of course he didn't have a glimmer into her past, didn't realize that Victor Nash, over his wife's protests, had decided his only daughter would be ranch tough and sometimes, mean-tempered. "This time you're wrong, Zachary. Believe me, I can take care of myself. I grew up on a ranch in Montana and—"

"And you're getting threatening letters."

"From a chicken shit."

"Whoever it is could be dangerous."

"He's just trying to scare me off, but it isn't working." She sipped from her glass and felt the cool wine slide down her throat. "Tell me something," she said, looking directly into those erotic gray eyes with the lids set so firmly at half mast. "This bodyguard, are you applying for the job?"

He didn't reply but stared straight back at her with such an intensity she felt as if her diaphragm had slammed up against her lungs. Breathing was suddenly all but impossible.

"Don't you think it would be stupid of me, I mean really stupid, to have someone named Danvers protecting me?"

"You can't fight the world alone."

"Not the world, Zach. Just the Danvers family."

"They're powerful."

"You mean *you're* powerful, don't you? You're part of the family whether you like it or not."

He hunched over his beer. "For the record, I don't like it." One side of her mouth twitched up as if he found the situation with his family irritating but amusing. His irreverence touched a part of her. Hadn't she, too, always been a bit of a rebel?

"But you're tied to them, aren't you?" she said. "Because of Daddy's money."

Quick as a rattler striking, his arm snaked across the table and he clamped his work-roughened fingers over her wrist. His words came out in a low, menacing growl. "Listen to me, lady. I'm trying to do you a favor here and all you're doing by fighting me is pissing in the wind."

"I don't want any favors." She inched her chin up but she couldn't ignore the five warm impressions where his fingertips pressed against the sensitive skin of her inner wrist. Her throat seemed as dry as smoke and his gaze lowered, resting for what seemed an endless second on the pulse throbbing above her collarbone.

"I'm trying to help you."

She wanted to believe him, but she knew that he was probably lying, that he'd been sent on a mission to render her harmless. He'd come from the family—whether he admitted it or not—and that thought, of the Danvers kin deciding how to manipulate her, caused her temper to ignite. For as long as she could remember someone was trying to dictate to her, bend her will, and this time, by God, she wasn't giving in an inch. Gritting her teeth, she yanked back her arm and scrambled to her feet. "I don't need any help."

"That's where you're wrong."

"Bull." Radiating fury, her eyes flashing with renewed determination, she said, "Good night, Zach. And by the way. Go to hell!" Furious, she turned crisply on her heel.

He watched her storm out the door, noticed the curve of her hips and the stiff set of her back. Her legs were thin, but not skinny and he wondered what they'd feel like wrapped around his waist.

"Shit," he muttered under his breath, disgusted at the direction of his thoughts. Whenever he was around her, his thoughts turned to sex, like some randy stallion in a herd of mares in heat. He'd handled the situation all wrong again. It seemed with that woman there was just no winning.

Well, she could complain all she liked, but he was going to camp out on her doorstep. Dropping some bills on the table, he took out after her. He stepped into the lobby just as the elevator doors were closing, but that suited him just fine and he paused, leaning against a pillar to watch as the elevator's indicator lights mounted over the closed doors blinked on in succession, then held steady for several seconds at the fifth floor. Smiling wickedly, he waited, noticing that there were no other stops as the car descended. Without a second's hesitation, he waited for the doors to open and rode the empty car back up. He'd sit out in the hallway if he had to, but he'd damn well see for himself if there was anyone set on stalking her.

The elevator bell rang softly as it reached the fifth floor. Zach stepped into the empty corridor and spied a chair and fake tree nestled against windows at the corner of the hallway, with a view down both wings. Zach settled into the low-backed chair and wondered who, if anyone, he'd find lurking about. The night could prove very interesting. If Ms. Nash found another note tomorrow morning he could nearly prove that she'd written it herself. With a satisfied smile, he shifted to the small of his back, stretched out his legs and crossed his ankles to wait.

Adria slammed the door of her room. Like ghosts that were determined to haunt her, Zachary's taunts had followed her up the elevator shaft. His arrogance disturbed her, the way he tried to order her around made her want to kick at something. The gall of him! Telling her she needed someone to protect her, for crying out loud! He and the rest of the family acted as if she didn't have brain one, as if she couldn't take care of herself, as if she were some kind of naive farm girl who just wanted to rip off all their money. She unclipped her hair and threw the barrette onto the bed in frustration. "Bastard," Adria muttered and caught herself as the word rolled easily off her tongue.

There was more than a little truth to the name, wasn't there? If she looked inside herself, really looked, she knew she'd discover that a part of her wanted Zach to be sired by another man—any man other than Witt Danvers, whom she believed to be her own father.

Because, damn it, she found Zachary sensual and disturbing and like no man she'd ever met before.

Her head began to pound. Was Zach really Witt's son? Oh, who cared? Did it matter? All she needed to know was if she were really Witt's daughter. Zach's paternity wasn't something she needed to think about. Zachary Danvers wasn't anyone she needed to think about.

She picked up the newspaper lying in sections on the small table in her room and snapped it open. With furious fingers, she flipped through the pages and stopped at the section marked Rooms For Rent. Tomorrow, first thing, she'd find a new place to live, then she'd waltz into the *Oregonian* and tell a tale that would leave the reporters with their tongues hanging out as they scrambled to get her story into the next edition. Later she'd talk to the television and radio news stations.

If the Danvers family wanted to play hard ball, so be it. She was more than ready to pitch them a curve ball the likes of which they'd never yet seen.

Trisha parked in her usual spot, between the garage and the cabin in the woods of the Polidori estate. A gardener's cabin that was supposed to be unoccupied, Mario had converted the little vine-covered cottage to serve as their secret rendezvous for over twenty years. Her heart was beating a light little tempo and she chided herself for being foolish as she ducked under the dripping clematis and knocked softly on the front door before turning the lock.

He was waiting for her. Backlit by the lights in the kitchen, he strode across the dark living room and her breath caught in her throat. Though she'd grown cynical and calloused over the years, the sight of Mario never ceased to cause a wave of anticipation to race through her blood.

He was bare-chested and his pants hung loosely, his suspenders falling past his hips. "You're late," he said in the smoky voice that had always caused her bones to turn liquid.

"Problems at home."

"Forget them." He reached over her shoulder and pushed the door so hard that it slammed in the casing before the lock latched. His arms surrounded her and his lips crashed over hers—hot, hungry, possessive. Her entire body quivered. He smelled male; all sweat and after-shave with the faint hint of smoke. His hands were anxious as he slipped her jacket from her shoulders and concentrated on the buttons of her blouse.

"Come," he growled, once she was naked to the waist. Taking her hand, he led her to the bedroom where mirrors lined one wall. "Watch me make love to you." His eyes gleamed as he gently cupped her breast and, falling to his knees, took her nipple into his mouth. His tongue was wet and warm and familiar. His lips anxiously tugged on her. His teeth teased and nipped.

Trisha sagged against him, welcoming the current of sexual energy running from his blood to hers.

His mouth still suckling, he worked his magic. His hands splayed upon her naked back and he shoved her slacks over her hips.

With Mario she could do anything, be anyone, and he didn't care. He was a responsive lover, gentle when she wanted to be cuddled, rough when she needed the thrill of quick, hot sex.

"Tell me what I can do for you," he said as the slacks fell to her knees and he found the tuft of soft curls at the apex of her legs.

"You . . . you're doing it," she murmured, though she could barely draw a breath. She felt the gentle probing of one of his fingers, tenderly parting her before exploring more deeply and causing the tension in her shoulders to fade. Desire, a murky hot flame, glowed deep within her.

"Then I'll give you more . . . so much more. I'll make you beg for it, my sweet." Her throat caught as another finger slid into her cleft. Liquid heat consumed her as he stroked, opening her wider and wider. "What do you want, Trisha, my love, tell me. I am but your slave."

She nearly melted. *Trisha, my love.* "I want you. All of you."

"Then you shall have all of me," he said, his lips curling back in satisfaction. In one quick motion he released her, unzipped his fly and lifted her onto his rock-hard sex. She gasped as he pierced into her, but her legs wrapped around his waist and he braced her shoulders against the wall, pumping and thrusting, holding her tight with each soul-jarring push that sent her mind into wild circles of flight. "Fuck me, Trisha," he whispered roughly against her ear. "Fuck me." The room seemed to spin and across the room, in the mirror's stark reflection, she saw his smooth back, the muscles rippling as he jabbed into her, her own haunted eyes looking back at her. She began to sweat and move with his fast, jerky rhythm and soon her shoulders were raw from the pressure of rubbing up against the rough wall.

He convulsed, threw back his magnificent head and let out a primal scream equaled only by her own hoarse wail of surrender. They tumbled onto the bed and Trisha ignored the fact that the bed sheets were already mussed, that the scent of sex lingered heavy in the air.

"I missed you," Mario whispered hoarsely.

"Oh, God, Mario, I've missed you, too." Tears seemed to well in her eyes but she held them back. He caressed her breast, rolling her nipple between his thumb and forefinger.

"You can spend the night?"

She smiled briefly. "Of course."

"Then I will love you over and over again and you'll forget whatever it is that's bothering you."

If only she could. Rolling over, she reached into a drawer of the nightstand and found an open pack of Winstons.

"What's bothering me isn't going away." She lit up, took a deep drag and passed the cigarette to him. She didn't want to think of his other lovers though she suspected that he had several. What could she expect? Years ago, when she was young and foolishly naive, she had believed that they were destined to be together, that they could thwart the fates and profess their love, that the passion they shared was like none other and could never be destroyed. How wrong and young and foolish she'd been. She'd learned the hard way.

Mario drew deep on the cigarette and blew smoke rings to the ceiling. The frail rings lifted upward, only to drift apart—like star-crossed lovers.

"You have problems?" he asked, nuzzling her neck.

She laughed and took the cigarette. Around a cloud of smoke, she sighed, "Always."

"Tell me."

"You must know. Your father took her out to dinner."

"Ahh. Adria Nash," he said with a familiarity that caused the sting as sharp as the bite of a whip to cut into her heart. "I met her."

"You what?" She jabbed out the Winston in a clear glass tray.

"At the dinner. I was with Dad."

Jealousy spurted through her blood though there was no reason for it. "What did you think?"

"The obvious. She is beautiful." A knife twisted in Trisha's heart. "She looks like Katherine. She could be your half-sister, but odds are she's just another phony."

"And your father, what did he think?"

"I thought we had a deal. We don't discuss our fathers."

"Witt's dead."

"But my father's very much alive unfortunately. Want a drink?"

She shook her head. The only time she didn't feel the need of booze or coke was when she was with Mario. It had been her blessing and curse to fall in love with him so many years ago. Like a dormant disease, it never seemed to go away. She'd married once and the marriage had fallen apart because she was still infected with love for Mario.

He climbed out of the bed and moved across the room in a way she found heart-stoppingly sexy. She watched his buttocks in the mirror, and his powerful sex, now at half-mast. He poured a tumbler of bourbon.

"What do you think of Adria?" he asked and she felt a prick of annoyance.

"She's as fake as rubber dog shit!"

He chuckled deep in his throat. "But still she bothers you."

"Not much," Trisha lied, tossing her hair over her shoulder and tucking her knees beneath her chin. Was it her imagination or was Mario more than just idly curious? There was a spark of interest in his eyes that he was trying to hide.

"What are you going to do about her?" he asked.

"I suggested we get a hit man," she teased. "Know any good ones out of work?"

He clucked his tongue. "My father is not Mafia. You know it. Besides, you can't just have her killed."

"It was a joke."

"A bad one." He capped the bottle and his eyes met hers in the mirror. "I think Adria won't give up. She stood up to my father and that's something most men and very few women would do. She's going to be a sharp thorn in your family's side for a long, long while." He smiled thoughtfully as he picked up his drink and turned back to the bed. Crossing the small room, he said, "Jason . . . or someone . . . will have to do something."

She stiffened a little as he sat next to her and the mattress sagged with his weight. The conversation made her uneasy and though she'd once trusted Mario with all her young heart, she was now cautious. Pillow talk had the capability of destruction. What was the old expression? Loose lips sink ships.

"Then again, maybe she is your long-lost sister."

Trisha's insides roiled at the thought. "Don't try to bait me."

"I'm just playing devil's advocate," he said taking a long swallow from his glass and offering it to her. "I know how much you loved little London."

"She was a brat," Trisha said bitterly. "I hated her. Dad seemed to think she could walk on water but even at four she was a manipulative little bitch, just like her mother."

Mario clucked his tongue and set the glass down. "Sounds like you're still all tensed up. Maybe we should take care of that." His smile was pure seduction and he roughly caressed her breast. Her nipple responded. "This time, my way," he said, his face turning wicked.

Trisha shivered in anticipation.

Adria was jarred out of sleep at six when the bedside alarm jangled in her ear. She felt as if she'd barely drifted off after a night of tossing and turning and worrying subconsciously that someone was sneaking into her room. Sleep had been nearly nonexistent and her mind had swum with images of Zachary sometimes as her enemy but more often than not as her lover. Over and over again she remembered the night in the Jeep when he'd kissed her with a raw animal passion that made her insides turn to hot, soft wax. In her mind's eyes, she replayed the scene in the bar when he'd reached across the table and captured her wrist with a possession that took her breath away. Desire had shimmered through her blood, then, as it did every time her thoughts turned to him.

It was ridiculous, of course. She couldn't want him. Her fantasies were only because he was the sexiest man she'd been around in a long while and the simple fact that he was forbidden fruit—a rough man whom she couldn't have.

"Character flaw," she told herself as she brushed her teeth and saw her tousled-haired reflection in the mirror over the sink.

She stepped under the hot spray of the shower until she was awake. Today was the day she was going to the papers. A knot of dread twisted her stomach at the thought. She had hoped it wouldn't come to this, but she'd been foolish. Talking to the press was inevitable.

But first things first. She needed a permanent residence. She dressed quickly and armed with yesterday's paper, she walked out of the room and stopped dead in her tracks. Her heart jolted and she could barely find her tongue as her gaze collided with Zachary Danvers's interested gray eyes. Still in the clothes he'd worn the night before, his long legs stretched out in front of him, his chin shadowed with more than a day's growth of beard, he rubbed the crick from his neck and gave her a crooked smile.

" 'Mornin'," he drawled, as if they saw each other at the crack of dawn each and every day.

"What're you doing here?" she managed to ask.

"Waitin' for you."

Another jolt. "Why?"

"I thought someone should hang around and see if you're really being harassed." He glanced pointedly down the empty corridors, "or if you invented the whole story."

"Why would I do that?"

"I can't explain anything you do, Adria," he said, shoving himself upright.

"Whatever I do, it's not as crazy as sitting all night in a chair at the end of the hall. I'm surprised security didn't throw you out."

"Only a few people saw me. The early-risers this morning. Joggers and guys with briefcases off to important meetings." He stretched, his tall body seeming to grow longer and leaner as he reached over his head, then winced as the cramps left his muscles. "So, no one bothered you?"

"No one called, but I asked the desk to take messages and no,

I didn't have a cheery little breakfast note this morning." They climbed into the elevator together.

"Maybe I could buy you breakfast."

She slid a glance in his direction. They were alone in the elevator car and he seemed to fill it with his presence. For once, there wasn't a trace of hostility in his eyes and she was tempted to let down her guard a bit even though he had the innate and maddening ability to make her see red at the drop of a hat. Be that as it may, she needed one friend, one contact in the family, someone who didn't outwardly hate her, and yet being close to Zach was dangerous on an entirely different and deeper emotional level.

As the elevator car ground to a stop and the doors whispered open, Adria stepped into the lobby and let out the breath she hadn't even realized she'd been holding. She paused at the desk to ask for her messages. The clerk offered her a plastic smile. "You're a popular lady," he said, handing her a stack of eight or ten pieces of paper.

"What's this?" she asked aloud as she fingered through the pages: Mary McDonough from KPTV news, Ellen Richards with a local magazine, Robert Ellison, a reporter for the *Oregonian*. Her throat tightened. "Looks like the cat's out of the bag," she said to Zach just as a short man in a herringbone jacket and shiny brown slacks pushed himself out of a chair half hidden by large-leafed ferns.

"Are you Adria Nash?" he asked with a smile. Beside her, Zach tensed. "I'm Barney Havoline with the *Portland Weekly*. He shoved a card at her and she checked it quickly, her fingers curving over the crisp edges. "I'd like to ask you a few questions if I could." He didn't wait for her to answer, but rushed on, "I heard that you're in town claiming to be London Danvers. Is that true?" He clicked on his microphone and grinned at her as if she were his long-lost friend.

Zach took a step closer to her.

Adria managed a thin smile. "That's essentially true, yes."

"And how do you know you're the Danvers heiress?"

"I found out from my father."

"Witt?"

"No, my adoptive father. Listen, Mr. Havoline, I don't know how you found out why I'm in town or where I'm staying, but—"

"Can you prove you're London?"

"—I was planning to call a press conference later in the day and explain everything."

He flashed her a condescending smile and she was aware that several patrons of the hotel were staring at them, even a bellboy had stopped to watch the unfolding drama.

"Really," Havoline insisted. "This will take just a little while. I only have a couple more questions."

"She said later," Zach cut in, stepping between the pushy reporter and Adria.

"But we're here now." Havoline forced a smile, though it was obvious from the wrinkles forming on his bald pate that he was worried about losing his prey. "I could buy you both a cup of coffee or breakfast . . . and who are you?" he asked, before his eyes met Zach's and the light dawned on his face.

"Your worst nightmare." Zach's expression had turned murderous and veins began to show in his neck.

"What—"

"Get out."

"Zachary Danvers." The reporter's eyes gleamed as if he realized he had more of a story than he'd first guessed. "So this woman could be your long lost—"

"I said 'get out'!"

"Not just yet, creep. What are you to her, some kind of personal bodyguard or is it more than that?" He tried looking over Zach's shoulder to catch Adria's eye, but a huge hand clamped over the lapels of his jacket and propelled him past the magazine stand and a few guests wandering in the lobby and toward the entrance. "Hey, you can't do this! I've got rights!"

Zach shoved Havoline through the glass doors and he stumbled onto the street. "I'll sue you, you bastard!" he yelled, brushing off his jacket as a news van for a local station pulled up to the front doors.

"Hell," Zach muttered and clamped his fingers over Adria's arm. As reporters climbed out of the cab, he spun her around and half ran back to the desk. "We need to leave," he told the clerk who had witnessed the entire scene. "You must have a back way out so that we don't have a mob scene here in the lobby."

"I don't know—"

Another van from a rival station pulled up and reporters started through the doors.

"Now!" Zach ordered and the clerk called over a security guard.

"Give these people an escort out and have Bill come up to handle the rest."

"This way!" The guard, a burly black man with a grim I've-seen-it-all expression ushered them to the back of the lobby and through a set of double doors toward the kitchen. Excited voices drifted after them and Adria ducked gratefully into the stainless-steel elevator. She wasn't ready for the press. Not just yet. She needed time to prepare a statement, time to get herself ready for all the questions and accusations that were sure to be hurled her way.

Minutes later they were on the street and walking the short distance to the Hotel Danvers where another crowd had gathered. Holding her arm fiercely, Zach guided her to a private entrance, through a tangle of hallways, down to the parking garage and into his Jeep.

"Where are we going?"

"Does it matter?" he asked, throwing the rig into gear and backing out of the narrow parking space. His countenance was as stark and harsh as the rugged Montana plains.

"I think I have the right to know."

"You got yourself into this mess. I could just leave you here to the piranhas."

"I didn't call the press."

"Like hell." Zach aimed the nose of the Jeep toward the exit of the parking lot.

"You don't believe me, do you?" she said, disappointed as they sped out of the lot and joined the sludge of traffic clogging the city streets.

"No," he admitted, glancing in her direction. "But if it's any consolation, I haven't believed a word you've said since you blew into town."

16

Her face was a mask of calm resolution. Her chin was thrust forward with determination and her eyes, so blue, moved from one reporter's face to the other. As the clouds overhead threatened rain and the cool wind caused the leafless tree branches to sway, Adria stood on a small rise in the park blocks and addressed the throng of reporters. Her cheeks, stung with the wintry wind, were pink, her smile sincere and Zach guessed that she'd had years of public speaking in college.

So far, her hastily convened press conference had gone well and along with the reporters a few passersby hesitated and listened to her strong voice. ". . . that's why I'm here. To find out the truth. To find out for myself if I'm really Witt and Katherine Danvers's daughter." Six microphones were thrust in her face while photographers snapped still pictures and shoulder-held minicams rolled. The wind teased at her hair, whipping it across her face and traffic continued to flow, the sounds of engines running, tires throwing up water and hydraulic brakes squealing as a backdrop.

A pushy reporter with thin lips and a pointed nose asked, "Do you have any proof, aside from this tape of your adoptive father, that you're London Danvers?"

"No, not really—"

"Isn't that a little thin? Home video cameras are a dime a dozen now. Anyone could put together a stunt like this."

Zach's eyes narrowed on the man and he hooked his thumbs into his belt loops just to make sure he didn't start pushing the little bastard around.

"It's not a stunt," Adria replied firmly.

"You don't think. But you don't know. You have no idea what your adoptive father's motives were."

A red-haired woman with a brassy voice asked, "What happened to Ginny Slade?"

"I wish I knew."

"Why didn't she demand ransom?"

Adria lifted her shoulders as a truck roared past, sending pigeons scattering through the park and trailing a plume of blue exhaust.

"What about the million-dollar reward that Witt left for anyone who found his daughter. Wouldn't Ginny have wanted a piece of that?"

"I can't speak for her."

Another woman thrust her microphone under Adria's nose. "At the time of the kidnapping, lots of people thought a local businessman, Anthony Polidori, was behind the plot. Witt Danvers always maintained that Polidori was involved."

"I don't know who was behind it."

"Polidori was harassed by the police but he swore on the lives of his children that he was innocent."

"I can't comment on that."

"Who was behind the kidnapping?"

"I don't know—"

"What about you, Mr. Danvers? What do you and your family think?"

Ignoring the thickening mist, Zach responded by skewering the woman with a gaze meant to strike fear into her heart. "I have nothing to say."

"But you're here, with a woman claiming to be your half-sister."

He felt his blood beginning to boil. "This is her circus, not mine."

"So that's what you think about it?" the woman asked, glee lighting eyes surrounded by thick mascara. "What about the rest of the family?"

"I can't speak for them."

"Just for yourself."

"I have no comment."

"Weren't you one of the prime suspects at the time?"

Zach's eyes flashed. "I was sixteen, for Christ's sake," he said, then forced a lid on his temper. "You'll have to ask the police that one." He grabbed the crook of Adria's arm and if he could have he would have bodily carried her away from this ridiculous sideshow. Reporters were jackals. The whole lot of them. He'd learned that firsthand when London had been kidnapped.

"What do the police have to say?" the redhead asked.

Adria shot a glance in Zach's direction. "Nothing yet." She didn't add that, at Zach's insistence, she'd spent the last three hours at the station, explaining her story, giving the police a copy of the tape, showing them the threatening notes. "Thank you all for coming. If you need to get hold of me, please leave a message at the front desk of the Orion Hotel."

"The Orion? Why not the Hotel Danvers?" The pointed nosed man yelled.

"Hold on a minute—"

"Just a few more questions—"

Zach's fingers clamped firmly around her elbow and he propelled her to the jeep. "Goddamned zoo," he ground out as he helped her inside, then slid behind the wheel. Glancing in his rearview mirror, he spotted more than one of the hungry reporters dashing to their cars and vans, hoping, no doubt to follow them. *Good luck,* Zach thought humorlessly. He knew the city like the back of his hand and had spent most of his teenaged years trying to outrun the law. He slammed the rig into first, popped the clutch and took off. A few cars gave chase and he had to suppress a grin of satisfaction.

"I think it went well, don't you?" Adria asked.

"It was a fiasco."

"Spoken like a true Danvers."

He braked around a sharp corner and the tires skidded.

"We're being followed?" she asked.

"Yep." He glanced in the side-view mirror, frowned and

turned down an alley that opened onto Burnside. "Some of the vultures weren't finished getting what they wanted." He sped across the bridge over the dark Willamette, heading east toward the mountains, then doubled back on the freeway, crossing the river again and turning south, continuously checking his rear-view mirror until he was satisfied that the cars shifting from lane to lane behind the Jeep weren't following him. "You've really stirred up a hornet's nest now."

"It's time."

"You shouldn't have called the press in the first place—"

"I told you I didn't."

"Well someone did."

"Yes," she agreed, her thoughts whirling as they left the city. "Someone did." *Who?* Someone from the Danvers family? Anthony Polidori? The creep who had left her the ugly notes? Someone who had overheard one of her conversations? Trisha? Jason? Nelson? *Zach?* A headache thundered behind her eyes and she realized that other than some dark, bitter sludge the police department called coffee, she hadn't had anything to eat all day."

"You'll have to check out of the Orion."

"I know."

"You have another place to stay?"

"Not yet."

"Jason thinks you should move to the ranch."

"With you?" she asked. The Jeep's interior seemed suddenly close, the atmosphere thick as she considered what life would be like living far removed from the city—with Zachary. How would she stand every day cooped up with him? She glanced at his profile, strong, determined, a craggy face marred by a scar on one side. Her heart began to beat more loudly. Of course she couldn't accept his proposal, she had work to do, here in the Willamette Valley. She didn't have time to dawdle across the mountains. This was just another ploy by the family to derail her from her goal. "I don't care what Jason thinks."

"It wouldn't be a bad idea. You'd be safe."

Alone with Zachary Danvers? Safe? She didn't believe it for a minute. Being alone with Zachary was dangerous on too many levels to count. She was never safe with him. "You'd like that, wouldn't you?" she said, touching the inside of the passenger window with her finger and erasing the dew that had collected on the glass. "Then I'd be trapped in a place where the family could watch me night and day, could tape my phone conversations, could monitor whom I saw and whom I didn't. Thanks, but I don't think so."

He eased off the freeway and found a truck stop where huge eighteen-wheelers were parked helter-skelter between several gas stations with overhangs high enough to cater to the massive rigs. A diner with a flickering neon sign that advertised breakfast was served twenty-four hours each day, was set back from the service stations. Zach parked close to the front door. "Come on, let's eat something and then you can decide." He reached across her and opened the door on her side of the jeep. The feel of his body, warm and hard, leaning over her thighs and brushing her breasts caused an unlikely but tingling sensation to inch up her spine. *Stop it!*

His gaze found hers and for a ridiculous heartbeat she thought he might kiss her again. His eyes darkened for a second, searching hers and his breath fanned her face. He smelled of leather and coffee and musky male and his jaw was nearly black because he hadn't shaved.

Earthy and raw.

Primal and wanton.

Passionate and wicked.

Zachary Danvers was all these and more. She licked her dry lips and held her breath. Waiting . . . sensing he could read her thoughts.

"Sweet Jesus," he whispered before he straightened and yanked the keys from the ignition.

She could barely breathe, let alone think.

"What the hell am I going to do with you?"

"I'm not your responsibility."

"Aren't you?" His dark brow lifted sardonically and her spine stiffened in defense.

"Look, Zach, I guess I should thank you for helping me out this morning, but I don't really need a baby-sitter."

"You might be surprised." He sent her a smile that cut past all her defenses. Pure male animal. The back of her throat turned to sand. He hopped to the gravel and she had to scramble out of the Jeep and hurry to catch up with him.

She wanted to tell him to get lost and leave her alone, but she couldn't. He'd been nearby when she'd needed him and when she'd decided to hold the press conference, he hadn't argued with her, even helped her pick the spot and stayed with her throughout the entire, nerve-fraying ordeal. She didn't know his motives, but she doubted they were pure. She'd just been thankful to have his strength, his presence during the press conference, but she was certain she could have handled the situation herself and she believed that he was probably sticking like glue to her in order to spy on her for his family. But why then did he insist she go to the police station with her complaints? Maybe he had no choice and felt backed into a corner since the word was out on the street that another woman claiming to be the little lost daughter of Witt Danvers had shown up in Portland.

They walked into the diner and were greeted with the smells of coffee, cigarette smoke, and grease. Zach pointed out a worn booth wrapped in dingy yellow Naugahyde and she slid onto a bench seat that sank decidedly with her weight.

Within seconds, a bulky waitress in a gingham uniform two sizes too small poured coffee and promised to be back for their orders. Adria picked up her plastic menu and tried to concentrate on the daily special, but having Zachary seated directly across from her was a distraction—the kind of distraction she didn't want.

Once they'd ordered, Zach drained his coffee and settled onto the small of his back. "You'd better tell me what you're planning,

Adria," he said, staring at her with eyes that seemed to see into the darkest corners of her soul, "because from here on in, it's not gonna be much fun."

The intercom beeped.

"I know you said you didn't want to be disturbed, Mr. Danvers," Jason's secretary, Frances, said in her most annoyed voice, "but your brother is on line two and he insists on speaking with you right now. I tried to get rid of him—"

"It's all right. I'll take it."

Jason crossed the thick forest-green carpet and picked up the phone. Nelson's voice was agitated and high-strung. "Channel Two. The news." A click signified that he'd hung up.

Like a hangman's noose, dread took a choke hold on Jason's neck. He grabbed the remote control, pointed it at the television in the opposite corner of his office and, with a sick feeling, dropped the telephone receiver back into its cradle. The television flickered on. As Jason stared at the program in progress, his worst fears crystallized. She'd done it, that bitch. She'd held her own goddamned press conference in the middle of the park blocks and standing to her side, sometimes in the camera's eye, often not, was Zach. Good old pain-in-the-ass Zach. A day's growth of beard discolored his chin and his eyes were dark and unreadable. He was wearing clothes that were mussed and he looked like a damned range cowboy, but he didn't seem to care that the cameras weren't being particularly kind.

Jason swore loudly. A tic started beneath his left eye as he watched, transfixed.

God, she was beautiful. Standing straight, her wild black hair tossed in the wind, her eyes clear and blue, she looked so damned much like Katherine, Jason could barely breathe. He remembered Kat's sexy little come-hither smile, her teasing laugh, the mischievous light in her gaze. At first she'd only had eyes for Zach, even though Zach had been a kid at the time, but later, after Zach had been banished from the family, when Witt had discovered his errant son in bed with Kat at the ranch, things had changed. Kat had finally begun to notice Jason.

It had started slowly at first. A smile. A wink. A naughty little joke. A finger touching the back of his neck that lingered a second too long. Witt's long absences on business trips didn't hurt, either.

The first time had been on a cold winter night with the wind howling through the attic. The electricity had gone out and Jason and Kat had been alone in the house. She'd feigned being frightened and he'd wrapped his arms around her to settle her down and to keep her warm. When she'd tilted her face up to his, it had been the most natural act in the world to kiss her, to touch her, to rip her robe from her and to claim her like a wild buck stealing another's mate. She'd been an untamed one, her passion pent up from years of frustration.

After their first night together, they'd begun sneaking around, experimenting with drugs, getting high on coke and marijuana and sex. Even thinking of her now, he was harder than he'd been in years. His wife, Nicole, was and always had been frigid and Kim, she was a hot little piece, frantic to please him, willing to play out all his fantasies, but she kept pressuring him to file for divorce and she'd never had the raw sensuality, never shown the primal lust for sex that had set Kat apart from all his other lovers. While Kat enjoyed sex, Kim tried too hard to act as if she were enjoying it. Even though she'd do anything he asked, Kim's responses seemed forced and inhibited.

There had been no one to equal the pure nymphomania and narcissism of Katherine LaRouche Danvers.

And this Adria woman—whoever the hell she was—looked so damned much like Kat it scared him to the pit of his soul.

She was fielding questions and smiling, for God's sake, handling the crowd deftly. Jason leaned his hips against the desk. Adria Nash was an enemy to be reckoned with and she couldn't be taken lightly. He wondered fleetingly what she was like in bed. Sexually charged like Kat or dispassionately accommodating like Kim?

He frowned at the thought of his mistress and her increasing demands. He couldn't divorce Nicole. Wouldn't. His wife, though a limp dishrag in bed, was shrewd. She'd take him for half of everything he owned, which, he hoped, would soon be the largest fortune in Portland. Somehow he'd have to find a way to keep Kim appeased—as well as discredit Adria Nash.

Checking his watch, he scowled. This afternoon he was supposed to inspect some of the smaller mills in the state. The company helicopter would fly him to Lebanon, Mill City, Pendleton, and the Dalles.

Through narrowed eyes, he watched the end of the segment, listened to the two anchors speculate on the fact that the missing heiress had stepped forward to claim her fortune, then watched as old footage taken the night London had been kidnapped rolled in front of the screen. His guts twisted at the sight of his father and Kat and there was a photo of little London. An artist, using the latest computer technology, had provided a simulated portrait of what the girl could look like and the features weren't far from Adria's. Dread settled like lead in his spine. What if? Oh, God, what if?

But there was no way she could be London. It was damned impossible.

He clicked off the television as the intercom beeped again. "I'm sorry, Mr. Danvers, I really am, but Mr. Sweeny insists that you'll want to talk to him. I tried to tell him you were busy and he used the most foul language—"

"It's all right, Frances. I'll take it."

"Oh, well, uh, line two again."

"Got it." Jason's palms began to sweat. He picked up and braced himself for Sweeny's news. "Jason Danvers."

"You told me to call you when I got to Memphis and I'm here," Sweeny said, his voice sounding smug.

"You've found Bobby Slade?"

"I've found a whole mess of 'em. Robert E. Lee Slade seems to be a family name or somethin'. It hasn't been easy, but I got the list narrowed down to a few prime candidates."

"Just be sure you end up with the right one."

"Piece of cake. Oh, by the way, thought you might like to know that your girl Adria's been busy."

Jason's fingers tightened over the receiver. "Has she?"

"Yep. I found out from an insider in the Polidori house that she's big news over there. The old man thinks he can use her if she is London because, as you probably already know, he's interested in buying out big chunks of Danvers International."

"Go on," Jason said through clenched teeth. Damn the Polidoris.

"Well, that's about it. Except that the younger Polidori seems to be very interested in her."

"Mario?"

"Mmm, could be messy, don't you think? Your sister's still seeing him, you know."

"I know," Jason ground out. Trisha would never learn.

"Fun family you got there, Danvers. I'll call you when I have more."

Click.

"Wait!" Jason said, hating to be dismissed by the slimy detective. Sweeny's information usually was good and if he'd managed to make an informant out of one of the servants in the Polidori house, then Jason felt as if his money had been well spent. But he wanted to know more. Lots more.

The noose around his neck tightened a notch.

Glancing at his watch he frowned and yanked his briefcase from the top of the desk. In the reception area, Frances was talking on the phone. He headed to the elevators, but she flagged him down. "It's Guy in security," she said, hanging up. "Seems we've got a siege of reporters downstairs wanting to talk to you or someone in the Danvers family. And these"—she held up a small pile of messages—"are all from reporters and columnists from as far away as Seattle. They want to talk to you about London." She raised her eyebrows over the tinted lenses of her glasses. "Do we have a new one again?"

"Yes, and a very convincing one," Jason said, unable to hide his irritation.

"Oh, dear." Her small lips pursed in her fleshy face. Frances Boothe would lay down her life for Danvers International. "Well, Guy said you might want to avoid the lobby."

"I am," he said, flashing her a not-to-worry smile. "They won't expect me going off the roof. Anything else?"

"Miss Monticello called twice. Wanted you to call back."

Jason's fingers clenched over the handle of his briefcase at the mention of Kim. She could stew for a while; it wouldn't hurt her to wait for him. Now that Adria had gone to the press, Kim held nothing over his head—except his affair. Frowning to himself, he dashed down the hall with two vice presidents, a bland man in charge of operations and an energetic wiry guy who led the sales team. They were both talking to him at once, two yes-men who cared more about Danvers International than they did their own families. He managed to respond automatically as they rode the elevator to the helicopter pad on the roof.

The chopper was waiting and Jason was grateful for the roar of the whirring blades that drowned out conversation for the next few minutes. As the helicopter lifted off and he looked down at the city he felt a premonition of doom. At one time he'd been certain he would be the crown prince of Portland. Now, because of Adria Nash, he wasn't so sure.

Zach glanced at Adria. She was huddled in the far corner of his Jeep, staring at the middle distance through the windshield, but, he guessed, seeing nothing as cars sped around them. She acted as if she didn't know he was in the rig with her and he couldn't forget how close she was. Whenever he was with her, his instincts seemed to sharpen and his nerves were strung tight as bow strings.

Her lower lip protruded slightly and her fingers drummed impatiently upon her leg. Her hair was loose and windblown and fell down one shoulder in thick, unruly curls. Beneath her jacket he noticed the outline of her breasts and he wondered if her resemblance to Kat stopped at her face or continued beneath her clothes . . .

Angry with himself for the single-minded track of his thoughts, he switched on the headlights and pulled out of the parking lot of a seafood restaurant where they'd split a bottle of wine, dunked crab legs in drawn butter, and torn off thick chunks of crusty bread. He'd tried not to stare at her over cups of espresso, but he couldn't keep his eyes from gazing at the curve of her cheek, the precocious little dimple when she smiled, the smooth column of her throat, and the roundness of her breasts.

He'd been hard half the day, silently cursing himself for feeling like a sex-starved teenager all over again. It was more than just her looks that attracted him; her mind was just as sexy as the rest of her.

Adria had given one interview after another and though Zach had disapproved, he didn't have a death wish and didn't do anything as stupid as try to stop her. He'd stood in the shadows, watching her handle the reporters' questions deftly though she couldn't have missed the innuendos that she was just a cheap fortune hunter out to steal a dead man's money. She had managed to stay calm, even injecting a little humor into the situation. From the newspaper-reading and television-watching public's point of view Adria Nash was going to look good— damned good—and if the Danvers family didn't accept her as an honest woman searching for the truth, they would have one hell of a public relations problem.

Zach snorted in disgust. Public relations and public image were Nelson's department. The kid was certain to be sweating. "Okay, where to?"

"I guess back to the hotel."

"You'll have reporters swarming through the lobby," he predicted. "Your phone will ring off the hook."

She smiled a little. "I'll leave that to security." Stifling a yawn, she added, "Besides, I think I can handle them."

"It's your funeral," he growled and she even managed a laugh as he drove to the Orion Hotel. She was tougher than he'd first thought and as she'd so vehemently claimed on more than one occasion, she didn't run scared easily. Her tenacious and independent spirit had earned her his grudging respect. "The press can be ruthless."

Her gaze slid in his direction. "I'm used to it." For a split second he read something more in her eyes than her usual hostility, a dusky look that caused a forbidden quivering deep in his gut. "Don't worry about it, Zach. I'll be fine."

Silently cursing the lust that continually teased the corners of his mind whenever he was around her, he parked near the hotel. "Let's go," he said gruffly, hustling her through the gathering mist to the hotel. Their footsteps rang on the wet sidewalk and Adria ducked her head against the wind.

He expected to be crushed by a throng of scandal-hungry reporters, but the lobby was nearly deserted. Only a few people, carrying raincoats and umbrellas, were hurrying in and out of the restaurant and bar.

Adria relaxed a little. It had been a long day and she'd been on edge, if not because of the reporters and their questions, then because of Zachary. He'd been apprehensive, his gray eyes brooding as he'd watched the crowd and tersely answered the few questions cast in his direction. She'd felt his tension hovering in the air, noticed the muscles of his neck flex when a reporter asked a particularly pointed question and knew the minute he turned his gaze on her. He was with her most of the day, only leaving her for about an hour when she was in an interview with a woman reporter from the *Oregonian*.

She found it impossible to believe that he was her half-brother. He was just too sexy, too darkly sensual to be related to her. Surely she wouldn't find him so attractive, so dangerously alluring if in fact the same blood ran in their veins. As if he read her thoughts, he turned his eyes on her and she saw it, that tiny flicker of passion that he tried vainly to hide.

Her throat closed in on itself and time seemed to stand still.

She felt as if she and Zach were the only two people in the world. One man. One woman. Licking her lips nervously she noticed that his gaze was drawn to the movement at her mouth. He swallowed hard.

"Miss Nash?" The clerk at the registration desk was trying to catch her attention.

"Oh, yes," she said, glad for the interruption. Clearing her throat and praying she wasn't transparent, she asked, "Are there any messages for me?"

"Does it rain in Oregon?" the desk clerk asked dryly, trying to make a joke as he handed her a thick stack of small papers that filled her fist. She flipped through each missive quickly. Some of the people were reporters, others she didn't recognize at all, probably just the curious, star struck that someone dared claimed to be London Danvers.

They walked to the elevators and Zach cast one final look over his shoulder before he touched her arm. "You don't mind if I come up to your room and see if your friend left any more notes?"

Adria's heart nearly missed a beat. She hesitated and bit her lip. *This is stupid—just plain stupid, Adria. You've always been a smart woman, so don't blow it now! Think, for God's sake! Being alone in a hotel room with Zachary is asking, no, begging for trouble so deep you're sure to drown! He's asking the impossible!* With a lift of her shoulder as she punched the elevator call button, she replied, "Whatever you want." Oh, God, had she really said that?

They stepped into the elevator car and the atmosphere seemed close, making breathing difficult. Zachary placed both hands on the back rail, leaning his hips against the smoothly polished brass, not attempting to close the distance between them. The elevator car shuddered, then ascended quickly and as soon as the doors slid open, Adria escaped. She strode quickly down the hall, breathing again, telling herself that the electricity in the air was all in her imagination.

Already realizing she'd made a huge error by inviting him up, she unlocked the door, stepped inside, snapped on the lights and stopped dead in her tracks.

She held back a scream at the smeared blood on the mirror and told herself she was overreacting when she wanted to run. Slowly, with Zach on her heels, she walked across the room to the mirror and the blood-splotched note taped to the glass. The words were simple, but concise:

LEAVE TOWN WHILE YOU STILL CAN, YOU GOLD-DIGGING BITCH

She started to rip the offensive letter off the glass, but Zach grabbed her hand. "The police should see this just as it is."

"The police?" she repeated. "Oh, God, I don't want to call them again."

Zach's jaw became rock hard. "Like it or not, Adria, you've got no choice."

"How does he get in here?" she asked, shaken, though the message made her more angry than frightened.

"Doesn't matter." Without waiting for her, he found the card Detective Ned Fisk had given him earlier in the day.

Fisk was off duty, but a coworker, Detective Celia Stinson, showed up with a team who took the note and dusted for prints. Stinson was a petite woman with curling blond hair and a no-nonsense disposition. She took one look at the situation and advised Adria to move. "And I'm not just talking about taking another room down the hall," she said, eyeing the interior of the room. "Go to another hotel, preferably far away. Now that you've gone public, this"—she said, pointing to the letter in its resealable plastic bag—"is bound to get worse."

By the time the police left, it was nearly two in the morning and Adria was bone weary. The tension of maintaining her calm during all the interviews, of being "on" for the camera, of being close to Zachary all day had taken its toll.

Zach rubbed a hand around his neck. "I think you should take her advice."

"Tonight?" Adria said.

"Right now."

"In the morning I'll—"

"Damn it, Adria, you don't get it, do you? This isn't a kid's prank anymore. We're talking some major sicko is on your case. You're leaving and you're leaving now." He strode to the closet, found her suitcase and threw it onto the bed.

"Hey, wait a minute! You can't tell me what—"

His face was grim, his nostrils flared as he turned on her so quickly she stepped backward to avoid having him run into her. His hands clenched, then opened again in frustration. "Listen, whoever wrote that seems to be getting a lot more deadly—"

"Or desperate."

"Call it what you will, he's obviously unhinged. No telling what he'll do next." He snapped open the suitcase.

"I'm not afraid."

"Then you've got fewer brains than I gave you credit for." He whipped open a drawer from the bureau and dumped it into the open suitcase.

"Zach—" she argued and his fury exploded. He dropped the drawer and advanced on her. The muscles in his face were set into a determined, I-don't-give-a-damn countenance that bordered on fury.

"Don't give me any shit about this, Adria. I didn't fight you when you wanted to go to the press, and I stood by like a friggin' wooden Indian while you gave your interviews. I was even glad to take you to the police station, but I'm not going to have something happen to you just because you're too bullheaded to recognize a threat when it's pasted above your panty drawer!"

"Wait a minute. I can't—"

"You can and you damned well will, lady." She stared him hard in the eyes, trying to get him to back down, but he didn't budge an inch and his nostrils flared in silent fury. "The way I figure it is either I spend the night right here with you in this room, or you move out. Now, what's it gonna be?"

17

Hell.

That's what the last three days had been: pure hell.

Zach had spent most of his time with Adria, either dealing with the media circus that her announcement had created or camped out on her doorstep at the run-down hotel in Estacada, miles away from the city. He'd taken the room next to hers and insisted they keep the connecting door unlocked should she need help. Every night since then he'd spent hours looking at the unlocked door and thinking about her—how warm and innocent she would look with her hair fanned around her face, her dark lashes curled over her rosy cheeks, and her breasts peaking over the edge of the sheets. The image had nearly driven him out of his mind.

He'd even given in once, opened the door and looked in, watching as she lay sleeping. Moonlight had spilled through the window and she'd sighed, her lips parting gently as she rolled over. Her eyelids had fluttered for a second and he'd stood still as death, but she hadn't awakened and he'd somehow found the strength to turn away from her. He'd gritted his teeth, slept little, and spent more time taking cold showers than he wanted to admit.

So far, it seemed, no one knew where she was staying. He hadn't told a soul and unless she opened her gorgeous mouth, she should be safe. She had talked about more permanent quarters, but he'd managed to convince her that mobility was important should her personal letter-writing nut case find her and force her to leave in a hurry.

Now, as he stared across the table of the little out-of-the-way tavern where neither of them would be recognized, she was smiling up at him with a wicked little glint in her eye.

"You're paranoid," she accused over clam chowder.

Men in work clothes bellied up to the bar, where peanuts, pretzels, and popcorn were offered for free and the television was tuned into a football game. From the sounds of the crowd, the Denver Broncos were ahead.

"Family trait." He pushed his platter aside. "Guess you can't be part of the Danvers clan if you don't have it."

"Guess not," she said with a teasing smile that caught on the strings of his heart. Damn, but he was becoming a fool over her.

She looked suddenly guilty, as if she'd been keeping something from him. "I got a phone call," she admitted. He waited for the rest of it and guessed that she'd spent hours, maybe days, deliberating on whether or not she should confide in him.

"Who called?" he asked as his patience gave out. He felt the brackets near the corners of his mouth deepening.

"Mario Polidori."

"He knows you're here?" Zach's smile faded and his entire countenance turned to stone. *Polidori!* Always one of those damned Italians or another. Part of the Danvers's curse.

"Probably a lot of people do," she pointed out as she waved the end of her spoon at him. "Your family's having me followed, I'm sure of it. And they're probably not the only ones. With all the interest in the media . . ."

"Christ!" He rubbed the back of his neck in agitation and his gut wrenched; a sure sign that he expected trouble. He didn't often foresee it and find out that somehow trouble had managed to slip him by. Why hadn't she told him earlier? They could have moved to another fleabag somewhere farther up in the hills—or toward the beach. Somewhere safe. "Anyone else call?"

She shook her head and her wild hair brushed across her shoulders. "Just Polidori."

"What does he want?"

"To talk to me, obviously." She let her spoon clatter back in her empty bowl. Should she tell Zach about the Polidoris's offer? She considered it, but decided to hold her tongue. What good would it do? Knowing that the Italian family was looking for ways to buy chunks of Danvers International would only serve to make him more angry and suspicious than he already was. And she didn't need to be on the receiving end of his particularly bad temper. Since she, if she did prove to be London, had no intention of selling the hotel or any part of the vast businesses to Polidori or anyone else, it seemed a moot point.

"Stay away from him," Zach advised.

"Why?"

"There's bad blood."

"Oh, don't give me that old feud thing." Someone turned on the jukebox and the Judds began to sing through a cloud of smoke that drifted their way.

"It exists, Adria. I've got the scars to prove it." Her gaze shifted to the fine line cleaving along the side of his face. It was barely visible, but seemed to serve as a constant reminder to him. No doubt he was still convinced that his attack at the Orion had been orchestrated by the Polidori family.

Near the bar, there was a roar of approval from the patrons watching the football game. Hoots and hollers filled the room, obscuring the announcer's voice and drowning out Naomi and Wynonna. The Broncos must have found the end zone again.

"Why don't you fill me in on the details of the feud," she suggested once the din died down and some drunk offered to buy the house a round. "Then I'll decide if I want to meet Mario."

"The feud," he said, obviously reluctant to talk about it.

"I know some of the story already."

"I'll bet."

"Come on, Zach. Tell me about it."

Gazing at her thoughtfully, he rolled his long-necked bottle of Henry's between his palms. He frowned silently, then shrugged.

"Okay, why not? You probably know most of the gory details anyway. It's always been there—ever since I was a kid—this . . . intense hatred of a family I'd never even met. You've probably read about most of it," he said, and she nodded, deciding it best not to mention talking to Maria Santiago.

The waitress came with a fresh bottle of beer for Zach and after she'd swept away the empty bottle and glasses, cleared the platters and bowls, slapped a bill on the table, and left balancing her precarious load, Zach continued, "The feud's all a bunch of horse shit if you ask me. It goes back generations to old Julius Danvers and Stefano Polidori. The long and short of that part of the story was that Anthony, Stefano's only son, believed that Julius was behind his father's death in a big fire at the Polidori's hotel, which was the major rival to the Hotel Danvers at the time. Who knows if it's true or not? Anthony swore revenge and two of Julius's three sons were killed, one in the war, another in some kind of fluke boating accident. Witt insisted Anthony was behind them both, though, of course, it's all speculation and a kind of farfetched, wouldn't you say? I mean one guy was shot down over Germany or something."

"A little unbelievable."

Zach scowled. "A lot unbelievable, if you ask me." He downed part of his beer, left the rest and paid the bill. They walked outside. The night was cool but clear and a million stars glittered in a soft ebony sky. Fir trees loomed like ancient sentinels around the old tavern and the sounds of a creek splashing over smooth stones cut through the still night.

Her defenses were down as she climbed into the Jeep. It seemed natural to be with Zach and she wondered at the fact that she'd met him only a short while ago—or had she? She felt as if she'd known him all her life.

He drove her up the foothills of the mountains and on a zigzagging course that followed the Clackamas River. At a wide spot in the road he parked and helped her down a seldom-used trail that led to the water's edge. Even in the darkness, she smelled the clear water mixed with the scents of damp earth and fir trees, and felt the force of the river as it roared and surged through the cliffs.

A cool breeze sped down the canyon as if riding on the back of the river and Adria felt its breath upon her face. She shivered, rubbed her arms and Zach slipped out of his denim jacket, then tossed it over her shoulders, his fingers never touching her. "I thought you might like to see this," he said, as if he needed a reason to explain himself. "Whenever things are cloudy or unfocused for me, I usually spend some time where the power of nature is the strongest. Sometimes it clears things up. If I'm near the coast, I walk on the beach and stare at the breakers, if I'm on the ranch, I ride into the mountains to the creeks that feed into the Deschutes River and if I'm in the city, well, I usually drive up here."

"Alone?" she asked and his smile slashed in the night.

"Always."

A night bird cried plaintively and the forest with its ancient mossy trees seemed to close around them, separating the rest of the world from this little stretch of water. "You were telling me about the feud," she prodded and she saw the tension return to his hard features.

"It just goes on and on, doesn't it? Good old Witt—the great man you hope to prove is your father—was as tough and single-minded as Julius. Witt had learned well, you see, and he was willing to do whatever he had to in order to preserve the Danvers fortune and name. Like his father, he managed to trap more than his share of politicians, judges, and policemen in his pockets."

"You didn't like him."

"Never," Zach admitted.

"But you respected him?"

"I hated the son of a bitch." Zach stared at the river and in the pale moonlight, Adria could see his features, stark and harsh, set without a trace of remorse.

"What about your mother?"

He snorted, his lips thinning thoughtfully. "Eunice . . . she's something. Complex," he said as if weighing his words. "She says one thing and does another."

Adria had heard the story of Eunice Patricia Prescott Danvers Smythe. As a young woman Eunice had been the socially correct choice as a bride for Witt Danvers. Only child of rich parents, she had her own money, a quick wit, regal bearing, though, it was reported she had been cursed with a mind of her own. Some people had thought her spoiled and disdainful and a woman scorned. There were sketchy references to other women in Witt's life, especially when he was younger, and Maria, the maid, had admitted that Witt's affairs had been whispered around town as well as into Eunice's ears. Though she'd borne him two children, a son and a daughter, Witt hadn't been satisfied with his willful wife and had spent many nights out.

Maria had mentioned that she'd overheard an argument in which Eunice had accused Witt of impotence, but it had to have been just the vindictive words of a bitter woman for it hadn't proved true. Eunice had given Witt two more children, Zachary and Nelson.

From the beginning, there had been speculation about Zachary's paternity.

In retaliation for Witt's whoring, Eunice had allowed herself to be seduced by Anthony Polidori. During that time, Zach had been conceived and more than one person had commented on Zachary's complexion—so unlike his siblings. Whereas Jason, the oldest, was brown-haired and blue-eyed like his father and even Trisha, Witt's second child, was fair, Zachary's skin was much darker, an olive shade, his hair black, his eyes a hue between green and gray. Nasty jokes had abounded and it had been widely speculated that Zachary had been fathered by Polidori, Witt's old nemesis.

Witt and Eunice's marriage had deteriorated and the house had shook often with Witt's bellowing rage. According to Maria, no one in the family had been left unscathed. A vengeful, violent man, Witt had made sure that everyone in his family bend to his will or suffer at his hand.

Eunice and Witt had divorced soon after Nelson was born. Witt, with his wealth and bevy of powerful attorneys, had managed to keep the kids with him while Eunice had been given enough money to keep her quiet.

Witt had been sought after by many women, but he eventually married Katherine LaRouche and when he was nearly forty-six, Witt had become a father again. London had been born and Witt seemed to feel rejuvenated, a new man.

Zachary was still staring across the dark, angry river.

"Your mother seems to care about all of you," Adria said tentatively.

"My mother left us."

"Because she had no choice."

His jaw worked. "That's what she claimed." He bent down, gathered up a rock and hurled it over the river with all the pent-up fury in his muscles.

"You expected her to stay with your father?"

"No," Zach said, his lips compressing in the darkness, as he reached for another stone and flung it over the canyon. Then, as if sensing the futility of his actions, he walked to the base of an ancient fir tree and leaned against its rough trunk. "I expected her to take us with her."

"But she couldn't—"

"She wouldn't, you mean. Back then, divorce courts and judges usually favored the mother, even if the father was as powerful a man as Witt Danvers. But Eunice was too scared to go public, didn't want her reputation ruined by the fact that my father was a womanizer and she'd had an affair with Polidori—" He cast a hard glance in Adria's direction, assessing her reaction. "You didn't really think I was naive enough not to know what people thought or deaf enough not to have heard the talk." His smile was as cold as the bottom of the river. "For as long as I can remember, I've heard people conjecture that I was Polidori's son. It's just not true."

She walked closer to him and stood beneath the drooping boughs of the massive tree. The smells of damp earth and spring water mingled in the air and carried with them the underlying scent of musk, unadulterated and male. The night was seductive as it folded, like a gentle black cloak, around them. "Even then there were blood tests. You could have proved that you were—"

"Are you kidding? Witt Danvers go to a doctor to prove that he had fathered his own son?" His voice was harsh, barely audible over the rush of water cutting through the trees. "You don't have any idea what kind of man he was. A mean bastard who thought nothing of slapping his wife around, or controlling his kids with a belt, or buying up smaller businesses on the verge of bankruptcy for a song. He clear cut forests, stripping the land bare, never once thinking about reforestation or erosion or anything but how the chain saw could bring him more money. Without batting a eye, he closed sawmills and logging camps, putting families out of work and never gave a damn, not if the bottom line told him there was a chance to make more money elsewhere. He was unbending and ruthless and proud of his power. He would never, *never* have submitted to paternity tests. You have to understand, Adria, that he didn't care about anyone or anything except himself, the bottom line, his own damned pride, and London, hell, yes, he cared about London." He turned and the moonlight caught in his furious eyes.

"You didn't like her."

"She was spoiled and manipulative—"

"She was only four—"

"Didn't matter," he said staring at Adria's face, his eyes moving slightly as if he were trying to find a flaw in her features, looking for certain proof that she couldn't be the little girl he remembered. Adria's heart kicked into double time and she found it suddenly hard to breathe. One of Zach's fingers touched the side of her face, stroking her cheek as he stared at her. "London was precocious, stubborn, and smart as a whip. She had Witt wrapped around her little finger and she knew it. I was sixteen at the time and she followed me around like a damned puppy. I didn't need it, but I wouldn't say I didn't like her. In fact, I thought it was kind of funny the way the old man made a fool of himself over her." He reached up and captured a strand of her hair. Her throat, suddenly scorched as if by a gusting summer wind, closed in on itself. "I don't know if you're London," he said slowly, his teeth flashing white in the darkness, "but if you are, it's gonna make things a helluva lot more complicated." He paused for a heartbeat, his eyes locking with hers. She swallowed hard and her pulse pounded in her throat.

In that forever instant she knew he was going to kiss her and touch her and wrap his fingers around her heart.

She gave a small sound of protest as he slowly lowered his head, but she didn't stop him. His lips found hers in the darkness. Warm, anxious, burning with a forbidden hunger, they molded over her mouth with a primal possession that was frightening.

Her heart drummed in her ears as his arms closed around her, dragging her close, forcing her to feel the heat of his blood, the fire in his loins.

Hot and hard, his body pressed hers and his tongue slid between her parted lips. She knew she should stop him, told herself she should think beyond this minute, but she couldn't and the feel of his tongue as it darted in and out, flicking against the roof of her mouth, playing with its mate, teasing her into moaning for more of him, was magic.

A pool of wanton desire began to swirl deep within her, flowing in ever-widening ripples, leaving behind an aching dark void that only he could fill.

She wound her arms around his neck, feeling the brush of the hair over his collar on the back of her hand, tasting the salt on his skin, smelling his musky scent, feeling the bulge in his jeans where he held himself so intimately against her.

Still the kiss deepened and she felt a pounding deep in her soul, a need that throbbed through her, chasing reason away. His hands delved beneath her sweater, touching her abdomen before scaling her ribs with hard, work-roughened fingers.

Her breasts ached for his touch. "God, you feel good," he
moaned as he slipped his hand beneath the flimsy lace and
searched for her nipple. She groaned, wanting more, ignoring all
the warning bells ringing insistently in her head.

"Adria," he ground out as the tip of one finger brushed against
her taut, waiting nipple. He kissed her again, harder still and his
mouth was insistent, urgent as he shoved the jacket off her
shoulders and pulled her sweater over her head.

Cool air swept up her abdomen, whispering across her
breasts. His mouth moved slowly and sensuously along her jaw
and her neck, his tongue licking a hot path to the circle of bones
at the base of her throat where her pulse hammered impatiently.

Adria sagged against the tree.

When he lifted his head and stared into her eyes, her bones
turned to water. "I want you," he whispered, his voice as tortured
as the wind racing through the trees.

"I know."

"We can't do this."

"I . . . I know."

His hands cupped a breast and she closed her eyes and threw
back her head, telling herself that she wouldn't, couldn't make
love to him, but as his mouth surrounded her nipple her will
vanished as quickly as if had been ripped from her by the angry
wind before being carried far away. His supple tongue and lips
suckled through the wet lace of her bra and her knees gave way.
They tumbled to the ground, disturbing the thick carpet of needles beneath the tree. The river rushed at a furious, wintry pace,
and Adria cradled his head closer, her fingers twining in the
thick strands of his hair.

Dangerous thoughts mingled with reckless abandon. *Why not
make love to him? You don't know that he's your brother . . .*

"Adria, for the love of God," he said hoarsely and buried his
face in her abdomen. His breath was a tempting desert wind,
trickling past the waistband of her jeans, touching the most
feminine part of her. She kissed his crown.

He drew in a long shaky gulp of air, then rolled away from her.

Curses damning them both cut through the silence as he turned
his back to her and plowed the stiff fingers of both hands through
his hair. "Son of a bitch. Son of a goddamned bitch."

"Zach—"

"Leave me alone."

"But—"

"For Christ's sake, get dressed," he ordered, not even looking
over his shoulder.

"It's all right."

"It's *not* all right. Put your damned clothes on and pretend this
didn't happen." He jumped to his feet, kicked the flashlight
toward her and started hiking up the path in the darkness.

Damn the man! He could be so maddening! Scrambling into
her clothes, she refused to feel an ounce of remorse. She hadn't
tried to seduce him and what had been simmering between them
for over a week was just starting to ignite. She knew she had to
tread carefully, and that deep down, he was right. She couldn't
make love to a man who could be her half-brother, but she'd be
damned to hell before she accepted sole responsibility for the
desire that sizzled between them. Grabbing the flashlight, she
marched up the path, muttering under her breath as the small
beam bobbed ahead of her and the rush of the river faded into
the distance.

As she rounded a final bend in the trail, she spied the Jeep,
headlights splashing twin beams on the grizzled bark of a huge
trunk. Someone had carved initials into the rough bark, surrounding their art with an imperfect heart. How ironic.

As she climbed into the passenger's side of the Cherokee, she
shot a furious glare in his direction.

"That was a mistake," he said.

"You'll get no arguments from me."

"Good."

"Just don't act as if I started it."

"It just happened, okay? It won't happen again." But even as
the words passed his lips, he knew they were a lie. There was no
way in hell he could keep his hands off her.

*   *   *

Hours later, Adria saw no reason to tell Zach she was going to meet Mario Polidori. Zach had been furious when she'd mentioned that Mario had called and decided she'd had enough with his overprotective attitude. Half the time he acted like her damned older brother, the other half he seemed as if he wanted to be her lover.

Warring emotions battled inside her and she decided she needed to get away from him to clear her head, to set her sights back on the path of her quest. She had to find out if she was London. If she was, she'd fight the entire Danvers clan to gain her birthright, if she wasn't . . . then she'd leave. Or she'd become Zach's lover. Either way she was risking emotional suicide.

She parked her battered Nova on the street near the old vegetable market where Stefano Polidori had first made his fortune. Located only four blocks from the Hotel Danvers, the market was now closed, and a new high-rise office building was being considered for the property.

Mario was waiting, smoking a cigarette at the corner near an Irish pub. "I had just about given up on you," he said, his teeth flashing white in the night. He flicked the butt of his cigarette into the gutter.

She was uneasy, but managed to hide her case of nerves. I said I'd be here."

"I know, but I thought your friend might have persuaded you to stand me up." Again the engaging, brilliant smile.

"My friend?"

Mario held the door to the bar open for her. "Zachary Danvers. Your brother."

Adria's stomach plummeted.

"Hasn't he been playing the part of bodyguard?"

"Among others," Adria said as Mario followed her into the smoky interior. Laughter and loud conversation filtered out from the bar. Glasses clinked and pool balls clicked and darts zipped through the air. A jazz band was playing from a makeshift stage, but most of the music was drowned out by the raucous patrons.

Without asking, Mario ordered two Irish coffees and lit a cigarette before he got down to business. "My father and I were wondering if you had thought about our proposal." He blew a stream of smoke out of the corner of his mouth.

"A little," she hedged as a slim waitress slid two glass mugs in front of them. "And the truth of the matter is that I can't make any deals with you or your father." With a thin plastic straw she stirred the green drizzle of crème de menthe into the whipped cream floating on her coffee.

"You don't know that."

"What I don't know is who I am. But if I do find out I'm London, then I won't be making any big demands on the company."

His dark brows lifted in surprise. "You would own over half of it."

"I'd still be the outsider."

"But—"

"Where I come from, Mario, you look before you leap and I can tell you this straight out, I don't have plans to sell or change anything at Danvers International. In fact, unless I find glaring incompetence, I probably won't make any big waves."

"That surprises me." He sipped his drink thoughtfully, his dark eyes assessing.

"I believe in the old adage 'if it ain't broke, don't fix it,' " she said, thinking of the long, hot summer days under blistering Montana sun and how many times her father had said those very words to her. Her father. The man who had raised her, who had often placed a work-roughened hand on her shoulder in a tender gesture reserved for her. She missed him now and knew that even if Witt Danvers proved to be the man who had sired her, Victor Nash would always be her father.

"Tell me more of yourself," Mario suggested, but Adria only smiled.

"It's boring. Really. I grew up on a Montana farm. Worked all week, went to church on Sundays. End of story."

"I doubt it," he said slyly.

"Why don't you tell me about you and your family—it has to be a lot more interesting than hauling hay and making jam."

"You're playing with me."

"No, I honestly want to know," she said. "Come on. What was it like growing up as Anthony Polidori's son?"

Mario's smile widened and his dark eyes sparkled. "It was hell," he said, taking a drag from his cigarette. "Servants, chauffeurs, two houses in Portland, a condo in Hawaii, and a villa in Mexico. No child should suffer as I did."

Adria laughed at his joke.

He told her interesting stories about private Catholic schools and nuns with quick tempers and long rulers that they were ready to rap against the palms and knuckles of those children whose piety wasn't convincing. She heard about his mother's early death, probably from the frustration of dealing with her hardheaded son and husband, and his own run-ins with his father.

"But you seem close now," Adria observed.

"I was younger. Rebellious. Horny." He reached across the table and touched the back of her hand with smooth fingers. "You must know how that is . . ."

"Do I?"

"Your turn, Adria. Tell me about you."

Staring into his slumberous dark eyes she experienced a sudden rush of insight. No matter how she felt about him, this man planned to seduce her. His fingers stroked the back of her hand and she managed a thin, forced smile as she drew her fingers away from him and folded all ten of them under her chin. "Why did you ask me to meet you?"

"There was the business about Danvers International," he said, seeming amused that she would so quickly draw away from him. Obviously he liked a challenge. "But also, I wanted to see you alone because I find you a fascinating woman. I would like to get to know you better." He took a swallow of his drink, frowned, and added sugar. "Does that bother you?"

"Not particularly," she said, lying a little. She didn't trust him but knew he could supply her with information on the Danvers family that might help her cause. "But I'm not a pushover."

"This, I know. And I like." He snapped his fingers at the waiter and indicated that he wanted another round. "I think we could learn a lot from each other." His smile was decidedly wicked.

Trisha watched from the shadows of the alley across the street. She saw Mario—her Mario—with Adria and her heart shattered into a thousand pieces. How much she'd given up for him, how much she'd loved him, how much they had shared and suffered together meant nothing to him.

Tears clogged her throat and her lower lip quivered. She prided herself on her tough exterior, her ability to hide the pain that never seemed to go away, even with drugs and booze.

With trembling hands she lit a cigarette and drew the smoke deep into her lungs. She should have ended her affair with Mario years ago, but she never had been able to completely forget him. Just when she was certain he was out of her system, that she was over him, he'd call or send a single flower and she would run into his waiting arms. Even during her brief marriage she'd carried on with Mario in secret, lying to her husband, cheating on him, cuckolding him because she couldn't give up her most deeply imbedded vice: Mario Polidori.

She'd been only a girl when she'd met Mario and it had been a thrill to see him behind her father's back, behind _his_ father's back. He'd introduced her to wine and marijuana and in return, she'd given him her virginity in the backseat of his father's red Cadillac Eldorado. Her interest in art had waned and she'd skipped lessons just to meet with him at the river, in a room rented by the hour, in a farmer's field, wherever they could be wild and free and laugh at their stodgy old fathers and their silly feud.

The lump in her throat turned hard as she stared past the café curtains of the Irish pub. Mario tossed his head back and his brilliant white teeth flashed as he laughed. Trisha's stomach wrenched and her fingers balled into fists of frustration. She wouldn't stay here and watch him humiliate her with that woman—the bitch claiming to be London.

At the thought of her half-sister, Trisha felt she might be sick. It would be hard losing Mario to someone pretending to be London. London, who had managed to steal all their father's attention. London, born to be a beauty. London, the princess, the treasure of the Danvers family.

Nauseous, Trisha turned away from the damning view and headed back to her car. She held her cigarette between her teeth and walked more quickly, faster and faster, exhaling smoke like a locomotive, her high heels clicking like wheels on a runaway train. Tears came unbidden to her eyes and she silently swore that Mario would pay and pay dearly for this slap in the face. Spitting the butt of her Salem Light into the gutter, she ran to her car and tried to erase the image of Mario laughing and joking, sharing a drink and a smile with the imposter.

No doubt he would try to seduce Adria. Mario believed himself to be a great lover and Trisha certainly couldn't argue with his skill in bed. Unfortunately, his appetite was insatiable and he'd never been faithful to her, not even when Trisha had turned up pregnant. She remembered that night with soul-jarring clarity.

She'd finally worked up the nerve to tell him about the baby after they'd made love in the cheap motel near the airport.

His body was still dewy with sweat and she stretched out beside him, running her fingers down the sleek muscles of his arms.

"I have a secret," she said as he reached for a pack of Winstons.

"Do you?" He struck a match, lit up and blew smoke from the corner of his mouth. With a smile, he asked, "What is it?"

"Something special."

"Oh, yeah?"

"You're going to be a father."

Silence. Dead silence.

"In September," she rushed on as his eyebrows pulled to-gether and smoke drifted from his nostrils. Then he smiled—that winning, cocky grin and she knew everything would be all right.

"A father. Me? Yeah, right." His words were filled with sar-casm as he laughed and the cigarette wiggled between his teeth. Slapping her on her naked rump, he added, "Good one, Trisha, you nearly had me believing that you were knocked up."

Her back stiffened and she felt the sting of tears behind her eyes. She'd fantasized that he would smile and twirl her off her feet and promise to marry her when she told him of the baby. She'd even been silly enough to believe that their love—and this baby, this precious, precious baby—might put an end to the horrid feud that existed between their families. Love would con-quer over hatred.

"You're kiddin', right?" he said when he saw the tears filling the corners of her eyes.

"I'm going to have a baby, Mario," she said angrily as she climbed out of bed and threw her sweater over her head. "Your baby."

He stared at her for several long seconds, the cigarette dan-gling neglected from his lips, the ash growing. "No—"

"It's true, damn it. Whether you like it or not, we're going to be parents!"

"Oh, God, Trisha, how could you do this?" he whispered, his dark complexion turning pasty white. He rubbed his forehead as if he were trying to erase the entire conversation.

"*I* didn't do it. *We* did."

"But are you sure?"

"I had a test at the free clinic."

"Fuck." He fell onto the cheap mattress of the motel and cradled his head in his hands. "How could this have happened?"

"You know how it happened."

"This couldn't have come at a worse time. My old man's—"

"For crying out loud, Mario. I didn't plan it. Sorry if it's inconvenient for you," she snarled, hurting inside. The room shook as a great jet roared through the sky and Trisha felt like dying inside.

Jabbing out his cigarette in an overflowing tin tray, he looked up at her. As if finally realizing how distressed she was, he opened his arms and motioned for her to join him on the bed. "Come on, Trisha. It's not the end of the world."

"It's a miracle," she said, defensive of her unborn child. "A miracle."

" 'Course it is."

She didn't trust him and tears threatened to overtake her again. "You aren't happy."

"Sure I am," he said, though his voice sounded glum. "I . . . I was just shocked that's all. Hell, it's not every day you get news like this." He patted the bed beside him and she sat on the edge of the stained mattress. His strong arms surrounded her and she wanted to trust him again—to believe in their love. His breath, smoky and warm, teased her ear. "You want this—this baby."

"Don't you?"

"Oh, sure. Sure."

She relaxed a little, though she wished she heard more conviction in his voice.

"I guess this is the part where I should ask you to marry me, huh?"

Sniffing back her tears, she nodded. "I think that's the proper thing to do."

"Hey, well, proper. That's me. Okay, then I'm askin'. Trisha, will you marry me?"

"Of course I will," she'd vowed, throwing her arms around his neck and tumbling into the bed with him. "I love you, Mario. I've always loved you and I will love you until the day I die."

"That's my girl," he'd said, kissing her and touching her breasts through her sweater. He climbed atop her and rather than kiss her gently he made love to her roughly, as if fighting some inner demon that only hard, furious sex could subdue.

Two weeks later they'd broken the news to their parents and both Witt and Anthony had hit the roof.

According to Mario, Anthony called his son a dumb fuck and forbid him from ever seeing Trisha again. If Mario needed girls to screw around with, Anthony would find some clean whores. If he wanted to fall in love and get married, there was always that nice Lanza girl who lived in the neighborhood; and if he wanted to be so stupid as to knock someone up, Mario should have his head examined. He'd been told to quit thinking with his cock and start listening to reason. Anthony had even come up with alternatives—Cynthia Lanza—a nice Catholic girl with big tits and no brains, but Mario hadn't been interested. Anthony had warned his son never to see Trisha again.

Mario had broken that promise the next week and told her about the scene with his father. To Trisha, Mario had seemed spinelessly relieved.

Witt had even been more furious than Mario's father. When Trisha broke the news to her father who was working in his den, he'd turned a shade of red bordering on purple and been consumed by a rage so deep, Trisha feared for her life.

"You'll never marry that dirty dago!" Witt roared, rounding the desk and kicking an antique vase that shattered into a million pieces.

"You can't stop me!" Trisha could be just as bullheaded as her father.

"You're under age, Trisha. Sixteen, for crying out loud! We could have that fucker up on statutory rape."

"He loves me, Dad. He wants to marry me."

"Over my dead body," Witt bellowed, rage mottling his face. "This is one helluva blow, but we can still take care of things. There's still time."

"What do you mean?" she asked, refusing to understand. But her stomach began to flutter in anxiety.

"I know a doctor who'll—"

"No!" she screamed. "I'll never have an abortion! Oh, God, Dad, you can't be serious!" Panic screamed through her blood. Lose the baby? No! She'd run away before she'd let her father snuff out the life of her unborn child. Protectively she held her middle.

"Either you take care of this my way or the boy gets arrested," Witt insisted, his face twisted in hatred. "And don't fuck with me, Trisha, 'cause there's nothing I'd like better than to see Polidori's only son in jail."

"You wouldn't—"

Witt's lip curled and his blue eyes gleamed with pure malice. "He defiled you, Trisha. Raped you and got you pregnant. He used you—like some common slut. And if you think I'll allow you to give birth to that slimy Italian's bastard, you can think again."

"I won't—"

Witt had raised his hand, intending to strike her and Trisha let out a bloodcurdling wail.

"I'll handle this." Kat stepped into the room, as if she'd been hovering in the hall, waiting for the right moment to appear.

"She's my daughter."

"And you're out of control." Kat's lips compressed. "I said, I'll handle this, Witt. It's women's business."

"I'm not backing down," he'd growled and stalked out of the den, kicking the door on his way out.

Quietly Kat had shut the door and the lock clicking into place was like the knell of doom. Trisha's eyes filled with tears because she knew she'd already lost.

"Come on, Trisha, let's talk sensibly about what's going on here," Kat said. "I know you're upset and your father, well, he is, too. It's just because he loves you so much."

"Bull shit!"

"He does. In his own way. But he hates the Polidoris as much as he loves you and he's serious when he says he'll press charges.

Mario will probably spend time in jail and how good would that be for you and your baby?"

Trisha began to sob brokenly, already relenting to the steady, unstopping pressure her family was sure to put on her. Like Chinese water torture, with the drip of water that keeps right on coming, second after second, minute after minute, hour after hour, and day after day, her father would keep after her until he eventually got his way. That was the way it always was with him. Her baby wouldn't change it.

In the end, Kat had convinced her that the only reasonable thing to do, the best thing for all concerned, was to abort the baby and the next day, before Trisha could change her mind, Kat had shuttled her to a private clinic where she'd given up the only person—the only thing—that had meant anything to her.

She'd never gotten pregnant again. She'd lost the baby and Mario's love. Though he claimed to still care for her, their relationship had never been the same. They had lost what little innocence they'd once shared.

Now, so many hateful years later, she rested her head on the steering wheel of her sports car. She and Mario were just illicit lovers, running through the shadows to private rendezvous of hot sex with no strings attached. Trisha tried to hide the fact that she still loved him, even from herself, but then something always happened to awaken all her old, long buried emotions, as if that little bit of life that had been so frail, existed for so little time, had linked Trisha to Mario forever.

Love, coupled with the possession and jealousy that came with it, always resurfaced. She would love Mario Polidori until the day she gave up her last breath. Tonight, watching Mario with Adria, Trisha had felt the old pangs of pain and loss, love and jealousy. She sniffed loudly and her hatred grew white-hot, settling in the pit of her stomach and burning.

Mario had been with Adria.

Beautiful Adria. So much like Kat. Too much like London.

18

"I'm going out," Jason said as he paused at the door to his wife's bedroom.

"Now?" Sitting in her dressing gown, brushing her hair, Nicole caught Jason's reflection in the mirror and she wondered why she'd ever been foolish enough to think that he loved her. She glanced at her watch. "Why?"

"Late meeting."

"It's nearly midnight," she said, hating the wheedling sound of protest in her voice.

"I know."

Closing her eyes, she tried to pull together whatever it was that kept her going. She set her brush down and said calmly, "You know, Jason, I should just divorce you and get it over with. Then you wouldn't have to lie anymore."

"I'm not—"

She held up a smooth hand before lifting her eyelids. "Please. Give me some credit, will you?"

When she looked up, Jason was smiling that waxen, tight little grin that she'd grown to hate over the years—the smile he seemed to reserve just for her. "The skillet suddenly too hot for you, darling?" he said and her insides revolted at the endearment.

How far they'd drifted apart over the years. Too far to ever find each other again. "What's too hot isn't the skillet, or the fire, it's that damned little mistress of yours," she said evenly though her insides churned. She'd thought she'd quit loving him years ago, but still the lies hurt.

At least he had the decency to blanch.

"She called here. Kim, isn't it? The little blonde with legs that won't quit and no breasts?" Nicole applied a little night cream to moisturize her face and hopefully forestall a few of the determined little lines that remained on her skin as the years crept by. "You really didn't believe I didn't know, did you?"

He seemed to puff up a bit—like he used to do when he practiced law and stood in front of a particularly recalcitrant witness on the stand. "I don't know what you're talking about."

"Come off it, Jason." She wiped off the excess cream. "Contrary to what you would like to think, I'm not stupid. And I know what's going on with this London thing. You're running scared, aren't you?" She tossed her pale hair over her shoulders and removed her earrings, clusters of diamonds and sapphires that sparkled in the soft lights arranged over her vanity. She'd picked the earrings herself, though Jason had bought them for their fifth . . . or was it their sixth . . . anniversary? "This new little London, she just could be your sister."

"I don't think so."

Sometimes, when the pain wasn't too great, when she could distance herself from him, it amused her to watch him lie. He did it so well, with such grace and such . . . conviction, as if he really believed all the untruths that fell from his thin lips.

"Zachary wouldn't be hanging around if it weren't serious," she said. "Nelson looks like he's unraveling at the seams, Trisha's worse than ever—I shudder to think what she's on these days—and your mother, usually so remote, she seems to have taken a sudden interest in the family. Oh, you're worried," she said, dropping her jewels in a velvet case and snapping it shut. "All very worried."

"And you're not?" He walked up behind her and placed his hands lightly around her throat. Their gazes locked in the mirror and she tilted her chin up a fraction as she felt him squeeze, ever so slightly. It would be so easy for him to cut off her wind and strangle her, but Nicole wasn't afraid. She slid a meaningful glance to the framed eight by ten picture poised on the corner of the vanity.

Their daughter, Shelly, laughing, her hair windswept in the breeze that had been rising off the ocean that day, gazed back at her. Shelly was the one thing that both she and Jason cared about. The only thing.

Jason's gaze dropped to the picture and his fingers relaxed.

He would never do anything that might cause him to lose his daughter for, as overly doting as Witt had been with London, so was Jason to Shelly. In his eyes, his daughter could do no wrong. The little imp had him wrapped around her slim little finger.

"You know, I'd hate to see anything happen to us," Nicole said softly, though there was a steel thread running through the words. "It would be devastating to Shelly."

Jason's smug smile faltered. "Kids are survivors."

"Are they?" she asked pointedly. "What about you?"

"I'm doing okay."

"Are you? I'm not so sure. Then there's your brothers and sister . . ."

His gaze met hers again in the mirror. "Zach always seems to land on his feet. The others . . . who can say?" He turned away from her and started for the door.

"I won't be publicly mortified, Jason. If your little girlfriend wants to get down and dirty, I won't be a part of it and neither will Shelly. Either stop seeing that little bitch or control her, I don't really care which." That was bending the truth a little, she did care, it bothered her to think that another woman, a younger woman, could turn his head, but she was shrewd enough to understand that Jason needed more than just a wife. He needed to be adored and fawned upon and he always needed a hot little number warming his bed and stroking his male ego.

The thought made her sick, but she'd live with it. For Shelly. As long as one of his slutty little mistresses didn't go public. Nicole had never before been concerned, not really, but she was

worried about this Kim. It took nerve—hell, it took brass balls—
to call up Jason Danvers's wife and start issuing orders.

Things had changed since Adria Nash had waltzed into town.
And not for the better.

She heard a pounding on the front door and her heart leaped
to her throat. Now what? For a minute she thought Kim had
become desperate enough to show up here. Jason probably gave
her the code to the gate and she had just enough nerve to
confront her lover and his wife.

Shelly! Her thoughts flew to her daughter. She couldn't let
Shelly meet the woman! Grabbing the satin robe left at the foot
of her bed, she slid her arms through the sleeves and hurried
down the hall, looping the belt, damned if that little tramp would
meet her daughter. Jason was two steps in front of her and he
opened the door, letting in the slice of wintry cold wind that
preceded his brother.

Zachary, in jeans and a denim jacket, looked out of place in the
house where he'd grown up. He was tense and the restless
energy that Nicole had come to associate with him was evident
in the way he paced the room, the manner in which his eyes took
in everything at once, the feel of electricity that he generated. His
hair was a little too long, uncombed, and he looked as if he could
use a shave—like he'd just come in off the range. He was so
innately sexy, that Nicole tried to avoid looking in his eyes for
fear that she would see the promise of sweet seduction lingering
in those hot gray orbs.

She offered him a chair, but he shook his head and stared at
his brother. "I want Sweeny's number."

"I was just on my way out—" Jason said.

"Now?"

"Late meeting."

Zach didn't press it; as if what Jason did with his own time was
his business. "Fine. Go out. Just give me the number."

"Sweeny's out of town." Now it was Jason's turn to be nervous.

"Then tell me where he can be reached." There was a desperate edge to Zach's voice, one that dared to be defied.

"He's in and out, you'll never catch up with him," Jason said and his voice sounded strangled. Out of control. All that practiced courtroom poker face shot to hell. He was lying again, Nicole surmised. And the untruths seemed to come harder when they were told to his steel-jawed brother. Would this chain of deception never end?

Zach's eyes grew dark. "Give me the number, Jason, or place the damned call. I want to talk to him."

Jason backed off. "You look like you could use a drink. I've got a bottle of—"

"I don't need a drink," Zach snapped. "Just give me the number."

Jason eyed his brother and finally relented. "All right. Come on. In the den." He checked his watch. "You know it's nearly two o'clock in Memphis."

"Good. He should be in."

"Sweeny could be asleep."

"Then it's time to wake up," Zach said, unable to tamp down the raw, naked tautness that had been with him ever since he'd kissed Adria and held her in his arms. Her lips had offered such sweet promise, her head thrown back in absolute abandon, her breasts straining against that little scrap of a bra. He'd come close to making love to her, so damned close and it had been all he could do to break it off. She'd been willing and soft, her body yielding to his. He'd argued with himself as he'd kissed her, sworn at himself when he touched her breasts and nearly lost all reason as she'd cradled his head to her nipple. He'd never been so hard in his life. Never wanted anything more. Never been so repulsed by his own desires.

Just thinking of it now caused the beginning of an erection to swell in his jeans. He stuffed one hand into a front pocket as Jason showed him the numbers scratched on a pad across the desk. Cradling the receiver with his shoulder, Zach punched out the numbers and waited impatiently, tapping the fingers of his free hand on the corner of the desk. "Come on, come on," he muttered as Jason closed the door to the den.

Sweeny's groggy voice answered on the seventh ring. "Yeah."

"This is Zachary Danvers."

"Jesus, do you know what time it is?"

"What've you found out?"

"I was gonna call Jason in the morning."

Zach glanced at the clock. "You're in luck. It is morning and Jason's right here."

"You're a fucking prick, Danvers." The voice cleared and he heard the sound of a lighter clicking. "Okay, it's not much, but a start." Zach's stomach twisted. If Sweeny confirmed the fact that Adria was a fraud, then she was little more than a cheap hustler—a gold digger. But if he'd discovered she was London . . . hell, that would be worse because he'd be related to her. His heart drummed frantically in his chest. Either way he was bound to lose. "It's kind of been like lookin' for a needle in a haystack," Sweeny was saying, "or trying to find that damned guy in the puzzle, you know what I'm talking about? The guy in the red stripes? Where's Whosit?"

"Waldo," Zach said tersely.

"Right. That's it. Anyway, I narrowed it down and it looks like the guy who was married to Ginny Watson moved to Kentucky a while back. Lexington, in the seventies sometime, near as I can tell. I'm gonna visit him tomorrow."

"You got his phone number?"

Zach heard nothing but silence for a few seconds.

"Well, do you?"

"Sure, I got it, but I figured a visit in person would be better. Seeing people face to face makes it damned hard to hang up."

"I want to speak to him."

"Easy, boy. You'll get your chance," Oswald said smoothly. "Just let me break the ice. I'll call you as soon as I have more news. I'll leave the message with Jason."

"Where will you be staying?" Zach demanded.

"Where will I be staying? That's a good one. Maybe at the goddamned Ritz? Or how about the Hotel Danvers, you got one over in Kentucky? Shit, how'm I s'posed to know?" He hung up and the phone clicked loudly in Zach's ear.

"What was that all about?" Jason asked, pouring two glasses from a bottle of Scotch he kept in the bar. His eyes were trained suspiciously on his brother.

"I'm just tired of waiting around and I don't trust Sweeny."

"Neither do I, but he keeps his mouth shut and if he finds out something, he'll let us know, but it'll cost. Now, where's Adria? Are you hiding her somewhere?"

Zach didn't answer and his older brother's lips curved into a hard little smile. "Keeping her all to yourself?"

"I thought you wanted her low profile."

"She's already been on the news and in the papers. Hardly low profile." Jason walked to the desk, opened the drawer and flipped out clippings and copies and faxes. "She's made the national news, you know . . . and I mean more than just the little blurb that was reported through the AP. The networks are beginning to call and even a few papers back East are showing a little interest. Every time I turn on the goddamned television, some one seems to be talking about her and during the day, at the company, there's a fucking siege in the lobby."

"Free publicity," Zach said sarcastically.

"Go to hell, Zach." Jason tossed back his drink. "It's started here, too, at the house. It upsets Nicole and Shelly and . . . I feel like I did when London was kidnapped—all the reporters camped out at the gate."

Zach remembered the throng of newspeople that had pummeled the family with questions, called at all hours, crowded around the gates to the house and he'd heard from his crew still cleaning up at the hotel, that the press had been ever-present in the lobby. Even his office in Bend wasn't immune; Terry had phoned and told him that a few reporters had shown up looking for him ever since Adria's meeting with the press.

"It's worse than I'd imagined," Jason was saying as he reached for the bottle again. "Even the lawyers are beginning to worry. They want to talk to Ms. Nash, but I advised them to wait a while."

"Just let me handle her." He didn't want her hustled away by a herd of bloodsuckers like the attorneys for the Danvers family. Impatiently he jammed one hand through his hair.

"Has she hired an attorney yet?"

Zach lifted a shoulder. "I don't think so. But she's with Mario Polidori tonight."

"Polidori?" Jason's face muscles flexed in disbelief and his nostrils flared in disgust. "Why?"

"Don't know. She didn't say."

"So, the vultures are already circling. Great, Zach, that's just goddamned great," he said sarcastically, then pointed a finger at his younger brother. "You can't let him get to her."

"It's none of my business."

"Like hell! Polidori, through a smoke screen of lawyers and holding companies and silent partners, has been trying to buy off chunks of Danvers International for years—waterfront property and the old hotel, downtown real estate, even a couple of saw-mills. You name it, he wants it. As long as it's got the Danvers logo attached. He has this thing about acquiring our castoffs; so far we've held him off."

"His money no good?"

"It's not the money, it's the idea that he wants it all," Jason said and Zach smiled at the irony of it all.

"Aren't you the guy who said 'it's always money'?"

"Not with the Polidoris. With them it's revenge," Jason said, staring morosely into his glass. Zach didn't argue; he'd grown up being told that the Polidoris were no-goods, out for blood, the worst of the worst. Zach had changed his mind over the course of the years, but he still didn't trust them, especially with Adria.

Before Jason could ask a lot of questions Zach didn't want to answer, he pushed himself away from the desk and left. Jason's case of nerves was getting to him.

He drove downtown and stopped at Hotel Danvers, picked up some blueprints that had been left there for him and grabbed a stack of messages, which he gave a quick once-over, then tossed into the trash. Reporters and more reporters. Jason was right on that score. Once they smelled the blood of scandal, the vultures kept circling until they finally swept in to pick the carcass.

He climbed into his Jeep and headed out of the city. Back to Adria. His foot pressed harder on the accelerator. The truth of the matter was that he was bothered that Adria was with Polidori and it had nothing to do with the feud or the family fortune. It didn't even have anything to do with London Danvers. The problem was more basic than that. It hit him at a gut level. Like it or not, Zach was jealous. He denied it to himself as he drove hell-bent-for-leather on the winding road to Estacada but when push came to shove and he was honest with himself, the truth of the matter was that he didn't like the thought of her with any other man.

"Idiot," he told himself and snapped on the radio. Squinting against oncoming headlights, he listened to a half hour dedicated to Bruce Springsteen songs, but his mind drifted from the lyrics to Adria. Christ, what was he going to do with her? He knew what he wanted and it was either obscene or just plain stupid, or maybe a little bit of both, depending upon whom she turned out to be.

Adria pulled into the parking lot of the Fir Glen Motel and swallowed back a welling sense of disappointment. Zach's Jeep wasn't in sight and the drab little motel with its dark units and only a few lights blazing in the windows did nothing to lift her spirits. A headache throbbed behind her eyes. Her meeting with Mario Polidori had turned out badly. Though she'd gained some insight into the Polidori family as well as the feud that still simmered between them and the Danvers clan, she'd been on edge the entire night.

Mario's interest in her had crossed the barrier of mild curiosity to friendliness and was fast approaching territory she didn't

even want to contemplate. She'd recognized a spark of challenge
in his eyes as he'd looked at her and she'd been hit with the
sudden insight that he wanted to seduce her. At first she'd told
herself she was imagining things, but as the evening had worn
on and he'd become bolder, his eyes darker, his smile just a
teensy bit more wicked, she was certain that he planned to sleep
with her. Not because he found her fascinating, but because she
was new blood—perhaps even new Danvers blood and a challenge. If nothing else, Mario Polidori seemed to love a challenge.

The idea that she was next on his list of potential conquests
caused her stomach to turn over. She told herself she should
have been flattered, that he was only flirting with her, but deep
down, she knew that she was playing with a dangerous fire and
she was glad to be away from him. Maybe, she thought, as she
cranked off the engine and listened to the sounds of the night,
all her mother's sermons about dirty sex had finally sunk into her
heathen brain.

*Except you didn't feel that way with Zachary, and getting involved
with him could be much more treacherous.*

Biting her lower lip in frustration, she closed her mind to that
worrisome way of thinking. She'd come close to making love
with Zach, damned close. If he hadn't broken off the embrace,
she would have given herself to him. Just the thought of his hard
mouth moving hungrily against her fevered skin caused an unwanted, forbidden warmth to steal through her blood.

"Stop it!" She yanked out the keys from the ignition and folded
them into her palm.

The breeze was cool and she rubbed her arms as she crossed
the gravel lot, unlocked the motel room door and reached for the
lights. She didn't get the chance.

A hard body flew through the dark room, hitting her square,
knocking the wind from her lungs as she fell. Her head cracked
on the floor and she struggled to get up, but her attacker was
strong. Heavy. A dead weight on her.

Pain ripped down her spine. She screamed and her mind spun

back to that horrible day in the school yard when Tommy Sinclair straddled her ribs. Pain and rage roiled within her. "No!" *Let me go! Who are you? Why are you doing this to me?*

The attacker held her facedown and she could barely breathe, much less scream again.

"Bitch!" a hoarse voice growled as she tried to writhe free.

Fear turned her blood to ice. She attempted to cry out again, but a gloved hand clamped over her mouth. Just like Tommy! Mind-numbing fear bubbled up inside her. "You don't learn, do you bitch?" Oh, God.

She bucked upward, but was rewarded with a knee to her back, threatening to crack her spine.

Dazed, Adria attempted to think past the sheer terror that streaked through her mind. She tried to strike out, lashing wildly with her hands, kicking upward, trying to pry off the horrid weight.

For her efforts, she was slapped. The smack seemed to ricochet through her brain. Lights erupted, causing a blinding, pain-riddled explosion behind her eyes, and her stomach turned over.

"You money-hungry idiot." Whose voice was it? Had she heard it before? Something smelled different—blood and fear, but something else, something that reminded her of a rare blend of tea, but she couldn't concentrate on anything other than saving herself. She scratched and clawed, but the attacker was heavy and determined. "Go back to Montana before you really get hurt." Forcing her tired muscles to work, she tried to climb onto her knees and bit hard into the gloved hand covering her mouth.

Just like with Tommy!

The assailant let out a hiss of pain and let go. Adria was ready. She moved quickly and screamed for help. She was almost free. Kicking madly, inching toward the door, she yelled just as, from the corner of her eye, she saw it coming. An object, dark and heavy, aimed at her face. She recoiled, holding her arm over her face. Smack! The object hit her on the back of the head. Pain exploded in her skull and she thought she might black out.

Faintly, she heard a door open and a man's voice yell. "Hey, what's going on?"

A dog, as if picking up the scent of blood, bayed in the woods.

Her attacker froze. Adria clawed her way to a sitting position. "Help me!"

A kick landed in her chest. Painful and crushing the blow made her wretch and curl into a protective ball.

"You goddamned bitch!" Breathing hard and limping, the intruder climbed off her and scrambled with an uneven gate through the door. Breathing hard, the metallic taste of blood in her throat, Adria struggled upright and crawled to the threshold. Just one look, that's all she needed and she was sure she could identify the intruder. It was someone she'd met, she was certain of it, but the ache in her gut prevented her from thinking clearly and the edges of her vision blurred as if she might black out. She tried to concentrate, to hold onto consciousness as the attacker fled through the shadows of the huge trees surrounding the motel.

She took in deep breaths and held onto the door casing in a death grip as she squinted into the night. She saw the stars and lights switching on in nearby units, but her attacker had disappeared. Damn it all, she thought as she spit blood onto the porch. She tried to yell again, but could make no sound.

A second door opened, just two doors down. Light spilled onto the small porch.

In the distance the dog barked in frustration.

"Hey, you! Hey, are you all right?" A male voice. Unfamiliar. She drew in a long, painful breath.

Footsteps. Crunching on gravel. Running in her direction. Ready to kick her again. She cringed. A man loomed over her as the lights in the unit blazed on. Her stomach heaved suddenly and she retched.

"Oh, shit," he said, looking around the small room before bending on one knee. "Now, don't move, miss, you're hurt!" She squinted up at him, but couldn't make out his features as he turned toward the open door. "Marge!" he bellowed in a voice that pounded through her brain, "Marge, wake up the damned manager and call 911!"

"What?" a woman's voice screamed back as doors creaked opened and banged closed, rattling the loose windows in their panes. The man knelt beside her again. "Now you just lay still, help's on its way."

Voices filtered in through the open door and pierced Adria's pain-racked brain.

"What the hell's going on?" a woman said.

"Hey, shut up! People are trying to sleep over here!" A man this time.

"Holy shit, what's going on in unit thirteen?" A younger man. "Mary, come look at this, will ya?"

"Don't get involved." Mary wasn't too willing to help out.

Adria blinked and tried to stay conscious. There was something familiar about the attacker, familiar and horrible and . . . it teased the edge of her consciousness. What was it? Who was he?

"Hey, lady, I don't know what happened here, but it looks bad," the man who was tending to her said.

She lifted her hand to the back of her head and felt sticky blood matting her hair. Groaning, she pulled herself upright, her eyes squinting, trying to get used to the bright lights. As she did, her heart squeezed in fear. The room had been destroyed. Chairs turned over, the television set smashed, sheets torn and ripped from the bed, as if someone had been in a fury so wild—so blind, he'd needed to lash out at something, anything to vent his rage. On the mirror over the bureau, scribbled in a grease pen's bold black letters, was a simple and horrifying message: DEATH TO THE BITCH.

"Oh, God." She felt suddenly sick again and the brightly lit room seemed to spin around her. Her nose and mouth tasted foul, and she had to fight against the overwhelming sensation that evil still lurked beneath the bed or behind the curtains.

"What's going on here?" the man asked. "No—wait. You just lie still. Don't talk. Save it for the police."

Footsteps. Shouts. People closing in, some curious, some concerned. She hurt so badly she didn't care.

"Sumbitch, would you look at that!"

"Did someone call the frickin' ambulance?"

"Hell, yes, but Jesus H. Christ, it looks like a bear came in here and went on a rampage."

"Yeah, sure, and now bears can spell."

"Hang on, miss. Marge—the manager—?"

Headlights flashed against the window and tires crushed the gravel in the lot.

"Adria!" She heard his voice, roaring through the crowd, a life line to reach out and cling to.

Zachary! Tears filled her eyes as she tried to scramble to her feet.

"You lie still!" she was ordered.

Zachary broke through the crowd beginning to collect at the door and gathered her into his arms.

"Adria, oh, God, Adria," he said, holding her as if he could protect her, as if the strength of his body could fold over hers and stave off the pain, the fear. Clinging to him, she fought the horrid sobs that suddenly clogged her throat as relief flooded through her. She was with Zachary and safe. So safe.

"Hey, you, I wouldn't touch her!" a man advised. "Leave her for the paramedics, they're on their way. She's bleedin', man, no tellin'—Hey, are you her old man?"

"What the fuck happened here?" the manager yelled, only casting Adria a cursory glance. "Who did this? Holy Saint Peter, what a mess!"

"Did anyone call the police?" Zach demanded.

"911, you get it all," the manager said. A short, balding man in boxer shorts and a nightshirt, he swore at the mess. "The insurance company will shit over this one."

"Don't worry about it." Zach kissed her forehead and wrapped her in his strong arms. "You'll be okay," he said, as if to convince himself. She shuddered and he pulled her tight against his chest. "You'll be okay."

Far away, the first wail of a siren split the night. Zach closed his eyes and held her as if he were afraid she might disappear. His pulse was thundering, his blood pounding in his ears as he kissed her crown, gently rocking her, praying that the ambulance would arrive soon.

Adria was released from the hospital that night, but before she could go anywhere, deputies from the Clackamas County Sheriff's Department wanted to talk to her. As the motel was just outside the city limits, the Estacada police weren't involved.

She and Zach spent two hours with the deputies and another on the phone to detectives Celia Stinson and Ned Fisk in Portland. Everyone suspected that someone from the Danvers family, or a nut case intrigued with the newsworthiness of her story, was to blame.

Adria tried to answer the questions hurled at her, she even managed to smile at the deputies' weak jokes and swill down some of their bitter coffee, but by the time Zach tucked a blanket around her in the Jeep, she was dead tired. Her head throbbed and her body ached all over. They drove back to the Fir Glen Motel and before he reached the parking lot, Zach swore under his breath. She turned her attention to the little motel and noticed that despite the police barrier there were camera crews clustered around the doorway of unit thirteen.

"Great," Zach muttered.

Rather than stop and deal with press, he cranked on the wheel and turned the Jeep around. He headed directly east and started climbing the snow-dusted mountains that were being gilded with the first rays of the rising sun.

"Where're we going?" she said, though she really didn't care. Her body ached and her head pounded despite the medication she'd been given at the hospital. She just wanted to stop running, to end this quest, to quiet the questions that raged in her mind and to stop the pain.

"My place."

"Your place?" she repeated, her tongue thick as she stared

through the windshield. The Jeep was climbing steadily. Snow-capped peaks of the rugged Cascade Mountains loomed ahead. "I didn't know you had one."

He slid her a glance—hard and stubborn yet laced with worry. "We're going to the ranch."

"In Bend?" she said, shaking her head before she sucked in her breath through her teeth and winced in pain from the movement. "I can't go there."

"Why not?"

"It's too far away. I've got people to see. Meetings in Portland. Interviews and appointments with attorneys and reporters."

"They'll wait," he predicted, his voice stern. He'd been silent through most of the interviews but as she'd explained what had happened, how she'd been with Polidori and come home to be attacked, he'd grown increasingly grim.

"No, Zach, really, I can't—"

"You were almost killed tonight," he shouted, clamping her wrist with one strong hand. Steering with the other, he kept an eye on the road as it wound snakelike through the foothills. "Maybe you don't take that seriously, but I do. Whoever sent you those warnings has just gotten a little bolder and if he would have hit you a little harder, or in a little different place, we might not even be having this conversation right now."

Suddenly chilled, she tried to rub her arms, but his hand was digging into her muscles. "But I can't—"

"Of course you can. You've waited nearly twenty years to find out the truth, I think you can wait a few more days."

She thought of Tommy Sinclair and his evil leer and wicked taunts. God, she wanted to prove him and all the other people who had thought she was the daughter of a whore wrong. Tommy Sinclair, who had been so close to her tonight, brought to her by the fear that still coiled in her heart.

"Come on, Adria. Give yourself a little time to pull yourself together."

She wanted to argue, to tell him he couldn't run her life, but she couldn't find the words. And she was frightened. More frightened than she'd ever been in her life. "This is just temporary, right?"

A slow, wicked smile spread across his beard-darkened chin. "I'm not holding you hostage, if that's what you mean."

Her throat turned to sand and she nervously licked her lips. "That's what I mean," she said.

"You can come and go as you please."

"But my car—"

"I'll send for all our things. Including that bucket of bolts you call a car—after I have it checked by my mechanic."

"It's fine," she protested.

"It's on its last legs."

"Please, I need the Nova—"

"It'll get there. In a couple of days. In the meantime there are plenty of vehicles at the ranch—cars, trucks, hell, we've even got a tractor if you get desperate."

"Very funny."

"I thought so," he said, but the laughter died from his eyes. "Come on, Adria. Give it a rest for a few days."

She was touched by his kindness and wondered fleetingly if his concern was genuine or if he was just doing his duty, baby-sitting her and keeping her out of trouble. "You . . . uh . . . you don't have to do this you know."

He let go of her wrist and grabbed the wheel. Lines of worry etched across his forehead. "Of course I do." He didn't add that he planned to stick to her like glue, that he was afraid for her life, that he felt sick with guilt because he hadn't followed his gut instincts when he'd known, he'd *known*, that he should never have let her out of his sight.

The sun, rising over the craggy, snow-covered spires, sent harsh rays through the valley. Zach switched on the radio and glanced to the passenger side of the Jeep where Adria, tucked in a blanket, was resting her head against the window and breathing steadily, as if she was soon to give into exhaustion and fall asleep.

Good. He tromped hard on the accelerator and the Jeep leaped forward. His jaw clenched so hard it felt like granite and he swore silently that if he ever found out who'd done this to her, he'd kill the bastard with his bare hands.

19

"Idiot! What did you think you were doing?" Anthony Polidori hadn't struck his son since the boy announced that he'd knocked up the Danvers girl years ago, but right now Anthony had to control himself to keep from rapping his cane sharply across Mario's thick skull. Clamping his jaw shut, he jabbed his cane in the soft grass of the backyard.

"I just wanted to feel her out—"

"I'll bet. That's the problem with you. Women. Any woman. For the love of God, stay away from her, you're only causing trouble!" Anthony's jaw was clenched so tight it ached and he wondered what he'd done to deserve such a stupid son. Stiffly he crossed the backyard and tried to rein in the anger that had kept him awake all night—ever since the phone call from his informant watching the Nash woman. He knew there would be trouble and he'd been proved right.

He paused by the tennis courts where he'd spent so many hours coaching his only boy. Now dandelions and long grass grew through the cracks in the cement courts. A climbing rosebush, untrimmed, sprawled up the tall fence, mistaking the mesh of chain links for a trellis. Dear God, where had the time gone? Had it all been spent feeding that hateful beast called the feud? Had he, along with the Danvers curs, lost all sense of what was real? Curling his fingers through over the heavy wire of the fence, he remembered the years of hoping that his son would someday grow into a shrewd businessman, a leader capable of handling the considerable businesses that his father had passed to him and he had hoped to hand down to his son—his only child, but Mario had never been much interested in business. He'd been an athlete, and even while he was in school his decided lack of brains—or at least of discipline—had been evident. That was the problem, the boy—well, man now—had enough gray matter if he only knew how to or wanted to apply it. But he never had. Aside from a little gambling business he'd run for a time, Mario hadn't worked a day in his life. Life had been too easy on him. Handsome by Hollywood standards, skilled on the tennis court or racing down the ski slopes, Mario had seen no reason to study and learn; his showing in school could only be described as poor, but he'd developed a way with girls. All girls. Including Trisha Danvers.

When Trisha had gotten pregnant—which was probably part of the slut's scheme to trap Mario and make life miserable for his father—Anthony had been furious with his son, but had blamed Mario's considerable lack of judgment on his youth. But this . . . this courtship of the Nash woman was asking, no *begging*, for trouble, especially since the girl had been attacked last night. Mario was long past the time when Anthony could write off his stupid actions as part of the folly of adolescence.

With a heavy sigh, Anthony said, "The police have already been here asking questions and guess who I got a call from? Remember Jack Logan—the police captain, now retired? He was a detective sergeant at the time of the Danvers kidnapping. Apparently he's still working for the Danvers family and more than happy to start in on us again."

Mario seemed unruffled. Wearing a Ralph Lauren polo shirt, expensive slacks, Italian leather loafers and sporting a day's growth of beard, which he mistakenly deemed fashionable, and an I-don't-give-a-damn attitude, he walked with his father but he showed no outward signs of remorse. "How was I to know she'd be attacked? Jesus, Dad, I didn't have a clue! How could I?" His dark brows crammed together. "Oh, shit, don't tell me one of your men was behind it!"

"Of course not!" Anthony snapped and felt a quick pain under his breastbone, the same pain that shot through him whenever he was under a great deal of stress. He took a deep, calming breath and ignored the irritating little jab. "We're in negotiations with her, aren't we?"

Mario's lower lip protruded thoughtfully and he shook his head. "Apparently not. She claims she's not interested."

"But she will be, if we make it worth her while." Anthony was sure of himself. He'd played this game before. Many times. And he always won. "But we must be careful," he said, gesturing futilely with his hands. "We must use a little decorum, be patient and cautious so as not to tip our hand."

"What's the point? She already knows what we want. You told her yourself that you were interested in the old hotel. I wasn't tipping anything."

"No?" They walked along the brick path leading through the rose garden to the back of the house. Mario held the door of the breakfast room open for his father and Anthony, able to breathe now that his heartbeat was regular again, stepped smartly up the stairs. He sat in his usual chair, spooned some sugar into his coffee cup and tossed this morning's edition of the *Oregonian* onto Mario's plate. The paper landed squarely over Mario's neatly sliced grapefruit.

"What the—" Mario stopped when he saw the picture of a cheap motel and below it a smaller photograph of Adria. Even in grainy black and white she was beautiful; the smooth lines of her face and her wide eyes reminded him that he wanted her. Badly. And what he wanted, he took. He could almost taste her and he imagined what she would be like in his bed. Years before he'd fantasized about Katherine Danvers and now . . . this woman was so much more real. So ultimately attainable.

"Read it," Anthony advised as he snapped his napkin across his lap, then waited impatiently while the maid brought juice and coffee. "You'll find your name in paragraph three, I think. A Detective Stinson is coming by to take your statement this morning. She's with the Portland Police Bureau and she's handling her end of the case because Ms. Nash seems to be the target of some rather nasty letters." He stirred his coffee, rattling the hundred-year-old porcelain cup with his silver spoon.

Mario's mouth flattened into a thin line of disapproval as he read the article and realized that he had been the last person to see Adria before she was assaulted.

"This is only an educated guess," Anthony said, dropping his spoon and lifting his cup to his lips. "But I think you've probably made the early-morning news broadcasts as well."

The maid silently deposited a basket of muffins swaddled in a checkered napkin, then slipped quietly back to the kitchen. As Anthony opened the linen napkin, steam smelling of cinnamon and orange escaped. He eyed the choices. "From now on, son," he said as he reached for a bran muffin, "let me know when you plan to see Ms. Nash." He broke the crumbly muffin in half and spread a sparing amount of butter on it. As the butter melted, he added, "I just might be able to save you and the family a lot of embarrassment."

Zach paced from one end of the den to the other, stretched the telephone cord to its limit. He muttered curses under his breath and nearly slammed the receiver down with enough force to break the woman on the other end of the line, Ellen Rigley's, ear drums.

"If I could just set up an interview with Ms. Nash at her convenience—" Ellen wheedled. She was pushy; a reporter who didn't seem to understand the word no. Zach glanced out the windows to the acres of ranch land that spread as far as the eye could see. It wasn't enough land. There wasn't enough to hide Adria.

"I'm sure she wants her side of the story told—"

Zach held firm and stared down at the front page of the local newspaper that lay open on the desk. Adria's picture was on page one, along with an old photograph of Witt, Kat, and London. The headlines were thick and black and seemed to scream—WOMAN CLAIMING TO BE DANVERS HEIRESS ATTACKED.

It didn't take the press long to react. They'd only been at the ranch two days and it was already a madhouse.

Zach felt as if he were trying to plow through quicksand. The faster he went, the farther he tried to get, the deeper and deeper he sank until he felt as if he were choking and there was no way out. No way to save Adria.

Great, he thought sarcastically. Being this close to Adria and keeping his hands off her was hell, trying to keep her from getting herself killed was proving to be damned near impossible. The woman was already talking about returning to Portland, for crying out loud, when the bump on her head was still fresh, her stitches not yet healed.

The all-business female voice hadn't given up. "—so I could fly out this afternoon or tomorrow morning, meet her at the ranch and—"

"I told you Ms. Nash has no comment." Zach had enough.

"I need to talk to her, Mr. Danvers." She was obviously trying to bully him. "Adria Nash showed up claiming she was London Danvers, then was attacked in a tiny motel way out of the city by an unknown assailant. The *Post* wants to have an interview with her so that she can tell her side of the story —"

Zach slammed down the receiver and pressed a button for the answering machine to pick up. He was tired of reporters and police and the whole mess. The phone jangled instantly and Zach, ignoring the impatient ring, threw his keys on the counter.

He'd just returned to the ranch house after spending three fruitless hours at the office. A bevy of reporters had kept Terry busy on the phone or shown up and made themselves at home, swilling and complaining about his coffee, waiting for a quote from Zach. He'd given one, largely unprintable, and most of them had taken the hint and slunk out the door with their tails between their legs. But a couple of tough, salty types had lingered, hoping that he'd crack and give them some bit of news that would make their copy different from the others that were being written into word processors around the nation.

Zach had given up trying to get any work done, told Terry to close up shop for the rest of the week, stuffed some papers into his briefcase and tucked a couple of blueprints under his arm. He'd locked the press out of his office, climbed in his Cherokee and driven like a madman back to the ranch, to the eye of the storm. He would have turned off the phones to the house except that he wanted to stay in contact with the sheriff's department in Estacada and the police in Portland. Then there was Sweeny's report. Zach's stomach clenched at the thought of it. Two days had passed since he'd talked to the slimy private investigator and, according to Jason, there was still no word.

The sleaze-ball detective was probably holding out on him. Or Jason was.

Ever since the attack on Adria, Zach trusted no one.

Yanking his jacket from a hook near the pantry, he stormed down the hall and out the back door. A blast of icy air greeted him and though the snow had melted at the lower elevations, a fine layer of white powder was visible in the foothills. The sky was clear, the sun high but without any warmth and only a few clouds clustered around the highest peaks of the surrounding mountains. On any other day, he'd be glad for the bracing air and cool promise of winter. But not today.

The ranch wasn't impregnable and before he'd thrown out the reporters and photographers who had insisted upon hanging around the front porch, he hadn't been able to hear himself think.

Fortunately Manny had decided to take matters into his own Native–American hands. Wearing his well-practiced stern-Indian expression, he'd wrapped a thick horsehair blanket over his shoulders and positioned himself in his pickup at the front gate. A no-nonsense rifle was propped against his dashboard and a NO TRESPASSING sign had been posted on one of the weathered fence posts, in full view of the road.

No one suspected the .22 wasn't loaded or that Manny Clearwater was the self-proclaimed worst shot in the county and one of the easiest-going guys Zach had ever met. His severe countenance, shaded by a black felt hat decorated with silver and feathers was enough to keep even the most ambitious reporters off the property.

For now.

Zach had envisioned bringing Adria here until she'd healed and hoped that the news about her attack would die a quick but quiet death. But his plan had blown up in his face and it seemed as if the entire world knew where she was.

Including the man who wanted her hurt. The muscles in the back of his neck drew together and his jaw clenched so hard it ached. Since she'd declined police protection, Zach had made it his personal responsibility to keep her safe. And alive. But it seemed as if the world, and Adria herself, were against him.

The bottom line was that she wasn't safe here. And that bothered him. It bothered the hell out of him.

He found Adria by the stables, the sunlight catching in her blue-black hair. Forearms bridged over the top fence rail, she watched a herd of mares and half-grown foals picking at the sun-bleached stubble of the field.

A whirlwind, laden with thick dust, danced across the dry paddock, picking up a few dead leaves and spinning them across the ground while the horses moved lazily from one tuft of dry grass to the next. Their hides were dusty and uneven, already beginning to change to the thick, longer coats of winter.

Unaware that he was behind her, she shifted, leaning on her opposite leg, her face turning in profile. His gut clenched at the sight of her and he told himself to forget that she was a woman. "You're a popular lady. The phone's been ringing off the hook."

"Why do you think I escaped out here?" She ran a finger along the dusty edge of the top rail and her cheeks had turned a deep shade of pink with the cold. "At first I talked to them, but the questions got too heavy, so I decided to take a break."

"Manny's keeping them at bay down at the gate and the answering machine should catch anything we need to know about." He propped a foot on the bottom slat and stood next to her. Pretending interest in the ridge of mountains on the horizon, he asked, "How're you feeling?"

"Kind of like an eighteen-wheeler drove up my back." Smiling a little, she showed off the hint of a dimple that he found incredibly sexy. "But I'll live and I'm afraid that's going to disappoint a lot of people."

"Don't even say it."

But she wasn't finished. "You know, Zach," she continued, turning to face him as the breeze teased soft, curling strands out of the band that held her hair away from her face, "I can't stay here forever."

"It's only been a couple of days."

"I have my life."

"You mean London's life." He cocked a dark brow and scowled at a few white clouds as a wavering flock of geese, trying and failing to maintain a V, honked into the wind and flew steadily southward, as if making up for lost time.

With one hand she shaded her eyes against the lowering sun. "It's time I settled this."

"How?"

"I think I need to hire an attorney and a private investigator. Get things moving along."

She was staring at him so intently, her gaze shifting from his eyes to his mouth, that desire swept through him like a hot prairie wind that no man could tame, no mortal could control. He remembered kissing her, nearly making love to her by the river and it was all he could do to slide his hands into his pockets to hide the swelling that was beginning to warm his groin. He wanted to reach out and grab her, press his lips over hers and kiss her until neither one of them could breathe. He imagined bending her backward till her hair swept the ground and her full breasts were pointed proudly upward to the clear Oregon sky. He'd place his face between them and—

Hell, this was getting him nowhere!

She was still talking about hiring a detective. ". . . best for all of us."

"Jason's already retained a guy—a creep named Oswald Sweeny. He'll get the job done."

"For Jason. And for you."

The corners of his mouth tightened involuntarily. "You said you wanted to know the truth."

"I still do," she said, squinting against the sunlight. "Correct me if I'm wrong, okay? Sweeny's working for the family, right? He's digging around, trying to prove that I'm a fraud. So he might not tell me—or the family might not feel the need to inform me—if he found proof positive that I'm London. Only if I'm not." She dusted her hands on her jeans. "So I think I'd better start looking for a few guys on my team. Good guys in white hats."

He dug in the dirt with the toe of his boot. "From what I hear you can't afford much."

She'd been expecting that, but not from Zach. From the others, of course, but not Zach and she couldn't stop the little stab of pain that reminded her that he'd found out things about her and hadn't confided in her—that he'd shared them only with the inner circle of the Danvers family. The chosen few. Her throat caught. She'd always considered him an outsider, but, as painful as it was, the truth of the matter was that she, and she alone, was the outsider. Obviously there were secrets Zach kept from her and she wondered how much he and the rest of his family discussed her behind her back. Had he told them the secrets she'd confided to him about her home in Montana, had he laughed when he'd discovered she was flat broke, had his eyes lighted with an evil little fire when he'd hinted that she'd nearly made love with him?

Being around Zachary Danvers was like walking a fraying tightrope strung taut across a yawning canyon. One false step in either direction and she would pitch down the steep emotional cliffs. Too much tension and the rope would give way. She wasn't fool enough to believe that he'd be there to catch her. "What is it you want from me?"

He hesitated, his eyes searching hers and she felt as if he could stare straight into her soul. "I just want to keep you safe."

"So that your family can prove me to be a liar." She felt the air shift between them. "You can't keep me here, not against my will."

"Is that what I'm doing?"

She licked her lips. "I think so. Yes."

His eyes were the color of flint, his brows pulled together in frustration though she didn't know if his vexation was with her, himself, his family, or the world in general. They were close enough to touch yet he moved closer, advancing upon her, his expression turned hard and suddenly cruel. As his shadow fell across her face, his fingers curled in the lapels of her old leather jacket. "Do you remember that someone tried to kill you?" he demanded in a harsh whisper. "Less than forty-eight hours ago?"

"I can't run scared." But her breathing was shallow and fast. The scents of coffee and leather and musky male cologne swirled around her.

He gave her a little shake and his eyes sparked with anger. "Can you recall what it felt like to nearly have your brains bashed in?"

She blanched. "Of course."

"Who do you think did it?"

"I—I don't know."

"Neither do I, but he's still out there, darlin', and my guess is that he doesn't give up easily."

"I don't either."

"Okay," he said, pressing his face close enough that she saw the striations of green in his gray eyes. "Let's talk about the sheets—the ones on your bed in the motel. Did you get a good look at them?"

She swallowed with difficulty but refused to give into the urge to step backward.

His fingers clenched more tightly. "They'd been ripped to ribbons, as if some enraged animal with six-inch teeth as sharp as razors had worked himself up to a maniacal frenzy and started shredding and just couldn't stop."

He yanked her closer, lifting her off her feet, drawing her nose to broken nose. "While we're at it, did you happen to see the message on the mirror, the one meant for you? What did it say?"

"It doesn't mat—"

"What did it say?" he repeated more loudly.

"Something about—"

"Not something about—it said: Death to the bitch. Fairly specific, I'd say. In fact, crystal-fucking clear. Do you know what kind of psychotic it takes to do something like that?"

"I—I really don't want to think about it."

"Well neither do I, but I force myself because it's not over yet."

She managed to notch up her chin and stare into eyes that glittered with determination. "I just can't run away from this, Zachary. I started it and I've got to finish it."

"Or wait until it finishes you," he snarled and looked at her mouth in a way that made her insides turn to jelly. As quickly as he'd grabbed her, he let go and she nearly fell as her heels hit the ground again.

Disappointment settled in her heart when he stepped away from her.

"The way I see it you've got no choice but to lay low for a while, wait until the police nail this guy or until the story dies down. Right now you're a target, not only for the psychopath who attacked you, but for any other copy-cat prankster looking for a way to get his jollies and his name in the press. These aren't nice people you're dealing with, Adria. So just stay put." He glared at her for a few silent, tense seconds, then swore loudly and stalked to the stables.

Heart thudding, she ran, catching up to him and following on his heels. She tamped down the fear that he'd managed to bring right to the surface of her mind and told herself to ignore the erotic message that had seemed to radiate from his eyes. "I'm not going to let anyone—not you and certainly not someone who runs around ripping bed sheets—intimidate me," she insisted.

"Then you're not as smart as I gave you credit for." He opened the door and strode inside. The door would've banged shut behind him, but she caught it and, clenching her fists in determination, followed him into the musty interior.

Several horses nickered a greeting. Dust motes swirled near dirty windows draped with cobwebs and littered with the brittle corpses of long-dead insects.

His boots rang on the old floorboards and the scents of horseflesh and dung, oil and leather, hay and dust mingled and assailed her nostrils, reminding her of the farm she'd left behind to follow this quest here, this damned quest! She touched a rough fir post supporting the hayloft where an old kerosene lantern, tarnished, rusted, and covered with cobwebs still hung, neglected.

Zach strode the length of the building and shouldered open a door at the far end. Old hinges creaked as he disappeared inside. She considered following him, but thought better of it and stayed near the horses, petting each curious velvet-soft nose that was thrust in her direction, feeling the hot jets of breath against her palm.

What was she doing here? What was she trying to prove? She should go back to the house and leave Zach and his lousy mood. Better yet, she should steal his damned truck and return to Portland where the answers to her life lay hidden.

Still she lingered, using the excuse of her injuries as reason to stay out here, away from civilization, alone with the one man who had touched her heart. For years she'd sheltered herself and her emotions, but with Zachary she'd let down her guard, willingly come to care for him . . . oh, God . . .

His footsteps echoed through the old building and she glanced up sharply. With only a cursory look in her direction, he hauled a saddle, bridle, and blanket and kicked open the gate of the first stall where a rangy buckskin gelding was tethered. The horse snorted and tossed his great head, but Zach managed to slip the bit between the buckskin's teeth and strap the bridle on. His will was iron-clad and he won the battle between man and beast.

Adria suspected he was used to winning—a man who discovered what he wanted in life and ruthlessly went after it. Not unlike Witt Danvers. His father. *Her* father.

Zach spread a blanket over the gelding's back, slid the saddle into place, and pulled the cinch tight. He was intent on his work, as if he'd forgotten her. The silence, aside from the restlessness of the horses in their stalls, was deafening.

"You're going for a ride?"

"What's it look like?" he said.

"Where?" The question fell off her lips. He glanced over his shoulder and their gazes caught in the dim light of the stables. His eyes were dark and still glinted with a silent, pulsing fury. For several breathless seconds he held her stare and she found it hard to breathe.

"Why?"

She lifted a shoulder, then didn't move. He was staring at her so intently she could barely breathe and she felt as if, with that harsh gaze, he was mentally stripping her—one piece of clothing at a time. She couldn't swallow and her heart was drumming wildly.

His eyes lowered to the base of her throat where her pulse was throbbing erratically. When his gaze touched hers again it was pure seduction. "Do you want to come?" he drawled in a voice so low it could barely be heard over the shifting of the horses' hooves and rustle of straw.

Oh, God! Barely able to breathe, she fingered a rope that had been left wound around a post. Her heart thundered. She stared into his intense, hot eyes and felt her joints go slack.

"Pardon?"

"Do you want to come?" he repeated slowly, the double entendre hanging heavy in the air between them.

She couldn't breathe, couldn't think.

"Well?" he demanded.

Yes! She licked her suddenly dry lips and heard the rush of wind whistle through the old rafters. "I—I think so." Her voice was so breathless she hardly recognized it as her own.

"You're sure?" One dark brow cocked dubiously and he hooked a thumb in his belt loop, his fingers riding low against his fly. "Could be a rough ride."

Her knees suddenly felt like they were made of rubber and she leaned her hips against the stall for support. "I know."

"Could be dangerous."

She swallowed with difficulty and felt a tiny spot of sweat bead between her breasts. "I'm not afraid," she said as though to convince herself. Her heart was racing, her mind spinning into wildly erotic images.

"Then you are a fool, Adria," he said and swore beneath his breath. Clucking his tongue, he led the gelding out of his stall and through the back door of the stables.

Adria, feeling as if she'd had the wind knocked out of her, stalked after him. He'd been playing with her, was only teasing her and she felt a new white-hot rage sear through her blood. "Wait a minute!" she cried as he swung into the saddle.

He ignored her and kicked his horse hard in the flanks and the buckskin took off, breaking into a gallop.

"Wait! Zach, please—" she screamed at the top of her lungs.

He yanked back on the reins. The horse reared and whirled, legs pawing the crisp air. Zach's eyes flashed like lightning sizzling through a night-dark sky and his lips thinned in anger. A rugged cowboy, determined to have his way. "You don't want this," he said, his nostrils flaring, his face set in stone.

"You don't know what I want!"

"Sure I do. All you want—all you've ever wanted was a way to get your hands on the family's money. Well, it won't happen through me."

The wind was beginning to rise, to whip her hair in front of her face and brush her cheeks. "That's not what this is all about, and you know it. Why don't you tell me what you're afraid of?"

"Afraid of?"

"That's right, Zach. You're running scared and it has nothing to do with what happened in the motel the other night."

His mouth curved into a self-deprecating smile. "What I'm afraid of. Isn't it obvious?" His gaze held hers in a stare that stripped her soul bare. "It's you, Adria. I'm afraid of you." With a whistle, he turned the buckskin again and leaned forward in the saddle. The horse took off, galloping rapidly across the dry grass, sending up a cloud of red dust, leaving her alone.

Adria sagged against the exterior wall of the stables. Closing her eyes, she leaned her head back and felt the rough-cut cedar walls press into her shoulders. Her fists curled in frustration and slivers jabbed at her bare knuckles. "Don't be afraid, Zach," she said, her eyes burning with unshed tears. "Please, don't be afraid." The man was so damned maddening and yet . . . Oh, God, and yet . . . she thought she was falling in love with him.

You can't!

But I can't stop myself.

He's your brother!

I don't know that. Not for sure.

But you can't afford to gamble! Not now! Not when everything you've worked for is at stake!

Like hell!

"He's right," she said, furious with herself. "You are a fool." Pushing herself upright, she headed toward the house. She was intent on forgetting him, on finding a way to escape, on putting as much distance between his body and hers as she could. She could take his Jeep or a truck or call someone to come get her. . .

Or she could go after him.

In the distance a coyote howled and the sun slid behind a cloud. Her footsteps hesitated for just a second before she realized that she couldn't let it lie. Rolling over and playing dead wasn't in her nature and she'd come too far and suffered through too many emotional struggles to just curl up and die and let the whole thing go.

Whirling back toward the stables, she faced her destiny. She flung the door open. Her legs moved of their own accord, her boots ringing as she ran along the smooth floor to the tack room. She found a bridle and hurried back to the row of stalls. A black mare poked her nose over the door and Adria didn't miss a beat. She slipped the bridle over the mare's head, then, running, led the trotting horse outside. Zach was nearly out of sight, only a speck in the horizon, but Adria wasn't going to let him get away. She climbed on the mare's bare back, leaned forward and clucked her tongue. "Let's go!" She dug her heels into the black's flanks.

With a surge of power, the horse moved beneath her, muscles bunching and stretching, the cold, hard ground flashing beneath steel-shod hooves. The wind screamed through her hair and brought tears to her eyes as the eager little mare ate up the distance, racing over the vast acres of grassland where the dry pastures rolled upward into foothills green with old-growth timber. In the distance craggy snow-covered mountains cut jagged ridges against the darkening sky.

She urged the horse faster and faster, afraid that if she slowed down for even a second she would see the folly in this dangerous chase, yank back on the reins and force herself to return to the ranch—to safety—away from the one man who could save her or destroy her.

Zach's horse galloped through the low-growing timber and Adria followed. "Come on, come on," Adria cried, the breath torn from her lungs, fear of facing her destiny shadowing her mind. But still she plunged on, chasing a man and her dream, moving closer.

Finally he drew back on the reins and his horse slowed at the banks of a wide river that sliced through the hills and fell in a wild silver torrent down the face of a cliff. Then, as if suddenly sensing that she was chasing him, he twisted in the saddle.

Her heart nearly stopped as she stared at his profile, all tough angles and planes, like the sheer mountains that rose behind him, wild as the river that slashed furiously through the canyon and cut a raging swath through the forest. His jaw hardened and his eyes narrowed in silent rebuke, but she didn't pay any attention. Instead, she kicked her horse faster. There was no trace of amusement in his face.

Zach's eyes followed her every move as she pulled back on the reins. When she was close enough to hear, he said, "You should go back."

"Back to Montana?"

"Back to the house."

"Not yet." She slid to the ground and Zach followed suit. Eyebrows drawn downward, his mouth pulled into a furious frown, he strode up to her, looking as if he'd like to strangle her . . . or worse, that he wanted to kiss her and never stop.

"For Christ's sake—"

"No. For mine. For yours," she said, breathing hard. She stared up at him stubbornly, squaring her shoulders and meeting his furious gaze with her own.

"You never listen, do you?"

"Not when it's something I don't want to hear." She felt the spray of the waterfall, cool against her neck and heard the roar of the water tumbling fifty feet to the rocky bottom of the canyon. She stood toe to toe with him, refusing to back down, silently challenging him with her eyes.

"You have no idea what you're asking," he said hoarsely.

"Tell me."

He stared at her long and hard, his eyes narrowing in the lowering sunlight, his breath fogging in the cool mountain air. "You never give up," he said and his voice sounded tortured, as if he was battling with himself and losing the war. Reluctantly he pushed an errant black curl from her face.

"No reason to."

"There are lots of reasons, Adria."

"None that I want to hear." She held her head high, angling her chin, daring him to argue, feeling the breeze tangle in her hair.

His gaze fastened to hers and held, causing her heart to trip in anticipation. Raw, unbridled passion glowed dark in his eyes as he looked down at her. Adria's chest was suddenly tight, as if bound by steel cords and she wondered fleetingly if he was right, if chasing him into the forest was so clever after all. She wanted him, yes, probably loved him, but being with him was treacherous and deadly, for she never seemed to get enough.

As if reading her thoughts, he struck, quickly wrapping his strong fingers around the back of her neck and pulling her roughly to him, branding her with his lips, kissing her with the heat of a savage prairie fire. His free arm circled her waist, dragging her willing body closer still, so that she could feel the thunderous beat of his heart, the thick evidence of his desire straining at his fly. He smelled of leather and sweat and tasted of coffee laced with liquor. The scents mingled and swirled in the fresh air and caused a slow-burning heat to start deep in her loins and spread throughout her body.

His tongue plunged deep into her mouth, tasting, delving, plundering, and claiming hers with a ruthless abandon that touched her own wild soul.

His hands splayed across her back, possessively, angrily crushing her breasts against the hard wall of his chest.

Winding her arms around his neck, she gave herself to him, refusing to listen to any lingering doubts in her mind, unable to think that he might be her half-brother—that this love, so special and pure could be tainted. She opened her mouth to him as she would willingly open her body.

She clung to him as he dragged her to the ground, pulling her with him, dropping to the bed of dry grass and leaves that were scattered over the forest floor. He spread kisses along her neck and over her eyes and twisted her hair in his fists. "You're sure?"

he asked, his voice breathless and dry as the wind racing through the trees.

"I want this, Zach," she said, staring deep into his eyes. "I want you."

He hesitated but she pressed her lips to his and all his defenses tumbled down. She knew why he was reticent, he still believed they were brother and sister, but she was certain there was a mistake. Surely they couldn't be related. She wouldn't believe it; she wouldn't fall in love with her own half-brother. Most people thought he'd been fathered by Anthony Polidori and he looked so much more like the Italian than Witt. This was right! So right! His hand cupped her breast and she arched up to him eagerly. He nuzzled her neck and she lolled back her head, offering him more.

His fingers found the buttons to her blouse and the clasp of her bra and soon she was stripped to the waist, her breasts bare, her dark nipples puckering in the cool air, her body heated by the inner fire that swept through her blood.

His hands were rough, but magical as he touched each proud little point before reaching around her and tracing the valley of her spine. Pleasure rippled through her body and she held onto his shoulders as if for life.

He kissed her breasts and she writhed beneath him, wanting more, feeling the pure joy of life as he teased the proud points. His tongue swirled and licked, caressing gently, pulling and creating a heat that sparked deep within her.

Whispering his name, she held her breast for him, letting him suckle, wanting more. So much more.

Love me, Zachary, she silently cried.

His fingers dipped beneath the waistband of her jeans, stripping her of the unwanted denim and leaving her in a scant pair of panties. She moaned as he took her breast between his lips again and her own hands moved to the front of his shirt tearing at the buttons, feeling the springy dark hair of his chest as her fingers grazed the strident muscles of his shoulders, the flat buttons of his nipples.

He moaned loudly—a primeval sound that made her quiver. "Adria," he whispered hoarsely as he gazed down at her.

She held a finger to his lips. "Don't," she whispered and a coil of warmth whirled in her midsection when he drew her finger between his teeth and sucked. Wet. Hungry. Hot.

Heat coiled at her center, pulsing and liquid, as he continued to pull on her finger and stare at her.

Her throat was like cotton and the moist darkness between her legs began to throb with desire. She wanted him, all of him, regardless of the consequences. Gaze fastened to hers, he slipped his hands lower, along the rift of her buttocks until she was squirming, her body silently pleading for more.

"You're sure?" he asked and his pupils had nearly obscured the gray of his eyes. Above him, clouds scudded across the sky.

"Y-yes."

"This could be wrong." Doubts shadowed his eyes and his fingers dug deeper into her flesh.

"Never," she whispered, guiding his head back to hers until his breath fanned her face. "Love me, Zach," she whispered, casting caution to the wind and closing her ears to the demons that screamed in her mind. "Love me and forget about everything else."

His throat worked and then the wind seemed to shift. Kissing her, he ran his fingers along her body, and beneath the silk of her panties. Lowering his head, he nibbled at her skin and lowered himself. His tongue slid around the circle of her navel and she bucked upward, wanting more, wanting him—all of him.

He slid lower still and she thought she would die when he stripped her of her panties and breathed hot and damp against the curls at the apex of her legs. Squirming, writhing, she felt him touch her, slowly at first and then more quickly, causing her to melt inside.

"Zachary," she cried.

"Not yet," he whispered and guided one of her hands to his fly. With a hiss, it lowered and she slowly pushed his jeans over his slim hips. With anxious fingers she caressed his buttocks, and felt the muscles of his legs flex at her touch. She ran her fingers up the flatness of his abdomen and felt him suck in his breath.

Heat flowed from his body to hers.

"You're sure about this," he said again when they were naked and breathing hard, their bodies slick with sweat, nerves strung tight in anticipation.

In answer she kissed him and he moved atop her, his strong hands holding her arms over her head, his eyes burning with a pulsing desire that seared into her soul.

He kissed her again and then roughly, as if he were fighting and losing an inner struggle, he prodded her legs apart. She lifted her hips off the ground as he drove into her and she felt his manhood, heavy and thick, break through the barriers of their lives and delve deep into the core of her soul.

She closed her eyes, but he kissed her cheek. "Watch me," he said hoarsely. "We can't forget that this is happening. We can't ever forget." His words were like the prophecy of doom, but she stared up at him and moved with his sweet, hungry rhythm. There was no pause, no minute to catch her breath. He pushed into her harder and harder, faster and faster until the colors behind her eyes began to blend and whirl.

She was moist and warm, like thick, hot honey and she felt him gather steam just as something erupted within her.

"Adria, oh, sweet, sweet Adria!" His voice, a raspy whisper, bounced off the walls of the canyons and the chambers of her heart. Lights exploded behind her eyes and her body convulsed around him, holding him tight within her as if she was afraid to lose the precious link they'd found, the ecstasy of loving each other. Her throat worked.

Love me, she silently cried, wrapping her arms around him as he fell against her, his sweating body melding perfectly to hers. *Love, me, Zachary Danvers, and don't ever stop.*

Tears touched the back of her eyes—from joy or relief, she didn't know—but she refused to give into the persistent drops and wouldn't think about tomorrow.

It would come soon enough.

20

"Tell me about my mother." Adria, shivering as afterglow faded, stared up the swaying, long-needled branches of the pines to the blue sky beyond. A few filmy clouds moved slowly through the heavens but didn't spoil the day.

Beside her, Zach tensed. "I didn't know your mother." He reached for his faded Levi's and slid into them. "She lived in Montana with you."

"My other mother," she clarified, refusing to let him vex her, but she wasn't going to let him put her off as he had in the past. They were lovers now, they could share everything. "Katherine." The ground was cold and goose bumps rose on her flesh as she found her jeans and sweater.

After making hot, furious love to her, Zachary had held her against his naked body. She'd seen the scar on his shoulder, been reminded of the night that London had disappeared and had convinced herself that she couldn't be related to him. Either he was Polidori's son or she wasn't London Danvers. Now, as her mind cleared, she wasn't so certain.

He seemed more remote than ever, as if the shock of what they'd done had been a slap of reality—cold water in his face.

"Katherine wasn't your mother," he said with conviction.

"You don't know that."

That much was true, Zach thought as he yanked on his boots. He had to get away, far away. Being with her was like being trapped in a seductive spider's web, sticky and warm and exciting but infinitely dangerous. Whether she'd decided to make love to him because she suddenly didn't believe they could be

related, or because she thought he would let down his defenses
and give her more information about the family, or because she
wanted to blackmail him later, or, God forbid, because her motives were pure and she was falling for him, he knew it just
couldn't happen. He should have been stronger. Ever since Kat,
he'd been in control and had never let a woman seduce him
since. He'd always been the predator. His will where sensual
women were concerned had been strong. Until now. With Adria.
He ground his teeth together in disgust and stood, swiping at the
dust covering his jeans.

He'd been unable to resist her—the defiance in her blue eyes,
the challenging tilt of her chin, her soft, sensual lips and the
provocative invitation that touched him in a deep, roughly animal place, where his body took over and his mind shut down.
He'd wanted sex. With her. Lusty, hot, get-your-rocks-off sex and
he'd ended up with more. Too much. An emotional whirlpool
that threatened to drag him under.

Just like Kat!

He slammed his eyes shut and told himself it was just a matter
of time. If he could maintain some distance from that sensual
body of hers, he could stay in control. At least until he had all
this figured out.

*Like hell, Danvers. How're you going to stay away from her?
Now that you've had a taste, a teasing nibble of her, how are you
going to fight the craving that even this minute is tearing you up
inside?*

The muscles in his back drew so tight they hurt. Angrily, he
forced his arms through his worn sleeves of his jacket and said
tersely, "We've got to get back. It's cold."

He stiffened as her fingers touched his shoulder. "You don't
have to feel guilty," she said over the roar of the river as it dived
from the cliffs to the gully far below.

"I don't."

"Then why—"

"Look, Adria, we can't do this. Not anymore. Not until we find out for sure." He placed firm hands on her shoulders and held her at arm's length. "It just can't happen."

"So you're starting to believe me."

"For Christ's sake, do you know what we're talking about here?" he said, nearly screaming. "Incest!" The word hung between them, seeming to haunt the forest, standing still in the chill afternoon light.

"It's not—"

"How do you know? If you're so damned sure that you're London, then how do you know?"

He watched her swallow with difficulty. "Because," she said, tossing her hair away from her face. "I believe that you're not Witt's son."

"Christ!" His face turned ashen. "Is that your rationalization?" He grabbed her arms so hard that she felt his fingers digging deep into her flesh through her jacket. "Now listen to me, *sister*, I'm *not* that Italian's son."

"How do you know?" she threw back at him, tossing the very words in his face that he'd spit at her.

"Don't you think that when Eunice and Witt split up, when she was stripped bare of everything she claimed she wanted, don't you think she would have turned around and laughed in his face, told him that his second son had been fathered by his enemy, insisted that I stay with her?"

"Not if she wanted her reputation to stay intact. Her reputation, as I understand it, was as important to her as you children, so she would never say anything to tarnish it."

"But she'd become an adulteress?"

"Her pride was on the line!"

He made a disgusted sound in the back of his throat.

"And she wouldn't have wanted to hurt you."

Eunice's words, uttered at his bed in the hospital whispered through his head. *I hate to admit it, Lord knows a mother shouldn't, but you've always been my favorite. Of all my children, you were the one closest to my heart.* Oh, God, no! All the spit dried in his mouth and he stared at Adria as if he were looking into the window of his future. "You couldn't have done this"—he motioned to the bed of pine needles under the tree—"on the outside chance that I wasn't Witt's son."

"I did it for the same reasons you did, Zach. Because I wanted to. Because I couldn't stop myself. Because from the first time I saw you, I knew it would happen. Because . . . because, damn it, I think I love you."

She lifted up on her toes then and kissed him hard on the lips. He told himself to back off, that they were playing with fire, that no matter what happened, there could be no good ending to this, they would both be burned and yet he couldn't stop himself. His arms fastened around her slim waist and he wouldn't let go. He kissed her and held her and stripped her of her clothes, watching in fascination at the beauty of her breasts, white, with a fine webbing of blue veins hidden deep beneath the firm flesh, her nipples perfectly round and hard as he touched them and kissed them and buried his face between the two warm mounds.

He kissed the skin of her abdomen, drawing lazy circles around her navel before he slid lower and she writhed in pleasured torment beneath him. She tasted of woman and earth and all things primeval.

While the wind teased her hair, her fingers and hands worked their own sweet magic on him, shedding him of his clothes, tracing intimate circles along his spine and chest, dipping low beneath his jeans to push the tight denim over his butt.

Her eyes shined like the blue Montana sky as she kissed him and tasted his hard buttons of nipples and skimmed her tongue down his breastbone and along the dark hairs that formed a line beneath his navel.

He fought the urge to close his eyes and stared at her, this woman who was forbidden, this woman whom he believed was only out for herself, this woman who could find the most hidden corners of his heart and expose them.

He shuddered as he took her with the same hot fervor that had consumed him the first time, driving into her with a force that was sure to chase the demons from his mind, thrusting hard and fast, hearing the catch of her breath, feeling her slick velvet warmth envelop him, losing all thought, all reason, all control as the world seemed to burst and he fell against her, breathing hard, unable to think with any sort of reason. He was lost in the magic of her and he wondered if he'd ever break free. Would he ever want to? Kissing the sweat-soaked curls at the nape of her neck, he wished the world would go away and leave them alone and that, God in heaven, that they could be lovers forever. Without fear. Without those horrid thoughts that nagged at his mind and tested his will.

God, this was dangerous. Never had he lost himself so completely, never had he let loose of that tether that held him in touch with what was real, never had he given so much of himself with total, uninhibited abandon.

Never had he made love to a woman who claimed to be London Danvers. His fists clenched and he drew dust and sand and pine needles into his palms.

She held him close and he listened to her heart pounding so wildly he wondered how she could breathe with his weight crushed against her. When he finally had some sense of control again, he lifted himself up on one elbow and stared down at her.

Her black hair swept the tops of her breasts, and he shoved the curling strands aside. "You're too beautiful," he said, believing her beauty was a curse. So much like Kat, yet so different.

"Why?" She gave him a curious smile that he'd never forget. Sunlight dappled her face and she had to squint and the tree branches shifted in the wind, causing slow-moving shadows to dance over her eyes and cheekbones.

"It's . . . well, dangerous, for lack of a better word."

"To whom?"

"Every male who comes in contact with you and to you yourself."

"You didn't make love to me because of my looks," she said,

rolling to her side and stretching lazily. He watched as the bones of her ribs showed beneath her breasts and her abdomen hollowed as she raised her arms over her head.

"Didn't hurt," he drawled, watching the play of shadow and light upon her skin.

"No, but that wasn't the attraction and you know it." She smiled up at him and in a glimmer of an instant she reminded him of Kat. "You couldn't resist because I was a challenge, someone you shouldn't have. Someone you didn't want."

"Wait a minute. You practically threw yourself at me. Chased me down." He motioned to the horses trying to graze on the grass that grew in patches between the trees. "In fact, you nearly ran me off the edge of the cliff."

She laughed and he let loose a crooked smile.

"After all those long, smoky stares you sent my way, after all the times you nearly kissed me, after you took me to the Clackamas River with the intention of seducing me, then backed out? Now, I'm the bad guy?" She winked at him and he felt his blood stir again. "I don't think so."

"You're missing the point."

"Which is?"

He took both her hands in his and regret softened the harsh planes of his face. "That this has gotten way out of control. *Way* out of control. We both know it."

"And how're we going to get back in control, hmm?" she asked as, once again he reached for his jeans. "By acting like this . . . attraction doesn't exist."

"Maybe."

"It won't work."

"Then we'll find whatever it is that does," he said gruffly. He started to dress, quickly this time. He didn't have time for this. He needed answers and he needed them fast. When he turned he was surprised that she, too, had thrown on her clothes, though her hair was mussed with pine needles and her face had the glow of a woman satisfied after weeks of deprivation.

She swung lithely onto the back of her little mare, sent a dazzling smile his way and said, "Race ya," as he was still yanking on his boots. With a holler that resounded through the trees, she kicked the black and galloped away, her laughter trailing after her.

"Damn that woman," he muttered, but he was up for the dare and hoisted himself onto the back of his buckskin. Within seconds he was chasing her, the trees and river flashing by in his peripheral vision, his objective, a woman with streaming black hair, in his sights.

Right or wrong, he was going to catch her, and when he did, he was damned sure the earth would move again.

The last thing Adria expected was for Zach to change his mind, and so quickly. But after she'd talked for hours with reporters and they were virtually assured that her face and story would be in the news yet again, he grew restless and told her that they'd leave and head back to Portland as she'd wanted. First thing in the morning.

Her feelings were ambivalent. She'd love to close off the rest of the world, to stay here with Zach and pretend that nothing else mattered, but she couldn't. She wasn't about to give up now.

While Zach was outside, cutting firewood, Adria poured herself a glass of wine and strolled into the den. Cedar walls and a river-rock fireplace surrounded a room filled with worn furniture, baskets of old magazines, and Indian blankets used as throws. Watercolors of horses and cattle and peaceful ranching scenes adorned the rough-cut walls. It was a cozy, well-used room that smelled faintly of ashes and burnt wood. She imagined Zachary spending his evenings here, his boots kicked off, the bottoms of his stockinged feet propped on the timeworn ottoman. A cozy vision, a warm thought, something she could envision herself being a part of. But that was crazy. Just because they'd made love, she was already fantasizing that they had a future together.

Stupid.

She ran her fingers along the spines of the books in the bookcase and found, tucked in a corner of one shelf, an old album with pictures of the family.

"I didn't know I still had that," Zach said, glaring at the album as he entered the room with a armload of firewood. The wind swept in with him and she smelled the scents of pine and musk mingling with the smoke as he struck a match on the stone hearth and lit the dry kindling. Flames crackled and sparked and she curled in a corner of the couch.

"I poured you a glass," she said nodding toward her wine. "In the kitchen."

He returned with a bottle of beer as well as the glass of wine and set the stemmed glass on the coffee table for her. Then he lowered himself into a chair opposite her, twisted off the cap of his beer and watched her as she sipped her Chardonnay and slowly turned page after page.

"You won't find much in there." He drank slowly, and she felt his eyes upon her. Restless eyes.

"Is that right?" She didn't stop gazing at the flat images. The pictures in the album were old and a little faded, some of the color washed out. Though there were none of Eunice, some spaces pointedly blank, a page yellowed around an empty spot where a snapshot had been removed, there were a few pictures of Zachary, never smiling, always sullen, glaring at the camera as if it were his enemy.

There were shots of Katherine, too, playful poses where she smiled and flirted with the lens, a natural tease in front of the camera. Adria bit her lip as she studied the pictures and her heart twisted at a photograph of Katherine carrying a dark-haired toddler on her hip.

Zach took a long pull on his bottle, then bent over the fire again, tossing in two chunks of mossy maple.

"You never really told me about her," Adria said, as Zach dusted his hands and stared at the hungry yellow flames licking the new wood.

"There wasn't much to tell."

Adria didn't believe him. Something in his tone bothered her. Instinctively she felt he wanted her to back away and that pushed her steadily forward. "Why all the ambivalence, Zach?" she asked, staring up at him. "What did she ever do to you?"

"Besides accusing me of taking London?"

"She wasn't serious. You were just a kid." She glanced up at him and didn't dare breathe.

His eyes darkened a shade and he gritted his teeth. He hesitated, looked guilty as hell and when his eyes found hers again, in that quiet little heartbeat as the fire reflected in golden shadows on his face, she knew. With deadly certainty, she saw the past through his eyes. As only a woman in love can discern, Adria understood that Katherine—her mother—her *mother*—and Zach had been lovers! "No," she whispered, shaking her head in denial. Her insides turned liquid and had she not been already sitting, she would have needed instant support. "Oh, no!" The vague suspicion that had been nagging at the back of her mind seemed to roar into the forefront.

The album dropped to the floor. "Zach, *no!*"

Mouth compressed and jaw rock hard, he took a step toward her, but she held up her hand—silently pleading with him to stay away. She knew her face had drained and felt as if she'd been kicked in the stomach. Consciousness teetered for a second. "Oh God. You couldn't. No, no, no . . ."

"Adria—"

"You . . . you and Katherine were *lovers?*" she said, her voice small and disbelieving.

He closed his eyes against the truth and his lips folded in on themselves.

She thought she might throw up. "She was my—"

"I know what she was," he snapped, swinging an arm as if to hit something, anything in his path. He jammed his hands through his hair and picked up his beer. "It just happened."

"Just happened?" she repeated, disbelieving. "For God's sake, Zach, she was your *stepmother!*"

His lip curled in derision. "And you could be my half-sister. Not a pretty thought, is it?" He took a swig from his bottle and gnashed his teeth.

Adria felt as if she'd been slapped. She struggled to her feet and backed away from him. "I'm not—"

He moved swiftly, pushing her back onto the couch, placing his hand on either side of her, imprisoning her in the old cushions. His head was so close to hers she could see the pores on his face, smell the beer on his breath. "Isn't that why you're here, *London*? Isn't that all part of the plan? To prove that you're my baby sister and—"

"No, no, no, no, no!" she cried, unwilling to believe what he insisted was the truth. She sprang from the couch and he caught her in arms as strong as steel bands. "You're not—we can't be—" Hysterical, she pummeled his chest with her fists, pounding away until he grabbed her by the wrists and held her, heaving, away from him.

"I warned you—"

"You made vague insinuations. But not this. Never this! You could have told me that you . . . you—"

"That I what?" he said, holding her gaze with his. "That I made love to the woman who could be your mother?"

The words cracked through the room like the sharp unleashing of a whip.

Her knees sagged and if it weren't for the strong arms holding her by the wrists she would have fallen to the floor.

"What would you have done then, huh? Would you have backed off?" His eyes narrowed harshly. "I don't think so." Jerking her roughly to him, he kissed her. His lips were brutal, punishing, his body coiled in anger. At her. At himself. At the whole damned world. When he lifted his head, they were both breathing hard.

"Did you do this . . . did you make love to me because I look so much—"

"Hell, no! I wanted Kat out of my life! Before she was in it! But she was determined."

"I don't want to hear this—"

"She was hot, Adria. And I was a horny kid. I don't have any excuses. It was wrong."

"So that's why Witt cut you out of his will."

His smile was hard. "One of the reasons."

"Oh, God. How did you ever—" she asked, not wanting to know.

"When she began sleeping with Jason, the old man kind of forgave me. It took a while, but we struck a deal. I got the ranch and he got his old hotel restored like he wanted it." His fingers cut into her flesh. "Why do you think Kat killed herself?" he said. "Because of me. Because of Jason. Because of London and Witt. Because of the curse of being a Danvers—the curse you're so ready to embrace!"

She shoved away from him, dragging in ragged gulps of air, her eyes as dark as midnight. "Don't make this any worse than it already is," she spat and watched as a muscle worked in his jaw. For a minute she thought he might kiss her again and a part of her still wanted to hold him, to kiss him, to make love to him . . .

"I don't think it could be," he said and stormed out of the room and decided to get drunk. No, not just drunk, but stinking, shit-faced, falling-down drunk. He grabbed his coat and strode outside. The temperature had dropped and a few light flakes of snow were beginning to fall. He'd find a woman. A woman without any strings attached. A woman looking for a one-night stand. A woman who wouldn't even ask him his name.

He slammed the door behind him, rattling the windows.

Manny, despite the cold, was seated in a rocking chair on the porch of a small cabin located at one end of the parking lot. A cigarette hung from the corner of his mouth and he was whittling as he listened to the transistor radio in the window. He looked up as Zach passed him on the way to his Jeep. "You leaving?"

"Yeah."

"Looks like you could spit nails."

"For starters."

"When you comin' back?"

"Don't know." He cocked his head toward the main house. "Watch her, will ya?"

"I'm a Paiute, Danvers, not a friggin' jailer."

"Just make sure she stays put."

"Woman trouble," Manny said, his expression unchanging. He drew on the cigarette and smoke shot from his nostrils. "The worst kind."

"Amen." Climbing into his Jeep, Zach stabbed the keys into the ignition, fired the engine and roared away from the ranch house. Damn it, what was it with him? First Kat, now a woman who looked so much like her it was eerie—damned eerie.

Somehow, someway, he had to get away from her and break free of this circle of sin that kept spinning around him, trapping him in its dangerous, life-crushing, erotic coils.

They left the ranch the next evening and didn't say a word on the way back to Portland. That suited Zach just fine. His head was pounding from his intimate relationship with Jack Daniel's the night before, his only relationship. He'd never gotten past a brief nod of his head toward the blonde who'd shown him so much interest last night. Her easy smile and freckles had been cute, her full breasts obviously restrained by a tight yellow T-shirt, but he couldn't drown memories of Adria with any amount of liquor. He'd turned down the blonde and she'd found another, more willing cowboy. Zach had nearly drowned himself in whiskey. Manny had come into town to collect him.

And today he was paying. Shit, was he paying.

He slid a pair of sunglasses onto the bridge of his nose to break the glare of sunlight off the road, but truth to tell, the sun was hidden behind a heavy bank of clouds and his eyes ached from too much whiskey, the sting of smoke, and lack of sleep.

He flipped on the radio, listened to the tinny sound of country music and wished he knew what the hell he was going to do with Adria when he got to Portland. She hadn't told him her plans, but he suspected she intended to ditch him. Hell, he couldn't blame her, he'd been cruel to her last night, but it was the only way he could get away from her, and he had to get away. For both of them.

As they drove into the city, he said, "I booked a room for you."

"Let me guess—it's not at the Orion," she said sarcastically. She didn't even glance in his direction.

"You'll be safe at the hotel."

Turning hostile eyes in his direction, she silently accused him of lying. "From whom?" A dark, skeptical eyebrow rose imperiously over her eyes. "The Danvers family? The person who attacked me?" *You?* "I don't think so." She saw the vexation in his eyes and told herself she didn't give a damn. She was wounded to her soul. To think that he and Katherine . . . God, he'd only been a kid at the time and Katherine was her mother . . . and . . . a quivering sensation in her stomach made her close her mind to the thoughts that had tortured her all night. In her mind's eye she'd seen him hot, and hungry, and eager, a sixteen-year-old boy, horny as hell, making it with his father's wife.

Is it any worse than you—making it with a man who could be your half-brother?

She nearly threw up before she closed the door to that particular thought and slammed the dead bolt into place. It couldn't be. It just couldn't!

"All right. You name it then."

"I don't know. Just take me to my car and I'll—"

"Your car isn't fixed yet."

"Not fixed? But it was running just fine—"

He snorted. The mechanic had called this morning. "I don't know what you call fine in Podunk, Montana, but according to a man who knows his way around a Chevy, you need new brakes, shocks, spark plugs, fan belt, the list goes on and on—"

"Great. Don't tell me. You authorized him to do it!" She couldn't begin to imagine how she could afford to get the little Nova out of hock.

"Don't worry about it. I'll get you a car. One that's dependable."

"I don't want your help, Zach—"

"But—"

"Or your pity."

"You need a car."

"Or your damned stubborn streak. Okay? Just take me to the airport. I'll rent one there," she said crisply. Everything was spinning out of control and she had to get a grip on her life, find out the truth, and then decide what she was going to do.

He shot her a glance. "You should stay with me."

"Oh, where it's safe?" she mocked, wanting to hurt him as he'd hurt her.

"Yes."

"Forget it."

He sliced her a look, then drove on, past the turnoff to the airport and heading straight into the heart of the city. He didn't stop the Jeep until he was in the parking lot of the Hotel Danvers.

So furious she could barely see straight, she said, "I'll just call a cab," as he hauled her bag out of the back.

"Fine."

"Being here is a big waste of time."

"Whatever you say." He punched the button for the elevator with his elbow and waited, holding her suitcase in one big hand, the toe of his boot tapping in irritation. The car arrived, he waited for her to step in and they sped upward to the lobby. At the front desk, he pulled the manager aside. Gray stare drilling into the shorter man's eyes, he ordered, "Ms. Nash needs a suite, a private suite with only one key. No one, save Ms. Nash, is to disturb her, and that includes any of the staff, or any of my family, is that understood?"

"Absolutely." The man's Adam's apple bobbed.

"And I want round-the-clock security by her door, a man posted—"

"No. Zach, this is ridiculous," she interjected.

"—twenty-four hours a day. When she's in the room and when she isn't a guard will be there. Got it?"

"Of course, Mr. Danvers."

"She'll take phone calls, and guests can wait in the lobby after she screens them, but no one, not even Jason, is to rescind this order. If anyone tries, I want to be notified immediately. I'll be in my usual rooms. And she doesn't need to register. She's my guest."

"Yes, Mr. Danvers," the manager said crisply before turning and taking a key from a hook. He slid it across the desk to Adria and she, grinding her teeth together in frustration, accepted it. For the time being. Just until she could rent a car and relocate.

Zachary wasn't finished. "I'll take her bag up myself and as far as you know the person who's in the rooms is a VIP and no one, I mean *no one,* is to know that she's here."

Adria started to protest, but held her tongue. Let him do this. It would take only a few more minutes and then she would be totally independent. Or would she? A contrary part of her heart begged to differ as she watched him, all quiet authority and rugged good looks. Telling herself that she could force herself to be immune to him, she followed Zach into the elevator where his presence all but dominated the little car and up to the sixth floor to a corner suite with several rooms, fireplace, private veranda, and Jacuzzi. He tossed her bag onto the couch and locked the door behind him. It clicked so loudly she nearly jumped.

"I'd feel better if I stayed with you," he said, cocking his head at the floral couch where her bag rested.

"I think, under the circumstances, that would be a big mistake," she said, but already, her pulse was jumping. The thought of being alone with him caused a warm, wanton sensation deep in the pit of her stomach, like a butterfly opening its wings for the very first time.

"I can't protect you if I'm not with you," he said. The distance between them was only a few feet and she could barely stand it.

"And I can't protect myself if I am with you." She rested her rear against the ledge of the window. "This has gone too far, Zachary, and I'm not blaming you. It happened between us and it was a mistake . . . I can see that now, but I don't know, I'm just not sure that I can trust myself if you're here with me." She spoke from the heart and she felt as if she were shredding inside because a part of her longed to be held by him, to kiss him, to feel his hands upon the crook of her waist. She bit her lip before she said something that she shouldn't.

A look of desolation, like the empty desert just before nightfall, crossed his eyes. "This is your call, Adria," he said, his voice low and soft, almost a caress.

Her heart shattered. She remembered the feel of his hands on her, the taste of his skin, the way he sighed against her ear. "Then it's the way it has to be."

Zach's shoulders stiffened and the brackets around the corners of his mouth grooved deep. "I'm in 714."

Her throat closed in on itself at the mention of the suite from which London had been stolen all those years ago.

"Call me if you need me."

I need you. I need you now! Her fingers curled over the window ledge and she held back the urge to run to him.

Back ramrod stiff, he walked out of the room and closed the door behind him.

Swearing under his breath, Zach pulled into the parking lot of the headquarters of Danvers International. The lot was closed, but he used a special card and the gates opened as if for royalty. Danvers royalty.

He hadn't been happy about leaving the hotel, knowing that Adria would probably bolt, but he had to find out answers and any he'd gotten from Jason on the telephone had been evasive and vague. He'd called, tracked his brother to the offices and decided that if he had to, he'd knock Jason senseless, because it was time to find out the truth.

Before he fouled up Adria's life forever.

Spoiling for a fight, he parked in a spot reserved for a vice president and took the elevator to the floor housing the suite of executive offices of Danvers International. During the day the building was crawling with people, at night it seemed a tomb.

He walked down the short hallway lit only by security lamps, past the empty reception area, and through the carved wooden doors to the president's office.

Jason, dressed in a crisp suit and tie, was sprawled on the leather couch angled in front of the television in the corner. He must've had one helluva day because his hair was slightly mussed and his tie was loosened. Propping one heel on a glass coffee table, he sipped from a glass of amber liquid.

Zach let the door bang shut behind him and studied the room where all the important decisions of the company were made. The two exterior walls were glass, offering a panoramic view of blazing city lights and two bridges spanning the Willamette River.

Inside, trophies and plaques were hung on a wall of rough cedar, a tribute to the forests that had been the source of so much of the Danvers fortune.

"You're angry," Jason guessed as he stood and tucked his shirt into the waistband of his slacks.

The understatement of the year. "A little."

"Adria?" Jason clicked off the television and reached for his drink.

"She's got a mind of her own."

"Thought you liked that in a woman."

"Not in this one."

Jason lifted a skeptical brow. "Help yourself to the bar."

"Not tonight." Propping his hip on the corner of Jason's wide desk, he said, "I just came here because I want to get in contact with Sweeny."

"He called earlier." Jason polished off his drink. "Big news." Zach's blood seemed to freeze.

"He called to crow really," Jason continued as he walked to the bar and added more Scotch to his melting ice cubes. "Seems he's found Bobby Slade, the one who we hoped would turn out to be Adria's real father. Robert E. Lee Slade. He's Ginny Watson's ex-husband, all right, and he's living in Lexington, Kentucky—has himself some kind of auto repair shop or something." Jason made a dismissive gesture with his hands, as if whatever it was that kept Bobby Slade employed didn't really matter. "According to Sweeny, Slade doesn't know where his ex-wife is, hasn't kept up with her since he heard from her two years ago when she'd taken some kind of nanny job in San Francisco."

Zach's hands began to sweat and he remembered Ginny Slade as a plain woman in dowdy suits and heavy shoes who looked ancient compared to Kat. But somehow the birdlike woman had managed to steal her precious charge right out from under Witt's nose.

"What else does the guy have to say?"

"Plenty. Bobby claims his wife was a nut case. Totally bonkers. She lost any grip on reality she had when their toddler daughter was killed in a drowning accident. She blamed him, he blamed her, and their marriage fell apart. Sweeny says Slade was glad to be rid of her."

"So what about London?"

"Here comes the clincher," Jason said, looking up at the ceiling. "Slade says that years ago—the midseventies, he thinks, just before he moved to Kentucky—she showed up in Memphis out of the blue. Ginny had a kid in tow with her, a dark-haired girl of about four. He thought it was strange at the time, but just assumed that the kid was hers as she claimed. She'd always had a thing about babies, even before losing her own." Jason looked straight at his brother and the hidden anger in his eyes bordered on hatred. "The odd thing about the situation was, and it kind of gave Slade the creeps, that she named the kid Adria, the same name she'd given their little girl who'd died."

"Jesus Christ," Zach whispered.

"My sentiments exactly. I hate to admit it, but it looks like Adria might just be London."

Zach gripped the edge of the desk. This was all wrong. It had to be. Adria couldn't be his half-sister. No way! She wasn't related to him! He thought of her lying beneath him, her body shiny with sweat, her voice moaning in gentle rhythm to his thrusts . . . for the love of God . . .

"Nelson's fit to be tied. He's on his way over here."

"What about Trisha?" Zach asked, though he barely could keep his mind on the conversation.

"Couldn't get hold of her," Jason admitted. "She's probably out prowling again."

"Let me talk to Sweeny. He's probably lying—"

"Shit, Zach, get a grip."

"I need to talk to him!"

"Why?"

"I just need to ask him some questions," Zach said and Jason favored him with a smug little smile that said he could read his brother like the proverbial book.

"The number's on the desk, Zach, but it won't do any good talking to him. The facts, as they say, are the facts. Adria Nash is probably our sister. The good news is that she doesn't know it."

"Yet," Zach said, with a sinking sensation.

"Ever." Jason's jaw hardened and he suddenly looked so much like their father, Zach winced. "As far as I'm concerned," Jason said with deadly calm, "she'll never know."

21

"We finally caught ourselves a break," Sweeny said, his voice self-satisfied and oily as it sang through the wires.

Every muscle in Zach's body contracted an inch and he could barely breathe. "You have an address where Ginny Slade can be found?"

"Nope, but I've got one where she worked a couple of years ago. Pacific Palisades in San Francisco."

"Let's have it."

The detective hesitated only a second, then gave Zach the name and number of Virginia Watson's last employer of record. It wasn't much, but it was all Zach needed. He hung up just as Nelson shouldered through the double doors of Jason's office, took one look around and paused, his face blanching slightly. "What the hell's going on?"

"Sweeny found Ginny Slade," Jason said. "Well, nearly. He thinks she's in San Francisco."

"Then it's true—?" Nelson was speechless as he plopped down in one of the side chairs and rubbed his temples with his fingers. It was obvious that he thought his life was unraveling. "I can't believe it. She's really London?"

"Looks that way," Zach said tightly.

"We don't have to believe it!" Jason was adamant. "We don't have to buy into it, we just have to keep our mouths shut."

"No way. She deserves to know," Zach said though it twisted his guts and a vile taste rose in the back of his throat when he realized that he still wanted her. Despite the nearly certain truth that she was his long-lost half-sister, he couldn't stop thinking of her as a woman.

Nelson pinched the bridge of his nose as if trying to forestall a headache. "First Mother, then this . . ."

"Eunice?" Zach's head snapped up.

"She slipped and fell chasing after that damned cat of hers," Nelson said. "She's all right, just banged around a little. A few scratches. Nothing serious, thank God. But this London business. It's goddamned unbelievable." He glanced up at Zach and his mouth twisted into a shadow of his former smile. "You know, a long time ago, you were my hero. Getting beat up, having yourself a prostitute . . ." His voice faltered and his gaze shifted to the floor. He sighed loudly, a tortured soul who'd been cast adrift years before. "I guess that's all gone now."

Zach couldn't think about the might-have-beens. Nelson had always been out of step; no reason that having London resurface would change anything. He clamped a hand on his youngest brother's shoulder, then let go. With renewed conviction, he crossed the room and thrust open the doors.

"Hey—where're you going?" Jason's voice followed him into the hallway. "Wait a minute. Zach! Oh, shit, what's he going to do now?"

"Who cares?" Nelson said. "It's over, Jase."

"Not yet—"

The rest of whatever he was saying was cut off when the doors closed. Zach pounded on the elevator call button with his fist. Though he was sick inside at the thought of Adria being London he told himself it had been inevitable and was probably for the best. Deep in his gut he didn't believe it. The good news was that they were closer to the truth and the pall that had been shrouding the family for years might finally be lifted. The bad news was that he'd never be able to touch her again.

Trisha was pissed.

She climbed in her Alpha and took off, putting the little sports car through its considerable paces, and driving through the night without knowing where she was going. She'd hoped to meet Mario, but her plans had fallen through. Again. Her fingers tightened over the steering wheel and she took a corner a little too fast, the tires screeching, the car skidding into the oncoming lane. Headlights bore down on her. The driver of the other car, swerved, nearly taking out a tree and laid on his horn as Trisha maneuvered her car back into the right-hand lane. "And fuck you, too," she muttered under her breath, then glanced at the rear-view mirror to make sure the jerk didn't turn around and chase after her. Well, let him. She'd show him what a real car could do. She was in one bitch of a mood.

Because of Mario. And Adria.

Mario claimed he couldn't meet her, that some kind of business had come up, but Trisha wasn't fool enough to believe him. Though he'd apologized over and over again, she hadn't heard the slightest hint of any true regret in his voice. She knew the reason—he had a new woman, someone more exciting, someone who presented him more of a challenge. She didn't have to be a brain surgeon to figure out that he planned the newest notch on his bedpost was going to be Adria Nash.

Ever since he'd been with Adria the other night, Mario had avoided Trisha, begging off with one flimsy excuse after another. But Trisha knew the score. Whenever he was involved with a new woman he became distracted and unapproachable, but eventually—sometimes only days, other times excruciating months—he came back, not the least bit contrite, resuming their affair with a renewed passion and vigor, claiming to love her.

The sex was always worth the wait.

The emotional strain was not.

So now he was interested in Adria and that bothered her— more than any of the others.

"Bitch!" Trisha hissed, thinking of the pistol locked in her glove compartment. She didn't know whom to shoot first. Mario or Adria. Maybe the two of them together. She'd bought the gun for protection and never had to use it, but tonight, her fantasies were running wild and if she caught Mario—her Mario—with that two-bit hustler from Montana, she was sure she could blow them both away.

Her fingers were sweaty and she shifted down for another curve. The thought of murder was appealing, but she knew it was only a fantasy, a girlish image of revenge that she would never carry out. Disgusted with herself, she pushed the cigarette lighter in and considered making a buy. A little coke would lift the old spirits and maybe give her enough guts to go through with her murderous plans. She shook out a Salem Light and placed it between her lips.

The cellular phone jangled and she smiled to herself. Mario had changed his mind. Steering with one hand, she picked up the phone. "Yes?" she said breathlessly and was disappointed when Nelson's voice crackled in the receiver.

"I thought you should know," he said, his voice heavy with despair. "It looks like Adria might be London."

"Shit, no—"

The cigarette lighter clicked and Trisha wedged the phone between her shoulder and head, while she stuck the burner to the end of her cigarette and pulled in a deep breath. Her eyes never left the road. Smoke puffed from the corner of her mouth.

"I don't believe it, either, but Sweeny seems to think he's got proof positive."

"That little prick wouldn't know his own dick if it weren't attached to his balls." She shoved the lighter back into the dash and took in another lungful.

"Do you always have to be so crude?"

"Has the press found out?"

"Not yet. But they will. Zach's running wild—"

"Zach?" she said, frowning as she blew out a stream of smoke that temporarily fogged the windshield.

"Yeah, he's back in town."

"With the bitch?"

"I think so." Trisha's blood ran cold as her suspicions proved true. No wonder Mario was busy tonight. "Jason's trying to keep the story quiet. He doesn't want anyone outside the immediate family to know, least of all, Adria, but Zach rushed out of here like a madman and I think he's going to tell her."

"Shit." Trisha's world began crumbling at a faster rate. First Mario, now everything that went with being a Danvers—her whole life, her future—falling into little pieces. Because of Adria.

"My feelings exactly."

"Where is she?"

"Get this," Nelson said, his voice tinged in irony. "Zachary's got her hidden in the damned hotel. Jason already checked, though that little creep of a manager, Rich, wouldn't tell him which room. Jason warned the guy that he'd fire him, but he still held his tongue."

"Zach must've threatened him with bodily harm." She braked for a red light.

"Probably. Sounds like our brother," Nelson said morosely.

"This just gets better and better," Trisha said, her mind already spinning ahead.

"Or worse and worse," Nelson complained.

"Why does Zach care if Adria knows?"

"You tell me, Trisha. You're always so good at reading everyone's emotions."

It all suddenly clicked into place. Her suspicions crystallized and she smiled wickedly to herself as she jammed the Alpha into first just as the light changed. The tires chirped as she stepped on the accelerator. "I bet our stoic, love-'em-and-leave-'em brother has fallen in love with her," Trisha said, disgusted at the thought of it. "I can't stand it. She's his . . . our . . . oh, hell, this is fucking unbelievable." She cruised through another yellow light. "You know, this could work to our advantage."

"I don't see how."

"You will," Trisha promised as she hung up the phone and turned toward the river. She flipped on the radio and began to sing along to an old Tina Turner song that blasted over the speakers. Finally she was certain she could handle Adria.

After Zach left, Adria went right to work. She called a rental car agency and reserved a car, dialed Zach's mechanic and left a message that she wanted her vehicle back as soon as possible. Next she'd have to find a way to hire a good lawyer.

She'd been approached several times since the press release and she had over a dozen business cards of smooth-talking men in expensive wool suits who had offered to look over the facts of her case. A few had hinted that they would work for her on contingency, with no money up front, but they all had seemed so slick . . . too smart for their own good, and she hadn't been ready to hire anyone yet.

Now, things had changed.

And for the worse.

She flopped back on the bed and draped her forearm over her eyes.

Forget him!

If only she could, but everywhere she went she thought of Zach, remembered the craggy angles of his face, felt again the tingling sensations of his lips touching hers, turned liquid inside with the want of him.

Fool! Do you think he's moping over you? You were probably just a quick distraction to him . . . and yet . . .

The phone rang and she nearly jumped out of her skin. Zach. It had to be Zach. No one else knew she was here. She picked up the receiver and forced her voice to remain calm. "Hello?"

"Adria," a female voice cooed. "So you are here."

Her heart somersaulted as she recognized Trisha's voice.

"Zach wouldn't tell anyone where you were, but I took a stab in the dark and though the desk is downright rude about letting me know your room number, they did deign to put me through." She sounded irritated.

"What do you want?" she asked, wondering if she really could be related to this woman.

"I need to talk to you."

"Now?"

"You got better plans?" Without waiting for an answer, Trisha said, "I'm in the parking garage now. I could meet you in the bar in five minutes, or . . . if you'd rather go somewhere else."

"The bar's fine," Adria said. "I'll see you there." So much for being safe, she thought, but really didn't give a damn who knew where she was. Maybe it was time to flush out the culprit who had jumped her and in so doing find out exactly what happened nearly twenty years ago. She ran a brush through her hair, slipped a silk jacket over her jeans and blouse and locked the door behind her.

She nearly stumbled over the security guard, a beefy red-haired man with a pockmarked face, posted in the hallway. "Mr. Danvers requested that I stay here," he said, almost apologetically. "You going out?"

"Just for a little while."

"Where to?"

"Just downstairs," she said, disliking the man for intruding into her privacy, though she knew he was only doing his job. She hurried into the elevator, tapped her fingernails nervously on the rail as the car descended and bolted through the doors as they opened silently.

Zach was waiting for her.

Lounging against a post, propped up by one denim-covered shoulder, arms crossed over his chest, he stood, staring at the elevator, like a cougar waiting to pounce on unsuspecting prey. "Goin' somewhere?" he drawled and a slow, sexy smile curved across his jaw.

A nest of butterflies erupted in her stomach.

"No, I—" she stammered, then held her tongue. "Have you been down here the whole time, waiting for me to try and escape?"

The smile disappeared. His eyes flashed angrily. "You're giving yourself too much credit, sister, way too much."

"If you'll excuse me," she said, trying to brush past him.

"Where do you think you're going?"

"To the bar."

"Thirsty?"

Narrowing her eyes up at him, she said, "Not that it's any of your business, but I'm meeting your sister."

"Trisha's here?" he asked, throwing a dark look toward the glass doors of the bar.

"Waiting. So if you'll excuse me."

He didn't. Instead he strode ahead of her. He threw open the door and scanned the room with eyes set into a hard-as-nails expression. His dark gaze landed squarely on his sister who was sitting in a corner booth, holding a short, fat glass of clear liquid in one hand and a burning cigarette in the other. With Adria at his heels, he crossed the patterned carpet. "What the hell's going on here?" he demanded, his lips barely moving.

"Just thought I'd have a drink with my . . . *our* sister." Trisha tapped the ash from her cigarette. "Join us?"

Adria's breath seemed to stop.

"Oh, God, don't tell me I ruined the surprise," Trisha said, feigning dismay, her fingers fluttering over her chest in mock surprise. "Didn't he tell you?" She threw her brother a look of shocked dismay and clucked her tongue. "Honestly, Zach, she deserves to know, don't you think?" She switched her gaze back to Adria. "They've nearly located Ginny Slade and it looks very much like you're going to end up the winner in all this. Oh, Zach, don't pretend to be so stricken. I know you knew all about it." Trisha took a long draw on her cigarette and held the smoke in her lungs before letting it drift lazily through her nostrils.

"No one's talked to Ginny yet," he said.

"Only a matter of time."

"*Yet?*" Adria whispered, hardly believing that after all these months, all the effort, she might be proved to be . . . Her gaze flew to Zachary's and she felt a wrenching deep in her soul. If she were London, then, unless Zach wasn't Witt's son . . . She knew her face drained of color and her knees felt wobbly for a second, though she'd known all along this could happen. Wasn't it what she'd wanted?

"This isn't a bad time to let the cat out of the bag, is it?" Trisha asked as Zachary slid into the booth opposite her, yanked on Adria's arm, and pulled her onto the soft leather bench beside him.

"Why didn't you tell me?" Adria asked, turning bewildered eyes on Zach. Zach who had protected her. Zach who had stolen her away. Zach who had made love to her. She could barely breathe.

"I just found out."

Trisha's gaze moved from her brother to Adria. "This makes things complicated, doesn't it?"

Zach glared at his sister. "It's always been complicated."

"I know, but I mean for you two."

The waiter came by with a refill for Trisha. Zach ordered a beer. Adria swallowing hard, asked for white wine and noticed the curl of Trisha's lip. "White wine the drink of choice in where was it—Elk Hollow, Montana?"

"Stop it, Trisha," Zach warned.

"Oh, little brother, you've got it bad, don't you? And for your half-sister. That's a real pisser." She picked up her first drink and finished it off. "A real pisser."

The waiter dropped off fresh glasses and Adria picked up the stem of her wineglass with trembling fingers. Her nerves were strung tight, but seemed jangled. Too much was happening too fast, she couldn't absorb everything. "Why did you want to meet me?" she asked.

Trisha's smile was brittle. "To tell you to stay away from Mario Polidori." At the lift of Adria's eyebrows, Trisha explained. "We go back a long time."

"I'm not seeing him."

"Oh?" Trisha rolled her eyes.

"Not the way you mean. I met him for drinks. We talked business."

"He held your hand, laughed at your jokes." Trisha took another drag and squashed her cigarette in the tray. "Look, don't play games with me, okay? I've played them all and know the score. Mario's off limits."

"Who do you think you are?" Adria asked, her temper, already frayed, finally splitting apart. "Both of you. You," she turned on Zach, "try to keep me a virtual prisoner and you, Trisha, telling me whom I can or cannot see. Give me a break. I'm outta here—" She started to leave, but Zach caught her arm and held her firmly against him.

"Just a second," he said, then turned his blazing eyes on his sister. "Is that it?"

"Not quite." Trisha took a long gulp of her gin and tonic. "Just in case you're not quite sure about a few things, I think you should know that if you two are involved, it's a big problem."

"Back off, Trisha," Zach growled.

"If you're London, Adria, and it's starting to look like you are, then you'd better accept the fact that Zach's your half-brother. I've heard all the rumors and so has Zach for all of his life, but I'll bet you both are banking on the fact that he's supposed to be Anthony Polidori's son. He's not."

Zach's jaw clenched so tight the bone showed beneath the skin of his chin. "I'm warning you—"

"That's right. Mom checked it out years ago. Remember, Zach, when you accused me of listening at cracks and peeking through keyholes? Well, I did. Every chance I got. It was the only way I could survive, the only way I knew what was going on. And I learned a helluva lot. I remember the day Mom, through rather discreet methods, found out Anthony Polidori's blood type. She was devastated because it proved beyond a shadow of a doubt that there was no way he could be your father. You, her favorite, the son she hoped didn't belong to Witt." Her eyes gleamed and Adria felt sick inside. "So, if you two have been screwing around, just remember that you're closer than you ever thought possible."

"Shut up, Trisha."

"It's sick, Zach. Just plain sick."

"Let's go—" He pushed Adria toward the end of the seat.

"Wouldn't the press love to hear this little twist, hmm?" Trisha asked in a thinly veiled threat. "I wonder what they'd say about all this . . . well, incest is such an ugly word. It could get tricky," she added, before plucking another cigarette from the opened pack sitting on the table.

"Do anything of the sort and I'll wring your neck," Zach warned.

"Sure you will. Christ, Zach, give up the melodrama. It doesn't suit you."

"Try me," he snarled and Trisha's mouth dropped open. "I wouldn't push it, if I were you."

Adria couldn't stand it another minute. She had to get away, to think clearly, to breathe fresh air, to put some distance between her and all the hatred, all the pain. Barely able to find her feet, she scrambled from the booth. She started running, across the carpet, through the doors, past the lobby and outside to the night. Rain was pouring from the sky, peppering the street and gurgling through the gutters. People on the sidewalk huddled under umbrellas, with their collars turned to the wind as they rushed from street corner to street corner.

Adria kept running, around the block, darting through traffic, ignoring the blast of horns, feeling the cold wet drops catch in her hair and slide beneath the collar of her jacket. The city was cloying, the emotions of the Danvers family as dark as the night.

"Adria!" Zach's voice boomed from somewhere behind her and she nearly stumbled over a man sitting in an alcove, his legs sticking out.

"Spare change?" he begged as she raced onward, blindly, running to an unknown destination and away from all the pain, the rage, the fatal mistake of loving the wrong man. Tears mingled with the rain and she gasped. Why had she come to Portland? Why? What did she care if she did turn out to be London?

"Stop! Adria!" He was getting closer, she could hear the soles of his boots slapping the wet the pavement and she willed her legs to move faster. *Run! Run! Run!* Get away. Go back to being Adria Nash. Give up this dream of being London Danvers! Leave Zachary forever!

At the crosswalk, she stepped off the curb, against the light. A car sped past her, nearly clipping her leg and throwing up a sheet of water that drenched the lower half of her body.

Zach's arms clamped around her and she screamed. "No!"

"Shh. It'll be all right," he said, pulling her close, back to the safety of the curb, letting her hit and sob and cry. She wailed like a wounded animal, striking at him madly, giving into the rage that consumed her.

Several people stopped to stare, then hurried along their way. "Adria, please . . . shh. It'll be all right. I'll make it right."

"How can you!" she cried wretchedly as rain drizzled down her cheeks. "It'll never be all right!" But the smell of him, the feel of his warm body pressed against hers, the soft, wet denim of his jacket brushing her cheek calmed her. Sobbing, her heart shattered, she clung to the lapels of his jacket and he held her beneath the street light, kissing her wet crown, promising her that everything would be fine.

"I didn't want this," she said brokenly, great sobs coming from her soul. "I didn't want to love you."

"I know. Hush."

"And now . . . and now." He kissed her then, silencing her lips with his own. She tasted sweat and tears and rainwater and saw, when she looked into his eyes, the torment, as deep as her own, the anguish of it all.

His dark hair was lank and flat against his head as he broke off the embrace and whispered her name, his voice cracking a little.

If only they could run away to a place where the truth and the press and the Danvers family would never find them. She watched his throat as he swallowed. "Come on," he said gruffly.

"Where . . . ?"

His lips thinned dangerously as he guided her back toward the hotel. "We have to go to San Francisco. This isn't finished yet."

* * *

Adria's nerves were struck tight as piano wires as they approached the house on Nob Hill in San Francisco. After camping out in the Portland Airport, then taking the first flight to the bay area, they'd landed and Zach had rented a car and located a hotel where he'd reserved separate, but connecting rooms. Just like before. Only this time, she knew, she'd never be able to love him again; never be able to trace the scar that lined his face, never touch his flat male nipples beneath his dark, whorling chest hairs.

She'd never make love to him again.

God, she was crazy just being alone with him.

Somehow, out of sheer exhaustion, she'd dozed for a few hours in the hotel while Zach had started trying to locate Ginny Slade. He'd begun by calling the number that Sweeny had given him, and then when a woman told him Ginny—or Virginia—no longer worked for her, he'd forced the issue, getting more numbers of people who had contacted the first woman, checking on Virginia's references, then dialing each and every one.

It had taken hours, but he'd finally gotten lucky and reached Virginia's current employer, Velma Bassett. Now they were walking up the steps to a grand Victorian house painted gray and trimmed in white. Wide brick steps led to a long porch and an oak door surrounded by narrow cut-glass windows.

Zach pushed on the bell.

Soft chimes responded in clear, dulcet tones.

Adria's stomach clenched.

Within minutes, the door was answered by a svelte woman of about thirty, with worried eyes and fingers that moved constantly from the door jamb to her throat.

"Mrs. Bassett?" Zach asked. "I'm—"

"Mr. Danvers, yes, I know. And this is Ms. Nash," she guessed. Her smile was friendly but nervous. "Please come in. I did as you suggested and called Portland; they faxed me pictures of you both along with the articles about this London thing. I have to apologize," she added, leading them past a grandfather's clock that ticked in the foyer, to a small room that had once been the parlor, "we don't pay much attention to anything other than the local news. My husband's a banker and he's more informed than I, but I really didn't know anything about the kidnapping. I was only a child when it happened and I lived in New York City . . . ah, well, I've rambled on, haven't I? I'll call Virginia down and you can speak with her in here. Please, please, have a seat. I'll have Martha bring you drinks—tea, lemonade, something stronger—?"

"We're fine," Zach assured her.

"Yes, well, I'm sure there's something. Now, if it does turn out that she's this Slade woman . . . oh, dear, well, she can't be looking after Chloe now, can she?" Still fluttering on, she left them alone in a room decorated in muted tones of peach and mauve and ivory.

Adria sat on the edge of a striped loveseat and Zach stood near the window, staring out across the bay.

While Mrs. Bassett was away, a maid slipped into the room and left a silver tea service on a glassed-topped coffee table.

Footsteps echoed in the hallway and Adria braced herself. Would she recognize the woman who may have stolen her away from her natural parents, the woman who had changed the course of her life forever?

"—but I'm not expecting anyone," a reed-thin voice protested.

"I know, but they say they're friends of yours, long-lost acquaintances."

"Really, Mrs. Bassett, I don't know anyone—"

The voice, like the scent of a sachet locked for years in a forgotten drawer, drifted into the room and caused Adria's heart to skip a beat. The floor seemed to fall away from her feet as a woman stepped into the room. She was small, birdlike, with graying dark hair and plain features, but when her gazed landed on Adria, she stopped stock-still. "No," she mouthed, but emitted no sound. What little bit of color had been in her face drained quickly away. "Oh, dear God," she whispered faintly. Recovering slightly she asked, "Who—who are you?" She forced a detached smile, but her lower lip trembled slightly.

"Take a guess," Zach suggested.

"I don't know—"

"Sure you do, Ginny. This is London."

Virginia's eyes darted from one to the other. "London?"

"London Danvers, the girl you took to Montana to live with Victor and Sharon Nash, the girl you pawned off as your daughter though your own child had been dead for years."

"No!" she said, but she licked her lips nervously. "Mrs. Bassett, I don't know what kind of lies these people have been telling you, but—"

"The police have been called, Virginia," Velma said calmly. "If they're lying—"

"Oh, Mother Mary!" Her hand flew to her chest, covering her heart. "You didn't—"

"Why don't you explain everything," Zach said, motioning to a chair. "There's a chance we can work something out."

"Oh, my Lord—" she protested, but dropped onto the sofa and gazed out the window to the clouds rolling over the green waters of the bay. Tears collected in the corners of her eyes and ran slowly down her cheeks as her gritty determination gave way to acceptance of what had to be. "I'm so sorry. So, so sorry."

"Tell us, Ginny," Zach said, relentless while Adria's heart went out to the woman who seemed to have aged twenty years since stepping into the room.

Velma Bassett stood near the doorway, bracing herself on the painted woodwork as she stared at the nanny she had trusted with her child for over eighteen months.

"I—I didn't want to do it," Ginny said, reaching into her pocket and finding a handkerchief to dab at her face. "But it was so much money."

"What was?"

"I was promised fifty-thousand dollars if I would take London away."

Adria's heart twisted painfully.

"I knew it was wrong, but I couldn't resist. All I had to do was disappear with the girl."

"But why? And who?" Zach demanded.

"I don't know."

Adria could hold her tongue no longer. "But someone paid you, met with you—"

"It was all arranged over the telephone. At first I thought it was a joke. Then I got a package. Ten thousand dollars. More money than I'd ever seen in my life, and I was called again, offered another forty thousand dollars. All I had to do was leave town. Five thousand dollars more was left for me in a locker at the airport in Portland, and the rest when I got to Denver. From there I was to head anywhere, to put as much distance between myself and Portland as I could. It was supposed to happen earlier, but London wouldn't go to bed and we almost missed our flight . . . I was so scared, but so desperate. Oh, God, what am I going to do now?"

"Well, you're sure as hell not going to take care of my daughter any longer," Mrs. Bassett said. "I'll pay you severance pay, whatever it takes, but, believe you me, you'll not be spending another night in this house!" So enraged she was shaking, she hurried out of the room and the soles of her prim red pumps clacked loudly on the steps as she hurried upstairs. "Chloe? Where are you?"

Ginny shoved a strand of hair from her face and her fingers quivered. "How did you find me?"

"It took some time," Zach admitted.

Adria leaned closer. "But surely you know who paid you?"

She shook her head and turned guilt-riddled eyes on Adria. "I don't have any idea."

"Man? Woman?"

"Really. I don't know. I never met with anyone and the money was all in cash—small bills."

She looked so miserable, her cheeks hollow, her eyes vacant as she dabbed at them, Adria believed her.

"Someone paid you off."

"Yes."

"Someone with a lot of money."

She nodded, but Adria got the impression she wasn't listening, that she was remembering the past and how she escaped with someone else's daughter.

"You'll have to talk to the police," Zach said.

"I know."

"It may not be easy."

She turned haunted eyes up at Zach. "It never has been," she admitted. "For twenty years I've looked over my shoulder, expecting this day to come. I knew you were back in Portland, you know," she added, staring at Adria. "I heard it on the news. Saw your face, listened to your story, knew that you'd be reunited with your family."

"You could have run," Adria said.

Ginny gave a self-deprecating little snort. "Where to? I really didn't think you'd find me." She pushed herself upright. "You look just like her, you know. It's . . . well, it's scary."

"So I've heard."

"Why didn't you come forward for the reward?" Zach asked.

She just stared for a minute. "Because Witt Danvers would have killed me for taking his little girl." She cleared her throat. "Would you give me a few minutes to get my things?" she asked with a weak smile. "Then I'll go with you to talk to the police."

"Fine," Adria said.

"I don't think we should let her out of our sight," Zach cut in.

"Don't worry, Mr. Danvers," Ginny said, studying Zachary as if for the first time trying to picture him as the man who'd grown up from the rebellious son of the richest man in Portland— the hellion who had given his father fits. "It's time for this to end."

She left and walked to a door at the foot of the stairs and slowly descended.

"So what do I call you now?" Zach asked as he paced to the window. "Adria? Or London?"

"Adria." she said, her throat thick, her eyes misting. This was the first of their goodbyes. "I hope to you, I'll always be Adria."

The minutes, recorded by the grandfather's clock in the hall, ticked by and outside the ever-present traffic moved sluggishly up the hill.

Adria wondered how much longer she had with Zach, how few minutes. Her heart felt as if it were breaking into a thousand pieces as she stared at him. His broad shoulders were rigid, tense with strain, one thumb was hooked through a belt loop and his fingers hung near the faded denim of his fly. His jaw was dark with a beard shadow and his eyes, beneath heavy black brows, were narrowed suspiciously. He shifted from one foot to the other, pretending interest in the view from the bay window before glancing back to the stairwell.

"Shit, what could be taking so long?"

"She's packing her things . . ." Adria said, but even she was conscious of the time.

Mrs. Bassett, with a golden-haired child of about seven in tow, clomped down the stairs and hurried back into the room. The child wore wild curls and a dress with a sailor's collar and brass buttons. "I don't know how I can ever thank you enough," Mrs. Bassett said, her eyes shifting quickly to the stairwell and back again. "To think that I trusted her with my precious Chloe. Oh, God, it just makes me shudder. I called Harry and he wants to press charges against her for false representation or whatever you call it. He's phoning our lawyer right now. Oh, dear." Kissing her child's crown, she said, "Why don't you go practice your piano, baby?"

"Don't want to," the girl said churlishly though her mother was shepherding her toward the upright near the fireplace. Chloe crossed her chubby arms stubbornly in front of her chest.

"Well . . ." Wringing her hands, Mrs. Bassett spied the basket of cakes near the tea service. "Here, then, how about a cookie?" She placed the platter in front of the girl. "Oh, my, I've completely forgotten my manners; could I please offer you a cup of tea? The least I could do, you know."

"Thanks," Adria said, but Zachary only shook his head and glowered at the stairwell as if he were afraid Ginny might disappear again.

Mrs. Bassett frowned suddenly. "I thought you called the police."

"We did. They should be here any minute—" Adria said.

"Is there another way out of the basement?" Zach asked suddenly.

"Oh, no . . . well, there's a coal chute, but it's been closed for years and some old cellar stairs, but they're boarded over. If there were a fire, the windows are large enough—"

"Christ!" Moving with the speed of a cheetah, he raced out of the parlor, across the foyer and down the stairs with lightning speed.

How could he have been so stupid? Vaulting over the rail of the stairs, he landed loudly on the cement floor and felt the cool rush of fresh air before he saw the curtains fluttering noiselessly in the breeze.

The basement was dark and he walked unerringly to a small cozy room in a back corner where the bedroom light glowed warmly. "Ginny?" he called, feeling an eerie breeze, the premonition of doom, scurrying up the back of his neck.

Muscles rigid, Zach stepped into the room. A suitcase, lying open, had been thrown on the bed. Clothes dangled from hangers in the open closet. One drawer in a tiny bureau was askew, underwear and nightgowns falling onto the floor. "Ginny?" he called again, but there was still no answer.

The hairs on the back of his neck raised as he crossed the room and threw open the door to a tiny bathroom. Red splashes were everywhere. Blood stained the walls and splattered the sink and toilet. Ginny Slade was lying on the cracked linoleum. Her tongue hung limply from her mouth, her eyes stared blankly at the ceiling and her wrists were slashed, blood still oozing from the open wounds. A straight-edged razor was clenched in her right fist.

Zach let out a sharp breath and stepped back, recoiling from the room splattered in blood and the sightless eyes that stared up at him. "Call the police," he yelled up the stairs. "Adria, call the police! No, 911! We need an ambulance."

He heard the thunder of footsteps and turned to find Adria on the landing. "Don't come down here and for God's sake keep the kid upstairs!" he ordered.

"What—" She stared past him to the blood creeping from the bathroom and onto the bedroom carpet. "Oh, God."

"It's Ginny—call the damned police."

"Mrs. Bassett already has."

But Zach wasn't listening. He forced himself to return to search for a pulse, to find some sign of life, but he knew that it was useless. Ginny Slade, the only witness to what had happened to London Danvers all those years ago, was dead.

22

"You're saying she didn't kill herself?" Adria asked after giving her statement to the police. She was seated in a dingy interrogation room, her chair on one side of an old Formica-topped table, Zach leaning on wainscoting near the door. The room was bare save for the ever-present smell of smoke, an overflowing ashtry and a trash can half filled with empty plastic coffee cups.

The man in charge was Detective John Fullmer, who wore thick glasses and whose one vanity seemed to be to disguise his baldness by combing long, sandy-colored strands of hair from the back of his head forward.

Fullmer was full of nervous energy. He smoked and chewed gum at the same time, alternately popping his stick of Wrigley's spearmint and taking a drag from his Camel.

It had been hours since Zach had discovered Ginny's body and Adria had believed that Ginny, knowing that she would be exposed as a kidnapper, had decided to end her own life. Fullmer had other ideas.

Warming her hands around a strong cup of coffee, Adria asked, "But how would someone have known where to find her?"

"We're not sure yet, and we don't like to give out the kind of information that only the killer would know, but there are clues. The window had been forced, so it looks like someone was in the house, waiting for her." He took off his glasses and polished them with the hem of his shirt. His gum snapped loudly.

Zach stared at Adria. "It's because she's left-handed," he said flatly. The razor was in his her right hand and she was left-handed. The slashes were angled wrong."

The detective's head snapped up and he stared at Zach, long and hard. "You know that?"

"I remember." Zach's gaze traveled to the center of the room but Adria guessed he was miles away, lost in a time when he was only a boy.

"How?" Adria asked.

"Because once . . . a long time ago when London was still living with us, Ginny had a pair of scissors—used them for mending, I think. She left them out once and I picked them up. I had to open some package and couldn't find my knife. I tried to use her damned scissors, but they didn't work. I couldn't figure it out for a minute, then I discovered they were left-handed. Unique at the time. Ginny caught me and had a fit, told me to leave her things alone." He shrugged. "We didn't get along all that well." His gaze focused on Adria again. "But that's no surprise."

The detective drew on his cigarette, then crushed it in the full tray. "I don't have an official report on cause of death. We'll have to wait for the ME for that, but it looks like someone subdued her, took the razor, wrapped the fingers of her right hand around it and opened her veins. End of story."

Adria shuddered and rubbed her arms.

The detective dumped the ashtray into the trash, before lighting up again.

They talked for a while more, then were allowed to leave. "Look, we know you two didn't do old Ginny in," the detective said, handing them each a card, "but we might have a few more questions . . ."

Zach's eyes met Adria's. "You can find us through Danvers International, or the Hotel Danvers in Portland," he said, scribbling the numbers on the back of a business card for his construction company in Bend.

They left the station and Adria felt drained, her entire life turned inside out.

So she was London Danvers.

So she would inherit millions of dollars.

So what?

"Come on, I'll buy you dinner," Zach offered, though he looked as tired as she. Beneath the shadow of his beard his tanned skin seemed paler, his eyes haunted. The strain was telling on them both and she wondered how long they could keep up this charade, pretend that the attraction they felt for each other didn't exist. "I know a great place in Chinatown. We'll stay in town tonight, then go home and break the news."

Home. Would she ever think of Portland as home?

She shuddered to think how quickly Ginny's life had ended. "Who do you think could have done it?"

"I wish I knew," he said, frowning as they stepped outside where darkness had fallen. The wind blowing in off the ocean was cold, cutting in icy gusts that climbed the steep hills of the city; it swept through her jacket and cut her to the bone. Or was she shivering from an inner frost?

Zach took her hand in his. She tried to pull away, but his fingers tightened over hers as they walked the three blocks to the space where he'd parked the rental car.

Once inside the Ford, he checked the mirror, then melded with traffic. "Watch in your side view," he said, moving from one lane to the other.

"You think someone is following us."

"Good guess, don't you think?"

"Here in San Francisco?" she asked, but she'd leaped to the same conclusions as he, the same one drawn by the police.

"You think that we led the murderer . . ." Her voice trailed off and she stared hard in the mirror, watching other cars switch lanes, seeing nothing out of the ordinary.

"Obviously there was a conspiracy of some kind years ago," Zach said, his brows drawing together. "And it didn't involve your mother or . . . or Witt. So we have to assume that whoever wanted you out of the picture then, was willing to kill Ginny to keep his secret."

"But who?" she whispered.

"Could be anyone."

"Someone in the family."

"Maybe."

"Or someone from the Polidori family," she said, though the list of suspects was shrinking. True, Anthony Polidori could have been behind the kidnapping and she was certain that he was having her followed, but the Danvers heirs as well, could have been a part of the kidnapping. Jason was power-hungry, Trisha a wounded animal wanting to hurt her father as much as she was hurt by him. Nelson would have been too young, only about fourteen at the time, and Zach, he was a kid, too.

Satisfied that they weren't being tailed, Zachary drove to Chinatown and parked in an alley. The restaurant was small, noisy, dimly lit, and packed nearly to capacity. Dishes rattled, people spoke in sharp foreign phrases, and grease sizzled through the open window to the kitchen. They were offered a table for two near the kitchen and Adria didn't object, though she could barely understand the waitress or any of the patrons who all seemed to speak rapid-fire Chinese.

Still, she was grateful for the crowd. It made things easier. Being alone with Zachary was the difficult part. They ate hot and sour soup, spicy chicken, and some shrimp dish that was so hot her nose ran and washed it all down with Chinese beer. She felt the tension drain from her shoulders and even managed a smile.

After the meal, she drank a thin tea with a flowery aroma that filtered up her nose and brought back a memory—harsh and ugly. The night of the attack, she'd smelled something sweet as this blend—the underlying scent of jasmine. Her fingers slipped. The cup slid to the table and rolled, spilling tea across the varnished surface. Hot tea dripped from the table to her thighs.

"Adria?" Zach asked.

She knew in the instant the smell of jasmine had reached her nostrils who had attacked her.

"What is it?" Zach demanded, staring at her with harsh gray eyes.

"Everything." She started wiping up the tea, refusing to look at him, telling herself over and over again she had to be wrong. But she knew. She *knew*. He grabbed her hand, squeezing it, refusing to let her keep mopping the spill with her napkin.

"What, damn it?"

"I think I know who attacked me in the motel," she said unevenly, wishing she didn't know the truth.

"What?"

"The person who sent me the nasty notes."

"How?"

"This tea." She motioned to the cups on the table. "It's jasmine, the same scent that was with the person who attacked me."

A knot formed at the hinge of his jaw and he sniffed the brew. Denial seemed about to fall from his tongue before he shoved the cup of tea away, sloshing hot tea onto the table. "Eunice," he bit out, his eyes mere slits.

Adria nodded, mutely, unable to form the words that hovered between them—that Zachary's mother had killed Ginny Slade.

Somehow they managed to duck the press—though the news was out: Adria Nash was London Danvers. The newspapers in San Francisco screamed the horrid truth and when they arrived in Portland the following afternoon, the television reporters had laid siege to the Hotel Danvers and Jason's house in the hills. Sooner or later, Adria would be forced to give a statement, but first and foremost, she had to face the woman who had tried to kill her.

Zach, tight-lipped, didn't say a word as he drove to his mother's house on the shores of Lake Oswego. The wipers slapped the rain off the windshield and Zach's knuckles showed white as he gripped the steering wheel.

Though it was early afternoon, lights blazed from the windows of the house. Adria's palms were sweating, her heart knocking as they walked up the stone path to the small porch. Zach knocked loudly, his fist hammering the door with the silent fury that was evident in the lines of his face.

He waited impatiently as the door was slowly opened and his mother, wearing a silk wrapper, opened the door. "Zach?" she said, her face lighting a little on her second son, but then her gaze landed on Adria and that little spark of hope, the tiny flame of joy in her eyes, was extinguished quickly.

Using the flat of his hand, he pushed the door open wider and walked into the house that had always seemed sterile to him with everything in its proper place, undisturbed by the reckless play of children. No grass dragged in off the lawn, no balls or bats or shoes left carelessly at the door. Not here. Now when she'd lived in San Francisco with her second husband, Dr. Lyle Smythe. As he passed her, the scent of her perfume with the underlying odor of jasmine reminded him of how vengeful she could be. "We need to talk."

"Do we?" She managed a thin smile. "Couldn't it wait?"

"Until the cops get here?" he asked cruelly and she flinched a little, her gaze hardening on Adria.

"What's going on?"

"It's over, Eunice," he said, refusing to use any kind of endearment.

"I don't know—"

"Don't bullshit me, Mom," he snarled and Adria saw it then, the deep pain in his eyes, the disbelief and silent agony of a boy who'd lost his last vestige of faith in someone he'd once loved.

Eunice, limping slightly, led them into a clutter-free kitchen. A cat was curled on one of the thick cushions in the caned-backed chairs at the table. A crystal vase was filled with fresh-cut chrysanthemums and ferns.

Lips pursed, Eunice seemed calm, outwardly going through the motions of being the perfect hostess, except that her hands shook as she poured three cups of coffee.

"We don't need coffee," Zach said.

"I do."

Somewhere in a neighboring yard a dog began to bark. Eunice's Persian cat lifted his head, yawned and stretched, then closed its eyes again.

"Sit down," Eunice said in a voice barely above a whisper.

"No thanks."

"Sit down, Zach, and drink a cup of coffee with me," she said lifting her chin proudly. "It might be the last one we'll be able to share together for a long time."

When he didn't respond, she dropped into one of the empty chairs and though her head seemed heavy, she sat as stiffly as if she had iron cables running through her spine. Adria ignored her cup and stood near the window. "You're here because of Ginny," Eunice said, pouring a thin stream of cream into her cup.

"That's right." Zach's voice was rough.

"I didn't kill her."

"Oh, come on—"

"It's true," she said desperately, her eyes pleading as she stared up at him. Even to Adria, he seemed to loom over the table, a big man with wide shoulders and sleek muscles and a fury so intense, his lips were flat and bloodless against his teeth. "Don't lie, Mother, it doesn't suit you," he snarled.

"I'm telling you the truth, Zach. Oh, I wanted to kill her, Lord knows I did, but I'm not a murderer. No matter what your father reduced me to, no matter how hard he tried to humiliate me, I couldn't kill." She took a sip from her coffee and stared vacantly at the cat. "If I was ever going to kill anyone it would have been Witt when he stole you kids from me."

Zach let out a snort of disbelief. He grabbed Adria's purse from her arm and poured it onto the table. Lipstick, comb, brush, wallet, keys, and letters fell out—duplicates of the letters she'd left with the police. Stabbing a finger at one of the ugly notes, Zach said, "You didn't send these?"

Her hand trembled as she rubbed a graying eyebrow. "That's my work, yes," she said. Drawing in a fortifying breath she looked up at Adria. "And I attacked you in the motel, I was so upset . . . the fact that you two were . . . oh, my God." She held out her hands in supplication. "I couldn't stand the thought of you together." She blinked rapidly. "You . . . You're brother and sister," she said, disgust evident in her features. Her nostrils flared. "You, Zach, my favorite and that tramp Katherine's daughter." Her fingers wiggled uselessly in the air. "And it was my fault, all my fault. If I hadn't meddled . . ." Her voice was reduced to a painful little squeak and she sniffed loudly, sagging against the back of her chair as the first tears dampened her dry eyes.

Adria leaned hard against the window.

"You mustn't believe those stories about Anthony. He's not your father. I checked, I wanted, oh, God, I prayed that you weren't Witt's son, but . . ." Her voice cracked and she battled against unwanted tears.

"I hated Witt. He did . . . unconscionable things to me. To you children. But during the divorce, I was weak, I didn't fight hard enough, I didn't want to lose what little self-respect I had and in the end I lost you. All of you, my children. Then Witt remarried to that . . . that god-awful crude woman who was barely older than Jason." Her nose wrinkled as if at a vile smell. "And somehow she managed to conceive. Despite the fact that Witt Danvers had been nearly impotent for years, that slutty little bitch managed to conceive and give him a daughter whom he thought was the most precious creature on earth. His 'princess.' His 'darling.' His damned little 'treasure.' It was sickening, believe me.

"Forget that he already had three sons and a daughter. He didn't care." She glared at Adria and pure hatred glimmered in her eyes. Venom seemed to drip through her words. "He would have done anything for you, little London, but not for my children. My family was unraveling at the seams and I thought if I could do anything, give my children any lasting gift it would be to get rid of you." She sighed heavily and stared at the vase of autumn flowers on the table. "But I couldn't kill you and that was my mistake. There was always the chance of this happening, of you returning to make my children's lives hell."

"After all this, you expect us to believe that you didn't kill Ginny Slade?" Adria asked, but Eunice's eyes focused only on her son.

"You'll believe what you want to believe, won't you, Zach? You always have and you always will. But as long as I'm unburdening myself, I'll tell you everything. Yes, I paid Ginny Slade fifty thousand dollars to steal London away; I didn't care where she took her just as long as she promised never to reappear." Eunice's shadowed eyes moved to Adria a minute. As if pulled by invisible strings, her lips pursed into a tiny tight frown. "Looks like Ginny didn't live up to her end of the bargain, did she?"

Sighing, she closed her eyes and rubbed her temples. "I was living in San Francisco at the time—remarried to Lyle and supposedly happy, so I assumed I would never be suspected and, really, since I knew Jack Logan, it wasn't hard to convince him that I had nothing to do with the crime. As far as anyone knew . . . oh, well . . . and then Lyle died and I moved back here to be closer to my family.

"When I first saw you," she said looking up at Adria with an expression of revulsion, "I knew you were the real thing, you look so much like *her*. You couldn't have belonged to anyone else. And then I saw how Zach was taken with you, how he was going to lose his heart to . . . oh, dear God, I couldn't just stand by and let it happen. So I wrote the notes, even managed to steal a key and sneak into your hotel room, and then when that didn't work, I thought I'd discourage you by physically confronting you."

"And when you got hurt you told Nelson that you tripped while chasing the cat," Zach interjected. "That's why you're still limping."

She lifted a shoulder.

But Zach wasn't finished. "And then you followed us to San Francisco and killed Ginny."

"No, Zach, no matter what you might believe of me, I'm not a murderer. Ask Nelson. On the night Ginny was killed he was here with me."

"He'd lie for you."

"I was here, Zach."

"I don't trust Nelson."

"Then trust his friend." She lifted her chin and met Zach's condemning stare. "Nelson was with someone the night he was here. They didn't stay all night, of course, because I'm not supposed to know that Tom is Nelson's lover, but they stopped by for a few hours—just old pals, you know—and we had dinner and played cards."

"You'll have to tell this to the police."

"I know," she said. "I've already contacted a lawyer. I did that after Ginny was killed. I figured you'd come back here." She smiled ruefully and reached up to touch his cheek, but he stepped back before her fingers grazed the line of his jaw. Pain contorted her features. "You always were the smart one, Zach. My best and brightest. My favorite."

Usually, Anthony Polidori didn't like to be awakened from sleep, but when the informant called and told him that Eunice Danvers Smythe had been arrested for the kidnapping of London Danvers, Anthony smiled to himself and thanked the man for his information. Too bad Eunice had been the culprit.

He felt more than a little sense of guilt thinking of her for, he knew, that she'd fallen in love with him thirty-five years before. He'd cared for her, yes, but he hadn't loved her with the same passion she'd felt for him and, in truth, he'd only bedded her to get back at Witt. Eunice had guessed his reasons. They'd been kindred spirits in that sense, enjoying each other at Witt's expense.

The bastard.

So Eunice had decided to destroy Witt's life. Although for years his family had been blamed for the deed, Anthony was amused at her gall. Maybe he shouldn't have been so hasty to drop her once Witt had discovered their affair.

He climbed out of his bed and found a striped robe that was worn in the sleeves and tattered at the hem. His wife had bought it for him nearly half a century before and though it was merely a rag, he had never had the heart to get rid of it.

He wondered if Mario was home or if he was with some woman; not that it mattered. Shuffling down the tiled hallway he thought back over his life and was surprised that the deep-seeded hatred he'd felt for the Danvers family had seemed to dim over the years.

He rapped on the door and waited. Nothing. Knocking harder, he scowled, then tried the knob. It was locked. "Mario, son, open up."

He heard a groggy response.

"Come, open the door."

"Jesus Christ." Growling and kicking things in his way, Mario finally appeared, his hair wild, his beard dark. "Wha—?"

"We need to talk."

"Are you out of your mind? It's four in the morning!"

"Get up and come downstairs."

Mario rubbed a hand over his face and yawned. As he stretched his back popped. "Let me get my cigarettes and slippers," he said, then turning, tripped over something else and swore under his breath.

The boy would never grow up.

Anthony made his way downstairs and had uncorked a bottle of champagne by the time his only son stumbled into the kitchen. "What the hell's going on?" Mario said. He rubbed his teeth with his tongue and shuddered.

"We're celebrating."

"Shit, couldn't it have waited until a decent hour—you know, six or seven in the morning?"

"No. And this is no time for sarcasm."

"Whatever you say, Pop." Mario clicked a lighter to the end of his cigarette. "Okay, I'm dyin' to know. What's up?"

"Several things. Come, come." Anthony patted the arm of his chair and indicated that Mario should sit on it as he had when he was a boy. Spewing smoke from the corner of his mouth, he obliged the old man. "Good. Here—" Anthony held a glass to his son, then, after Mario had taken the crystal goblet, touched the rim of his with his sons. "To the future."

"Yeah. Right. The future." Mario, thinking the old man had really lost it and was one step away from the loony bin, began to drink, but his father's hand stayed him. "And to the end of the feud."

"Christ!"

"All right. To God as well," Anthony said magnanimously.

"What're you talking about? The fucking feud is over? How can that be? You crack out the best champagne and just make some sort of statement that it's over and all the shit that's gone on for nearly a hundred years is forgotten? Just like that?" Mario snapped his fingers loudly. Then he rubbed his eyes. "I'm dreaming. That's what this is—a fuckin' nightmare."

"One more thing we are celebrating."

"Oh, great. What's that?"

"Your marriage."

"Now I know I'm dreaming."

"No, Mario. It's time. You need a wife. I need grandchildren. We have to think of the future and not the past. You'll be married and have children and we will all be happy."

"Oh, sure, right. What happened tonight, eh?" Mario asked. "When I went to bed everything was the same and now you're dragging me out of bed, talking like a goddamned fortune-teller. Did you get knocked over the head or what?"

Anthony ignored his son's raving and clicked his glass yet again to the rim of Mario's. There were many possibilities for a wife for his son and he hadn't ruled out Adria Nash—London Danvers—as a potential candidate. She was beautiful and rich and smart. Who could ask for anything more from a daughter-in-law? Of course there was the chance she wouldn't want him. Well, there were other eligible young women. Fertile women, beautiful, but not necessarily as smart as this London. Perhaps they would suit Mario better . . .

"There's only one woman I've ever wanted to marry," Mario said, suddenly sober and Anthony had to tamp down his old feelings of disgust. "Trisha."

Gritting his teeth, he said, "I won't stand in your way." Then, he took a sip of his champagne, stared up at his son's disbelieving face and laughed, long and hearty, as he hadn't laughed in years. He patted Mario on the knee with a fondness that he'd forgotten—a fondness he'd once felt when his wife was still alive, and Mario was four or five and hardly any trouble at all. "Drink up. Enjoy. And let me tell you what happened tonight. . . ."

Zach was grim as they walked out of central station in Portland. He'd watched without a word as the police, Eunice's lawyer, and Nelson had arrived, all arguing and shouting. Jason, too, had shown up and his mood had been sour. Trisha, when she'd deigned to appear in a full-length ermine coat, no less, had breezed past Adria and said to Zach, "Now look what you've done."

A crowd of reporters was clustered near the door. Voices shouted over one another, trying to capture her attention.

"Ms. Nash? Is it true that you've finally proven yourself to be London Danvers?"

"It looks that way, yes."

"How does it feel to finally know your natural family?"

"I haven't sorted it all out yet."

"You're inheriting a great deal of money, aren't you? What are your plans?"

"I don't have any yet."

Zach looked about to step in, but Adria placed a hand over his arm. "Look," she said, speaking into the microphones thrust in her direction. "I'm very tired right now. Of course I'm glad to know that I'm London," she said, refusing to meet Zach's eyes, refusing to listen to the pain in her heart knowing that he was her half-brother, "and I've no immediate plans for the future."

"Will you move to Portland permanently?"

"I don't know."

"What about the charges pending against Eunice Smythe?"

"I can't comment on them."

"Is it true she attacked you in that motel in Estacada?"

"I have nothing more to say at this time."

"But now that you're one of the wealthiest women in the state, surely you—"

"Excuse me."

She shouldered her way through the crowd and Zach was with her every step of the way. She couldn't meet his eyes, didn't want to think about her future. For nearly a year she'd thought that if she could prove that she was London, if she could find her real family, her life would change for the better. She could make a difference. She'd fantasized about the money, of course, and seen herself as a shrewd businesswoman who would sit on the board of charities as well as handle the affairs of Danvers International. Witt Danvers's little lost princess. The treasure he'd loved above all else, including his other children.

She'd been a fool. A silly fool with girlish dreams.

And she hadn't planned on falling in love with Zachary.

They climbed into his Jeep and Zachary nosed the Cherokee into the street. Half a dozen cars followed his lead. "Great," he muttered, eyeing the rear-view mirror. "Just great." He glanced at Adria. She was dead tired, leaning against the window, staring at him with those damned eyes that seemed to see straight to his soul. "They'll be at the hotel," he said, turning abruptly and watching the headlights follow him. "Vultures."

He drove crazily, changing lanes at the last minute and turning corners abruptly. She sensed the change in direction, saw the towering lights of downtown fade behind them.

"Where are we going?"

"Someplace private."

"Just the two of us?"

He hesitated, his fingers curling over the steering wheel until his knuckles showed white, then nodded curtly. Something inside her—something moist and dusky—began to awaken. "Just the two of us."

Jack Logan was too old to be driving like a wild man, chasing a lunatic in a Jeep. He was tired and grumpy and if it wasn't for the bottle of Irish whiskey that kept him going, he would have called Jason Danvers and told him to follow his own damned family. But he'd been paid and paid well and he figured that later he could sleep all day if he wanted to.

Retirement hadn't settled well with him; he missed the action and excitement of the department. True, his arthritis was bad enough to make him limp and he wasn't as quick as he used to be, but his mind was sharp and he could spend only so much time gardening or fiddling with the damned workbench his daughter, Risa, had insisted was so therapeutic. No, he missed the sport of it all, the feeling alive and hated the notion that just because he'd reached a certain age, he'd been put out to pasture.

So he kept taking Danvers money, not so much to supplement his Social Security and pension, but to keep his blood pumping, to make him feel alive again. He followed the Jeep, hanging back, turning off at different streets, nearly losing the rig several times, but always finding it again.

He had an uncanny sense about these things and he guessed where the rig was heading in its crazy, zigzagging course that always led north, toward the interstate bridge, toward the huge body of water separating the southern boundary of Washington from Oregon: the Columbia River and the marina where the Danvers yacht was berthed.

The Jeep turned off the interstate and Logan continued on, driving across the bridge, barely noticing the wide black abyss that was the Columbia. On the far side of the river, in Vancouver, just over the Washington border, he turned his car around and headed back to the freeway, this time heading south. To celebrate he took a little nip from his bottle and drove unerringly back to the marina. Flashing his outdated badge at the guard manning the gate, he drove quietly into the parking lot and saw Zachary's Jeep tucked in a darkened space.

Bingo.

"You still got it, Logan," he told himself and uncapped his bottle yet again before taking a long swallow that warmed the pit of his stomach and spread through his blood. He didn't have one of those cellular phones, but he knew there was a Safeway store nearby with a couple of phone booths near the front doors. He'd let Jason sweat a while, have himself a couple of drinks at a topless bar not all that far away, then call the bastard. While he was at it, he might just ask for a raise. Hell, he deserved it.

23

The smell of the river rose off the water and tickled
Adria's nostrils and a gusty midnight breeze teased at the wild
strands of her hair. She was here, on a gleaming white yacht,
alone with Zach for the last time in her life. She should be happy,
she'd gotten what she'd wanted and yet . . . a horrid weight had
settled upon her shoulders as she thought about the future:
barren, bleak, without love. Without Zach.

"Drink?" he asked, once they climbed down a short staircase
and entered the main salon that was decorated in gleaming teak
and brass.

"I—I guess," she said, though she shook her head and
dropped onto a burgundy sofa that was part of the wall. Tears
were suddenly very near. She crossed her arms over her middle
and sighed. "I don't know what I want."

"What?" he mocked, pouring them each a snifter of brandy.
"You've got it all, London—"

"Don't call me that."

"Why not? You worked hard to be her."

"I just . . . it just doesn't feel right." He stood before her, tall,
rugged, unshaven, his jeans riding low on his hips, looking like
he belonged on the range . . . or in her bed and he was off-limits.
Forever.

"Better get used to it." He handed her a glass and their fingers
touched ever so briefly, but Adria felt his heat. Damning the fates,
she took her brandy, sipped, then tossed it back, hoping that the
alcohol that burned down the back of her throat and settled in
her stomach would dull her senses so that when she looked at

him she wouldn't feel this painful agony in her heart, that she wouldn't remember the electricity of his touch, the power of his gaze, the texture of his skin rubbing intimately against hers.

She held her glass up for a refill and he cocked an interested eyebrow. But there was no amusement in his eyes, just flint-gray desire. His jaw slid to one side. "Getting drunk?"

"Maybe."

"Not a good idea."

"Don't lecture me," she said, standing quickly and marching to the bar. She poured herself a healthy shot and swirled the amber liquor in her glass. Already she felt the effects of her first drink, the mellow warmth running through her blood, a fresh boldness. Longing, deep and forbidden, began to uncoil and stretch within her. "So what're you going to do, Zach? Now that I'm your half-sister?"

"Run like hell."

"You're still here."

"There's still a murderer out there somewhere."

"And you don't think he's given up?"

"Never."

"So you're going to what—stick around until he's behind bars? Be my personal bodyguard?" she asked, sipping more of the brandy.

"That's the plan."

"Maybe I don't want a bodyguard," she said, giving into the impulse to say what was on her mind. "Maybe I want a lover."

"Then you'll have to find yourself one, won't you?" He downed his drink and ignored the urge to pour himself another and another after that. Getting shit-faced wouldn't help the situation. Adria was already losing control, not that he blamed her. They'd both been wound tight as watch springs.

She regarded the bottom of her glass sullenly, then pinned him with her erotic blue eyes. "But I want you."

He closed his eyes and swore under his breath. "You can't—it's impossible."

Finishing her drink in a flourish, she took a bold step toward him and shook her head. Black hair moved around her face like a gleaming ebony cloud. "You want me, too."

"Christ, Adria, don't do this," he said, his voice strained, his eyes dark as the night. She didn't stop until she reached him, then stood on her tiptoes, ran her fingers up his chest and pressed her full, anxious lips to his.

"We've done it before."

"Not when we knew—oh, God."

She nuzzled his neck, then touched the seam of his lips with her tongue. His bones threatened to melt and with all the will-power he could gather, he grabbed her quickly by both wrists.

"Don't, Adria!"

"Zach, please, I love you—"

"For God's sake, you can't! I can't!" His brain argued with him. *Why not? It's not as though you haven't stepped over this threshold before. One last time and then goodbye, adios, forever. Take her, take her now!* Desire thundered like stampeding cattle, racing through his blood and pounding at his temples. The pressure of his hard sex against his zipper was hot and urgent. He closed his eyes to block out the anxious, loving look shining in her eyes. "We'll regret this," he ground out, feeling like a powder keg ready to explode.

"Never," and the pain in her voice broke through his hard shell.

Shoving her up against the wall, he kissed her, brutally, angrily. He still pinned her hands above her head as his lips and tongue assaulted her. Her breasts were heaving, rising and falling beneath her jacket and he cupped one in his hands. "Is this what you want, London?" he said, forcing the furious words over his tongue as he wedged his pelvis between the V of her thighs, pressing hard against her mound.

Her eyes widened in horror. "I'm not—"

"You are! And you'd better face it!"

Inside he was shaking with desire, ready to throw caution to the wind and take her willing body. The barrier of their clothing was thin, easily destroyed and then they would be naked. Alone. Man and woman.

Brother and half-sister.

No! If they didn't stop this dangerous game, he would give into the urges running rampant through his body and take her. Hell, if she didn't stop looking at him like that— He kissed her again and this time the kiss wasn't punishing and he let go of her hands, dragging her body against him and losing himself in the wonder of her. He wound his fingers in the thick tangles of her black hair and felt her mouth open to him. His tongue explored, sleekly darting in and out and she moaned so softly he barely heard it.

He reached for her breast, delving into her bra, feeling the tense little nipple, hearing the sound of want deep in her throat.

"I . . . I can't," she whispered, tears streaming down her cheeks.

"I know." He swallowed back his lust just as he heard it—the sound that was out of place—of leather against boards. His galloping heart stopped for a second.

They weren't alone.

Hell!

Slowly lifting his head, he placed his hand over her mouth and motioned for her to be quiet. Over his calloused fingers he saw her eyebrows draw together for a second, then shoot upward. She got the message. "Stay here," he whispered against her ear.

"No—" she said against his hand, but he shot her a look that brooked no argument, motioned for her to go back into the cabins and slowly, quietly, mounted the stairs.

Her heart pounding, she watched in mind-numbing fear. What if the person on deck was the murderer—who else could it be? She couldn't let Zachary fight him alone. Quickly, she searched the salon for a weapon, found nothing and took the stairs silently to the deck.

"—so it doesn't matter if she's your sister or not, you still want to fuck her." Jason was leaning against the boom, standing on the main deck, the night wind causing his jacket to flap. Rain was beginning to fall in fat drops as he glared at his younger brother. "Christ, Zach, you never learn, do you? First Kat, now her daughter."

"You were with Kat," Zach reminded him. He stood with his back to the stairwell, his eyes trained on his brother.

"I didn't move on to London."

"But you killed Ginny."

Jason frowned darkly and Adria crouched in the shadows, hiding on the steps, her heart thudding as she bit her lip to keep from crying out. Maybe there was a phone in the cabin.

"Couldn't let her go shooting her mouth off," Jason admitted.

"But how did you know about her?"

"I didn't. Not until Sweeny located her and then I had you followed to San Francisco." Adria tried to slink back down the steps, but Jason only smiled as he saw her and waved her up to the deck. "Welcome, sister," he said. Her blood congealed as she saw the gun in his hand. "How does it feel to be the wealthiest woman in Portland?"

"What are you doing here?" she demanded.

"Just having a chat with my siblings."

"How'd you find us?" Zach said.

"I knew you'd be together somewhere, it was just a matter of figuring out where you'd want to spend your little illicit tryst. Jesus, Zach, I knew you were always a rebel, but screwing your own sister—?"

"You bastard!" Zach lunged and Jason smiled a cold, calculated grin that caused Adria's heart to freeze.

"No!" she cried, expecting to hear the sharp report of a gun. Instead, Jason sidestepped and shoved the boom, which was no longer tied down at his brother. The heavy wood swung free catching Zach across his midsection and throwing him against the rail. He nearly lost his balance.

"No!" Adria screamed, lunging for him, but it was too late. Jason tackled his brother and hit Zachary squarely in the back of his head with the butt of the gun. Zach kicked upward and caught Jason in the groin. Jason roared and doubled over in pain. Staggering, Zach tried to kick his brother again, but Jason was quick. He caught Zach's boot, jammed Zach against the rail and twisted his leg.

Adria jumped on Jason's back, kicking and clawing, fighting with every ounce of strength in her, but Jason turned Zach's ankle again. Zach let out a yell as Adria heard the sickening sound of tendons ripping from bone. Jason shoved, hurtling his brother into the cold dark waters of the Columbia. Into the river—just like Mark Kennedy all those years ago. "Oh God, oh, God," Adria cried, kicking harder.

Jason flung her off. "You've been trouble from the first time I saw you." His gun was aimed right at her heart, but she didn't care. Not while Zach was drowning.

"Ditto, *brother*," she said, fury surging through her veins. She started peeling off her jacket.

"You won't last two minutes in that water," Jason predicted, lowering his weapon when he realized he wouldn't need to use the revolver. She was going to kill herself. For Zach. "It's cold enough to freeze—"

"Rot in hell, you bastard," she screamed before diving into the brackish water and praying that she'd find Zachary.

Jason watched her slice through the air before he could hit her over the head and make sure she drowned. He charged forward, but it was too late. She was airborne, then disappeared beneath the surface and his only hope that she would drown or freeze. Either way the result would be the same.

He was certain Zach was dead and that bothered him a little. He'd always felt a grudging respect for his younger brother. Rebellious, irreverent, a pain in the ass, Zach did things his own way, by his own code of honor. Years ago, when he was just a kid, Zach hadn't told the truth about Sophia, the whore Jason had set him up with on the night London had disappeared. Of course, it had been a setup.

Though Jason had no idea that London would be kidnapped

that night, he'd been smart enough to realize that Sophia's room would probably be visited by Joey and Rudy or some other goons who'd been on the Polidori payroll because Jason had made a little bet and hadn't bothered paying off.

Just between him and Mario. Neither of the old men had any idea that Mario was running a little gaming on the side. Witt was too involved with his hatred of the Polidoris and his adoration of London, and Anthony thought Mario didn't have any brains at all. And Zach had kept his mouth shut. For all those years. Well, he was dead now and it was probably easier that way.

Slowly Jason walked the deck, looking in the water for any sign of life, praying that London was finally dead. Too bad that she was so damned beautiful, so much like her mother. He grimaced. Kat's suicide had started it all. She'd taken a bottle of pills and more booze than she could handle when Witt suspected that she and Jason were involved. For days afterward, Jason had carried around a shitload of guilt, but eventually, though he felt badly, he'd accepted her death and realized that her being dead made things much better for him. He and the rest of his siblings would eventually inherit all of Danvers International.

Unless London ever reappeared.

When Adria had shown up, he'd panicked. Sweeny's news that she was really London was a hard blow, but he'd known instinctively what had to be done. Surprisingly, he'd found it easier than he'd thought to kill—not that he'd actually butchered Ginny. He couldn't risk the alibi. But he'd found someone at the Red Eye Café who was willing to take care of it. For a lousy five grand. He'd done a decent job and Jason had his alibi all sewn up.

Paying for Ginny to be killed had been easy, he'd never cared for the woman, it was almost as if she'd been a stranger. But killing Zach—by his own hand—was much harder and Adria . . . He gritted his teeth and prided himself on doing a job well done. Then he began to scream.

"Help! Help! Can anyone hear me! Man overboard!" He raced downstairs, found the phone and punched out 911. He gave himself time until the first person on a neighboring boat appeared and the sound of sirens screamed in the distance. Then he kicked off his shoes, tossed off his jacket, and dove into the water to wait. By the time the police arrived, the current would have swept the remains of the newly found London Danvers and her lover—her half-brother—out to sea. The police might suspect him, but it would never be proven . . . two more lives claimed by the power of the river.

Zach coughed and drew in water and coughed again. He was cold. So damned cold and his head felt as if it had been hit by a two-by-four. Instinctively, he struggled upward, feeling the current pull him downstream. He surfaced, gasped deep lungfuls of air and was swept under again.

His muscles felt sluggish, one leg barely moved, but he forced himself to the surface and drew in another deep breath. Something was wrong—horribly wrong, but he couldn't remember what. He breathed in air and water and saw lights, not that far away, and he began to swim, still coughing, dragging his body through the water, feeling the icy fingers of the river try to pull him under yet again.

Then he remembered and he pushed himself harder, plowing through the water, wishing the dead weight in his right leg would fall off.

Adria! She was with Jason on the yacht. Oh, God, if she wasn't already dead. Adrenaline surged through his blood and he swam faster, ignoring the frigid cold, refusing to give into the cramping in his muscles and driving himself through the water. He only hoped it wasn't too late.

He was nearly a quarter of a mile downstream when he finally grabbed hold of a piling, and coughing and shivering dragged himself out of the water. He'd lost a boot during the ordeal and he kicked off the other, when the pain in his ankle reminded him that he couldn't walk. Gritting his teeth, he scrambled up the bank as best he could. Hopping on one leg, he pulled himself forward, over a concrete embankment, and discovered himself at an all-night service station.

Under flickering fluorescent lights, an attendant with a butt of a cigarette burning on his lips took one look at Zach and reached under the counter for his gun. "Jesus H. Christ, would you look at that?" he said to the empty room.

"Call the police," Zach ordered.

"No shit, I'll call the police . . ." With the gun aimed at Zach's midsection, he reached for the phone and dialed with trembling fingers. "Hey, this is Louie at the Texaco just off Marine Drive. We got ourselves a little problem here. . . ."

Within minutes a squad car arrived and Zach was given a blanket and driven, shivering, back to the yacht. Escorted by two officers, he hobbled onto the deck and found Jason who had just been plucked from the river himself. Boats were trolling, search lights skimming the whitecaps. Dread, like acid, ate a hole in his gut.

"Where's Adria?" he demanded and Jason, looking at Zachary as if he'd seen a ghost, couldn't say a word. "Where is she?" Zachary lunged at his brother, nearly falling as his ankle gave out, but his fists closed around Jason's sodden shirt. "If she's hurt, I'll kill you, you bastard!"

"Hey, take it easy," one of the cops yelled as Zach's fist smashed into his brother's jaw. "You can't—" Two men peeled him off his brother.

"You murdering bastard, you goddamned murdering bastard! Where is she?" Zach yelled.

One of the patrolmen who had been with Jason said, "Mr. Danvers reported that she dived in, searching for you after you fell into the water."

"Fell? Like hell!"

"Zach," Jason said, his voice full of reproach. "I'm sorry—" And Zach knew instantly what he wanted. As he had years ago, Jason was quietly asking Zach to cover for him, to hide the fact that he was involved. Screw that!

"You tried to kill me," he said through gritted teeth. "For all I know, you tried to kill her, too."

"We'll sort this out downtown," one of the officers said.

"No way! You've got to find her!" Zach insisted, trying to reach the rail. Desperately, he searched the black waters. "You've got to!"

"It's been over half an hour, Mr. Danvers—"

Zach flung himself to the rail, his eyes squinting against the darkness. He started to climb over but felt one hand being yanked behind his back, then the second wrenched behind him as handcuffs clicked into place.

"You can't—"

"Come on, Mr. Danvers.

He tried to struggle but his ankle gave out, sending pain jarring up his leg. The officers shoved him into a waiting car.

Zach hadn't slept in days. One twenty-four-hour period seemed to bleed into the next and he had no idea of the time, or the date, just lived with the sickening knowledge that both Jason and his mother were behind bars. Jason's accomplice, a burly man on parole, had been shooting his mouth off in a bar near Fisherman's Wharf and a police informant had nailed him. It hadn't taken much persuasion to get him to talk and Jason's name had come up.

Nicole, already having packed Shelly off to Santa Fe, was clamoring for a divorce and Kim had made a quick disappearance. No one had seen her, though many suspected it had been she who first told the press about Adria being London Danvers. As far as Zach was concerned, his older brother and his mistress deserved everything they got and more.

Trisha had sworn off Mario Polidori for good, telling him bluntly to get out of her life when he'd asked her to marry him. Zach didn't believe it would last. Trisha was and always had been a fool where Mario was concerned.

As for Nelson, he finally seemed to get some backbone and

was actually trying to help his mother. For years he'd been a lost soul, trying to balance who he was with who he thought he should be, still trying to please his father.

Most people thought that Adria was dead.

Pain zeroed in on his heart and spread through his body.

The police and volunteers had searched the river, dredged where they could, but the news reporters and the police speculated that her body had been washed out to sea, claimed by the giant Pacific. He closed his eyes and felt the hot pressure of tears against his eyelids. He hadn't cried for years and yet now he felt reduced to bawling like a damned baby.

In his mind's eye he saw her, a little wicked, a little innocent, her eyes round and blue and filled with desire as she'd laid beneath him, begging him to love her. Even now, knowing she was dead, he got hard thinking of her. She'd sacrificed herself for him, flinging her body into that ugly river when it should have been the other way around. He should have tried to save her. He should be dead and she should be alive and vibrant and starting life as London Danvers.

"Son of a bitch," he growled. "Son of a goddamned bitch." He uncapped his friendly bottle of Scotch again and poured a long stream into his empty glass—one that he'd picked up in the bathroom of this—his albatross—the Hotel Danvers. He wondered if his father could see him now. "Hope you're laughing your ass off!" He glared at the ceiling, then thought better of it, because if there was an afterlife, Witt Danvers wouldn't be wandering around on the other side of the pearly gates, no sirree, he'd be down in hell, trying to cut a deal with the devil.

Zach's teeth ground together in silent fury.

The press had enjoyed a field day with even more scandal, compliments of the infamous Danvers family and still they were camped outside the hotel, the yacht, the ranch, the sawmills, logging operations, and the damned company headquarters. He tossed back three fingers of Scotch and checked the clock. It was barely ten. Christ, he was a mess. His mouth tasted like shit and his guts burned. The phone rang near the bed and he picked it up, silently hoping to hear her voice, knowing that he never would again. "Yeah?"

"You in charge now?"

"Who's this?" he asked.

"Don't tell me you don't recognize me?"

"Sweeny," Zach said with a sinking sensation.

"That brother of yours, the one in jail, he owes me."

"I'm sure he does."

"Thought you might like to do the honors."

Zach found the half-empty bottle and took a long pull. "I don't think so."

"Got new information."

"Screw you."

"It's about London."

He should just slam down the phone, but he didn't. Just held his breath and waited.

"You gotta pay me first."

"Fine. I'm in room 714."

"I'll be there."

Click. Zach eyed the bottle and wondered if he could finish it before he had to deal with the likes of Oswald Sweeny.

Ignoring his crutches, he climbed off the bed, looked in the mirror and winced. His face was still discolored from the knock in the back of his head and what he'd thought was a two-day growth of beard looked like it was really about six. "Shit," he muttered as he stripped off his clothes and sat in the shower, trying not to get his damned cast wet, hoping the hot jets of water would sink into his flesh and flush away all thoughts of her. But the steamy spray did little to quiet the images that seemed to be with him always.

He shaved, looked at his reflection and glowered. He still looked like hell.

Sweeny arrived to find him dipping into the bottle again. Balanced on the crutches, the bottle swinging from one hand, he opened the door. Without preamble, he asked, "How much do we owe you?"

Oswald hesitated as he walked into the room.

"I'll check it out when I see Jason," Zachary said, knowing the man was going to bluff him out of a few extra bucks. He hobbled to the desk and rested a hip on the corner. "Want a drink?"

Sweeny smiled, showing off his little teeth, but something in Zachary's gaze, probably the hard, dead edge, convinced him to decline. "I got a bill right here."

He handed it to Zach, but he didn't bother opening it. "Tell me what else you know."

"Not before I get paid."

Zach didn't move a muscle, just stared at Sweeny, glaring at him like the cockroach he was.

"The papers will pay plenty for what I know."

"The tabloids?" Zach snorted. "Don't cut off your balls to spite your face."

"All right, all right." He held up his fleshy palms. "Look, I couldn't just give it up. The whole London thing was too intriguing. I thought, hey, I might just write myself a book, one of those tell-all exposés."

The look Zach sent him stopped him short.

"Anyway, I kept digging and guess what I found out? Your old man was impotent." He let that sink in for a minute, but Witt's limp dick wasn't big news. Not to Zach. What was he getting at?

"That's right," Sweeny said when Zach's eyes narrowed over the rim of his glass. "Witt Danvers couldn't get it up, at least not very often. Not often enough to ensure him fathering another child—fathering London. I checked, and it took a while, but I found out that your stepmother, while she was supposed to be visiting friends in Victoria, really ended up at a clinic in Seattle where she got herself artificially inseminated by a private donor."

Zach's head snapped up. "What're you saying?"

Sweeny grinned that evil little smug grin as if glad that he'd finally got Zach's attention. "I'm telling you that Adria Nash is

London Danvers, but she's not Witt Danvers's kid, not technically—or biologically—speaking."

The glass fell from Zach's hand and Scotch splashed on the floor and the bottoms of his jeans. His head pounded.

"If she were alive, she'd still inherit it all, I suppose. It would take a team of lawyers to figure it out, but since she was the kid Witt was so crazy about, she'd still be his princess—heiress to it all and since half your family is dead or behind bars, she'd get it. No doubt."

"If she were alive," Zach ground out, his lips barely moving.

"Yeah, well. . . . nothin' I can do about that."

"You can substantiate this, I assume."

"Of course. Records could be pulled, court-ordered, you know, and I found a nurse who's willing to talk. It's just a damned shame that London's dead."

"Shit," Zach swore, his throat thick. He needed another drink.

"Hey, Danvers," the round little detective said, as if he sensed Zach was blocking him out. "About that check . . . ?"

Zach carried his bags down to the hotel lobby. He'd stayed in Portland longer than he'd planned. It had been over a week since he'd talked with Sweeny and the media was no longer laying siege to anything with the Danvers name. He was still wearing a cast, but he could walk and he wanted to get the hell out of town. He doubted that he'd ever come back.

It was time to move on.

On impulse, he left his bags by the lobby desk, then mounted the stairs to the ballroom, to the first place he'd seen her. He opened the doors, half expecting her to appear, but as he snapped on the lights, he found the room empty and cold and without a breath of life.

He was left only with memories, a bad ankle, and the sober realization that he'd never be the same.

"Fool," he ground out, walking inside the huge room and letting the door swing shut behind him. He remembered London on the night she was kidnapped, how impish she'd been, how precocious. Well, she'd grown into one helluva woman. Adria in that swirling black cape or the shimmery white gown, her eyes blue, her lips teasing—a little naughty and a little nice. He felt dead inside.

But, he was a practical man. At least he always had been. Whether he liked it or not, he'd have to face the fact that she was gone, that he'd loved her, and that he'd never love again. It was probably all for the best. He wasn't cut out for emotional entanglements. Again the hot tears stung his eyes and he swore at himself. He didn't believe in grieving. It didn't solve a damned thing.

Angry with himself, he switched out the lights and left the room. He would drive to Bend and then get so drunk Manny would have to drive him home, but he wouldn't go looking for a woman. Not for a long, long time.

He had parked on the street and as he carried his bags outside he felt the pale heat of the winter sun filtering between the towering office complexes and past the leafless trees that had been planted in front of the hotel. Sunlight danced on the wet streets and he slipped a pair of shaded aviator glasses onto the bridge of his nose before he rounded the corner and stepped toward the Jeep, only to stop dead in his tracks.

She was there, one jean-clad hip propped against a fender, her eyes as blue as the sky, her witch-wild hair catching in the breeze. A vision.

"What the—"

"You gonna stand there all day with your mouth hanging open, or are you gonna take me home?" she said and her voice cut a slice right out of his heart.

"Adria—"

It couldn't be!

His heart kicked into double time, but he wouldn't believe the image. He couldn't.

"Well, cowboy?"

His throat worked. He dropped his bags and took a step forward. With a laugh, she ran to him and threw herself into his arms. Telling himself that she was real, he held her as close as he could, letting the warmth of her body seep into his. "But you're—what happened?"

She kissed him with a passion that burned through his skin and the tears he'd been fighting for a week fell from his eyes.

"I couldn't stay away," she said, her voice husky. "I tried." Her face was serious now. "I dragged myself out of the river and told myself that the best thing for you was to think I was dead. I had enough money in my pockets to rent a cheap room and I even managed to buy a few clean clothes. I waited, trying to figure out how to get my car, my ID, and go back to Montana without you ever finding out."

His jaw grew rock hard. "You would let me think—"

"Shh." She pressed a finger to his lips. "I still thought we were brother and sister and . . . well, then the story came out about Katherine and the fact that I wasn't Witt's biological daughter and I thought . . ." She smiled up at him, love glistening in her eyes. "Well, I thought we could do something about that."

His voice was hoarse. "Why didn't you come sooner—?"

"I wanted to be sure. And I didn't want to come back as London Danvers," she said, tossing her hair out of face. "I found out that I like being Adria Nash, that I don't need a birth right, nor any of the Danvers money." Her throat worked and she lifted her chin, daring him to argue with her. "I'm back here because I love you, Zachary," she said bravely. "I want to be with you. No strings attached."

He regarded her for a heart-stopping moment and his lips curved into a slow, sexy smile. "Well, how about that?" he said, then his eyes grew dangerously dark. "I've loved you from the first time I saw you and I've gone through hell and back for you. No bullshit no strings. There'll be strings, lady, and plenty of 'em." Grinning his crooked cocksure smile, he lifted her from her feet and, ignoring the dull throb in his ankle, carried her into the hotel. She laughed that throaty laugh that made him tingle inside and her black hair nearly swept the ground. People turned and watched, eyebrows raised, women gasped as he shouldered open the front door of the Hotel Danvers and climbed the stairs to the ballroom, but Zach hardly noticed.

Once inside the dark room, he dropped her to her feet and locked the door behind them. Taking her into his arms he kissed her on the neck, brushing his lips over her soft skin. She wound her arms around his neck. "Now, Ms. Nash . . . let's start over," he suggested as he toyed with the top button of her blouse.

Adria smiled at the man she loved. She wound her arms around his neck and knew that she'd come searching for her past . . . a life of luxury and wealth, only to discover that love was the richest treasure of all.

He stared into her eyes as her blouse parted. "This time, darlin', were gonna take it real slow and do it right. Trust me."

ABOUT THE AUTHOR

Lisa Jackson is a #1 nationally bestselling author with over three million copies of her romances in print. She is the author of *Treasures, Intimacies, Wishes, Whispers,* and *Twice Kissed.* Her newest romantic suspense, *Unspoken,* will be published in November, 1999. Lisa loves to hear from readers and you may write to her c/o Zebra Books. Please include a self-addressed stamped envelope if you wish a reply. Her Web site is www.lisajackson.com.

<u>BOOK YOUR PLACE ON OUR WEBSITE</u> AND MAKE THE <u>READING CONNECTION!</u>

We've created a customized website just for our very special readers, where you can get the inside scoop on everything that's going on with Zebra, Pinnacle and Kensington books.

When you come online, you'll have the exciting opportunity to:

- View covers of upcoming books
- Read sample chapters
- Learn about our future publishing schedule (listed by publication month *and author*)
- Find out when your favorite authors will be visiting a city near you
- Search for and order backlist books from our online catalog
- Check out author bios and background information
- Send e-mail to your favorite authors
- Meet the Kensington staff online
- Join us in weekly chats with authors, readers and other guests
- Get writing guidelines
- AND MUCH MORE!

**Visit our website at
http://www.zebrabooks.com**

Put a Little Romance in Your Life With
Fern Michaels

__**Dear Emily**	0-8217-5676-1	$6.99US/$8.50CAN
__**Sara's Song**	0-8217-5856-X	$6.99US/$8.50CAN
__**Wish List**	0-8217-5228-6	$6.99US/$7.99CAN
__**Vegas Rich**	0-8217-5594-3	$6.99US/$8.50CAN
__**Vegas Heat**	0-8217-5758-X	$6.99US/$8.50CAN
__**Vegas Sunrise**	1-55817-5983-3	$6.99US/$8.50CAN
__**Whitefire**	0-8217-5638-9	$6.99US/$8.50CAN

Call toll free **1-888-345-BOOK** to order by phone or use this coupon to order by mail.

Name_____

Address_____

City _____ State _____ Zip_____

Please send me the books I have checked above.

I am enclosing $_____

Plus postage and handling* $_____

Sales tax (in New York and Tennessee) $_____

Total amount enclosed $_____

*Add $2.50 for the first book and $.50 for each additional book.

Send check or money order (no cash or CODs) to:

Kensington Publishing Corp., 850 Third Avenue, New York, NY 10022

Prices and Numbers subject to change without notice.

All orders subject to availability.

Check out our website at **www.kensingtonbooks.com**